THE
DAVENPORTS

KRYSTAL MARQUIS

DIAL BOOKS

DIAL BOOKS
An imprint of Penguin Random House LLC, New York

First published in the United States of America by Dial Books,
an imprint of Penguin Random House LLC, 2023
Copyright © 2023 by Krystal Marquis

Dial & colophon are registered trademarks of Penguin Random House LLC.
The Penguin colophon is a registered trademark of Penguin Books Limited.

Visit us online at penguinrandomhouse.com.

Library of Congress Cataloging-in-Publication Data is available.
Printed in the United States of America
ISBN 9780593463338

10 9 8 7 6 5 4 3 2 1
BVG

Design by Jennifer Kelly
Text set in Minister Light

To my parents for accepting that med school wasn't going to be a thing. Your love, support, and sacrifice gave me courage to chase this dream.

CHICAGO, 1910

CHAPTER 1

Olivia

Olivia Elise Davenport pulled a bolt of vibrant yellow silk from the display and held it to her dark complexion. She was drawn to the bright fabric nearly hidden behind the muted pastels, a shock of sunshine peeking through the clouds, and wondered if it was too bright for so early in the season. In her free hand, she held a sample of beaded lace and tried to imagine the sound it would make whispering around her ankles while she danced. *There will be a lot of dancing*, she thought.

Anticipation bubbled in her chest. The season of ball gowns and champagne had arrived at the conclusion of the Easter celebrations. Now that Olivia was out in society, it was time for her to find a husband. It was her second season, and she was ready. Ready to do her duty and make her parents proud, as she'd always done.

The only problem? It was difficult to find eligible gentlemen—born into the right family, educated, and set to inherit a large fortune—who were also Black.

Olivia took a deep breath. The yellow silk fell from her arm. She knew what her mother would say: It was too loud. Besides, she'd only come here to pick up a few finished alterations.

"May I help you?"

Olivia started at the voice over her shoulder. A shop attendant stood next to her with her hands clasped. Despite the smile on her face, her cold blue eyes betrayed a different intent.

"I was just admiring the fabric selection." Olivia turned toward the display of broad-brimmed hats, ignoring the eyes of the shop girl digging into her back. "And waiting for my friend," she added. *Where is Ruby, anyway?* It was her best friend who insisted they send the servants ahead with their parcels and browse Marshall Field's unaccompanied. And now she was nowhere to be found.

The shop girl cleared her throat. "You may pick up your mistress's orders at the service desk. I could direct you, if you've lost your way."

"I know where the service desk is, thank you," Olivia said with a tight smile, ignoring the slight. All around them, pale faces watched the exchange with increasing curiosity. Someone behind her chuckled.

She remembered her mother's words: to always rise above. Because her family *was* rare. Wealthy. Beautiful. *Black.* Ruby wore her wealth like armor, usually in the form of jewels and furs. Olivia preferred the understated air she observed in her mother.

Today, those perfect manners didn't matter. Her beauty was no shield. All the young girl before her could see was the color of Olivia's skin. She stiffened her spine, pulling herself to her full height. Olivia pointed to the largest jeweled broach in the display in front of her. "I'd like this boxed, please. And I'd like that

hat as well. For my sister. She always gets cross when I come home without something for her," she said conspiratorially to the other patrons—though she knew full well Helen would prefer a pair of pliers to a hat. Olivia walked slowly around the room. "Those gloves." She tapped her chin thoughtfully. "Five yards of that yellow silk—"

"Excuse me—"

"Miss," Olivia provided.

The shop girl's cheeks reddened.

Good, Olivia thought, *she's realized her mistake.*

"Miss," the shop girl huffed, clearly frazzled. "Your choices are quite expensive."

"Yes, well," Olivia said, the playfulness vanishing from her tone, "I have expensive taste. You can charge it to my family's account." Her eyes cut back to the shop girl. "The name is Davenport."

There weren't many Black shoppers ordering white attendants around department stores. But Davenport, a name cultivated by her father's hard work and her mother's determination, was well known. It was powerful enough to get her father admission into most of Chicago's elite clubs, her mother on the most exclusive charity boards, and her older brother into university. Chicago may have been a beacon in the North, where many Black people thrived under laws enacted during and after the Reconstruction, but painful encounters due to the color of her skin still caught her off guard.

A second attendant, an older woman with more decorum, appeared from the crowd. "I can assist you, Miss Davenport. Eliza, you are dismissed," she said to the shop girl. Olivia recognized her as one of her mother's regular attendants. "How are you, dear?"

Olivia's anger began to settle as she watched the older woman flit around wrapping things in tissue. She knew she was being petty. Most things considered, her life was privileged. She thought about canceling the sale, asking that everything be put back, but she could still feel the eyes of the other attendant watching from afar. And pride was one of the many things Davenports had in abundance.

Finally, Ruby appeared. Olivia was relieved to see her friend, and to no longer be the only Black person in the room.

Ruby's face was flushed and her eyes glittered against her russet-brown complexion. "I heard there was a commotion over here," she said with a grin. "What happened?"

Harold, the coachman, pulled the carriage from the curb in front of Marshall Field's and into State Street traffic. It was late afternoon in the early spring, and Chicago was alive. Colonnaded restaurants shared walls with brick and glass factories churning man-made clouds into the sky. Bells from the streetcars competed with the horns of motorized cars. Men in their tweed suits rushed by newsies yelling from their corners. People of all kinds filled the streets as Olivia watched from the window of one of her family's many covered, luxury buggies, concealed by a silk-lined canopy.

"Oh, Olivia." Ruby reached for her hand. "That girl knew damn well that your dress cost more than what she makes in a month. Plain old jealousy, is what that was."

Olivia attempted a smile and refolded her hands in her lap. Her friend was right, but there was more to it. That girl had looked at Olivia as if she were a thief. A pretender. Less than.

Olivia would never get used to that look.

Beside her, Ruby examined the fox-fur trim on a pair of gloves Olivia purchased during her shopping spree. "Keep them," Olivia said, catching her best friend's eye. One less thing to remind her.

Ruby pulled on the gloves and cupped her face, preening. Then she wiggled her brows and stuck out her tongue until Olivia gave her a real smile and the two collapsed into a fit of giggles.

Harold stopped the carriage at the intersection. Straight would take them to the North Side, where Chicago's wealthiest and most affluent residents lived. It was where the Davenports called home.

"Oh! By the way," Ruby said, "did I imagine it or did Helen come out of your garage covered head to toe in grease the other day?" She stifled a laugh.

Olivia rolled her eyes. Her younger sister was determined to be as unmarriageable as possible. "She should be more careful. If Daddy sees her, he'll have a fit."

As children, Olivia and Helen had been close. Together with their maid Amy-Rose, and later Ruby, they turned the grounds of their family estate into their very own kingdom. They spent hours in the gardens, evading their governess. When the time came for Olivia to make her societal debut last spring, she decided to do away with childish things, hoping Helen would follow her example. Instead, Helen seemed to be barreling in the other direction.

As Harold guided the carriage through the gates of Freeport Manor, Olivia couldn't imagine a more beautiful welcome after a long day. The Davenport mansion stood at the edge of one of Chicago's most elite neighborhoods, where their estate dwarfed those around them. When Olivia was younger, she thought it was because of her family's money. Later, she realized it was because no one wanted to buy property that bordered a Black family's estate. The grounds included several acres for gardens, stables, and fields for the horses to roam. The newest addition was a garage for the repair of Davenport carriages and the automobiles John collected.

The Davenport Carriage Company was a leap of faith her father had taken years ago. As a very young man, he had escaped enslavement and made the treacherous journey north, where Black folks had a chance at something like freedom. He dreamed of creating a horse-drawn carriage so luxurious, it would be more than a means of travel. And he succeeded. Shortly after being laughed out of the garage where he worked, William Davenport took his savings and a few disgruntled employees and began his own business. It thrived, and in time his carriages became the most sought-after in the world.

But now, with automobiles competing for space on city streets, John had started to pressure their father to update with the times.

"Look." Ruby pointed to the phaeton near the garage. "Is that one of yours?"

The phaeton was spartan in design. Matte black with thin spindly wheels and no driver, the opposite of the Davenport models with their velvet-tufted seating, thick sturdy tires for a smooth ride, and a finish so lacquered, one could see their reflection above the gold-leaf Davenport crest emblazoned on the back.

Olivia straightened up and gathered her skirts. "Probably one of John's projects. Though, I don't see why he'd bring it here. Ever since he came home with his automobile, it's been all he and Helen talk about."

"Will John be at dinner tonight?" Ruby asked, feigning nonchalance.

Olivia rolled her eyes. Her best friend was terrible at hiding her interest in her brother. "He does have to eat," she teased.

Olivia descended the steps of the carriage and looked up at Freeport, the only place she'd ever called home. The three-story Victorian was painted a pale blue with steep, gabled roofs and a pair of turrets. The wood railing of the wide porch had been carved with an ivy pattern so lifelike, the leaves appeared to flutter in the breeze. Large oak doors opened before them, revealing a grand staircase that snaked up the side of the foyer, brightly lit by the late afternoon sun filtering through the stained-glass cupola above.

Edward, the butler, waited patiently for their hats and gloves. "You're late for tea, miss," he whispered.

"Tea?" she asked. Her mother hadn't said anything about tea. Olivia tugged at the ribbon below her chin and gave Ruby a confused look.

The girls quickly made their way over the polished hardwood floors and past the gilt-framed mirrors toward the sitting room. Olivia held her breath, her brow furrowed, as she opened the door. "I'm sorry I'm . . ."

Her apology faded when she caught sight of a handsome stranger sitting across from her parents. His camel-colored tweed suit wrapped his smooth dark skin.

"Oh, and here she is now." Emmeline Davenport rose from the couch, the skirt of her gown falling gracefully around her. She stood impeccably straight, whether from the stays of her corset or sheer determination, Olivia could not tell. Mrs. Davenport cut a quick look at her daughter with the expressive almond-shaped eyes they shared and gently turned her guest from Mr. Davenport and the tea service. "This is our daughter Olivia. Darling, this is Mr. Lawrence."

The gentleman before Olivia was not like any of the young bachelors she'd met. He towered over her, forcing her to take in the breadth of his shoulders. His hair was parted to one side and brushed flat. Not a single hair out of place. Not even in his thick mustache, which framed full lips that parted at the sight of her to reveal straight white teeth and a self-assured grin. His smooth cheeks ended in a blunt, cleft chin.

He was very handsome.

"It's lovely to meet you." Olivia extended her hand.

"It is my pleasure," he said, accepting her hand and bowing his head. His voice, which had an accent, was so deep, it sent a vibration up her arm.

Olivia watched the smile form on her father's face. Mr. Davenport's large brown eyes softened. He slid his glasses off his proud nose and placed them in the pocket of his jacket. He left his cane against the chair and met her mother at the windows across the room. They made the ultimate picture of what Olivia wanted. A perfectly matched pair.

A flutter at her side brought her attention back to their guest.

"Ruby Tremaine. I don't believe we've been acquainted," Ruby said, her hand shooting out between them. Olivia met the gentleman's eyes, a twinkle of humor at her friend's boldness passing between them.

"Jacob Lawrence. It's a pleasure to meet you as well," he said.

"Mr. Lawrence recently moved here from London," Mrs. Davenport called with a smile, before returning her attention to Olivia's father.

"Oh? And what brings you to Chicago?" Olivia asked.

His eyes found Olivia's. "Looking for new opportunities."

Indeed, Olivia thought. "What sort of opportunities?" She could barely keep the flirtation out of her voice.

Mr. Lawrence grinned. "I'm looking to expand my shipping business beyond the British Isles. I met your father at a newsstand a few days ago and he graciously offered to make some introductions. I called to give my thanks."

Olivia felt her parents' stares from across the room and moved closer to Mr. Lawrence. "I apologize for my tardiness. If I had known you were coming, I wouldn't have kept you waiting."

Without taking his eyes off Olivia, Mr. Lawrence said, "No need to apologize. My visit was not planned. I only regret that we aren't able to spend more time together."

Olivia's heart raced.

Ruby near-shimmied her way between them. "I absolutely insist you attend my father's party this Friday."

"It's a campaign fundraiser for Mr. Tremaine's bid for mayor," Olivia's mother said, walking over. She turned to Mr. Lawrence. "The Tremaines' ballroom isn't as grand as ours, but it's sure to be a cozy, intimate gathering."

Olivia shot an apologetic glance at her best friend and said, "I have always found the Tremaines' garden to be lovely this time of year. Will it be open for exploration, Ruby?"

"Of course." Ruby sniffed. "We've spared no expense."

Mr. Davenport appeared at Mr. Lawrence's elbow. "It will be a perfect opportunity to meet Chicago's major players."

"You're very kind. I can't think of a better way to spend a Friday evening." Mr. Lawrence turned to Olivia. "Will I see you there?"

Olivia felt a flutter in her stomach. The season had only just begun, and here the most eligible suitor she'd ever laid eyes on was quite literally in her drawing room. Maybe finding a husband at last would be easier than she thought.

"Of course," she said, a smile playing across her lips. "I might even save you a dance."

CHAPTER 2

Helen

This looks nothing like the diagram, Helen thought as she inspected the undercarriage of the damaged Ford Model T John towed to the garage earlier that morning. A delivery like this reminded Helen of Christmas morning: the anticipation and the suspense, each vehicle a mystery. Even though automobile repair wasn't specifically in the Davenport portfolio, John quietly accumulated the best mechanics in Chicago to help him service and modify the new horseless carriages sweeping the nation.

That roster of mechanics included Helen. She stared at the deformed entrails of his latest find, convinced that her brother gave her the wrong schematics to study. The sketches appeared simple enough, but looking at the inner workings of the auto-mobile now was like staring at a tangled web. It didn't help that John and the other mechanics made suggestions above her head. It was only a matter of time before the twins, Isaac and Henry, began bickering. She rubbed her temple, postponing the stirring headache.

"Hand me the wrench," John said. His hand bumped her face as he reached blindly in her direction.

She swatted his hand away and sat on the floor, dirt and oil altering the pattern already stained into a pair of John's old overalls. "I don't know why you won't just let me do it. My hands are smaller than yours."

"Fine then, you fix it." John's frustration barely disguised the challenge in his tone. The men around her stopped talking. Even Malcolm, who kept a scowl permanently etched on his face, took a step closer. She knew they would be watching her every move. The first time John turned a repair over to her, the whole garage erupted in protest, Malcolm loudest of all. Since then, most of the mechanics watched her with a mixture of amusement and awe. Malcolm, however, preferred to grunt from a corner about women knowing their place. About wealthy children using his workplace as their playground.

All of the men were sworn to secrecy.

Helen Marie Davenport searched among the scattered tools and wiped the back of her hand against her chin. Kneeling in a puddle of oil, she felt more herself here than anywhere else. Here no one expected her to know the right things to say or be aware of the latest gossip and trends. Here she let her curiosity run wild.

John didn't mind her constant questions. He let her speak her mind. Helen adored her older brother. They even had the same look about them, contagious smiles, and their father's proud nose and quiet nature. And they were dreamers.

"Did you forget what a wrench looks like?" John teased.

The men laughed at his joke. Isaac reached for the diagram she'd left on the floor. An architect by trade, he'd followed his brother to the Davenport Carriage Company after seeing an ad in the paper. "I can look these over for you, if you'd like, Helen."

That was another thing. Here, she wasn't *Miss* Davenport or *Miss* Helen. With the exception of Malcolm, who never addressed her directly, the men called her by her first name. She'd earned her place with them and they treated her like an equal for it.

Inside the garage, she was a true apprentice.

The garage wasn't as fancy as the factory where the carriages were made, but it suited their needs just fine. The outside was painted the same shade of pale blue as the manor house. Two large bay doors allowed them to work on more than one automobile at a time, especially since John's Ford was parked in the carriage house. The walls were lined with a mix of new and secondhand tools mounted above the wooden workbench that hugged the back wall as it stretched toward the small office, where she and her brother often discussed the business's future.

But before Helen could hand over the diagram, something caught her eye and suddenly the engine's secrets revealed themselves to her. She gathered the tools she needed, and the rest of the garage faded into the background. She leaned forward over the open engine, alert and breathless. This is what she was meant to do.

The men watched for a while, but in time they returned to their own work, and John's shadow fell over her. John, the first-born child and only son, was groomed to take over the family's carriage company. His easy smile and smooth manners made every lady swoon over him.

Then there was Olivia. Olivia, who always knew the right thing to say and didn't get ink on her sleeve or grease on her chin. She'd marry well and make their parents proud and continue to shop and entertain her way through life, just as she'd spent the last year doing.

Helen closed her eyes and took a steadying breath. She missed her sister—the way she'd been. Helen intended to use her mind to do more than plan dinners and pick china.

John tugged on her ear. "Where'd you go?"

Helen shook her head. "I think you should tell Daddy about converting the business to an automobile factory. Just repairing Ford and General Motors automobiles is not the future of our company. Studebaker and Patterson are already—"

"Helen." He sighed. "We've been over this. He won't even allow us to advertise automobile *repairs*. He would never agree to a factory."

She looked up at him. "He would if you present it the right way. He may be set in his ways, but Daddy likes facts. It's a risk, I agree. But one we need to take."

"I couldn't argue it the way you do." John juggled the planetary gear between his hands. "You tallied the numbers, made the plans, figured out the budgets."

"And you predicted the trend in the market, secured a space downtown to open a larger factory, and"—she poked him in the chest—"recognized what I have to offer."

"You're right. We're a team." He massaged below his left shoulder and frowned. "I wouldn't feel right presenting your work to Daddy as my own."

Helen grunted. Her face hot and prickling from the indecision on John's face. "You know very well that Daddy would laugh me out of the room."

After making a few minor adjustments to the Model T's undercarriage, she took the gear from her brother and fitted it into place. Her stomach clenched at the thought of voicing her secret wish—to work, officially, for the Davenport Carriage Company— to her father. John would keep her secret until she was ready, until she had the experience to *prove* to their father that she had as much to contribute to the family name as her siblings.

"I just think you're not giving him a chance," her brother said. "He could surprise you."

Helen chewed her lip. What if John was right? Helen pictured herself walking into his study with her notes and numbers. She'd played her speech out in her mind so many times, she could recite it in her sleep. In her best, wildest dreams, Daddy was impressed—*proud*.

The corner of John's mouth twitched. "You both get the same look on your face when you have an idea. You're more alike than you realize."

Hope swelled in Helen's chest. Just when she thought she would float away, the garage's side door swung open.

Amy-Rose stood in the doorway. Flour coated her sleeve and a few stray curls clung to the side of her neck. Her expressive hazel eyes were set in a medium-brown complexion spotted with freckles. Now those eyes settled on Helen.

"There you are! I swear—" Amy-Rose tripped over the threshold. "Your *mother* asked for you," she said, clearly out of breath. "I told her you were in the bath."

Helen didn't believe her friend's face could have flushed any brighter until Amy-Rose spotted John sitting on the floor beside her.

John stood first. "Thank you, Amy-Rose." He stretched his

arms down to his sister and hauled her up. "Get inside before Mama and Daddy find you like this."

Some days Helen wished they would, just so she wouldn't have to keep part of herself hidden from them.

But for now, Helen wiped her palms on her thighs and hugged her brother quickly, not sure which one of them smelled worse. Then she followed Amy-Rose, scanning the windows of the manor as she sprinted back inside.

CHAPTER 3

Amy-Rose

Amy-Rose picked up Helen's soggy towel from the bedroom floor and hung it in the adjoining bathroom. After she found Helen in the garage with John, she had quickly ushered the youngest Davenport into the bath and gotten her dressed for dinner. Now Helen was downstairs with the rest of her family while Amy-Rose tidied up. After this, she would be needed in the kitchen.

Through the next set of doors was Olivia's bedroom. The girls' rooms may have been mirror images of each other—great four-poster beds, thick Persian rugs, rich vibrant wallpaper—but that's where the similarities ended. Olivia kept her room pristine: Every object had its place. She never left discarded garments on the floor. Her books sat erect on their shelves. A few family photos dotted the fireplace mantel.

Amy-Rose had spent hours in there as a child, hosting elaborate teas with the Davenport girls and their dolls, whispering hopes and dreams late into the night when their mothers were fast asleep.

When her mother was still alive.

Amy-Rose thought back to the day she and her mother, Clara Shepherd, arrived at the long gravel drive of Freeport Manor, the biggest house she'd ever seen. Everything was large here, glittering and beautiful. Especially the family who called it home. The Davenports were the only family in Chicago that would take a maid with a child; no one else wanted the extra mouth to feed. In this new, strange place so far from home, Amy-Rose had found friends.

It had been three years since her mother had passed. Some days she could pretend that her mother was just in another room, dusting a chandelier or turning down a bed, singing French lullabies. Amy-Rose would run up to their shared bedroom and the pain of remembering her passing would force her to her knees. When the ache eventually subsided, happy memories would fill her mind. The best were the stories her mother used to tell her about Saint Lucia—the colorful birds that visited their home, the bright mangoes that grew in the yard, and the sweet smell of the bougainvillea mixing with the salty sea air. She missed the views of the mountains, Gros Piton and Petit Piton, reaching for the sky. Amy-Rose had been only five when they left the island, so she didn't remember much. Her mother's memories felt like hers.

They rarely spoke about the storm that took the rest of their family or their home. This was their new home.

A carpeted hall led into the small drawing room where the girls spent most of their time. Deserted except for the small terrier lounging on a grand silk pillow in the corner, the room was a mix of Olivia's ordered and classic style and Helen's latest interests: books about Rome and manuals about automobile engines. Even

Ruby left her mark here in the samples of perfume from Marshall Field's dotting a small rolling tray used for tea.

With a sigh, Amy-Rose descended a set of stairs to the Davenports' impressive kitchen.

"Good, you're here," a voice boomed from inside the pantry. "Take this. And this." Jessie, the head cook, dropped a carton of eggs into Amy-Rose's arms without looking to see if she was ready to catch them.

Jessie heaved a sack of flour onto a cutting board with such force, Mrs. Davenport's favorite tea service rattled on the tray. The cook set her fists on her wide hips and turned slowly toward Amy-Rose. "It don't take that long to lace that girl into a corset." She pivoted again, her broad hands shoved dishes into the sink.

Clearly, Jessie had never tried to dress Helen Davenport. "Helen needed a touch-up," Amy-Rose said. "Her hair doesn't hold the curl as long as Olivia's."

Henrietta and Ethel appeared through another passage and immediately began straightening up the kitchen. Jessie didn't spare them a glance, even when Ethel placed a hand on her shoulder. Instead she stared at Amy-Rose as if she knew the young maid's thoughts were far from the task at hand.

"I think you're helping that girl get away with mischief you have no business being involved in." Jessie sighed long and deep, softening her gruff tone. "I know you care for those girls like sisters, but mind me, they *ain't* your sisters. You need to stop dreaming of how things used to be and start thinking about how they is. The girls will be married soon." Jessie pointed to the pots piled high in the sink and the maids polishing the fine silver. "The Davenports won't need you then."

Amy-Rose edged in to wash her hands and grabbed an apron from the hook, ignoring the truth of Jessie's words. Instead, she let herself be transported to Mr. Spencer's storefront and the day she'd flip the sign from Closed to Open on the door. The day the storefront would have *her* name above the entrance, and customers waiting for her wares and trained stylists. The apron hanging from her neck wouldn't be to protect her clothes from potato peels or sauce, but hair butter and shampoo. "Who's to say I'll even be here when that happens?" she huffed. "In a few weeks' time, I aim to have enough saved in Binga Bank to lease Mr. Spencer's storefront."

Amy-Rose looked at the older woman who, for years, had hovered over her like an overbearing godmother. Telling Jessie her plans made her plans that much more real—more than a daydream she shared with her friend Tommy. Out in the stables with him, it was a wish. Tommy was the only person who really knew of her desire to leave and strike out in business for herself. He'd gone with her to apply for a loan after securing enough for a down payment. His belief in her was almost as strong as her own.

"About two months ago," she continued when Jessie didn't reply, "I asked Mr. Spencer if he'd be interested in selling one of my deep conditioners in his barbershop." Amy-Rose felt a warmth spread through her. "They were a hit. He said they practically walked off the shelf. Since then, he's been reunited with his daughter down in Georgia. He's a grandfather and—"

Jessie brushed excess flour from the top of the cup in her hand. "Girl, get to the part about the store." She turned then, and watched Amy-Rose with misty eyes, a hand settled back on her hip. "Well, go on," she said after clearing her throat.

Amy-Rose flushed. "Mr. Spencer agreed to rent his barbershop to me so he could move South." The words came in a rush that blew all the air from her lungs. She watched the other women stop their work. Her heart raced as she took in their wide eyes and their slow turn to Jessie. The Davenports' cook and self-appointed leader of the household took her face in her hands as she walked around the butcher-block table to embrace Amy-Rose.

"Oh, your mama would be so proud!" Henrietta cried from her station at the silver cabinet.

"Hetty's right. Your mama'd be proud." Jessie patted Amy-Rose's cheek. "Now, until then, separate the yolks from the whites." Her order lacked any of its usual sternness and Amy-Rose obediently picked up a knife.

Hetty sidled up to Amy-Rose and said in what she may have thought was a whisper, "What about Mr. John?"

"He'll inherit his father's company one day." Amy-Rose chased away the image of John in the garage, his worn trousers and shirtsleeves pushed up to his elbows. The way the muscles in his forearms moved under his skin. "And I'll have mine."

Jessie turned, her face screwed up for a lecture, when something outside the window caught her eye. "What does that boy want now?'

Amy-Rose followed the cook's gaze and saw Tommy, Harold's son, waving from the garden. He had warm brown skin and wide, eager eyes such a deep, calm brown, they could set anyone at ease. After Amy-Rose's mother had died, she'd spent time watching Tommy feed and brush the horses as she feed them apples and other treats. Long rides on the grounds led to a close friendship between the two. When Amy-Rose shared her dream of one day opening a salon for the care of Black women's hair, Tommy congratulated her as if she'd already done it. His hope buoyed her own.

"It can wait," Jessie complained, but Amy-Rose was already on her way outside.

Tommy paced along the fence, wringing a hat in his hands. There was an unusual fervor in his eyes and an energy about him that filled her with both excitement and dread. Like Amy-Rose, Tommy had grown up alongside the Davenport siblings, but he'd always respected the line that separated the help from the family. He'd never befriended John, a boy his own age, even though the Davenports' only son had spent as much time in the garage and stables as the lead coachman's only child. Tommy seemed to be the only person immune to John's endearing charm.

"I'm leaving," Tommy said by way of greeting.

Amy-Rose skidded to a stop.

Tommy barreled on. "I spoke to the conductor of the Santa Fe Railway, and he agreed to give me a reduced fare on a transcontinental headed west."

"West?" Amy-Rose said, her mind still struggling to catch up with Tommy's words. It should have come as no surprise. He'd been trying to escape Freeport ever since he was old enough to work, or "earn his keep," as his father said. Tommy vowed he would leave this place and make a fortune of his own.

"I've been talking to a member of the Chicago chapter of the National Negro Business League. He said that there's new cities growing like daises all over the country. Full of new opportunities."

"Where could you have more options than here?"

"I need to start somewhere new, where I'm not *one of the Daven-*

ports' boys. I'm not trading in a bridle for a shoe-shine kit when they eventually switch to horseless carriages." Tommy twisted his hat some more. It was barely recognizable. "Amy-Rose, the man offered me a job at his insurance company."

Amy-Rose was confused. "You want to sell insurance?"

He laughed. "They do more than that. They secure loans and real estate for Black entrepreneurs. It's what built the South Side." Tommy closed the distance between them and took both of Amy-Rose's hands in his. "I aim to be on the California Express in six weeks' time." He cupped her shoulders. "I wanted you to be the second person I told, after my dad, of course." He let her go and shook his head, as if surprised by his own news. "I also wanted to thank you."

"Thank me?"

"You've inspired me. I listened to your plans for a salon, watched you pepper every business owner downtown until they chased you out and onto the street." They both smiled at the memory of the dry-goods store owner, Clyde, doing just that. "You were a force to be reckoned with when you brought your savings to the bank." He laughed. "Not sure you needed me at all." Tommy looked at her with a genuine warmth that made her heart swell. "You're on your way to make everything you want a reality. And I want that. For you, and for myself."

Amy-Rose threw her arms around his neck. He smelled like hay and horses, sweat and determination. Tommy was a salve to her battered soul when she needed a friend. A good man, hard-working and proud. How could she not want the best for him?

"Don't worry," he said. "I'll come back to visit my father. And for your grand opening."

She laughed around the lump in her throat and pulled away. She tried to imagine Freeport—Chicago—without him. Already, the world around her seemed less bright. As if he knew what she was thinking, he brushed a finger against her cheek, catching a tear before it fell. He said, "Everyone has to leave home sometime."

CHAPTER 4

Ruby Tremaine loved her best friend, truly she did, but nothing highlighted the change in her circumstances more than lying on Olivia's four-poster, silk-canopied bed after a long day of shopping for items Olivia cared so little about.

Ruby's own life had been reduced to budgets and polite smiles, as Margaret, the maid she and her mother now shared, tore up her old dresses and attempted to make them look different and daring enough to pass as new purchases. Luckily, the latest trend of narrow, shorter skirts meant there was enough fabric to work with.

Ruby had tried to ignore the signs of her father's tightening grip on her purse strings, especially when the city's influential lawmakers continued to appear at dinner each week, or when her family enjoyed the view from their private box at the racetrack. But then last spring, Henry Tremaine sat his wife and daughter down in the study and told them he was running for office. "We will all have to do our part," he said.

Our part.

Our part felt more and more like their decisions and her consequences. Ruby still tried to focus on the positive outcome of *when* her father succeeded in his bid for mayor. She was in much better circumstances than her cousins in Georgia, who, with her father's help, recently secured ownership of the land where her uncle was a tenant farmer. The cotton they harvested supplied the raw materials for the textiles produced at the Tremaine mill and boardinghouse. But failing crops down south coupled with the financial stress of the campaign were taking their toll.

At first it was fun. New, handsome politicians to flirt with, even if she had to suffer through endless debates about wages and the overcrowding in factories.

Less than a year later, though, Ruby wasn't sure if her father was any closer to becoming Chicago's first Black mayor, much as she hated that stab of doubt. She *did* know that a summer holiday in Paris was drifting farther and farther from reach.

Of course, Ruby had intended to confide all this to her best friend several times before today, but the words always got stuck somewhere in her chest. Every purchase Olivia ordered seared a hole in Ruby's pride and forced her to bite back the poison bitterness rising in her. She'd disappear between the displays of the department store and admire the wares, telling herself the lack of pressure to purchase was a relief. At least it allowed her to sulk in private, which she seldom did around her friend.

Olivia entered from the drawing room she shared with Helen. "What have you heard of this Jacob Lawrence?" she asked. Her eyes glowed as she stared out her bedroom window.

Ruby shrugged. "You?"

Olivia shook her head. "He is something, isn't he? I'd like to know more about him, but I'm afraid showing too much interest will have Mama hovering closer than ever." She smiled. "Do you think there's a secret catalog where parents find suitable husbands?"

"If there is, I'd like a subscription." Ruby sighed, her chest tightening at the thought of John.

Olivia's delicate brows wrinkled. She must have sensed Ruby's anxiety, because she said, "We are to be true sisters soon. Once John is over the stress of impressing Daddy, I'm sure he'll make you a grand proposal."

Ruby reached instinctively to twirl the pendant at her neck, remembering too late it wasn't there. She clutched the decorative pillow in her lap instead, holding on to her friend's encouragement just as tightly. "I hope so."

Being near John made Ruby's throat dry and stomach twirl; she had loved him for as long as she could remember. Yet despite little flirtations and stolen kisses, and the clear encouragement of their families, John had yet to propose.

It worried her.

Like Olivia, Ruby was now of age. It was time to settle down and get married. And, with her family's situation growing more dire, the pressure was on to find a good match, one that would secure Ruby's wealth and position in society. John would do that, but more importantly, she had never wanted anyone but him.

Ruby looked down and realized she had unraveled the pillow's braided fringe. She tossed it aside and her hand flew up to her neck again, where her namesake gemstone once sat in the hollow of her throat. She was suddenly filled with an urgency to see John. To remind him of why they belonged together. "Let's head downstairs," she suggested. "We were so late this afternoon, maybe we can make up for it by being early for dinner?"

Ruby led the way, Freeport as familiar to her as her own home, not too far from here. They descended the grand staircase and followed the voices in the hall to the living room, where the rest of the family was indeed already gathered. This space, decorated in deep reds and rich golds, was where the Davenports did most of their entertaining. The person Ruby most wanted to see stood apart from the others. John positioned himself in front of the fireplace, a glass of amber liquid cradled in his hand.

This is my chance, Ruby thought. She walked up to the fire, her skin already prickling from the sight of him. She fixed a soft smile to her face and touched his shoulder.

"Good evening," she said, hiding her nerves behind a casual tone.

John flinched in surprise and turned to her.

She placed a hand on his wrist. "I didn't mean to startle you."

"My mind was somewhere else." John smiled, the full force of his gaze on her.

In a moment, she was transported back there: under the white oak trees that lined the Davenport property. Helen had challenged Ruby and Olivia to a race. Ruby's horse had thrown her from the saddle and run off into the woods. Helen and Olivia were too far ahead to see what had happened, but their brother came running.

As John had inspected her ankle, Ruby could only think of how handsome he was. How much she wanted to kiss him. Before she could lose her nerve, she leaned in.

His body had stiffened, one of his hands still encircling her ankle. Then he softened and returned the gentle pressure of her lips. A violent fluttering had erupted in her chest. Ruby had risen onto her knees and closed the space between them. She'd shivered as his hands brushed the top of her shoulders, slid across her back, and settled at the nape of her neck, deepening their kiss.

When he'd finally pulled away, gasping for air, Ruby had almost fallen forward into his lap. His heart had thudded under her palm, and he'd smiled at her. Wordlessly, he had helped her to her feet and escorted her back to the house. It was their first kiss, and certainly not their last.

He stared at her lips now as if he was trapped in the same memory.

Ruby's face warmed, and she took another step closer.

"Do you still ride?" John asked, practically reading her mind.

"Not as often as I'd like," she replied, a smile on her lips. She did not mention that her family had sold all but two of their horses.

John took a small sip from his glass. "Weather permitting, we should arrange an afternoon ride for next week."

Ruby kept her grin demure. "I'm sure we can find the shade of an oak tree when the sun is high."

John's eyes widened, but just when she finally had his full attention Amy-Rose suddenly appeared, holding a bottle filled with the amber liquid John was drinking.

"Thank you, Amy-Rose." John extended his glass, the effects of their shared memory quickly vanishing. "And thank you for this afternoon. I know Helen can be a handful."

"No trouble at all," Amy-Rose said, casting her eyes downward. She was, as always, infuriatingly beautiful for a maid. Ruby had never seen a girl whose features, unadorned with jewels, gloss, or rouge, appeared so flawless up close.

Ruby stepped closer to John. Between him, the fire, and the

look he was giving Amy-Rose, she felt a ribbon of sweat unfurl down her back. "Come. Let's go someplace a little more private," she said to John, eager to get their conversation back on track. She cut her eyes to Amy-Rose, who nodded and walked away.

Ruby needed to remind John of what they once were and what they still could be. And that would not happen if he was staring at the maid like that.

From outside, Ruby's brick-faced home seemed empty, abandoned. Tremaine Mansion was nestled closer to the bustle of downtown Chicago. Ruby alighted the carriage in front of the grand entrance. She couldn't help but think it looked like a haunted mansion compared to Freeport. It lacked the warmth of the Davenports' home, and the family that breathed life into it.

Standing in her empty foyer, Ruby felt like a ghost, a specter who flitted silently in and out. She was glad for the darkness. It hid the changes that opened a hollow sadness in her—missing paintings, sold mementos, items that were, to her, priceless trinkets. The list was endless.

"Ruby, darling, is that you?"

She had nearly reached the landing of the staircase when her mother called from the dimly lit room down the hall. Her shoulders sagged. "Yes," she replied quietly. Her stomach rolled as she dragged her feet across the hall where a plush Aubusson runner once warmed the corridor.

Mr. and Mrs. Tremaine sat on either side of a slowly dying fire, drinking sherry. Ruby came to a stop before them as if called to the mat for some transgression.

"How was your evening?" her mother asked.

Ruby stared at the embers glowing red in the firebox. "Lovely." She tried not to fidget; her mother despised fidgeting.

"The Davenports are well?" she pressed. Ruby looked at her mother and saw what she would look like in twenty years. Even in the low light, she could make out her regal nose and full lips. Though her figure was fuller, Mrs. Tremaine could easily be mistaken for Ruby's sister.

"Yes."

Mr. Tremaine placed his crystal glass on the side table with a crash. "Enough pleasantries. Did you speak with John?" Her father turned in his chair and frowned at her. He was a tall man with a rounded belly. Ten years older than his wife, his hair showed a light dusting of white at his temples, but the sharp, piercing gleam of his eyes had not dimmed a bit.

"John and I shared a moment alone after dinner," she began. "He and I lingered in the dining room when everyone else retired next door for coffee or brandy. We laughed about some of our adventures as children—"

"Ruby," her mother said, "you're rambling." Mrs. Tremaine didn't raise her voice, but there was something in her calm, composed tone that made the hairs on Ruby's arms rise.

"He invited me to go riding." She took a step closer to them.

"When?" Mr. Tremaine's voice was loud in the quiet, and made both his wife and daughter flinch.

Ruby looked between her parents, realizing that she had played this all wrong. She should have said she was still priming John to ask her the question they so dearly wanted. "We . . . haven't decided on an exact date."

Her mother's mouth puckered into a tight bow.

Mr. Tremaine slapped his knee and shot up from his chair. "I had intended to announce your engagement to John Davenport at the party this Friday."

Ruby sucked in a breath. How could he plan an announcement before a proposal?

"Darling." Her mother stood and took Ruby's hand, her face softening ever so slightly. "John is a good man, from a wonderful family. Your marriage to him could save *this* family. Together, the Tremaines and Davenports can be the example of what's possible here. I do hope you are trying." Her tone was supportive and yet her fingers were tight around Ruby's hand.

"I am, Mother," Ruby said, keeping her voice controlled and stepping out of her mother's reach. How could she even ask Ruby that? Ruby had been trying with every modest smile and well-timed laugh, with every arch of her eyebrow or accidental run-in on the estate grounds. How could she explain to her parents that perhaps no matter how hard she tried, it may not work out the way they'd planned? No one asked her if she wanted to be the face of Black progress. They were gambling what they had—her future and their own—to convince a city full of people that the Tremaine family's success could be easily replicated.

With her heart in her stomach, Ruby left the room, wondering who wanted her engagement more.

CHAPTER 5

Olivia

"Make sure you bring this right inside."

"Yes, Mama." Olivia's arms ached from the weight of the basket she held. Her mother had arranged the muffins for the soup kitchen on the South Side.

Mrs. Davenport added two more muffins to the basket. "It's important to help those with less, Olivia. Your father and I wouldn't be where we are today without help along the way."

Olivia straightened. "I know." It was a beautiful afternoon, perfect for walking by the lake or a ride in an open carriage. Then her mother had asked her to make this trip downtown. Technically it was Helen's turn, but she'd disappeared some time before breakfast. Olivia was more than a little annoyed, though she chided herself for the feeling. Of course her mother could depend on her.

"I'll see that these get to the volunteers."

Emmeline Davenport pressed her hand to Olivia's cheek. It was all the encouragement she needed. The basket bounced off her hip as she left the kitchen for the stables. Just outside the door, Tommy was readying the horses.

"Miss," he said, taking the basket and offering her a hand into the horses-drawn carriage. She settled into the soft leather with the basket beside her. Freeport Manor disappeared between the trees.

In the city, restaurants and shops blurred by. Soon they were on South Street's scaled-down version of State Street, full of boutiques, markets, and Black-owned businesses, including salons, law firms, and a hospital. Before Amy-Rose began styling the Davenports' hair, Emmeline and her daughters made a day of shopping and visiting the salon. Olivia had never seen so many people who looked like her in one place. Some were formerly enslaved people like her father. Others were born free back east like her mother. All were hoping to build a new life in a city that offered opportunities to remake oneself. Here, music seemed to be the dominant sound as brassy jazz permeated the air like fresh baked bread. Men traded information outside the barbershop as they got their shoes shined, and mothers held their children close. It excited her and, if she was being honest, made her nervous, all at the same time.

Olivia stepped out of the carriage with the basket in hand. "I'll drop these off and be right back," she said to Tommy over her shoulder.

Visiting the community center was always humbling. She knew her life was much different from those of the people who lined up for canned goods or a hot meal.

"Miss Olivia, nice to see you again." Mary Booker organized the clothing and food drives and oversaw the soup kitchen.

"Hello, Miss Mary." Olivia placed the basket on the table behind the buffet.

Mary leaned over her shoulder, her hands buried in an apron. "I bet those taste as good as they smell. Thank your mother for us."

"Of course." Happy to be rid of her small load, Olivia took in the room. The walls were unadorned, and empty chairs sat under many of the tables. She remembered how vibrant the room had been for the Easter celebration three weeks ago. The room was far less crowded than usual. "Am I late or early?" she asked.

"Neither. Everyone has someplace better to be, it seems." As Mary spoke, a young man brought his tray to the table and hurried out the door.

Olivia said goodbye and told Mary that her sister would retrieve the basket next week.

On her way out, she spotted a group of Black men and women about her age. They whispered in a corner, laughing nervously. Curiosity gnawed at her. Of course Olivia had friends—she had Ruby, and her sister, and Amy-Rose, and a few other girls with whom she could have a chat—but something about seeing this group of friends whisper and laugh stirred something in her.

Before she realized what she was doing, Olivia followed them outside and around the corner of Newberry Library. The group stopped in front of a nondescript house on a cobblestone street. The plain brick edifice was clean. The shades were drawn. She watched them disappear inside, and three more people too—a man her father's age and an older woman on the arm of a young man, who was whispering in her ear. She somehow knew that whatever was going on in there was why the center was empty—and that it was important enough to draw young and old into its darkness.

The porch stairs slanted to the right as a tall man in a too-small suit greeted her. "The meeting's downstairs. Watch your head."

She ducked under the low beam at the landing. The hushed voices below reminded her of a hummingbird, full of energy and too swift to catch. The basement was darker than the main floor, light entering through narrow windows cut high into the ceiling. Faces, all different shades of brown, took turns peeking at the other entrance near a makeshift stage. She paused when she spotted the occasional pale face among them. None were from the social circles Mr. and Mrs. Davenport kept their children closed within.

"You look a bit lost," a voice said behind her.

Olivia's hand tightened around the purse and gloves clutched to her chest. "I am not lost." She peered at the stranger under the brim of her hat, still fastened to her head. The young man lifted his chin to see over the crowd.

"Oh," he said. "You're meeting someone." He hooked his thumbs on the lapels of his jacket. His gray-striped suit was perfectly tailored, but showed some signs of wear. They were of a similar height, with her in her heeled boots, making it difficult for her to avert her gaze. His strong jaw tilted back to her, and Olivia was struck by the light honeyed color of his eyes, high cheekbones, and bright white teeth revealed by a disarming smile.

"No," she began, then stopped. He was a stranger. She didn't need to tell him anything.

"So, you *are* lost." He nodded as he examined her carefully planned outfit. "Fine dress. Polished boots. Those hands look like they've never done a hard day's work." He laughed at Olivia's open mouth and the shock written across her face. His laugh was smooth, and so full of joy, it spilled over. She almost forgot he was laughing at her expense.

"Just because my clothes are nice—"

"Nice? Miss, open your eyes."

Olivia followed his gaze. The people gathered in their second-hand shoes and ill-fitting suits knew hardships she couldn't imagine. She assumed some, like her, were one generation beyond enslavement. Mr. Davenport never really talked about his family, of the life he left behind, or what it took him to get North. It was as if his life began in Chicago when he met Emmeline Smith while working in a carriage repair shop.

Now Olivia's hands drifted to the large gold buttons of her blouse. The realization that each one could probably feed someone for a week made heat prick her cheeks. The crowd pressed closer. She felt trapped between the man beside her and an older woman to her right, who left Olivia in a cloud of powder and shea butter when their shoulders collided.

"Mrs. Woodard." Olivia recognized her as a close friend of Reverend Andrews. Both were strong supporters of the community center.

The middle-aged woman gave Olivia a firm handshake before folding her arms over her chest. Her double-breasted coat was the same shade of cream as her skirt. A pearl barrette kept her voluminous coils away from her face. "Will you be joining the women's gathering?"

Olivia glanced around the room. There were indeed as many women in the crowded room as men. When her attention returned to Mrs. Woodard, the older woman's sharp gaze made Olivia's throat dry up. If *I* recognize her, *then*—

"We're pushing for the vote, you know," said a young woman on the other side of Mrs. Woodard. She wore a dress that looked like a uniform, deep blue, with white stockings and shoes. She pushed her chin forward. "We deserve a say," she said, her eyes on the men in front of them. "Just as much as they do." Soon Olivia found herself surrounded by women discussing their work and politics. They possessed a confidence and directness she immediately liked. They were like Helen, self-assured and determined. Olivia was painfully aware of the rudely opinionated young man next to her, watching her every move from the corner of his eye.

"And what are your reasons for visiting the old Samson House?" he asked. The tenor of his voice was a startling contrast to the ladies' higher ones.

"I don't know why I'm here," she confessed. "I followed a group from the community center." She gestured to the teenagers crowded at the front of the room.

He nodded. "They're here to see a Mr. DeWight."

Olivia waited for more information. "And he is?" Her frustration was mounting. First, he implied she did not belong there. Now he was being deliberately obtuse.

"A lawyer from Alabama."

The crowd around them continued to swell and the temperature in the room increased. This was all for a lawyer?

The young stranger went on. "His articles in *The Defender* got people talking 'bout their rights and Jim Crow."

"Jim Crow?" She looked away, trying to remember the snippets she heard about of the restrictions on Black people in the Southern states. She chewed her lip, embarrassed at how little she recalled.

The beginning of a smirk tugged at his mouth. Olivia had a feeling he knew just how to play those high cheekbones. "It's worse than I feared," he said. The desire to set him straight raised her temperature, but he continued before she could respond. "It is a good thing you're here," he said, his chin pointing behind her, where Reverend Andrews appeared, brushing past them to walk onstage and step onto an overturned crate. He faced the crowd. A hush fell over the room, like the quiet that falls over a congregation before the organ bellows the opening hymn. But this was not a service Olivia was used to.

The reverend cleared his throat. "Thank you all for coming here today. I know these are trying times, dangerous times. It may seem as if a force greater than ourselves means to pull us back after each stride toward equality." Women nodded into their fans and men's jaws hardened. A few offered mumbled prayers through barely parted lips.

"But we must not lose faith." The people around Olivia responded to his words with a chorus of *Amen*. "Without further delay, Mr. Washington DeWight."

"Excuse me," said the mysterious young man, the one who had interrogated her. She watched him gently part the masses on his way to the stage.

It took her a moment to understand.

He *is Mr. DeWight?*

He skipped over the crate to the spot where the reverend just stood. He found Olivia in the crowd and winked at her, setting her pulse raging in her ears. She wished she could disappear, run back up the stairs. But she didn't want him to know how much he'd rattled her. She forced her feet to stay rooted to the floor and to not turn from his gaze, which seemed locked on her.

Alabama lawyer Washington DeWight spoke with a steady confidence as he described growing unemployment and restricted access to employment and education, famine and violence that forced Black people north and west. He painted a picture so unlike the world she knew, despite insulting behavior from the occasional store clerk, that she couldn't help but question its veracity. But then she looked at the men and women beside her, the tears that lined many of their proud faces. Her stomach clenched and her breaths turned shallow.

"The Jim Crow laws of the South are spreading north." Mr. DeWight's words rang out, impassioned. The crowd jeered at the news and chattered. The reverend attempted to settle them. A small boy shoved a tattered blue pamphlet into Olivia's hands. She read the laws recently passed in Mr. DeWight's home state of Alabama. Each sentence started with *It is unlawful* in bold black letters. Each one struck down a right she'd taken for granted her entire life: Negros prohibited from entering establishments, owning businesses, sharing public spaces with white people. The list continued onto another page.

"The sentiment that the dark color of our skin is something to be feared continues to dictate policy, corrupting public places, stripping us of our only too recent freedoms!" he continued. His words sparked more and more side conversations in the audience. The woman beside her nodded as her companions began whispering amongst themselves. He shouted, "I ask that we all keep a watchful eye. The malevolent times of the recent past are still upon us." His words felt like ice water running down her back. She tucked the pamphlet into her purse as her mind struggled to imagine the ways these *laws* could impact her family, destroy everything her parents had worked so hard to build, everything her brother was set to carry forward.

Rare, is what her mother called their family. Her father had been enslaved, as had his father and mother before him and on and on. He didn't discuss his experience. Their mother preached patience, that he would share in time. The Davenport children had known only what history had been taught by their governess, leaving them to imagine the worst. Olivia remembered the moment she'd realized that every Black person she knew was touched by the horror of slavery. Sometimes Olivia felt it like a wound hidden deep under smooth skin—one that she didn't remember receiving but that ached nonetheless.

Every month or so, her father locked himself in the study with Mr. Tremaine and their contacts from the South, men who were in the business of finding lost family members. Her uncle, her father's brother, who aided in his escape, had yet to be found.

John was the first to notice that their mother filled those days with activities that kept them out of the house. Mama had been born free, but carried a weight of her own. She didn't share her burden either. Instead, she armored her children with the best things money could buy. Her mother's foresight allowed them safe passage throughout the city, seats at tables where they drew unwanted attention, but also served as an example of success in the Black community. Their excess allowed them to help others. It seemed impossible that a world in which her parents had built the Davenport Carriage Company could be dismantled.

Olivia's cheeks burned. Her chest felt tight. Was it true that everything she knew—her entire world—was being threatened by an assailant she couldn't see, one her parents hadn't fully warned her about? Did they even know? *They must.* Olivia remembered how closely her parents kept them when about town. Even when traveling to the community center, they had a member of the staff accompany them. Oh no—how long had she been down here?

Olivia pushed her way toward the entrance as the voices around her rose.

"You're not leaving so soon, are you?" Washington DeWight had left the stage and now caught up to her.

"I—I lost track of time. I'm late for a previous engagement," she stammered. Her eyes darted around the room.

"What did you think of my speech?" Mr. DeWight called up the stairs after her.

"I . . . I . . ." She was unsure what to say. She both believed him entirely and emphatically did not.

"Miss Olivia!" Tommy jumped from the driver's seat as soon as she emerged into the sunlight. A sheen of sweat covered his brow, and his cap was mangled cloth between his fingers. He glanced at Mr. DeWight and frowned. "I'm sorry to frighten you, miss, but I've been looking high and low for you. We have to go."

"Yes, of course," she replied, distracted, still feeling stunned.

Washington DeWight touched her shoulder lightly and some of the fog around Olivia's mind cleared.

"Will you be at the next meeting? We've rented this space for the next few months."

"Mr. DeWight—"

"Please, call me Washington."

Olivia's stomach flipped at how easily he brushed aside formality, like they were old friends. She watched Tommy open the carriage door for her. "Mr. DeWight," she said, feeling a small flutter in her chest. "I don't think that would be for the best."

He laughed again, but this time it did not feel kind. "I understand." Mr. DeWight took her hand and helped her inside the carriage. He leaned forward. "Don't you trouble your head over these silly things." His eyes flicked to the luxurious interior of the carriage and back to her eyes. "I'm sure your mind is much too crowded with pearls and parties and all the fine things in life. You just enjoy."

With that, he shut the door and the carriage took off. Olivia watched him standing there on the sidewalk as the horses veered into the street, his insult burning her cheeks.

CHAPTER 6

Helen

Helen, still in her dressing gown, stared at her reflection in the vanity. Tonight was the Tremaines' big gala, and Amy-Rose had done her best to tame Helen's curls and pull them up to the crown of her head. She never understood the need to straighten her hair before curling it when her hair dried into tight coils all on its own. Didn't she get a say on how her hair looked? And who decided what hair was supposed to look like anyway?

All she could think of was the hours she'd spent sitting in her room when she could have been in the library or the garage. Somewhere beneath the spiderweb of bobby pins, her scalp itched, but she knew if she so much as stuck the tip of her pinkie in there, her mother would be able to tell.

She looked at the dress draped over the chaise behind her and sighed. It had a high waist and a skirt that fell like a column. The crystals around the neckline glistened. Helen had no interest in going to this party. She dreaded the small talk of how much she'd grown and how her piano lessons were coming.

Helen was lost in her thoughts when she heard a knock at her door.

"Come in."

William Davenport inched his way inside the doorway. Helen took in her father's stiff white shirt, stark against the midnight of his slacks and shirtwaist. She followed his gaze as it traveled around her room, which she refused to let anyone clean but herself. It was cluttered not only with books and sketches, but also discarded shoes and abandoned cups of tea and empty plates. Amy-Rose and Olivia complained about the mess. Helen argued that all the best minds lived like this. She'd read in one of her books that it fostered creativity. Now she turned slowly in her chair, wondering if her father thought she was a slob.

Once upon a time, she had been the apple of her father's eye. He would sit her on his knee as she pulled on his ears and traced his profile and asked him questions. Questions about anything—including his horses and carriages. She recalled one afternoon when her father was in a carefree and playful mood. He let each of his children drive a buggy up and down the drive. Olivia kept a slow and steady pace. John, who had driven several times before, drove with a confidence that got under Helen's skin. When it was Helen's turn, she snapped the reins and set the team barreling down the drive. The air whipped her cheeks red and snatched the hat from her head. Mr. Davenport threw his head back and laughed. "That's my girl!" he had called out.

"Helen," her father said now, removing his glasses, "shouldn't you be dressed for the party?"

"Why are people always trying to dress me?" she muttered under her breath.

Mr. Davenport leaned over her desk and tapped his cane, shifting some of the atlases she'd left out. "I had an interesting conversation with John today," he said.

"Oh?" Helen asked, curious now. She turned back toward the mirror, watching his reflection move across the room and pick up another book on her bedside table. She noticed their resemblance—the stubborn nose and large brown eyes he'd passed on to her.

"Yes. He told me he bought a Model T that didn't run. Bets have been placed on who will uncover the reason. One person is close."

A small smile tugged at the corners of her lips. She'd spent the past few days in the garage working on the engine. John shooed her away before lunch.

Mr. Davenport was standing over her now. Without a word, he placed a car manual on the vanity in front of her. "The mechanics say every morning another part is removed. And cleaned. Exceptional problem-solving skills. I wanted to congratulate the mechanic. They may be able to repair it. But none of them had the slightest idea who was behind it," he said, sending her heart into overdrive.

Helen stared at the manual, grasping for words like straws. Was he upset? But he seemed impressed . . . She took a deep breath and met his gaze in the mirror.

She faltered.

"Curious thing to bet on a person you can't even name." His voice dropped to a whisper. "Let me see your hands."

Helen's stomach fell. Reluctantly, she did as he asked. Gently, he pried one of her fists open. Even after scrubbing with a fine-tooth brush, the telltale tar peeked through the corners of her fingernails. His next breath held more disappointment than she could stand.

"It's dirt," she said, the lie a piercing betrayal to her pride. "I was in the vegetable garden with Jessie."

"I will not suffer a liar, Helen," he said sharply. "You are not to go into that garage and mingle with those ruffians."

She cast her gaze downward. "They're my friends."

Mr. Davenport grunted. "They are not your friends. They are my employees. Malcolm expressed some concern—"

"Malcolm!" Helen said. Indignation twisted her stomach. The ornery mechanic held fast to outdated notions. She should have known this day would come.

"The garage is no place for a lady. It is a place of work, for those who need to, and not your playground. You're a beautiful girl, and you should take pride in that. It's time for you to grow up, Helen."

Helen slouched in her chair. Her image of his approval, the broad smile he'd direct at her for her accomplishment, it drifted out of reach. "I'm not a lady. And I can be a valuable part of the company if you would just give me a chance. If I could just—"

Mr. Davenport's silence was the loudest sound Helen had ever heard, louder than her own quick breaths. The hardened look in his eyes stopped her, but fatigue returned them to their warm, deep brown. Her father pinched her chin and met her eyes. She could have sworn his were tinged with a sadness that equaled her own. "John will take care of the business."

Her father's words tore open her heart and squeezed the hope from it.

"Now hurry up and get ready," he said. "We'll be leaving soon."

Mr. Davenport's figure blurred in Helen's vision as he left her bedroom. She pressed her palm to her lips and took a deep, shuddering breath, hearing the door click firmly shut behind her father.

CHAPTER 7

Amy-Rose

The house was quiet after the Davenports finally left for their evening at the Tremaines'. Amy-Rose and the remaining staff did not expect them back much before dawn, just in time for their long day of service to begin again. However, she was one of the lucky ones.

Her personal list of chores related mostly to the upkeep of Olivia and Helen. Olivia, who was so neat, left nearly nothing for her to do, and Helen didn't let Amy-Rose straighten her room lest her creative sanctuary be disturbed. So, Amy-Rose's mornings were filled with pressing their dresses and styling their hair. After that, she was free to do as she pleased.

She sighed. What must it be like to stay out all night, dancing and drinking champagne, not a worry in the world? She placed Olivia's powder and rouge in the makeup kit and turned off the lights.

She moved to the opposite wing of the house, where Henrietta—Hetty—was preparing Mr. and Mrs. Davenport's room. This side of Freeport Manor may have had fewer rooms, but they were grand. Mrs. Davenport surrounded herself with plush rugs and oversized couches that were as firm and unyielding as she was. Her closet was bigger than the apartment Amy-Rose had shared with her mother before they came to live here. Amy-Rose leaned against the doorframe as Henrietta straightened the duvet with quick flicks of her wrists.

"I'm just about finished here," Hetty said. "Why don't you head down to the kitchen and make sure everything is ready for Jessie when she gets back?"

Amy-Rose nodded. The Davenports' cook had left for the Tremaines' home early this morning to help prepare. Mrs. Tremaine requested her services, hoping to serve Jessie's signature desserts for her guests.

Once in the kitchen, she saw that Jessie had already scrubbed and polished everything. Amy-Rose said a silent prayer of thanks and took a seat at the long kitchen table to work on her salon plans and salves. She spent hours each night after her chores were finished, listing and experimenting and drawing and erasing and redrawing until she was satisfied, only to begin again on a clean sheet of paper. Her fingers traced the edge of one of the pages like her mother would her cheek before tucking her into bed.

She read through her recipes, gathering the items to try a new one. A jar of honey. Bananas to be mashed and blended with the reduced sugary syrup. Oils pressed from the plants and herbs in the garden that she kept in the highest cabinets. All the makings of a perfect pre-wash treatment. Amy-Rose didn't know what it took to run a business, but she knew what hair needed to be shiny and healthy. Mixing her treatments calmed her, left her mind free to wonder the what-ifs the future held.

Amy-Rose sighed and scratched the pencil across the pages of her journal, doodling design ideas for her salon next to her honey and banana recipe. The salon would be bright and welcoming. She wanted a tea service and finger foods. Everything would be lavender, her mother's favorite color. She imagined large gilded mirrors at each styling station that would multiply a delicately patterned wallpaper. Proper sinks for washing and rinsing, an elegant label gracing the product bottles, and on the sign above the door . . . If only she could decide on a name.

A set of footfalls came crashing into the kitchen. It was John Davenport, with his tie undone and his jacket over his arm. His finely tailored pants hugged his long, lean legs. Amy-Rose had thought all the Davenports had left for the party already. *What is he doing here?*

John glanced up quickly and smiled. His easy, playful disposition softened his features, which were so like his mother's. "How do you think that pressing comb will do against intruders?" His fingertips reached toward her. "Not hot, is it?"

"What?" Amy-Rose looked down. She was clutching an iron to her chest. She hadn't even realized she'd picked it up. "I'm sorry. I thought everyone had left." Heat rose in her cheeks.

"I got caught up in the garage. And then in my rush to get dressed, I tore one of my buttons right off," he said, gesturing to his shirt. "How is your sewing?"

"Fair," she said, her eyes staring at the floor between them.

"I tried to do it myself, but I kept sticking my finger."

"I'm not sure fixing a button counts as sewing," she joked. Amy-Rose regretted the words the instant they left her mouth. Her tone assumed a familiarity that was lost during her transition from playmate to servant. A pinch in her chest reminded her of Jessie's advice. The past should stay where it is. Now her own mouth felt dry at her boldness, but John just laughed. She watched the knot in his throat bob and a dimple appear on his freshly shaved cheek. Soon her shaky laughter joined his.

Then John deftly unbuttoned his shirt. "You'll need this," he said, handing it to her.

Amy-Rose tried to keep her attention on his shirt and not the toned muscles of his arms, exposed in his sleeveless undershirt. Or the way his just-steamed trousers hugged his waist. Her fingers picked through the sewing kit for the right needle and a silk thread strong enough to keep his shirt together over his broad chest. "What would you have done if you hadn't found anyone to stitch this for you?'

"Walk around naked, I guess."

Amy-Rose nearly stuck her own finger with a needle at his response. She blushed and pretended not to hear him.

John moved closer to her to watch her work. His hip brushed against the side of the counter, so close she smelled the soap on his skin and felt the heat from his body. Her skin tingled at the nearness of him. A few more strokes and the button was secure.

"Thank you, Amy-Rose." He brought the shirt close to his face. "Better than 'fair.' Not even my mother will be able to tell." He shoved his arms through the sleeves, the fabric pulling against his broad shoulders.

Amy-Rose smiled as she packed up the sewing kit.

"What are these?" he asked, gesturing to the papers on the table.

The question caught her off guard. John held the sketch of her salon. His brow furrowed as he studied her dream put to paper.

Could she share this with him? Not even Jessie had seen her plans.

John's fingers grazed her own. She looked into his eyes. Something in them made her brave.

"I want to open my own salon," she said. "Specialize in Black women's hair—styling it. So much of what we do is dictated by magazines filled with people who don't look like us." Amy-Rose turned back to her notebook and flipped through the pages filled with ingredients for pressing and curling kits in a mixture of French and English. Her shoulders relaxed and her voice grew louder. She'd done her research, following the work of other pioneers in hairdressing. Peppering the ladies at the drugstores on the South Side about what works best for them. And her mother. She'd written down everything her mother ever taught her. "There is more than one kind of beauty."

When she looked at John, he was staring at her. How often did she imagine a moment like this? John's strong jaw was inches from her face. His skin was a rich, smooth brown against the stark white of his tuxedo shirt.

John's eyes searched her face. "I think it's a wonderful idea," he said. His fingers brushed hers again, sending an electric jolt through her hand that traveled all the way down to her toes. It left her skin buzzing with energy and the fine hair on her arms lifting with a wave of gooseflesh.

"*There* you are!" Ethel skidded to a halt when she saw the young Mr. Davenport's untucked shirt and Amy-Rose's burning face. The two broke apart like opposing magnets. "Excuse me, Mister John," she said, eyeing them both. "I was looking for Amy-Rose."

"Good evening," John replied, his voice formal. "I was just heading out." He turned to Amy-Rose. "Thank you again, Amy-Rose. I don't know what I would do without you." He held her gaze, and Amy-Rose's heart raced.

CHAPTER 8

Ruby

The band had arrived shortly after the temporary help. Maids for hire and the Davenports' cook bustled in through the side entrance early in the morning to prepare the Tremaine home for the festivities. All were sworn to silence at the state of affairs concerning the family's dwindling resources. Without textiles from the factory, the Tremaines' main source of revenue was hobbled. Increasing the rent of the tenants of the Tremaines' boardinghouse was out of the question, even though it barely covered the cost of the building.

But mayoral races didn't wait. And neither did Ruby's father.

Ruby dressed without Margaret's help, trying to push the thoughts from her mind. Her dress hugged her curves and was a bit more scandalous than her mother preferred. But appearances were everything, and being seen in the latest style was peak Tremaine, even if it meant sacrificing a garment from a past season's wardrobe. Ruby had pulled her hair back to show off her long neck and graceful shoulders.

She felt like a gem. Still, something was missing.

Ruby stared at her bare neck and frowned. She glanced at the door behind her, a little afraid her mother might appear.

Just a quick look, she told herself. Music drifted from the mahogany box on her dresser as she lifted the lid. The tinny music reminded her of a lullaby. She placed the earrings and fragile gold cross on a chain to the side. Carefully, she pried the bottom of the box up. The light glinted off the sharp edge of the ruby hidden beneath, teardrop-shaped and lovely.

The sight of it still took her breath away. The namesake stone was a gift for her sixteenth birthday from her mother and father, before their dreams grew bigger than her happiness. With one more quick glance at her closed door, she lifted the necklace by the ends of its lobster claw closer.

The deep red stone sat in the hollow of her throat and matched the rich fabric of her dress. *This would go perfectly*, she thought with a sadness she wished she could swallow down. Her father's reasons for running for office were noble. But she couldn't help the bitterness that welled up at having to hide her most prized possession. It rankled almost as much as the bitterness of her parents asking her to sell it. How could they? This gift from *them*—it was more than a trinket. It was strong, beautiful, and set in gold. A perfect reflection of her own self-confidence, when she wasn't feeling second chair to her best friend. When she held her parents' gift, much less wore it, she felt bold and strong.

Ruby harbored no regrets about the necklace of her mother's that she'd pawned instead. Served her right for asking such a thing of her daughter. And the fact that her mother never missed it only confirmed that Ruby had made the right decision.

The music died and in the sudden silence, Ruby heard footsteps stop outside her door. She watched the knob turn as she fidgeted with the clasp behind her neck. There was no time to hide it now. But no one could know she kept it. The stone and its delicate chain disappeared into the neck of her dress.

"Are you about ready?" Mrs. Tremaine asked from the doorway.

"Yes," Ruby answered quickly. She shifted her weight, hoping to block the broken-looking jewelry box on the dresser. Her skin warmed as she took in her mother's stare.

Mrs. Tremaine sighed. She walked up to Ruby. "I know things are more difficult than we expected when your father entered this race, but this isn't forever. The whole harvest isn't lost. And your uncle is working on contracts with other farms. We just need to give it time."

Ruby nodded stiffly as her mother adjusted the fabric draped over her shoulders. The chain of the necklace slipped further, tickling her skin. She hoped that the bodice of the dress was tight enough that the stone wouldn't clatter to the ground beneath her feet.

"Your father may not always show it, but he is proud of you," her mother said.

Ruby's body tensed. She wanted to hold on to the anger a bit longer.

"Just stick to the plan, and everything else will work itself out."

The plan. Anger flared in Ruby's chest again. The plan that she had no say in. She decided she would continue to protect what was important to her, starting with the little piece of her identity caught between layers of her clothing. She longed for the day when she would be the mistress of her own home, adored by an affectionate husband and surrounded by their children. And not treated as a means for her parents to achieve their goals.

"Ruby, what have you done to your jewelry box?" Mrs. Tremaine picked up the seemingly broken pieces.

"Is it a jewelry box, if it doesn't have any jewelry in it?" she asked.

Her mother looked at her steadily, her expression not without compassion. Then she seemed to make a decision, her face hardening. Quietly she said, "You better fix your attitude before you head downstairs."

Your attitude. Ruby exhaled, her temper escaping her lungs with enough force to shift the bodice of her gown. Her prized necklace clattered to the ground. It skittered across the hardwood floor, and came to a stop at the rounded toe of her mother's silk shoe.

"Ruby," Mrs. Tremaine said, her voice trailing off as she bent to retrieve the jewel. "I thought this was included with the other items you brought to the adjuster? You were supposed to bring all small items of value to him when he was here."

Ruby watched the light glisten off the delicate chain. The bright stone had disappeared into her mother's palm and with it any excuse she could muster.

"Ruby?"

"I replaced it with something else," she said. Her pulse began to pound behind her ears. "That is mine. I don't understand why I can't keep it. You've sold nearly everything else."

Mrs. Tremaine stayed firm. "Do you know how many people this could help?"

Other people, Ruby thought. Never her. Not their daughter who had to smile and pretend nothing was amiss. Plus the money technically went to the campaign. "What about me?" Ruby's voice had risen to a louder than acceptable volume. Her chest heaved with each breath. All she wanted was to snatch the chain back, to feel the comforting weight around her neck. She knew any move to do so would guarantee its loss. Even now she pressed against the boundaries of her parents' thinning patience. "What about me?" she asked again, calmly, as if her heart weren't at risk of breaking.

She watched silently as her mother weighed a decision. Ruby knew the instant it was done. Mrs. Tremaine pulled her shoulders back, palmed the necklace, and hid her hands in the folds of her skirt. "One day you'll understand. Now, please, finish getting dressed."

A small sound escaped Ruby's lips. Her feet remained where they were. The door closed with a firmness that echoed around the room, and a hollowness expanded within her.

There was only one way to get back what was hers.

Ruby stood in the foyer beside her mother, a smile plastered on her face. Her jaw ached from the words she kept to herself and the pleasantries forced out instead. Good behavior—it was her only hope. She watched their party guests as they glided across the foyer under the vaulted ceiling. The women wore their hair high and their gowns long, escorted by gentlemen in finely tailored tuxedos. A live band played, waiters offered champagne and hors d'oeuvres on silver trays, and a hundred lanterns decorated the patio outside.

It was a glamorous affair, but all Ruby could think was: Could they see the darkened paper where the work of an old master once hung? Her mother had told everyone it was on loan to some distant museum. "Isn't it grand how Mr. Tremaine supports the arts?" they said. But Ruby wondered if they whispered behind their backs, "Oh, how the mighty have fallen." Running for office was one thing, but going penniless as a result was another. She fought the urge to reach for the necklace she knew wasn't there.

"Could you at least look like you are enjoying yourself?" her mother said behind a smile.

"I would enjoy it more if I had my necklace," she muttered.

"You can be sure it'll be sold by the end of next week." Her mother gave her a pointed look.

Ruby knew it would be a lot easier once she lost herself in the music and the crowd. With a glass of champagne to calm her nerves and banish the sour feelings settling in her gut.

She escaped the receiving line the first chance she got and deftly fielded questions about her plans for the summer as she hunted for a sparkling cocktail.

Olivia seems to be enjoying herself, she thought. Her best friend and Mr. Lawrence were the talk of the ball. She was happy for her, really, she was. But earlier that day, Ruby had suffered another lecture from her parents about making the most of this night with John. So here she was, and yet John was nowhere to be seen. Rather, Ruby was stuck with Louis Greenfield, a childhood friend who did nothing but talk about racehorses.

When John finally walked through the door, a hush fell over the room as if every single lady, with the exception of his own sisters, held her breath. The tuxedo hugged his shoulders and concealed the muscles moving beneath. John was the most sought-after bachelor in the room, and yet he carried himself in such a carefree way, it was hard to determine whether he was simply oblivious or couldn't be bothered with such nonsense. Either way, it made him even more magnetic.

Ruby placed her empty glass of champagne on the table and knifed her way through the crowd. The beads of her dress clinked at her heels. She arrived at his elbow a few steps before the doe-eyed daughter of one of her father's new city council friends.

John turned at her touch on his forearm. The dimple in his cheek set her heart to fluttering. The smell of soap and aftershave still clung to his skin. She was glad for the shawl hanging over her elbows—it gave her something to keep her hands busy.

"How lovely of you to join us," she said, cringing inside. She had meant to sound teasing but it came off chiding.

Thankfully, John didn't seem to notice. He smiled. "I'm sorry, Ruby. I lost track of time. Working on a new project," he said by way of explanation.

"I admire your dedication," she said. "I hope to one day find something I love as much as you do automobiles." Ruby adjusted the pin in his lapel, leaning close to make the most of how her reconstructed dress hugged her body.

"Would you like to dance?" she suggested at the same time John asked, "Have you seen Helen?"

"No," she said, disappointed by this question. She tried to think of something, anything, to keep him near. "I can help you look for her? Perhaps she's in the garden." She thought of the maze and the privacy it would offer them.

"I appreciate the offer, Ruby," he said, still searching the room. "But you have guests. I would hate to take you away from them." He pressed his lips to the back of her hand. "You look lovely to-night, by the way."

A small sound escaped Ruby's mouth as she searched for the words that would persuade him to stay. But before she knew it, she was alone at the edge of the dance floor, staring at John's back as he moved to the opposite side. She felt the stinging glare of her mother from the couches of gentleladies near the fireplace.

Ruby kept her face calm while she reached for a glass of champagne, and upended the drink after her mother finally turned away. The champagne was tart and fizzy, the complete opposite of how Ruby felt. She wondered if there was a ladylike way to retrieve the strawberry stuck at the bottom of the flute. Not that anyone was paying any real attention to her. Olivia and Mr. Lawrence twirled across her parents' "modest" ballroom, as Mrs. Davenport had put it, drawing the gazes and sighs of all in attendance. Even Helen had captured more attention when she first arrived, dressed in a faint pink gown that swayed beautifully as she'd stomped from table to table looking for someone to sneak her a cigarette.

Ruby grabbed yet another flute from the tray flying past her. She swayed slightly, but luckily the table was there to steady her.

"In need of liquid courage then, are you?"

Ruby looked up from her glass, startled at the voice over her shoulder. Harrison Barton pointed to the glass in her hand. He had moved to Chicago from Louisiana last summer. His wealth had gotten him an invitation, but there wasn't enough money in the city to make people forget his white father once owned his mother. He had the same fair complexion as Olivia's old playmate-now-maid Amy-Rose. And as Ruby lifted her gaze, she was reminded of his eyes—a pale, watery brown fringed in green. Many in this room would have him bear the guilt of his parents' mixed union. Features like his were typically the result of violence, a reminder of unspoken pain. His very existence challenged the comfort of Black and white people alike.

It didn't faze Ruby. "And what would I need courage for, Mr. Barton?" she asked. She let him take the glass from her hand and replace it with a bite-sized raspberry tart. Its buttery crust melted in her mouth, followed by the burst of sweet fruit and cream filling.

"Did I say courage?" Mr. Barton corrected himself, color rising above his collar. Ruby felt her skin prickle and couldn't quite keep a smile off her face. She liked the musical way he pronounced each syllable. "Perhaps you're just in need of fun." He sounded less sure of himself, but kept his warm smile.

"Fun is my favorite pastime. My, if you're not having fun, what's the point?"

Mr. Barton shifted his weight, revealing John talking with his father across the room. But to her surprise, John's eyes were on her and Harrison Barton, his face in a frown. Was he . . . jealous? She placed her hand gently on Harrison's forearm. Through her eyelashes she saw John freeze. *Typical*, she thought. Men never outgrew the instincts of playground possession. Well, if this is what it took to capture John's focus, then so be it.

"Would you like to dance?" Harrison asked.

Ruby tore her gaze away from John and toward the man standing in front of her. "I would have asked you myself, but you beat me to it!"

He placed his hand at the small of her back and guided her to the center of the room. She felt John's eyes as she and her handsome dance partner glided across the floor and smiled genuinely for the first time all night. A plan began to take shape . . . Ruby turned the full wattage of her charms on Mr. Barton. She leaned in as close as was acceptable, and after making a mental note of John's last location, she willed herself not to look in his direction and instead focus all her attention on the man in front of her.

Harrison Barton proved to be a magnificent dancer, and shockingly, an even better conversationalist. He described his family and the small town he grew up in with such fondness, it made Ruby's heart ache. She was so invested in his story about how his brother broke his arm climbing a tree, she didn't notice the song change or her mother sneaking up behind her.

"Ruby," she said through her teeth when she reached her daughter. "You must make yourself available to *all* our guests."

Ruby, the champagne bubbling in her veins and her anger simmering beneath her skin, spun to her mother.

"I beg your pardon, Mrs. Tremaine," Harrison broke in before Ruby could utter her frustration aloud. "Your daughter is an excellent partner. I enjoy her company and never intended to steal so much of it." Harrison's words may have been directed to her mother, but his hazel eyes never left Ruby's. And if he saw Mrs. Tremaine's eyebrow twitch, he showed no sign of it. "Thank you for the dance, Miss Tremaine," he said. She watched Agatha Leary approach him, and the two melted into the crowd. Yes, a popular bachelor would do nicely.

Ruby made a break for the bar, leaving her mother's side before she said something she'd regret. She took a hard left when she spotted the crowd. Instead, she found comfort in the hallway. The air was noticeably chilly, but refreshing. Ruby leaned against the wall and closed her eyes. *Only a few hours more*, she told herself. Hushed whispers made their way through the music to where she hid. Ruby couldn't resist. She tiptoed closer to the drawing room, repurposed as a ladies' lounge for the night.

"Well, I hope for their sake he wins."

Ruby jolted upright and stood still, hidden by the wall of the hallway.

A second voice chimed in. "He'll need the white vote if he wants to win. More than the few here tonight."

"Mm-hmm," the first speaker said. "If he doesn't, the Tremaines will have nothing left."

Ruby's chest strained against her dress with each breath.

"May I have the next dance?" a voice murmured in her ear.

She started. Then the smell of bergamot and balsam wrapped around her, easing the tension she felt. Ah yes, the real reason she had danced with Mr. Barton in the first place. She'd nearly forgotten.

Ruby smiled and twirled slowly toward John Davenport, the satisfaction of knowing her plan would work tugging at the corners of her lips.

"I thought you'd never ask."

CHAPTER 9

Olivia

Olivia was breathless. She clutched Mr. Lawrence's shoulders as he spun her around the dance floor. With his hand pressed flat across her spine, they fought to outlast the other couples trying to keep up with the band's increasing tempo. Eliminated dancers joined the spectators, clapping with the beat. All eyes were on her, and for once, Olivia didn't find herself second-guessing her every move. She wasn't striving for perfection.

She was having fun.

Her face felt warm and sweat gathered at her temples. And though her calves burned and her toes smarted, she didn't want to stop.

"When I asked you to dance," Mr. Lawrence yelled over the music, "I pictured something a little slower."

"We can slow down if this is too much for you," she said, an eyebrow arching in a challenge.

"And lose?" He shook his head and stared into her eyes. "When I set my mind to something, I mean to win."

His words made her blush deepen.

Faces blurred around them. Their steps grew clumsy as the pace increased and another couple bowed out. Olivia missed a step, her feet tangling with Mr. Lawrence's. They stumbled from the dance floor, his arms around her waist and his face merely inches from hers. They broke into laughter.

"I'm sorry," she breathed.

Mr. Lawrence considered the last couple celebrating on the floor. "We gave it a good run. And there will be a next time." He smiled. "I'll get us some drinks." She nodded and watched him walk across the ballroom.

"Olivia." Mrs. Davenport stepped quickly toward her daughter and squeezed both her hands. "You two make such a lovely couple," she whispered.

Olivia smiled as her mother lovingly pinched her chin and walked on.

Jacob Lawrence had barely left Olivia's side since he'd arrived at the party. He was gracious as she carried out numerous introductions, and he made her laugh several times. He was witty and charming. Handsome. Everything she was looking for in a match. And, she was quite positive he felt the same way about her. After a year of wondering how she would find a match, could it truly be this easy?

She watched him at the bar, two champagne flutes in hand, talking to Mr. Tremaine. He glanced in her direction and smiled.

"Of course this is where I would see you again." A familiar voice shook Olivia out of her reverie. She turned.

Washington DeWight was standing behind her, a smirk on his face, dressed in a simple dark suit and all the confidence he'd had onstage. His hands were in his pockets, shoulders thrown back as he lazily looked around the room. "You do look more at home here, don't you?"

Her stomach flipped and her mouth felt dry. "What are you doing here?" she asked. Her voice was rougher than she'd intended.

He laughed. "Well, it's lovely to see you too. The Tremaines invited me."

"Oh?"

Mr. DeWight pursed his lips. "Any candidate for public office knows how important it is to get the support of the working class." He nodded to himself. "I was right about you."

"How so?" she asked, her eyes narrowing, picking up on his tone.

He gestured to the room. "Rich girl, slumming it on the poor side of town."

"I was not *slumming* it. I was bringing donations to the community center. I—"

"My apologies, a philanthropic rich girl—"

"You don't know anything about me," she said. Olivia found herself closer to him than she was before, her fists clenched at her sides.

"You and that gentleman of yours have been the talk of the ball," he offered, switching topics so quickly, Olivia found herself blinking dumbly in response.

Out of the corner of her eye, Olivia caught Mrs. Johnson, a friend of her mother's and an intolerable gossip, watching them, a slight frown on her face. A few others were looking in their direction too, whispering. Olivia gave them her widest smile and kept her chin level.

Mr. DeWight's smile grew wider too as he took in her visible frustration. "Curiosity may have led you to the meeting, but I think compassion kept you there. This is a beautiful world you live in." He took in the room around them before bringing his eyes back to hers. "But now you know what's at stake." He held her gaze.

Olivia's breathing slowed. His words had left an impression on her, hard as she'd tried to push them out of her thoughts. She'd nearly asked Hetty to fetch her a copy of *The Defender* the next morning, but . . . what would that accomplish? Her father had spent his life working to protect her from the horrors of the South. He wanted her to live exactly the life she was so lucky to have.

The band started up a new song and the Tremaines' guests scrambled to the ballroom floor. Their half-eaten delicacies and empty champagne flutes littered every flat surface. A sea of silk, tulle, and satin, the guests moved to the current of the rhythm. She looked down at her own dress and thought of the neat, thread-bare frocks worn with fiery confidence by some of the women she saw in that crowded basement. None of the young ladies in her set attended rallies. They threw charity galas and fundraisers, they donated money and goods to acceptable causes.

Mr. Lawrence suddenly appeared beside her. "Are you all right?" he asked. He handed Olivia a glass and searched her face.

"Yes!" she said, shaking her head free of these thoughts. "Mr. Lawrence, this is Washington—Mr. Washington DeWight." She practically inhaled the champagne as the two men roughly shook hands.

A muscle in Mr. Lawrence's jaw twitched. "How do you two know each other?"

Olivia looked to Mr. DeWight for help. Mr. Lawrence's reaction to her use of his first name did not go unnoticed. Now it had her flustered and scrambling for words. Mr. DeWight stood silently, his hands hidden again in his pockets, an almost amused look on his face. He was deliberately staying quiet while she squirmed in the too hot, too loud room, under the scrutinizing eye of the English gentleman. "We—" she started, then stopped. What should she say?

Finally, Mr. DeWight spoke. "Miss Davenport and I were just having a laugh." He chuckled as if they shared a private joke. "I mistook her for an old acquaintance. Though now that I think on it," he said, pinning her with his stare, "I must have just seen a picture of you in the society papers." The air rushed back into her lungs with such speed, Olivia became dizzy. "If you'll excuse me." Washington DeWight gave Olivia a tight smile and tipped an invisible hat to Mr. Lawrence.

Olivia watched him walk away, her heart pounding, gooseflesh rising all over her skin. She turned back to Mr. Lawrence and smiled wider than she had all night. "Now, where were we?" she asked, her hand fitting nicely in the crook of his elbow.

As Mr. Lawrence guided her to the dance floor, Olivia was relieved to see the lawyer from the South had disappeared into the crowd.

CHAPTER 10

Helen

Helen knew it was going to be a long night. As soon as her family had ascended the stairs to the Tremaine home, she'd made a break for it. She saw no need to wait in a receiving line to be introduced to people she already knew. It was always the same players at these events, with the same outdated notions of how young ladies ought to behave. After that talk with her father, she didn't need any more of *that* right now, thank you very much.

The first chance she got, Helen snuck into the ballroom, ducking between guests. She stole a tray of crab cakes and two flutes of champagne and found a chair nestled in the corner. She watched the party around her, the younger girls her age whispering and giggling to one another. They seemed altogether unconcerned with the fact that they were basically here for the amusement of their parents, with the eventual responsibility of finding a husband. They'd all be coming out soon enough, and the pressure to select a good match—or rather, to *be* selected—would take up every waking breath. Helen herself would be eighteen by the end of the summer, and if Olivia had been matched last year, Helen would now be stuck dancing with the new crop of bachelors. She couldn't stand the idea. Helen rolled her eyes and turned to the large windows overlooking the gardens. Maybe some fresh air would do her good.

The Tremaines' garden was a legendary maze of neatly manicured hedges, now strung with tiny lights that flickered like fireflies. Once outside, Helen cornered the son of one of her father's business partners, Josiah Andrews, and convinced him to give her a cigarette and a light.

Once Josiah had walked away, Helen took a drag from the cigarette and blew the smoke out in a swirling cloud above her head. She tried to dislodge her father's words from her mind. Couldn't he see that she had so much to offer? That she was more than a pretty face? She flicked the ash into the wind and cleared her throat. She would not cry again.

"Oh, hello."

Helen stilled, cursing herself for getting so caught up in her thoughts, she didn't hear someone approach. It could have been her father, or worse, her mother. Emmeline Davenport saw smoking as a pastime for women of lower classes.

She turned to the intruder.

Jacob Lawrence. The young man Olivia had spent most of the night with. They'd met briefly before dinner. Helen noticed right away that he was tall, lean, and carried himself as though he could have anything if he only asked. Indeed, it appeared quite likely he would soon have her sister.

He came to stand next to her. But not too close. He tapped a cigarette on an engraved gold cigarette case and waited. "How about we come to an agreement?" he asked when she didn't move. His voice was smooth and accented. "I'll not breathe a word of you being out here and you'll share that light in your hand."

Helen eyed him, not sure if she could trust him. His smile was too wide and his eyes too intense. They didn't break contact with hers as she held the matchbox out to him.

"I'll want another cigarette too," she said, stubbing out her spent one beneath her toe.

Mr. Lawrence laughed and Helen felt a chill run up her spine.

"Beautiful night," he said, holding the light steady for her.

"Yes," she said, wishing he would go away and leave her with her thoughts.

"Is this a true maze?" he asked. He stepped down into the wet grass.

She nodded. "There's a fountain at the center." She stuck out her chin and crossed her arms.

He looked at her. "You don't seem impressed by me."

"Should I be?" she asked.

He laughed again, further unsettling her nerves. Helen felt his laugh like an engine turning over under her hand—powerful, eager, and a little dangerous.

"Most people find I'm very impressive."

She couldn't help it; a laugh of her own escaped her lips and echoed through the night. In the shadows, she could see his smile widen and his confidence, so strong already, grow.

"I'm wealthy. Well read. Well traveled," he said, listing these traits on the fingers not holding the cigarette.

"Oh, don't forget handsome too," she said.

"I thought that was a given." He cleared his throat and climbed the stairs to stand beside her again. The heat from his body drew gooseflesh on her arms. She breathed deep. The smell of his cologne—cedar—and the smoke from his cigarette generated a strange sensation in her chest.

"What about you?" he asked.

Helen was confused. "What *about* me?"

Mr. Lawrence laughed. "Tell me about yourself."

His request caught her off guard. Helen realized she'd never met anyone who didn't already know who she was, who her family was. She was the youngest of the Davenport children, Olivia's sister, the one who couldn't needlepoint, sing, or serve tea correctly. What else was there to say?

"I too am well read," she began. He nodded as if he expected this and she pouted. She squared her shoulders and said, "Mostly mechanics' magazines and manuals. Poetry is such a bore." She looked at him, a challenge in her eyes.

"Fantastic. I'm rubbish with machines," he replied. "How are you with electrical work? There is a switch in my hotel room that shocks me every time I turn out the lamp."

"I'm sure I could manage." Helen's face grew hot at the idea of being in his room.

He lifted his eyebrows a fraction, but recovered quickly, his features forming a smile. "I'll keep that in mind."

Suddenly, Helen's skin was too tight. What was she doing? He may not be engaged to her sister, but it was only a matter of time. Helen recalled the way Olivia smiled as Mr. Lawrence led her across the dance floor. Even from her chair in the corner, Helen heard the relieved sigh of her mother above the music. This is what Emmeline Davenport had always wanted.

And yet, what was this feeling stirring in her chest?

"I must head inside," he said. With that, Mr. Lawrence took her hand and kissed it, holding it to his lips a moment too long, she thought. Helen stilled. Her mind grew quiet and all she could see was the handsome young man standing before her.

"Good night, Miss Davenport."

"Good night, Mr. Lawrence," she said, pulling her hand away. "And until you call that electrician, consider lighting a candle instead."

He laughed, his hand hovering above the handle on the patio door. "Ring me first. I'll put a pot of tea on."

CHAPTER 11

Amy-Rose

Amy-Rose combed her fingers through Helen's hair, removing pins along the way. She tried to keep her focus on the task at hand, but one pin had stuck her, just lightly, reminding her of the sewing needle she'd used to stitch John's button back on. And the bitter tang of Helen's coffee, black, just the way John drank it, clawed at her senses. Everything, however small, reminded her of John. They'd had a moment, the two of them, hadn't they? Amy-Rose felt the flutter in the stomach as she imagined his calloused hands against her wrists. The warmth of his palm against her skin. She was overreacting. They were just having a bit of fun.

"Are you well, Amy-Rose?" Helen stared at her, a hand clasped around Amy-Rose's wrist.

Amy-Rose could feel her pulse bounding against the soft pressure applied by the girl, whose hands were as rough as her brother's. Thoughts of John crowded her mind again. She cleared her throat and shook her shoulders. "Yes, of course," she said.

Helen's eyes narrowed. Amy-Rose held her gaze and tried to

remember what it was Helen had been talking about. Was it about cars? Helen was usually talking about cars. Or some new invention she'd read about in her father's papers.

"So, what do you think I should do?"

"Do?" Amy-Rose turned Helen in her seat. Her mind scrambled to piece together the words Helen had said while her mind wandered, imagining she was caught in John's arms.

Helen rolled her eyes. "My birthday is at the end of the summer. I'll be eighteen and Mama will have no reason to hold off finding me a husband. The only thing that's saved me so far is how picky Olivia can be." Helen sighed, and for a moment she looked like the young scrawny girl she'd been a year ago. But over the past months, her figure had filled out, she'd grown into her face, and the intelligence in her eyes hinted at a fierceness within her Amy-Rose hoped wouldn't scare off eligible bachelors.

Helen's words about her older sister were harsh, and Amy-Rose thought to remind her of the pressure Olivia must be under, to decide her future at nineteen, please her parents, and live up to the expectations of society.

"Is she being picky? Or does she know what she wants and is willing to wait for it?" Amy-Rose hadn't meant to say those things out loud. Her fingers quickened their pace about Helen's head. She feared she'd say more. Last night's chance encounter with John disrupted her composure, and now Amy-Rose didn't know up from down. Sleep evaded her and she woke with a pounding headache. Not even penciling ideas for her salon had calmed her nerves.

"I think you're right." Helen picked up another paper. "Livy knows what she wants, and she's not one to settle." Her eyes met Amy-Rose's in the mirror. "Obviously, neither should we."

The wind whipped the dresses on the line with a crack. Amy-Rose held the hem of one of Olivia's shirtsleeves to her skin. Still damp. For a moment she weighed the chances of the gust tearing the clothing from the line against the trouble of hanging the garments in the small room where she did the mending. The arrival of dark clouds made the decision for her. She began removing the shirts and dresses off the line, folding them neatly to prevent creases. The less she had to press the better.

With the only sound the rustling of the wind through the trees, Amy-Rose's mind wandered again to her encounter with John in the kitchen. Her skin tingled at the memory of his body so close to hers, the way his cologne made her head spin. Balsam and bergamot, and a hint something else that was uniquely John. He'd spent the past several months away at university. At first, the house seemed so empty without him. Helen was completely lost, but Amy-Rose welcomed the distance. It lessened the sting of how invisible she felt around him.

They were no longer children who played in the gardens or told stories around a roaring fire. Still, she never forgot the day he told her she was the prettiest girl he knew after Tommy teased her to tears over the freckles that dotted her nose. Like dirt. John had taken the bar of soap from her hand and pulled her away from the basin. The warmth of his hand and his smile had made her forget the sting of her chapped hands and the shame that burned her face. He'd said it matter-of-factly. She'd realized then that she would never see him the same way again. His simple observation spurred the most unshakeable beginnings of a crush, though she'd been too young to know what to call it then.

She knew what to call it now. Trouble.

But then he'd bounded into the kitchen and asked her to sew on a button.

Now she was confused. *Could he just have been flirting?* Doubt grew by the minute. She held a blouse to her chest and tried to remember the way his voice moved through her. She pictured what their life could be like together, after he'd graduated school and was ready to take over his father's company. She would likely be there to celebrate. But not as the maid.

She would be a brand-new version of herself. Her salon would be up and running. Her business successful, and she his perfect match. He was the heir to the Davenport family business and fortune. He needed a well-bred lady at his side, one who could host dinner parties, dress in the latest fashions, and eventually raise the next heir.

"Is that me?" she whispered into the dim afternoon. *Is that what I want?* Amy-Rose thought of her notebook of dreams and everything she held dear. Helen's words came back to her. *Livy knows what she wants, and she's not one to settle.* Amy-Rose felt the words surge through her and heat her blood. *Obviously, neither should we.*

A sudden tap on her shoulder made her jump. She spun quickly, losing her balance. John steadied her with a hand at her elbow. The playful tilt to his mouth captured Amy-Rose's attention a beat too long. *Oh, and that dimple!*

Amy-Rose glanced over her shoulder. Her throat felt tight and dry. The heat blooming in her cheeks began to spread as she noticed the top buttons of his shirt were undone. His skin was smooth and dark and her fingers ached to trace the line of his jaw.

She remembered the warmth of his body when he stood next to her in the kitchen, making her shiver.

"Cold?" he asked, concern furrowing his brow.

"No—yes."

John's smile widened. "Do I make you nervous?"

"Of course not." Her words held more conviction than she felt. Amy-Rose forced herself to look up from the damp blouse in her hands and stare into his eyes. She watched them begin to smolder.

"Thank you again for your help the other night. You not only saved my shirt, but my ears from a lecture I'm sure I deserved about being prepared and presentable."

"I was glad to help. Did you enjoy the party?" she asked. Amy-Rose had never attended one of the lavish events thrown by the Tremaines. And as a maid, she had only watched from the sidelines of the Davenports' dances, blending in and out of the shadows like a good and reliable servant.

"Yes, it was nice seeing some of my friends. Strange too. Away from here, I choose everything, big and small. From what I wear," he said, gesturing to the coveralls and bleached shirt with rolled-up shirtsleeves, "to bigger things, like . . . managing my time or where I live. Then as soon as I turned down the drive, all of that"—he snapped his fingers—"disappeared. And what goes with it? My confidence, brought on by this . . . *illusion* of being self-sufficient."

"I'm sure it wasn't an illusion," she said. Amy-Rose couldn't help how differently she felt coming back here to Freeport after selling her hair treatments at the small general stores on the South Side. How quickly the boldness of her business attitude dissipated when she donned an apron and picked up a dishcloth. Maybe the two of them weren't so different. "There must have been something about it you enjoyed. The music?"

John laughed and Amy-Rose had to suppress a sigh. "Yes, the music and dancing were fun." He looked at her. "What's wrong?"

Amy-Rose finished folding the blouse and dropped it into the basket. "I was imagining it, that's all. The glamour. I've been to the dance halls with Tommy and Hetty, but nothing fancy. The dancing alone . . ." Her voice trailed off.

"It's not so hard. The gentleman will lead."

"I don't—" Her words faded at his outstretched hand. Her own were hidden between the folds of her skirt. She knew they were dry and chafed from the washing.

"May I have this dance, Miss Shepherd?" he said, placing his other hand over his chest. Amy-Rose couldn't help the smile slowly spreading across her face.

She stared at his open palm—an invitation to step into a make-believe world where they would be two people meeting at a dance. One where she was not a maid and he wasn't the son of her employer. It was just pretend. Her fingers tingled until her skin made contact with his. He gently placed a hand at the curve of her waist and began counting. She knew the steps. She'd danced with the girls when they were learning, watched them practice with their instructors, and stood against the wall at the many dances held at Freeport Manor. Today, she held John instead of a tray behind a banquette.

They ducked under the clotheslines. The shirts twisted in the wind and Amy-Rose pretended they were other dancers circling elegantly around them. John commended her on her form and joked about how happy he was to not have to worry about toes crushed underfoot. He began to hum softly, drawing her closer, close enough that their movements slowed. She angled her face closer to his. She didn't think she'd ever stood this close to him before. Her breath stuck in her throat, the heady smell of his cologne too intoxicating.

Amy-Rose's heart raced. Her foot stepped into the basket of folded laundry. Before she knew it, the ground and sky tilted. John fell with her, pulling clothing from the line around them. The two of them were a tangle of limbs and damp garments. He gently removed the petticoat covering her face. She sat up and looked at the mess they'd made, all the things she'd have to rewash, but beside her, John looked at her like she was the world. His laugh escaped in a great, infectious rush.

"At least I didn't step on your toes," she said.

CHAPTER 12

Olivia

Olivia looked out the window as the breeze scattered white petals across the back lawn. She sat in her new day dress, pale blue with an ivory lace trim. Smart. Modest. And a host of other important qualities her mother said clothing can convey. If Mr. Lawrence was anything like her brother, whether a dress was becoming or ugly often depended on the figure of the woman who wore it. "It's not about size," he'd said to her once. "But proportion. Line." As if he'd been talking about a motorcar. She took shallow breaths now due to the corset and shook her head gently.

She and the new English bachelor, Jacob Lawrence, were the talk of Black society since their turn about the Tremaine ballroom floor. The only person more excited about the blossoming romance than Olivia was her mother.

In the week following the Tremaines' party, Mr. Lawrence had had tea at Freeport Manor, lunch with her father downtown, and just this past Sunday, attended service at their church, sitting in their family's pew. The whispers were loud. Suffocating. As encouraging as they were frightening.

It was everything she wanted.

Olivia had done what was expected of her and this was her due: a strong, handsome gentleman who fulfilled her parents' every wish and her quiet hopes.

She shifted in her seat as the thought of the young lawyer Washington DeWight eased into her mind. His life appeared to be full of choice and intention. But he also seemed to be unimpressed by all that Olivia had accomplished. As if all her own hard work was a waste of time. The idea of him thinking she was some frivolous girl made her grind her teeth.

Emmeline Davenport burst into the morning room then, humming loudly to herself. Olivia noted she was in a particularly good mood. Her mother was graceful, and though she had faced hardships of her own, Mrs. Davenport, her hair styled neatly at the base of her head, had an approachable face that disguised nothing. Her almond-shaped eyes smoldered like twin coals, warm and mesmerizing. Every joy and disappointment wrote itself clear across her brow and the tilt of her mouth. Their small angles guided Olivia's reactions—when to bargain, challenge, and relent. After all, the only thing Emmeline wanted was for her children to have the best of everything and to want for nothing. How could Olivia fault her for that?

Olivia emerged from her thoughts to find her mother smiling at her as if she held a secret.

"I think someone is a bit lost in a daydream," Mrs. Davenport said, more like a statement than a question. "How flushed you look."

Olivia placed a hand on her cheek. It was indeed warm. Her mother would be alarmed to know it was thoughts of Mr. DeWight—not Mr. Lawrence—to blame for her blush. In fact, Olivia was a bit alarmed herself.

Emmeline Davenport patted Olivia's hand and sat on the chaise across from her. "I am very pleased at the reception you and Mr. Lawrence have received. You two make such a lovely couple." She turned to the window Olivia had just been gazing through. Olivia's stomach did a little flip. This was everything she wanted. It was all going to plan. She felt a great weight was being slowly lifted from her shoulders with each passing day spent in Mr. Lawrence's company.

Her mother sighed as if she felt it too. Mrs. Davenport picked up a pair of gloves from the small table beside the large wingback chair and tapped Olivia's knee. "It's a beautiful day for a stroll and a picnic." As she stood, the footman entered the sitting room to announce that Mr. Lawrence had arrived.

Olivia glanced at the clock on the mantel. It was exactly one in the afternoon—Mr. Lawrence was nothing if not punctual. She followed her mother to the grand foyer where Mr. Lawrence stood with his hat in his hand, examining the painting of a shed in a lonely cotton field, where the small white tufts appeared to be swaying in a breeze under a cloudless sky. Like every suit he'd worn, whether houndstooth or herringbone, today's was impeccably tailored, the fabric a luxurious tweed.

He turned at the sound of their approach, a smile already on his face. The power of his gaze made Olivia pick at the buttons of her gloves. She pointed to the painting. "Daddy received this as a gift. It's the plantation where he and his brother were enslaved.

The artist is one of the men charged with locating my uncle. He painted it from my father's description."

"It's a powerful piece."

"He nearly threw it into the fire when it arrived. But if you look here . . ." Olivia pointed to two figures in the background.

Mr. Lawrence followed her fingers. "Your father and his brother?"

She nodded. The stricken look on her father's face when he'd spotted them was one of the few times Olivia had seen her father cry. Her mother, who was born free, if poor, in a loving family, had embraced him from behind, her face pressed to his back, where he would not see her tears. The painting had hung in the entryway ever since.

"Mr. Lawrence," Mrs. Davenport said, fitting her hat to her head. She beamed at the pair, her gaze lingering briefly on the painted scene behind them. Olivia saw the fleeting glimpse of sadness that passed over her mother's features. "How are you this afternoon?"

"Good afternoon, Mrs. Davenport," he said, his voice smooth as butter, his accent clipping his words pleasingly, bespeaking his London upbringing. "I am well and hope you don't mind, I took this rather hefty basket from your cook."

"Yes, Jessie does love to spoil us," Mrs. Davenport said. She cast a sidelong glance at her daughter.

Olivia cleared her throat. "I've selected the dishes myself. A mixture of English delicacies and American sweets—and some French favorites for fun. I hope you'll enjoy them."

Mr. Lawrence shifted the weight of the basket to his left hand and offered her his arm. Olivia tilted her head higher as she looped her lace-gloved hand into the crook of his elbow. He leaned in to whisper, almost conspiratorially, "I am sure to like anything you have chosen." Olivia fought the urge to hide her smile behind her hand.

At the bottom of the front steps, one of her family's grander carriages waited. An open-air design, it allowed the riders an unobstructed view of their surroundings—and the public an unobstructed view of its riders. Olivia glanced back at her mother, sure this was her doing, as Jacob Lawrence helped both women in. Mrs. Davenport's eyes sparkled, her obvious enthusiasm reminding Olivia of everything that was at stake.

Once inside, Olivia found herself tongue-tied. But her mother and Mr. Lawrence kept up a steady conversation about the weather and Chicago's many offerings. Mr. Lawrence stole glances at Olivia. She felt a heat rise under her skin each time he looked at her. She had the distinct impression he had looked at women this way before—intentional, and in plain view of their parents as they calculated their good fortune. Olivia discovered herself relieved to not have committed some faux pas that would drive him away. He was smart, cultured, and well traveled. Everything she and her parents had hoped for.

After the short carriage ride, Mr. Lawrence, ever the gentleman, helped the ladies down and carried the large basket.

Olivia loved this park, and the grand, gray-blue sweep of Lake Michigan beyond.

She was aware of the eyes on them as they made their way to a shaded knoll overlooking the lake's expanse. Some of the park's mostly white patrons frequented the same tearooms—she recognized a few familiar faces enjoying picnics of their own. The gentlemen were sons of the various white business owners her father worked with. Those who recognized her offered a nod or polite smile or some discreet gesture of acknowledgment. Brown faces were few and far between, obvious among the scattered patrons.

Mrs. Davenport opened her fan and waved to Mrs. Johnson and Mrs. Tremaine near the gazebos, a tea service laid out beside them. "I'll leave you young people to yourselves," she said, patting Olivia's wrist.

Olivia tried her best not to show her true feelings as her mother's smile widened. She suspected her mother had planned for her friends to be here under pretense of running into them. She would be only a short distance away, and Olivia and Mr. Lawrence were in a public park. Still, she got the strange feeling that today was to be some sort of turning point in their relationship.

Relationship. It seemed too weighty a word for what she and Mr. Lawrence had. There was so much she didn't know about him.

He placed the basket at the foot of a tree on a bed of pale pink petals fallen from the branches above. The blanket opened with a crack at the flick of his wrists. His eyes bore that same confidence that drew her in the very first day in the sitting room.

"After you," he said. She took his hand and lowered herself to the ground, careful to tuck her skirts under her. Her corset dug into her hips and she felt each of its bones against hers. Jacob Lawrence sat silently across from her, watching her in a way that made her skin hot and cold at the same time. She chewed her bottom lip and then instantly released it, remembering that her mother was close, analyzing their every gesture with a hawk's keen eye.

"The crêpes are my favorite," she said, hoping a neutral topic would get the conversation going. Olivia pulled Jessie's creations from the basket and arranged them on the blanket.

"It was hard not to take a peek inside, with it smelling as sweet as it does." Mr. Lawrence's words were playful, his eyes more interested in her than the food. She offered him the pastry, his fingers gently grazing hers.

"Well?" she asked.

"I think I may need another one," he said, mouth slightly full. "I'm not quite sure how I feel yet."

Olivia laughed. It was a good sign that they agreed on this, right? She added crêpes to the list of things she and Mr. Lawrence had in common and took a bite of her own.

"What do you suppose those two are talking about?" Mr. Lawrence nodded to a white couple Olivia recognized—older than them but younger than her parents. The gentleman looked off into the distance, a pained expression on his face. His wife clutched his arm, her lips moving too quickly to be the sweet nothings of two lovers on a stroll.

"That is Mr. and Mrs. Weathers. She is most definitely telling him the latest gossip around town."

Mr. Lawrence rubbed his chin. "No, I don't think that's it." Olivia watched his well-manicured fingers smooth his mustache down. She turned back to the couple before her mind could imagine what the full lips below it would feel like . . . just as another face, and Washington DeWight's smile and high cheekbones, slid into her thoughts. And as it did, she'd have bet her new hat that the name Davenport passed the lips of Mrs. Weathers. She opened her mouth to say as much, when Mr. Lawrence continued. "Just as I thought, she's going over the plans of their diamond heist for the hundredth time. Can't you see how tired he is of hearing about it? The poor man has the whole thing memorized."

The twinkle that never seemed to leave Jacob Lawrence's eyes brightened. For a moment, Olivia forgot her mother's watchful gaze and the weight of onlookers' glances. A laugh bubbled up at his absurd story. They carried on like this for several minutes, people-watching and inventing more elaborate stories as they picked at the sweet feast between them.

But as available players for their tales ran out, the silence between bites grew. Olivia cleared her throat, remembering her teachings. Men enjoyed talking about themselves. An attentive wife makes a strong marriage. She knew hardly anything about Mr. Lawrence's life back in London. Sure, he spoke at length about the city and its attractions, but not what excited him. Or about his family.

This was the first time the two had been left in relative privacy. Her mother was just beyond earshot. There were no crowds of dancers or curious bystanders to hear their exchange. She examined his profile, chiseled jaw and brow. Every hair from his head to his mustache perfectly in place. From this angle, she could see a faint scar beneath his ear. His focus was on the little boys pushing wooden boats across the smooth surface of a reflecting pool.

"One last couple?" Mr. Lawrence asked. "Hopeless romantics." He pointed to a Black couple a short distance away. Olivia felt her shoulders relax as she took in the confident and familiar stride of her friend. Spotting them too, Ruby veered off the pathway, Harrison Barton at her side. She was a splash of warmth and color in the muted spring hues around her. Her smile at Mr. Barton was playful, if guarded. They seemed to have enjoyed each other's company at the Tremaine party, but Olivia knew Ruby to be as practical as she was impulsive.

"You may be partially correct," she said to Mr. Lawrence.

A few onlookers tracked the couple's progress but seemed to lose interest once Ruby collapsed at the edge of the picnic blanket. She removed her wide-brimmed hat, the same shade of mauve as her skirt and jacket. "I just need a few minutes in the shade," Ruby said. "Mr. Jacob Lawrence, this is Mr. Harrison Barton." She offered Olivia a wink and inspected the spread.

After a moment of hesitation, Mr. Barton sat, completing the group. "Nice to formally meet you," he said, shaking Mr. Lawrence's hand. Ruby popped grapes into her mouth as Mr. Barton gave a brief account of his relocation to Chicago. He referred to the South Side as a city-within-a-city and all the beauty and excitement it had to offer. He never took his eyes off Ruby, though. Olivia couldn't help the smile on her face at how Ruby, always one for attention, let Mr. Barton's words wash over her without comment or her usual preening.

"What brought you into the park?" Olivia asked.

Ruby looked to where her mother sat with Mrs. Davenport. "Mother is finalizing the plans for the big fundraiser in June." Her eyes sparkled. "They're grateful your parents have agreed to host it in place of their annual ball. It's going to be fun."

Olivia laughed. "I don't know who's more excited, your parents or mine. Or *you*."

Ruby spread a thin layer of jam on a biscuit. "Just be glad they're too busy to shadow our every move. Otherwise we'd be stuck up there right now." She turned to Mr. Barton. "This gentleman was kind enough to take his lunch away from his desk to walk with me."

"I'm also looking forward to the fundraiser," said Mr. Barton. He beamed at Ruby's smug grin. "It's great what your father is trying to do for the community." He finally took his eyes off Ruby to scan the people walking the paths, their gazes flicking away from his. He turned back to the group. "If there were more Black folk like us around, maybe people wouldn't stare so much." The finery of their small set, the luxury of spending a workday enjoying the weather instead of toiling away in a shop or mill—it was unusual.

Ruby cleared her throat. "Yes, Papa would be happy to have your support. And vote. Now, the fundraiser will be a masquerade"— she waggled her eyebrows—"with many of the same people who attended our party, in addition to political leaders." She looked back toward the lake. "Both Black and white who share common goals."

"Sounds like it will be quite the affair," Mr. Lawrence said.

"It'll be the highlight of the season." Ruby gave Olivia a speaking glance and a small smile. "Many interesting things happen at the Davenports' spring-into-summer ball."

Olivia laughed. "You make it sound like a night at the theater!"

Ruby nodded. "Especially if you know where to stand." Her giggle joined Olivia's until she saw Mr. Barton glancing at his watch.

"I have to get back," he said. He took her hand and helped her to her feet.

Ruby pouted, which made his smile widen.

"I'll see you later," she said to Olivia.

After Ruby had joined her mother, Olivia asked, "Does any of this remind you of home?"

Mr. Lawrence dragged his eyes from the children at play. "No, I spent most of my time elsewhere."

Olivia picked a crumb from the napkin. "Did you grow up with many siblings?"

"I'm my parents' only child." He glanced down at the blanket.

"I don't know what I'd do if it were just me," she said. As frustrating as her siblings could be, she imagined it was far easier to share her parents' attention than bear the full brunt of their expectations. "It must be difficult. And lonely?" she offered. "I've always had my siblings."

"I know nothing else." He glanced briefly at her.

"I'm sorry," she said, embarrassed. "Ruby is an only child and has never complained."

"Don't be," he said. "It was, at times"—he nodded once—"lonely. But I have cousins who kept it at bay. I'm sure for Ruby, your friendship is cherished."

Olivia sucked in her bottom lip, not sure where to go next. "Do you enjoy your work? With your father?"

Mr. Lawrence brushed the ends of his mustache with his fingers. "Being in business with family . . . It's complicated," he said. He picked up another crêpe. "These really are delicious." He smiled as he took a bite, but there was a shadow in his eyes, an emotion Olivia couldn't quite read. She noticed the crease forming between his brows and felt the sudden urge to smooth it down, wipe away the stress that encroached on his features. She also noticed how he sidestepped the question.

From her spot on the blanket, Olivia felt her mother's eyes on them. It was a beautiful afternoon and the grounds had grown crowded with Chicago's "leisure class," as Helen would call it. White ladies and gentlemen with wealth and time to spend strolling through gardens and museums. Though her family subscribed to the "double-duty dollar" practice of shopping Black-owned business that supported the community, white patrons and business partners kept Davenport Carriage Company at the top of the market. Few people would be outright rude or hostile to a Davenport, but again, that didn't mean they didn't stare.

"Haven't you ever noticed the way people gawk at you?" she asked.

Lawrence followed her gaze and leaned back. With a cheeky grin, he said, "I have learned there's not much you can do about how people look at you." He smiled politely at the passersby. "I'm sure you've felt eyes following you before."

She remembered again the afternoon in Marshall Field's, the encounter that made her burn with anger and run up her family's credit.

"Most days, though, I find myself wondering how, or even why, I am where I am." Lawrence twirled his empty wineglass between his fingers. "I mean, I know my family worked hard for generations to build our name. But I am a Black man in England, where in every space I am the minority. The Other. And here, like at home, I am both exulted and cursed for my circumstances. None of which I can change or take credit for."

"There must be a kind of pride in being able to add to that legacy," she said, knowing that's how she felt every time she saw a Davenport carriage cross her path. It's why she imagined her parents held so tightly to the everyday workings of the business as it grew, and in the preparation they put into John's education. She wondered how the next generation of Davenports might feel, or be treated. *Better than us*, she hoped, looking at the gentleman beside her and trying not to let the contents of the Jim Crow pamphlet intrude on the present.

Mr. Lawrence dipped his head. His words were not what she'd expected. It was as if they were plucked from her heart and spoken with his lips. Jacob Lawrence understood. Born into his wealth and name like her. Behind his bravado, charm, and well-tailored suits lay a kindred spirit.

I may have misjudged him, she thought. Time and familiarity would close this gap between them. Olivia stretched her hand out to Jacob Lawrence like an olive branch. He placed his warm palm in hers and squeezed tight.

CHAPTER 13

Helen

Her mother's blue china glistened on the stark white linens arranged with a care Helen saw no point in adjusting. It was a beautiful day outside and about half an hour ago, John strolled past the dining room with his shirtsleeves rolled up and a towel and wrench sticking out of his back pocket. Her hands ached to hold that wrench herself, elbow deep in the horseless carriage he'd brought home. Instead, she stared at the place setting before her, trying to figure out what was amiss. The rigid woman beside her watched intently. Mrs. Milford's eyes, though a warm brown, followed her with a scrutiny that left her feeling raw.

Helen had come down that morning dressed in a simple roughspun dress she'd outgrown—perfect for the work she had planned. She'd intended to ask Amy-Rose to braid her hair away from her face in two neat rows, the ends just brushing her shoulders. Her mother and Olivia were expected to be out of the house for most of the afternoon, leaving Helen free to do as she pleased.

But then, "Helen, dear!" her mother had called from below.

Helen had paused at the top of the steps. Downstairs and to the right was the kitchen, where she hoped to slip unnoticed to John's garage. Her mother pitched her voice the way she did when company was present, when she was afraid Helen might commit some egregious social error without some subtle warning to reset her course.

Helen's chest tightened. As much as she wanted to flee, she knew she wouldn't get far. "Yes?" she said, dragging out the word and swinging around the newel post. She hoped whatever this was, it would be a minor delay.

A woman, older than her mother, stood in the foyer. Her expression was as bleak as her dress. Helen entered the grand space cautiously.

"This is Mrs. Milford," said Mrs. Davenport, smiling widely. "Mrs. Milford, Helen."

Mrs. Milford was a short woman in a severe black dress and sturdy boots, polished to a shine. All of which, when compared to Mrs. Davenport's mauve frock, made her a bearer of bad news. The newcomer held her hat in her hands, revealing dark hair streaked with gray, brushed smoothly away from her deep brown face, and painfully pinned at the nape of her neck in a tight, coiled poof. She analyzed Helen's every movement and appearance from head to toe.

"A pleasure to meet you," Helen said, not completely forgetting her manners as her stomach dropped.

"Likewise." Mrs. Milford's disapproval appeared to wane temporarily.

Afraid of what this visitor meant, Helen turned to her mother, dread growing with each loud *tick* of the grandfather clock beside them.

"Mrs. Milford is—was—a pastor's wife."

"Didn't agree with the pastor anymore?" Helen asked to her mother's shock.

"I am recently widowed."

Now Helen was shocked. Her brief elation that her mother would be embroiled in such scandal—and would have *shared it with her*—was quickly replaced with a compassion she didn't know how to express. She regretted her callous question, shame burning her neck.

"No need to say anything," Mrs. Milford said. "There shouldn't be any awkwardness between us if we are going to work together. And present tense is fine. I feel as though he is still with me." A gentle smile softened her features, but her glance at Mrs. Davenport, followed by a subtle nod, spoke of an ambush.

The feeling of queasy dread had returned as Helen followed them into the dining room. A heavy brocade cloth fell like liquid gold over the surface of the table. Each seat had a slight variation in the place setting before it. Helen looked at her mother.

Mrs. Davenport cleared her throat and regarded Helen with a warning in her eyes so severe, Helen held her breath. "Mrs. Milford, as I was saying, is a pastor's wife with strong ideas of how a lady should behave. She answered the ad in the paper."

"What ad?" Helen croaked.

"'Lady's Companion Wanted. Must be well read, have extensive knowledge of etiquette, and above all else, patience.'" Mrs. Milford folded her hands.

"What?" Helen shrieked. She hadn't meant to raise her voice, but this was *bad* news. Very bad news. "How could you do this, Mama? I don't need etiquette lessons. Again!"

"Clearly, you do. Your current behavior is not only childish, but rude."

Helen's plans for the day were officially scrapped. The first thing they did was send Helen back upstairs to change into something more "suitable." Her new *lady's companion* followed her upstairs, her mother close at their heels. Helen tried not to cringe when she opened the door to her bedroom.

"Helen," Mrs. Davenport said from the threshold. Helen watched as her mother toured her sanctuary in silent horror. Books and sketches strewn everywhere. A pair of shoes peeked from underneath the bed skirt. At her vanity, empty plates and teacups occupied the space where perfume and makeup should be. "This won't do," her mother said. She turned to Mrs. Milford. "Do you see how desperately we could use your services?" Helen bristled at the word *desperately*, but held her tongue.

A few humiliating moments later, Helen was dressed. Corset and all. She smoothed flat the tiered ruffles at her neck and blew at the awkwardly dangling feather on her hat. *I'm indoors*, she thought to herself, struggling to keep her emotions in check. Her clothes were heavy, abrasive in their newness.

Now back in the dining room, she stood hungry and breathless, looking at place settings that offered no promise of a meal. *What have I done to deserve this?* she thought. But she knew. These were things she'd be expected to know once she became the lady of her own house. The thought of a fast approaching future where she could no longer sneak into a garage and tinker, murmur her secrets to her father's horses, or genuinely do what she wanted when she wanted made her appetite disappear. Well, almost.

Helen traced a finger along the ivy detail of a fork's handle. *You should know this*, she thought to herself. *It's not as if you don't pick one up every day.* Her mother insisted the table be formally set each night. Helen suddenly wondered if she had been using the wrong forks at dinner all this time without knowing it. *This is ridiculous.* She moved a fork to the other side of the plate and glanced up at her new companion triumphantly.

The corners of Mrs. Milford's lip drooped, making her already long features stretch further in her narrow face. "Miss Helen, I was under the impression you were a clever girl."

"I am," Helen replied, hating the hesitation in her voice.

"Are you *trying* to be obtuse? Do you enjoy wasting our time and your parents' money?"

"No." Helen swapped two of the forks left of the plate.

Mrs. Milford's questions came in rapid succession. "What type of man do you hope to attract with such poor attention to detail?"

Helen swallowed a huff. She'd already endured one lecture on how to better control or conceal her emotions and did not wish to invite further scrutiny. Her mother no doubt expected daily reports on her progress. And she did a little *better* than paying attention to details! How else does one pinpoint the exact cause of an engine misfire or the myriad others things she was capable of doing? No mechanic worth their grit could do what Helen did without a cunning or a discerning eye. But that wasn't what Mrs. Milford wanted to hear. No, no. Nor her parents. If only they could *see* the significance of her skills outside the home. There must be a man who valued that.

Mrs. Milford continued to talk, and without meaning to, Helen allowed her thoughts to drift to Mr. Lawrence. Jacob. Her sister's soon-to-be-fiancé. She'd never had such easy conversation with a member of the opposite sex without a vehicle between them. He was funny. And Helen suspected, just from their brief encounter on the Tremaines' patio, that he saw the benefit of her interests, and in the skills that she nurtured in secret. She caught the smile spreading across her face. She shook herself, blushing hard. Worse, she became aware that she had missed something Mrs. Milford had said.

"Come, child. This is nothing to work yourself up over." Mrs. Milford walked over to one of the chairs along the dark-paneled walls. She reached into a beaten fabric bag with a faded floral pattern and pulled out a book, then came around the grand table.

Up close, Helen noticed the scars under her chin that dipped into the collar of her high-necked blouse. She wondered if Mrs. Milford may have some secrets of her own and if her severe dress went beyond the mourning of her husband. In her hand was a slim book covered in pale blue cloth. She offered it to Helen, never taking her eyes off the young girl's face.

"*The Art of Being Agreeable* by Margaret E. Sangster. Once you've completed this one, I will bring you another."

Helen enjoyed reading manuals. How-to's were always her first choice. Knowledge and books were her companions when her sister outgrew her to join this world Helen had tried so determinedly to avoid. Was she being childish? Digging in her heels, delaying the inevitable?

Helen took the book from Mrs. Milford, careful to keep her face neutral. It was a dead weight in her hands. So much heavier than the planetary gear she'd held in the garage just a couple of weeks ago.

"There is much for you to learn," her new companion said. "But this is a start."

Helen looked at the table, still unsure if her place setting was correct, and thought, *This is going to be a nightmare.*

CHAPTER 14

Ruby

The air was warm and sticky, and something sinister buzzed around Ruby's ear, deepening her irritation. Or maybe it was Agatha Leary. Agatha was nice enough, though her presence was a constant reminder that Ruby's best friend was otherwise preoccupied.

Olivia spent every free moment lately with Jacob Lawrence. Or with Mrs. Davenport, planning on ways to causally run into him. Ruby missed the afternoons they shopped the storefronts on the South Side. Or when they visited the museums during the hours allotted for Black patrons—or sometimes during normal hours, if Olivia was bored and in a suggestible mood, game for leveraging her family name. They always found something to pass the time.

Especially now, with her parents checking on her as much as they were—a girl could hardly breathe!—Ruby missed Olivia. She felt time quickly slipping through her fingers. John was losing interest. His focus always seemed to be elsewhere. And he had yet to call on her or schedule the ride they had talked about. She thought for certain after the ball he would have extended an invitation. He had positively steamed with irritation—the sight of Harrison Barton swinging her around the ballroom floor seeming to have lit a fire under him. But that was over a week ago and the flame was fading fast.

After the party, she had waited for a letter, racing down the stairs to meet the postman outside before her mother could. But there was nothing addressed to her save for the short notes Olivia sent to update Ruby on her own courtship. Hastily, Ruby would return to her room, with its leftover opulence, mostly untouched by the cutbacks made to support her father's campaign. Securing John's hand, her contribution to her father's endeavors—and the salvation of his greatest undertaking—grew less likely by the day. She thought of responding to Olivia, but she could hardly ask her oldest friend, *How do I keep your brother interested?*

That is why she stood behind a chain-link fence now with Agatha Leary droning at her back, watching the young men of her set play a game of baseball.

"Agatha, do you see Mr. Davenport?"

Agatha stammered at Ruby's sudden interruption. "I don't see him. I hardly think he'd be out here running bases on account of his limp. Why, Ruby, you should know that!"

"I meant Mr. *John* Davenport." Ruby suppressed the urge to roll her eyes. She hoped John would be among them or in the crowd so that they might have a few moments to speak to each other. The rest of the spectators would serve as a chaperone and a buffer from Agatha, who thought it her duty to shadow Ruby's every move in addition to talking her ears off.

"Oh, of course! He's not here. You know, I heard he returned from his first year at college with all sorts of ideas to change his family's business and no intention to return to his studies. Mr. Davenport was positively livid."

Ruby's head whipped around. "How do you know this?"

"My cousin is Mr. Davenport's secretary." Agatha smiled, relishing the fact she knew something about the Davenports Ruby didn't. Ruby imagined her spreading this news to anyone, whether they wanted to listen to her or not. It made the muscles in her neck tighten.

"I'd be careful if I were your cousin," Ruby said coolly. "I doubt the Davenports would appreciate their business being discussed like tawdry gossip." Smiling tightly, she folded her arms and turned back to the players on the field.

"Well," Agatha started, her tone husky. "If you're looking for something, or someone, to keep you interested, Mr. Barton is in the outfield."

Ruby let her jaw slacken before searching the field for herself. Sure enough, Harrison stood not ninety feet away from her, hovering over third base. His back was straight, his broad hands braced against his knees. His entire focus was on the man swinging the bat over home plate. She found herself smiling in his direction, with Agatha staring at her intently.

"Careful," Agatha warned. "Looking at a man like that may earn you some gossip of your own."

As Mr. Barton had escorted her through the park, he'd talked about his work at the bank and his plans for the future, investing in Black businesses and starting a family—"Really setting down roots here in Chicago," he'd said. She remembered how his eyes had lit up, and with a smile that was earnest and quietly confident.

When he mentioned he was joining clubs, she pictured a dark, cigar-smoke-filled room, not a baseball field. It made her wonder what *she* wanted, beyond meeting her parents' expectations.

Ruby glanced to where her mother stood. Always working for the campaign, Mrs. Tremaine was making her rounds, urging more Black voices to uplift the needs of the South Side. Oh, the scene she would make just to wipe the smirk off Agatha Leary's face! As if she read it plain on Ruby's, Agatha walked away, her nose turned up as she stalked over to the group of young ladies.

Though Ruby knew Agatha referred to the fact that Mr. Barton appeared to be calling on Ruby regularly, some part of her couldn't help dredging up the words she'd overheard in the ladies' lounge during her parents' party. It was why her plan had to go off without a hitch. John's attention was never so attuned to her as when she was on Mr. Barton's arm. It was as if he suddenly remembered her. Sure, they had never been officially declared for each other, but there was an understanding between them that went beyond their parents' expectations. They had both agreed to cool things off while he was away at school, but she didn't expect him to come back quite so driven and focused. It was like all he cared about now was the carriage company—making motorcars instead of racing them.

Ruby knew Harrison Barton was the key to securing a proposal from John. He was eager and sweet and wanted to belong to the close-knit circle of their set, to become one of the more influential people in Chicago. He already hung on her every word. *It'll be simple*, she thought. And once John returned to her, Mr. Barton could stay in the loop or fade back into obscurity.

Ruby eyed him now, noting his athletic build and the way his knickers hugged his calves.

This may even be fun.

At that moment, Mr. Barton glanced in her direction. He stood up, facing her more directly. He reached up and tipped his cap at her. He didn't see the pitcher pull out of his stretch and adjust his stance. He didn't see the release that quieted the crowd as it made its way to the player at home plate. The *crack* of the bat striking the ball was a warning with too-short notice. Athletes and bystanders alike watched helplessly as the ball made a line drive to his position behind third base.

It was like the world stopped. The game froze like a photograph. Then every player on the field turned to the body of Harrison Barton, sprawled across the clay and fresh cut grass. Ruby was sprinting before she fully registered what had happened. She crumpled the sides of her dress in her fists, freeing her ankles for speed as she rounded the fence, ran past the dugout, and onto the field. She gasped for breath, each one sharp at the back of her throat. She didn't want to scream. The press of bodies obstructed her vision. The crowd that formed around him increased her panic. Why were they just standing there? She had to elbow her way through. The sight of his feet, toes pointed up to the sky, nearly unraveled her composure. Still, she pushed on, holding her breath to the point of dizziness.

When she finally made it to the middle of the crowd, Mr. Barton was sitting upright. A player from each team knelt beside him. They helped him to his feet and held him steady as he tested weight on his left foot. Relief flooded Ruby's body so quickly, she missed many of the words they exchanged. She stopped herself from reaching for him. Her parents' party was made slightly less miserable with Mr. Barton at her side, but still. They barely knew each other.

Ruby wrinkled her nose at the mixture of perspiration and grass clippings that clung to her. *Did I just run into the middle of this ball game?* She shook herself and looked up in time to catch Agatha's smirk behind the fence. Agatha, the biggest gossip she knew.

"I'm all right," Mr. Barton said, gently untangling himself. He held his hands up to keep his teammates at bay. The palms of his hands were scraped raw and a gash on his right wrist stretched to the elbow. His first unsteady step had them reaching for him again.

"Oh!" The startled sound escaped Ruby's lips and her hand flew to her cheek. She slipped back into the fray, making sure she was still in Agatha's sightline. Smile, she told herself. "I've got it from here, gentlemen," she said to no one in particular.

He gave her a sheepish grin. "I'm sure it looks worse than it is," he said.

Ruby offered him a handkerchief. A stark white piece of cloth, embroidered with her initials.

"It looks plenty awful to me." She looked around at the spectators. "Let's get you in the shade." He let her steer him to a nearby tree. Close enough to the others that they were easily observed, but far enough that they may speak without being overheard. He sat down abruptly, taking her with him. It was silly and awkward and she laughed.

Ruby remembered the last time she had sat under a tree with a member of the opposite sex. It had been at the peak of a crush-come-to-life, and not nearly enough to satisfy her.

"Perhaps I should be struck by more fly balls," he said, smiling, then wincing.

She pulled her hand away. "Please! You could have been seriously injured."

The corner of Mr. Barton's mouth twitched, and Ruby's shoulders relaxed. *Stop*, she scolded herself.

"You're worried about me," he said.

"No more than I would be for any other person suffering from a similar injury. You should really pay better attention."

He smirked. "Well, someone on the sidelines stole mine."

"Ha," Ruby said. "Don't pin your lack of focus on me." Ruby turned her head away then, watching him clean himself up from the corner of her eye. "She must have been someone special," she added.

"Very special indeed. Maybe the most beautiful girl in all of Chicago."

Ruby's face warmed, and she gave him a challenging look. *"Maybe?"*

He released a surprised bark of laughter, wincing again as he did. Ruby liked the sound. And the way he looked at her. "Miss Tremaine, as soon as I can hold my own, I'd like to take you dancing."

Ruby smiled victoriously. "I'd love that."

CHAPTER 15

Amy-Rose

The kitchen was quiet. Clean and deserted. Amy-Rose liked working from the stool in the corner late at night, feet tucked under the counter where the oven, still warm from a pie or a roast, kept her warm. Most nights, only the sound of the pencil scratching against the rough pages of her notebook could be heard. She couldn't get her ideas down fast enough. And when she finished, she felt lighter, braver.

Brave enough tonight to reread the last thing her mother had written: a grocery list. Clara Shepherd had sat in the seat Amy-Rose now did, writing down the ingredients for her accra. She could almost hear her mother and Jessie argue over the proper way to prepare the fish cakes over a sizzling pan, the smell of chopped greens and onions in the air. She enjoyed listening to them go back and forth and to watch her mother mix the ingredients, measuring them out with her strong, slender hands. People from all over the house would be drawn to the kitchen.

Amy-Rose rubbed her temples and looked away from her work,

thinking how quickly everything would change. There'd be no real reason for her to stay on with the Davenports once the girls were married. But the counter by the window in the kitchen was where her mother had sat her after Amy-Rose scraped her knee trying to sneak horses out of the stable with Olivia and John. The room upstairs was the one they'd shared, where she listened to stories of Saint Lucia so detailed, they felt like her own. Everything around her sparked some little memory of the only parent she knew, the only real family she had.

That's not entirely true, she thought. The Davenport girls may not be her sisters, but for a time, that's what they'd felt like. Jessie and Ethel, in the role of aunts, bickered from dawn until they disappeared into their room at night. The moments of tenderness between the pair of them were rarely seen, though they had always had more than enough for her. Harold, Tommy's father and the Davenports' coachman, whittled the miniature horse figures she displayed by her bed. There was no corner untouched by a fond memory. The Shepherd family of two grew here.

What would life be like to wake up in a new place? Surrounded by different people? The thought made her uneasy, but excited too.

Amy-Rose gathered her notebook and pencil, and tiptoed through the door leading out to the garden. The brisk wind raced across her face, cooling the sudden flush of panic that overtook her. She moved across the Davenports' backyard, careful to stay out of the line of the windows, as she wasn't meant to be out on the grounds so late. She hugged her sweater closer and stepped off the path where an assortment of native foliage and sturdy New England greenery thrived. Mrs. Davenport took great pride in its maintenance, having grown up in a small Boston tenement far from the Boston Public Garden.

Now it served as Amy-Rose's refuge. Once the house was out of sight, she settled against the trunk of a great oak tree. Through its leaves she watched the stars wink in and out, her heart rate returning to normal. Just like the East Coast trees around her, she could be replanted.

"If I didn't know better, I'd say you're following me."

Amy-Rose's hands flew to her throat. In the bright moonlight, John sat with his elbows on his knees. He stood, revealing the creases in his fresh suit and the buttons undone at his collar.

"I didn't think anyone else was out here," she said. Tempted though she was to watch the notch where his neck met his chest, she kept her gaze on his. His steps were slow, purposefully side-stepping the tree roots, as he drew near. A chill raced through her as his body came close enough to block the next gust of wind rustling through the gardens, filling the air with the scent of freshly cut grass and his cologne with its heady balsam notes. She inhaled deeply and resisted the urge to close her eyes.

John bent down and picked up her notebook. "This is precious," he said.

Amy-Rose blushed under the power of his smile and reached for her book.

"Do you want to sit with me awhile?" He looked so earnest.

"I could sit a spell," she said. Amy-Rose followed John the short distance to the small bench beside a bed of red columbine. It was the perfect quiet corner for two lovers, she thought, as the heat from John's body warmed her leg where their thighs lightly touched. It was intimate and comfortable and only served to confuse her more. She watched his profile. His jaw was tight and brow scrunched to a thin line.

"Is something on your mind?" she asked. It wasn't her place. She was still the help. The words had bubbled up before she'd had a chance to caution herself.

John wiped his face with his hands and heaved a great sigh that she felt in her bones. It was a kind of weariness she knew too well.

"How did you end up here?" he said, instead of answering her question. Even in the moonlight, she could see his eyes burn with a curious intensity that made her look away. "I'm sorry for not knowing. It just feels like you've always been here, part of this family. I only just realized."

"That I had a life before here?"

"I meant no offense. I guess—it's just more of a realization that I've been caught up in myself—what my parents want for me. Things are different away from here." He pinched his bottom lip and those butterflies in Amy-Rose's stomach began to soar. "I know they mean well, but I—"

He stopped so abruptly, Amy-Rose feared he'd decided to leave her alone with her thoughts. Jessie's warnings played in the back of her head, taunting her. The Davenports will move on, and so should she.

"I apologize, here I am complaining about two parents worrying about me and—" He moved as if to place his hand over hers but stopped. She thought of his brief touch that night in the kitchen as he rushed to get ready for the Tremaines' ball. She took his hand, and found comfort in its warmth. He looked at their hands. "I'm sorry."

Amy-Rose remembered the day her mother was buried not too far from here. Everything had been arranged by Mrs. Davenport. Amy-Rose barely recalled anything that happened between her mother's passing and the moment her rose-laden casket was lowered into the ground. She closed her eyes and saw her mother and the journey that had ended at the front gates of Freeport Manor.

"I was pretty young when Mama and I came here. We're from Saint Lucia originally. It was always 'home' to Mama. All I remember was being surrounded by people all the time. I was never short of companions or adults spoiling me terribly, even as they whispered about my mama being fooled by a sailor who would never return when they thought I was too young to understand." A chill ran up her spine when she thought about what had happened next. The rain, the wind, the storm that took everything away. Her voice shook as she recounted the dread of waiting for it to pass. "When the sky finally cleared, it was bright and beautiful, as if nothing had happened. Most of our town was destroyed, even our home. Mama said neighbors offered us a place to stay, help to rebuild. But she said there were too many reminders of the people we'd lost."

"So you didn't stay long after?"

Amy-Rose shook her head and smiled. "Mama said it was the perfect time to have an adventure. We had nothing but a few belongings that fit into one bag. My father lived in Georgia." Amy-Rose glanced at John. His gaze fixed on her, he nodded for her continue. "He was a white man, from the States. Mama used to say they fell in love one magical summer while he was on holiday. She always believed he'd come back for her. She wrote him letters even after his replies stopped coming. I have a box of them in my room. You can still make out the design of the wax seal on some of them. A five-petaled flower with the letter G woven through." Amy-Rose picked at the fraying corner of her notebook. A sadness she rarely let herself feel washed over her. "It wasn't until we arrived on his family's plantation that we were told he'd died. Fever, they said, before turning us away."

A Black man with stooped shoulders had answered the door that day. He hadn't invited them in, but told them to stay put and closed the door. They waited. And waited. Clara Shepherd paced, pausing to readjust Amy-Rose's collar, to tell her daughter to stop fidgeting. It felt like forever before the door swung wide. Amy-Rose clung to her mother's leg as Clara spoke to the white couple on the porch. She didn't like the way they stared at her. They were frowning, their lips pressed into thin lines before they began speaking. As Amy-Rose listened to her mother tell them the familiar story of her father, she looked through the door and into the face of a blue-eyed girl, older than she was, with a pointed chin and a smattering of freckles like hers. Their voices rose in her memory, and with them, a tightness in her throat now as John watched her. He gave her hand a gentle squeeze.

She couldn't bear to hear him say "I'm sorry" again, so she barreled on. "My mother was devastated," Amy-Rose said, ignoring the way her eyes and nose stung. "Sometimes I wonder what life would be like if he were alive."

That afternoon was private and belonged to her and her mother and still hurt too much to share. The white couple's son was gone and couldn't be Amy-Rose's father. The blue-eyed girl looked from her to the adults and yelled, "Liars!" Amy-Rose would probably never forget how round the girl's mouth became or how swiftly she was carried out of sight. Amy-Rose also remembered how small her mother had looked, staring at the door as it slammed closed. The man her mother swore loved them and would one day make true on his promise to return was no longer there. Though sadness was etched into every line of Clara's face, her eyes were dry and her grip on her daughter was fierce.

"What happened next?" John asked.

"We moved around a lot, never staying more than a few days until we made it to Chicago. We came north on a train that let us off at Grand Central Station. My mother heard domestic work was the easiest to find, but your family was the only one who would take the both of us."

John smiled into the darkness. "Olivia and I were hiding behind the curtain, our feet sticking out underneath. I remember Livy whispered, 'I think we're meant to be friends.'"

"We were." Amy-Rose's thoughts drifted from what she'd lost to what she had gained—the companionship of children her own age, where her mother was always around, and a sense of belonging. Amy-Rose passed her free hand over the cover of her notebook. "My mother encouraged me to follow my dreams. She bought me notebooks so I could write them down, so I'd never forget." Her mother had also insisted her daughter choose for herself. Do what was best for *her*. Clara Shepherd rarely spoke about love after that day in Georgia.

Amy-Rose and John sat on the bench, hand in hand. Neither one of them making a move to pull away. The quiet was easy and comfortable. The bubbling in Amy-Rose's stomach calmed and she was able to relax. *I could count on you*, she thought, looking at his strong profile. "What were you thinking about, when I first came out here?"

John looked to where the Freeport Manor peeked over the hedges. "I want my parents to be proud." His voice was softer than before.

Even though her mother was no longer with her, Amy-Rose thought about how memories of her were imbedded in the decisions she made each day. Her dreams only seemed achievable because of how strong her mother had been.

"They already are," she said. "I can see it in the way they look at you. And I doubt there is much you could do to change that."

Amy-Rose didn't realize she was leaning closer to him until his face hovered inches from her own. So close, she thought he could hear her heart pounding in her chest. Her skin tingled as she waited. Her hand trembled in his, and her eyes fluttered closed in anticipation. John's lips brushed across hers, flooding her senses with warmth. A gasp escaped her lips. He stilled. Amy-Rose, worried she had ruined the moment, held her breath. He looked at her with an expression she couldn't describe. She sucked in her bottom lip and bit down.

"Don't," he whispered. He tugged her chin downward until her full bottom lip came free. Then covered it with his own. John Davenport was kissing her. He was gentle as his hand traced her jaw, slid down her neck where her pulse jumped in his hand. Shyly, Amy-Rose followed his lead. Her mind was mesmerized by the shape of his mouth. She'd thought about what this would feel like. Unsure of what to do with her hands, she slid them up the hard planes of his chest and wondered in amazement if he could possibly feel the same pleasure she did.

John drew her closer to him, one hand low on her back keeping her steady. Then, with increased pressure, John deepened the kiss. Her book dropped to the ground and she wrapped her hands around his neck.

She felt her back arch to meet the warmth of his body and he bent over her, his hands applying enough pressure at her back to keep her upright, and the taste of him intoxicated her. This was not at all like the chaste, comically romantic kiss she'd imagined. This was a hunger, a thirst that made her moan against his mouth. His growl in response left her breathless and dizzy. She tilted her head up to the sky and shivered when he breathed her name against her skin between the featherlight kisses he placed along her collarbone.

Behind her closed eyelids, she detected a brightness. "Who's there?" Harold's voice boomed into the night, too loud for her fuzzy senses.

The light came their way. Her heart leaped into her throat. John pulled her around a group of dense bushes. She held on tight. He laughed at the shrinking light of the lantern. A moment she had wished and wished for, after so long, was now passed. But the sound of his suppressed happiness made her giddy. She also felt closer to him, having shared her story, and he having revealed some of himself with her. Together, they raced back toward the house, laughing quietly into the night.

CHAPTER 16

Olivia

There were no romance novels that could hold Olivia's attention that afternoon. She must have read the same line five times. Her mind kept returning to the other day at the park. It had been nearly two weeks and, since then, she and Mr. Lawrence had enjoyed countless lunches and walks about town—always under the watchful eye of her mother, of course, with opportunities to speak freely few and far between. Still, Mr. Lawrence continued to surprise her.

Olivia dropped the book to the table with a thud, startling the terrier in her lap. "Sorry, Sophie," she said to the disgruntled pup. She pressed her fingers to her temples, kneading the frustration she felt.

Sleep was beginning to take her when a commotion outside her bedroom caught her attention. The door opened a slit. Helen slipped through and closed it tightly shut. Olivia watched her sister lean against it like she was the last soldier alive protecting a keep.

"What's got into you?" she asked.

"*Shh!*" Helen hissed. "I'm trying to hide from Mrs. Milford. Do you think I still fit in the wardrobe?"

"Absolutely not!" Olivia replied. "The woman can't be that bad." She examined the way her sister breathed quickly.

"Don't be fooled. She has all those etiquette books memorized down to the page numbers. And she sees *everything*. Between her and Malcolm, the snitch, I haven't been able to work at all on the automobile John brought home. It's last year's Model T and in great condition, when you look past some of the damage . . . and the mystery defect. And instead of getting underneath the cylinder head, I'm dodging a governess."

"She's not a governess. Helen, you're being dramatic," Olivia said. Then she sat up. "Are you wearing a *corset*?"

Helen cut her a pained look and Olivia tried her best not to laugh.

"Livy, please let me hide here. Just for a little while?"

Olivia softened at the sound of her nickname. "Fine," she said. Helen's face brightened. Olivia saw so much of their father there—a similar determination infused every angle. "I'm sorry about what happened with Malcolm. John told me," Olivia said, by way of explanation. Her heart ached when Helen only shrugged. "He also said that you are key to the repairs they're doing, and that he knows you *have* managed to get out to the garage to look at that vehicle."

Helen smiled at that, like Olivia knew she would.

"Come," Olivia said.

Helen joined her on the chaise and immediately pulled a book from her skirts. Her head rested against Olivia's shoulder. Her voluminous coils were pulled into a fragrant, still-damp puff at the nape of her neck. "It's not fair," she said.

Olivia sighed and brushed her sister's hair back. "I know."

"Malcolm thinks women belong in the home." Helen scoffed. Then in a smaller voice, with restrained hope, she said, "Daddy would never allow it."

Olivia peeked at what Helen was reading and instantly regretted it. The diagrams gave her a headache. How could the family business come so easily to her brother and sister? Sure, she wasn't expected to know much about carriages or how the company was run, but she saw how it brought the two of them together. And with Ruby spending all her time with Mr. Barton lately . . . She couldn't imagine what Ruby and Harrison Barton had in common beyond a few acquaintances. Surely she'd grow bored of him any day now. Olivia didn't like shopping, but she missed the hours she and Ruby usually spent together. With the exception of a few Tremaine family trips, they hadn't gone more than two days without seeing each other in years.

She longed to have someone to share the little things, someone to laugh and grow with. Jacob Lawrence and his slow smile popped into her head.

"Why does your face look like that?" Helen had closed her book and was staring at her.

Olivia pressed her hand to her face. "Like what?"

Helen sighed and stared over Olivia's shoulder, her eyes unfocused and a grin spreading across her face. "That. You get a lost-in-a-daydream look on your face. It's Mr. Lawrence, isn't it?" She pulled at her clothing, a stubborn set to her chin. "I don't understand the point of tea and social calls. Don't you ever get tired of walking around and talking? What do you do with your hands? And are these," Helen said, prying at the edge of her corset, "necessary?"

Olivia considered her words carefully, her smile widening. Helen had never asked questions about courting. She sat up straighter and pitched her voice low. "I keep my hands to myself, naturally," she said. "There will come a time when you meet someone who makes even the mundane things seem magical."

"And is that what it feels like? Magical?"

Olivia pressed a hand to her stomach and thought about the fluttery feeling she had around Jacob Lawrence. She thought about their conversations and how they moved from lighthearted teasing to more serious observations. "Sometimes it can be."

Helen rolled her eyes and opened her book. "If you say so," she grumbled.

Olivia laughed then and stood. "Aren't you coming?"

Helen gave her a horrified glare. "And forfeit the perfect hiding spot? Absolutely not."

Olivia's stomach tightened when she remembered she had hidden a copy of the Jim Crow laws in her bookcase. But Helen wouldn't go through her things. *She's already buried in her book.* Olivia adjusted the skirts of her simple day dress. Her mother had fussed at breakfast, but she didn't see the point in dressing to recline in a drawing room all day when the process would have to be repeated for Mr. Lawrence's attendance at dinner that evening. She took the stairs quickly in bare feet, having left her soft slippers under the couch upstairs. The polished wood floors were cool under her soles. The closed door to her father's study swung open. Olivia stumbled to a stop. In the doorway, an unexpected visitor stood, smile hiding a fleeting, guilty look.

"Washington DeWight."

His smile widened. He stepped forward and pulled the door closed behind him. "You recognize me? I suppose the lighting here is much clearer than in a crowded ballroom." He straightened, broad shoulders thrown back. One hand held a briefcase, the other gently tapped his hat against his chest.

Olivia folded her hands behind her back to hide fidgeting fingers. The smell of cheroot cigarettes reached her. Her father was within. She glanced back to Mr. DeWight, eyes narrowing.

"I met with your father," he said quietly. "Incredible journey he's had, I thought he would be interested in supporting the Cause."

"Yes, he is very influential. People come from all over to talk to him. Sometimes even ingratiating themselves with his children to get closer."

"And you? Have you come for your allowance to purchase ribbons? A hat perhaps?" He smiled and Olivia's mouth puckered to the side. He pointed his hat at her. "No, perhaps it's a new dress to entrap the poor, unsuspecting Mr. Lawrence into an arrangement?"

"Is that what you think I am? Some frivolous girl consumed with material gain who has to cheat her way into a good match?"

"You keep telling me you're more than that. I have yet to see it. Oh, I know your family is very charitable. You donate money to orphanages and the Negro-run hospital. You and your mother bring food for the shelter. All well and good. Important. But hardly dangerous. You do not risk your name or standing with any of these gestures when the impact of offering either could prove the difference. They could spark real change. The Cause demands it. Mr. Tremaine understands that."

"So, you mock Mr. Davenport's children just beyond his ear-shot?"

"Olivia—"

"Miss Davenport," she corrected, her eyes on the door behind him.

"No offense was intended, *Miss Davenport*. On the contrary, I see potential in you. A fire smothered by the demure feminine ideal to which you so meticulously subscribe."

Olivia stood speechless, shocked by the passion burning in the words that grew softer with each syllable. She stood inches from him, without shoes, even a corset. She listened to him diminish the work she did and heard their shortcomings with the heat of embarrassment coloring her cheeks. She wished nothing more than to show him he was wrong. That she was more than a doll waiting to be placed in a new playhouse.

"I see the fire now," he said, clearly pleased with himself. His stare challenged her. "Have you given a thought to what we talked about when we last met?"

She nodded. "I'm not as you say. I don't have to prove myself to you or anyone else."

He smiled. "True. But to yourself—is it not worth proving to you?"

The afternoon passed in a blur. In her father's study, Olivia stared at her book, turning the pages without seeing them as he read through his papers. Mr. Davenport's eyes weighed on her, but she kept her face down as her thoughts bounced back and forth on what William Davenport would think of Mr. DeWight's observation. She wondered what her father and the young Southern lawyer had discussed. If he had any inkling as to what that same young man asked of his elder daughter, he didn't say.

He folded the paper in his lap. "Olivia, you have been sitting here the better part of an hour. And I haven't seen you turn a single page in that book." Mr. Davenport removed his eyeglasses and tucked them into his jacket.

Olivia blinked her vision clear. Her father was watching her, a gentle smile on his face.

"I didn't realize," she said.

"What's on your mind?"

Her mouth was dry. Washington DeWight's words swirled in her head. She couldn't ask without revealing how she knew the young lawyer.

"Is this about Mr. Lawrence?" he asked. "The two of you have spent a lot of time together in a few short weeks. Don't tell me you're worried about a small family dinner."

Olivia was at a loss for words. It was not like her father to bring up the gentlemen who courted her. He left that to her mother, though she assumed he was disappointed that she had not found a husband last summer.

"Mr. Lawrence—yes. Well, Chestnut did let him give her an apple." Olivia's horse was notoriously picky, allowing only Tommy and Olivia herself to feed her.

Mr. Davenport chuckled. When he spoke, his voice had turned serious. "Your mother worries about you girls. She can't help it. Her childhood was difficult." He pressed his lips together. "Going to bed hungry each night as a child makes you hungry in other ways as an adult." They knew this. It's why Mrs. Davenport stressed the importance of giving to the shelter, the food pantry, and committed their involvement to the employment offices too. Olivia watched him look toward the door, his eyes softening. Her mother's voice wafted from down the hall. "We just want the best for you."

Olivia nodded, her throat still tight.

He used his cane to push himself out of the chair. "Let's see what Jessie has prepared for us." Olivia took his hand, warm and rough in hers. Mr. Davenport kissed the top of her head and Olivia could smell a hint of cheroot clinging to his clothes. She looped her arm through his as he led them to the dining room.

Olivia clutched a small glass of wine she hadn't touched during dinner. The meal had gone well. Better than she'd expected even. Mr. Lawrence sat on her left, where she could study him. His neat mustache and easy smile reached brown eyes as deep and rich as dark chocolate. Jacob Lawrence was funny and charming. He seemed to flit from conversation to conversation with her family as easily as a hummingbird. He was smooth. Practiced. Perfect.

"You did the tour?" Helen asked. The sound of her sister's voice pulled her back into the moment.

"The factories are a marvel, Mr. Davenport," he said, looking past Olivia to where her father sat at the head of the table.

Mr. Davenport dipped his head. His chest seemed to swell with pride. "It was a great leap of faith," he said. Olivia watched the tender look her parents shared across the table.

"Faith and hard work," said Mrs. Davenport.

Mr. Lawrence nodded. "Of course." He took a sip of his wine, the charm slipping for a moment. A shadow passed over his features. Olivia sat straighter, but it passed as quickly as it had come. Jacob Lawrence was his jovial self again. "What are your plans for the adjacent lot? Forgive me, I heard the gentlemen outside your office discussing an expansion."

Mr. Davenport smoothed the front of his shirt.

Helen's face brightened. "Daddy, are you opening a garage?"

"No—"

John propped his elbows on either side of his plate despite their mother's glare. "Why not? It would be the perfect place to repair automobiles instead of here at Freeport."

"We are a carriage company," her father said.

Helen set her knife and fork down with a clatter. "Automobiles are horseless carriages."

Mr. Davenport gave his younger daughter a stern look. Olivia watched Helen's stubborn chin work to either hold in a pout or a retort. Her father sighed. "And this is why we don't discuss business at dinner."

Helen looked at John, her brows raised, then sighed. Olivia felt a tug in her chest. *Though Helen should know better*, she thought.

John faced Mr. Lawrence, seated across from him. "The ponies or the ring?" He slumped back in his chair, shoulders still tense.

"I beg your pardon?"

"Do you bet on the ponies or enjoy a good boxing match?"

"I don't gamble, but I appreciate the skill of both sports," said Mr. Lawrence. He and John spoke at length about boxing, baseball, and cricket, though she couldn't recall John ever picking up a bat of any kind. Their childhood was full of piano lessons and horseback riding. They were tutored and kept mostly at home. Washington DeWight's words came back to her. She was sheltered. Her parents sat at the ends of the dressed table, the pain of their younger selves hidden under a veneer of silk and silver.

The struggles of the people on the South Side were as taboo to mention at this table as the scars on her father's back, as the business he had founded despite those scars.

"I saw in your appointment book, you were meeting with a lawyer." John's words cut through Olivia's thoughts. So much for keeping business away from the table. "Are you thinking of replacing the Howards?"

Mr. Davenport placed his knife and fork down on the table. "No, not all. The gentleman I met with is from Tuskegee, Alabama. He expects a lot of Black folks will be moving north for work."

"Because of the Jim Crow legislation?" Olivia asked before she could stop herself. Her father readjusted the front of his jacket. She could feel the weight of his gaze on her, and her family's curious looks.

"Yes," he said. "Among other things."

John frowned at her, ready to ask his next question, but she beat him to it. "What kinds of things?"

Mr. Davenport looked more uncomfortable now than when he shut down the conversation about the garage. He was slow to answer, but a look from his wife got him speaking again. "Lack of opportunity. Violence." He picked up his knife and fork.

"And the lawyer wanted?" Olivia felt, more than saw, the glances of her mother and siblings. Mr. Lawrence leaned slightly forward. From the corner of her eye, she saw his attention dart from her to her father.

"He wanted to make connections. He's looking for support in

creating unions for laborers and coalitions to protect the progress of equality. I said I could pass his card along to the people heading organizations started after the tragedy in Springfield." The table grew quiet then. No amount of interference from her parents could have sheltered them from the death and destruction in Springfield two summers ago.

"Tragedy in Springfield?" Mr. Lawrence asked.

"For three days, Black businesses were destroyed and Black residents burned alive in their homes," he said gruffly. "I can fund the Cause and direct them to those who can offer more help. Beyond that, I'm afraid my hands are tied."

Mr. Lawrence said, "I think that is prudent. It's best to leave matters like this to lawyers and politicians and activists."

Olivia looked down at her meal sitting on the bone-white china. The light above winked off the silver service Henrietta had polished to perfection. "Surely, more can be done."

Mrs. Davenport's smile froze. She glanced at Mr. Lawrence, but Olivia pretended not to see. She couldn't be the only person at this table who realized how removed they were from the news Washington DeWight had laid at their feet.

"I would not host such meetings here and put you all at risk." Mr. Davenport's eyes softened with a sadness that tempered Olivia's frustration. "And then there are the men I employ. Who would feed their families if the shop and garage were vandalized, or worse, in retaliation?"

His words were sobering. There was more at stake than the material possessions she knew she took for granted. "You're right," she said, though the words tasted sour on her tongue and her heart felt heavy. She smiled and let John redirect the conversation to horse racing until her mother said enough and ordered the dessert be served. A cherry pie. The scent of its sweetness turned Olivia's stomach. She pushed the fruit filling out of the pie, her appetite nonexistent. Instead, she studied Mr. Lawrence at her side. Leave it to the politicians and activists, he'd said. His words hung in the air, pressing down on her shoulders.

"You know," Mr. Lawrence whispered. "I admire your passion to champion this cause." The look in his eyes was encouraging.

"I'd like to do more than that," she said. She didn't know where to start, but she was sure she could find out. Even if it meant speaking with Mr. DeWight. Her father seemed in favor of the work he planned.

"I'm sure. Your mother mentioned you're a junior member of some of the charitable clubs across the city. You'll be helping with the Tremaine fundraiser?"

"Yes," Olivia replied, hesitant. "But it's not all I intend to do. I—" Her words stuck in her throat at her father's voice. Mr. Lawrence's attention pulled away, his opinion needed on another matter. His glass raised in salute to match Mr. Davenport's. Olivia found herself fixated on the patch of skin on her father's wrist. From underneath the sleeve of his outstretched arm, the smooth and uneven texture of the scar peeked out at the hem.

A burn to hide a brand.

Olivia remembered, as a young child, the way a white investor had looked at it one afternoon she and her mother visited him at the garage. Her father had rolled up his shirtsleeves to assist one of the mechanics. And although his arms and hands were riddled with scars, there was one that gave this white investor pause. The one that made some people cringe while others grinned. She didn't understand the stares then, their morbid curiosity. Now her father's mention of the Springfield Massacre, the lynching reported only in *The Defender*, and the threat of restrictions disguised as laws made her worried for every person she knew. She was glad to be sitting, a sudden light-headedness making her weak. Her pulse pounded to an unfamiliar beat.

Washington DeWight was ringing the warning bell.

"Is everything all right, Olivia darling?" Mrs. Davenport asked quietly. She held Olivia's wrist, steadying her full glass. Her tone was not lost on her daughter. Nor the fact that she had missed when her mother left her seat and came to stand at her side. Olivia pushed away thoughts of the lawyer and his call to aid, and everything his presence meant. The warning underneath her mother's question refocused her attention.

"Of course, Mama," she said. "Everything is perfect." Olivia finally took a sip of her wine, hoping it would quiet the thoughts of dread growing louder in her head.

CHAPTER 17

Helen

The big clock echoed with a force strong enough to rattle Helen's nerves. Each tick of the second hand brought her closer to a breaking point. The matron hired by her mother to *refine* her manners turned out to be a humorless woman who insisted every occasion be treated as if they hosted the Queen of England for tea. Lemon and the sugary scent of cake cloyed at her senses.

Every waking moment was carefully scheduled. Her music lessons continued, but everything else was endured under the watchful eye of her tutor. Today, she and Mrs. Milford sat at the corner table at Marshall Field's crowded tearoom. Helen's back was to the wall, where she could see other gentlewomen pick at their food, their packages herded around their ankles. They hid their laughs behind napkins and flipped flaxen and raven curls from their faces. She sipped more tea than she'd care to drink and realized that if she did everything right, she had a life of absolute boredom ahead of her.

Helen tugged at the bodice of her dress, hoping to get a gasp of air into her lungs and make room for the plate of macaroons before her. Mrs. Milford always knew when Helen wasn't wearing a corset, and would devise some torturous punishment like embroidery to remind her of the importance of proper attire. Marshall Field's latest fashions were all any of the girls her age talked about. Those and a catalog from a place called Bloomingdale's in New York City. None of the newer styles required a corset. Helen eyed her chaperone.

"Shoulders back, Miss Davenport," said Mrs. Milford, gesturing to the pot between them. As Helen refilled their cups, her companion said, "You don't have many friends your age, do you?"

Helen's stomach made an odd lurch. "I don't share many things in common with girls my age," she replied.

She wondered if things would have been different if she hadn't fallen in love with the weight of the wrench in her hand, the smell of oil, the feeling of accomplishment after building something with her own hands. Olivia called it soreness, that ache in Helen's muscles after crawling out from under a carriage or automobile. Helen didn't know how to describe it, but she knew no new dress or party could make her so happy. Her heart had sunk when she'd caught sight of John and the others walking to the garage as the carriage took her away this morning.

"Oh, I doubt that's true," Mrs. Milford said. "You think you're the only girl whose interests lay outside the domestic realm?"

Helen bit the inside of her cheek and gazed around the room. *Do they all have passions they keep hidden?* She remembered her sister. "Olivia used to ride," Helen said. "She could coax even the most stubborn of horses over hurdles or onto a carriage hitch. She loved riding."

Mrs. Milford brought her cup to her lips. "I'm curious to know how she handled the adjustment. I take it she doesn't ride like she used to." Her raised eyebrow was a kind of challenge. And she was right. Helen didn't often think of how Olivia might have imagined her future, only how well she carried the expectations placed on her.

Helen turned to the older woman. "Why did you take this position? To teach me?"

Mrs. Milford studied Helen's face as if she were imagining someone else sitting across the table. There was a small shift in the firm set of her shoulders. "Maybe this is enough for today?" She called for the waitress.

It was just as well. The tea had grown cold.

Helen grabbed her hat and a parasol, using the kitchen entrance as her means of escape. After a painful half an hour at the piano, Mrs. Milford had given up and dismissed the instructor. "Don't go far. Amuse yourself and return at three o'clock," she said. Helen was only too happy to oblige.

The noise from the garage tempted her more than anything. She had snuck out late last night to check the progress on the Model T. *Have they noticed the changes I made yet?* She heard Malcolm and Isaac, the architect-turned-mechanic, talking. Helen weighed the odds that her father wouldn't find out. She breathed around a tightness in her chest that she couldn't blame on her undergarments, and headed toward the drive instead, undecided about her next move.

A black-and-red Davenport buggy turned onto the Freeport

drive just then. Helen froze. *Who is coming up the drive?* She had a panicked feeling it was her mother and Mrs. Johnson in the latter's family carriage. Her mother would expect her to be with Mrs. Milford, or studying in her room—not skulking around the grounds and garage. She moved toward the porch, but it was too late to run back inside. Her feet were rooted to the steps, her hat still clutched in her hand. Helen tucked flyaway curls under her hat with hands slick with sweat. She cursed herself for not ducking into the garage when she had the chance.

As the carriage drew closer, Helen realized it was not her mother. The top of Mr. Lawrence's head was the first thing she saw. It struck her as odd that she had recognized it.

The horse halted at the bottom of the stairs. Jacob Lawrence stepped down and his eyes found hers immediately. He walked up the stairs, stopping a few risers below her so they met eye to eye. It reminded her of the way he stood in front of her in the Tremaines' garden the night of their party.

"Miss Davenport, I had hoped to call on your sister this afternoon," he said, smoothing down the corners of his mustache.

Helen took a deep breath, still recovering from her small panic. "Olivia is not here. She's out with Ruby. They should be back before dinner."

He nodded and stuffed his hands in his pocket. "Well, I'll be off then. You'll tell her I came by?"

Helen looked at the great gate at the end of the drive and then back at the house.

"Miss Davenport?"

Helen bristled at his tone, but decided to use it to her advantage. "I will. If you help me."

Mr. Lawrence removed his hat and bowed. "How may I be of service?"

She tapped her chin and pretended to think hard. "There is a damsel in great need of rescuing."

"Am I to assume you're the damsel?"

"Of course not, squire. *We* are going to rescue her." Helen waited.

Mr. Lawrence stepped closer and dropped his voice low. "Is it a dragon, or a sorcerer, that has our damsel?"

"Yes," Helen said. A laugh escaped her lips.

He raised an eyebrow at this answer, a smile tugging at his full mouth. "In that case, best not keep her waiting." His palm opened between them. "Where is their lair?" he whispered.

With one final glance at Freeport Manor, Helen grasped his fingers and climbed into the carriage. "There's a bookstore in town. I'm sure we can find her somewhere in there. I can direct you."

Riding beside Mr. Lawrence in a buggy made by her father's company felt like an illicit act. She ran her hand over the plush seat. "Where did you get this?"

"Your father was kind enough to let me use one. Perhaps he knew it was destined for great things."

Helen laughed. She was thrilled to have escaped the house, but equally appalled that she'd fled beside the man who was wooing her sister. The tree-lined drive of Freeport Manor disappeared behind them. The neighborhood gave way to louder, crowded traffic broken up by patches of green.

"Thank you," Helen said. "I had to get out of the house."

"Is it haunted?"

Helen's brows knit together. "No, of course not."

"You looked like you'd seen a ghost." He smiled. "Are you sure you're not the damsel? Is this a test?"

Helen smacked his leg with her parasol. "I am no damsel!" She fought the urge to cross her arms like a child. Mr. Lawrence was the same age as John and the other young men who worked in the garage. She was surprised at how comfortable she felt around him. Most of her interactions with men revolved around carriages or automobiles. Not her plight against conformity.

"I'm no damsel," she repeated. "But maybe I did need some minor rescuing."

His eyes cut from the road to her. "What horrid fate did I save you from?"

Helen looked at the storefronts without really seeing them. "I'm running away from my *etiquette* lessons. My manners have been found to be lacking, and though I am far too old for a governess, my mother has employed one to correct my behavior before I chase away all the eligible bachelors Olivia passes over."

Mr. Lawrence's mouth screwed to the side at the mention of her sister. Helen barreled on. Did he not know he would have competition for her sister's hand? "And it is horrid. None of what I'm learning has any practical value. I'd much rather be pursuing my own interests. There's bound to be someone out there who wouldn't mind a perpetually disheveled lady who can't run her own household, but doesn't mind helping saddle a horse or repair an axle or generally get her hands dirty."

Helen and Mr. Lawrence both looked at her hands: chipped nails and dark stains. Part of her cursed the gloves she'd left on her chair, but the larger, truer part of herself was defiant and proud.

Her breath caught when she saw the hint of a smile on Mr.

Lawrence's face. He lazily held the reins between his hands and stared straight ahead. Helen's stomach turned. This is exactly the kind of behavior her mother and Mrs. Milford were trying to lecture out of her. *Great, he must think I'm a lost cause. But why do I even care?* And with that thought, the rest of her grievances flew out of her head.

"It's no easy task balancing what you want for yourself and what your family wants for you." He sat up straighter in his seat. "I'm not only here looking for prospects for my family business, but ways to save it. The Lawrence family name means something in certain circles, as I expect yours does. I have been cursed and blessed to be an only child, all of the fortune as well as the burden of responsibility. Everything I do affects my parents and our future."

"I know how lucky I've been." Helen picked at the lace of her parasol. "Olivia shines under Mama's attention and John always knew the business would be his."

Mr. Lawrence looked at her from under his long lashes. "And you? What fills your days? I'm sure not having a defined role isn't going well either."

"What are you talking about? We're going to save a damsel!" She smiled. Helen knew that she used her parents' preoccupations as opportunities to do what she wanted. She wasn't ignored and never felt neglected, but understood her place in the family dynamic. "No, I still believe I'm very fortunate." Money and privilege set her family apart, and she was loved.

"I'm sure your future is not as bleak as you believe."

Helen frowned. "They brought in reinforcements." She remembered how she felt ambushed when her mother introduced her to Mrs. Milford. She knew she was capable of anything she set her mind to. "I once disassembled a bicycle at a birthday party just to see if I could. Everyone walked in ready to eat cake and there I was in the grass in a heap of twisted metal." When Mr. Lawrence remained unfazed, she continued. "It wasn't my party and the bicycle belonged to the nine-year-old son of one of my father's friends. No one cared that I was seven myself." She sighed as Mr. Lawrence laughed beside her. "They overreacted. I could have put it back together if they'd let me." The sound he made beside her made her proud. He wasn't appalled by her behavior. It was as refreshing as it was unsettling.

"I once swapped the ink in the well on my father's desk with invisible ink. I'm afraid that went over about as well as your bicycle repair."

Helen's belly hurt and they were both in tears. After a deep breath, she said, "I sewed the sleeves of John's favorite jacket shut after he called my stitching dreadful." She wiped a tear. "That was more recent. And it was a particularly awful attempt at needlepoint."

Mr. Lawrence threw his head back. The sound was wonderful. It washed away the frustration of her morning. She felt warm and light.

"I trust he didn't take it well?"

"No," Helen said. "He tore the lining when he punched his way through it." She turned to him. "My friend Amy-Rose was able to replace the lining. Oh, but you should have seen his face!"

Mr. Lawrence laughed, then looked at her, eyes still smiling. "Which way?" he asked when they came to an intersection.

Helen no longer wanted to leave the carriage. "Let's take a scenic route." She pointed to the road leading away from the city.

He hesitated before turning where she directed. "I imagine I'd never like to be on your bad side," he chuckled.

"Then you should do your best to avoid it."

Somewhere along the ride, Mr. Lawrence and Helen had closed the space between them. The full skirts of her dress draped over his knee and their shoulders brushed with the sway of the buggy over the uneven road. At some point, the stone and cobbled streets turned to dirt. Suddenly, the left side of the carriage dipped. Mr. Lawrence's arm wrapped around her shoulders and pulled her close. His other hand, still gripping the reins, braced against the front of the buggy as they bounced in their seats. The horse reared onto its hind legs. The sun glistened down its back as they jerked to a stop. The horse reared again and cried out. Mr. Lawrence jumped down, reaching for the bridle. "Calm down!" he pleaded as the frightened animal evaded his grasp.

Helen watched him struggle for several moments before she removed her hat and pushed up her sleeves. The drop to the ground was greater than she suspected. Her feet landed in mud that quickly enveloped her feet. *This will be difficult to explain*, she thought. She toddled to face the horse. "What's her name?"

Mr. Lawrence scratched the back of his head. "A flower? I don't remember."

She rolled her eyes, but softened it with a smile. "There's your first problem." Helen looked up at the beautiful creature with a coat of deep brown. "Hey there, sweet girl," she crooned. Helen placed her palm against the horse's neck. The majestic creature bucked at first, but Helen continued talking to her in a gentle tone until she calmed down.

"She's stuck." She nodded to the horse's hind legs buried in the mud. The ground made a sucking sound with every attempt to pull her free, as if it wanted to swallow her whole. Helen tried to ignore the way Mr. Lawrence watched her as she whispered to the horse, guiding the creature free. Her skin prickled with heat, and underneath the smell of the wet earth and animal, she caught snatches of cedar. *Focus*, she told herself.

"There we go," she said as the horse popped up from the mud and found solid land.

Helen cheered and looked to Mr. Lawrence. He clapped at her efforts. "I do like a girl who can get her hands dirty." He glanced at the mud covering the tops of her shoes. "Or in your case, your feet."

Helen laughed and took a beat too long to move out of the horse's way. When she did, she stepped out of the shoe held fast by the mud. Before she could catch herself, she stumbled back. Her other foot was trapped and she met the ground with a wet, messy slap.

Mr. Lawrence stood above her, chewing his bottom lip, mustache twitching.

Helen lifted her hands. The mud was up to her elbows. She felt a wet drip down her chin, saw it land on her blouse, heard the choking sounds coming from above.

Mr. Lawrence's control broke. His mirth was loud and infectious. Helen, pretending to be embarrassed and horrified, grabbed a handful of mud at her hip and tossed it. Her aim was true and landed square in the middle of his chest. She pressed her lips together. She waited for his reaction, confident she hadn't gone too far.

Slowly, Mr. Lawrence bent down. His fingers sunk into the ground, his eyes never left hers. His movements were deliberate. Helen licked her lips, and saw Mr. Lawrence do the same. In that split second, Helen let another shot fly, this one striking his shoulder. They used the horse and carriage as cover, running and shouting like children, until both were covered in mud and grass.

Helen slid against the side of the buggy, and Mr. Lawrence was there to catch her. He held her elbow, releasing her long after she'd steadied herself. He stood over her as they exchanged fast, laughing breaths. "Helen, I should get you back." She stilled at the sound of her name. Unsure of what to say, she nodded and they got to work freeing the buggy and coaxing the horse back to work.

It seemed like they made it back to Freeport Manor faster than it took them to get out of town. They continued to swap stories, each more ridiculous. In the back of her mind, Helen knew her behavior was monstrous. She didn't care. Talking with Jacob Lawrence was easy, easier than she would have thought with a man who wasn't John. The realization sat heavy on Helen's chest until the grand Victorian face of the manor house emerged from the trees. She instantly felt the stiff way her dress clung to her body. The dried mud cracked and flaked when she moved. "I think you should go around and drop me off by the garage," she said.

"It may be too late for that."

Helen followed his gaze to Amy-Rose fanning herself on the stairs. Her face a picture of shock. She knew Mrs. Milford must be waiting for her inside—it was past three o'clock. She only hoped her mother wasn't waiting for her too.

Mr. Lawrence made to get down, but Helen clutched his arm. "I can manage. We don't want to make things worse."

"Well, if she gives you any trouble," he whispered in her ear, "you could show her your curve ball."

Helen laughed despite herself and the lecture looming before her. It strengthened her as she made her way from the carriage to her friend's side. Just before disappearing inside the house, Helen glanced over her shoulder to see Jacob Lawrence still smiling at her.

CHAPTER 18

Ruby

Ruby held her glass lightly in her hand. The jazz club had been her suggestion. The music was loud. The crowd, and its constant chatter, buzzed through her, electric. She leaned against the bar and played lazily with the beads dangling at her waist, then looked across the room, enjoying the warm feeling of her drink spreading through her.

Harrison Barton had gone to the stage to request a song. She loved dancing, and he was all too happy to oblige. She had to admit, she was having fun. Now if there were just a chance meeting between them and John, or some mutual acquaintance who might tell the young Mr. Davenport that they saw her with a new beau and if he doesn't act soon he'll miss his chance, the night would be perfect.

Ruby took another sip of her cocktail and laughed as Mr. Barton danced to her side, dressed in a finely made suit, cut to perfection. He watched the other couples with an amazed look on his face.

"Don't they have dance halls like this where you come from?"

Mr. Barton nodded, his smile still in place, but a sadness had crept into his eyes. "They do. Most dance halls where I come from, whether for Blacks or whites, don't take kindly to mixed people, unless you're the entertainment. They're not all officially segregated. It might be easier for me to get into a white-owned establishment than my siblings with deeper complexions. In others . . . my face is offensive." He shrugged, but Ruby could see the hurt there.

She looked away, knowing she was guilty of making her own snap judgments.

"Now, don't go feeling sorry for me."

"I'm not," she scoffed. Ruby knew pity was the worst feeling to endure from someone else. She straightened and glanced over at him. "All I know are the rumors."

This time he broke eye contact. He stared into his glass, rolling it between his fingers. "My father and mother grew up together. Almost." He shifted, unsure, then seemed to make a choice. "My mother was enslaved," he said. He looked up and met Ruby's eyes. "They kept their friendship, and later their love, hidden until his father was dead and she was freed. Still, they've always kept to themselves." A small smile chased away the darkness that had fallen over his features. "They didn't seem to mind. Or need anyone else, except us—my siblings and me."

The rumors were worse than reality. Ruby's mouth puckered at the bitter tang at the back of her throat. She took a deep breath, realizing in that moment that even if Harrison Barton had been the result of a violent act and not a loving union, she wouldn't have liked him any less. "And so you left," she said.

Mr. Barton looked toward the dancing couples. "People don't understand that the love between my parents is as real as the love anyone else feels. They see it as a betrayal. My parents kept me and my siblings close for as long as they could. Much like your friend Olivia. Except we didn't have the money then to protect us from the worst of it. We did have each other." His voice was steady. His words not revealing any of the pain he must have been feeling. Instead, he had a faintly joyful expression on his face as he watched the movements of the more talented dancers. "It's not something I chose or can change. It's better to focus on the things I can."

Ruby studied him. How could he be so at peace? She knew she had a temper and a penchant for retaliation. Ruby Tremaine loved drama. *That's how you ended up here, pretending an attachment to a man so confident in who he is, he doesn't let the outside world affect what he knows inside.* She twisted the cross she now wore at her throat. His words slid under her skin where they settled alongside her own feelings.

Her family's wealth had dwindled to a shadow of what it once was. They struggled to keep up appearances in the hope that her father's bid for the mayoral seat would pay off, his dreams of pulling up other Black folks coming true. Ruby could only see her family through the eyes of the other influential Black families and white businessmen who traveled in and out of their circle. No matter how much she tried, their judgment raked her skin raw. No one knew the full extent of her family's circumstances. She suspected Olivia might, but was too polite to speak of it.

Ruby said something then, despite her parents' warnings to keep their situation within their ever-shrinking household. "We're broke," she said.

She'd blurted the words before she could think better of it, and waited for the regret to set in. It didn't.

Mr. Barton turned to her, his face open and waiting. He didn't know her family before—not like the Davenports did. Ruby knew Olivia wouldn't care, that their friendship was seeded in love and shared experiences. But the further the might of the Tremaines seemed to slip, the more Ruby felt unsure of herself. *I don't know how to be* Ruby Tremaine *without the money and the jewels and the parties and the laissez-faire lifestyle.* In the corner of her blurring vision, she saw him watching her, his face open and free of judgment. She blinked her vision clear.

"My father wants to be mayor—to be a part of the minority that *makes* decisions, not just lives by them. At first, I thought it was prestige he wanted. Another thing he could own, stamp his name on. I've run into enough of the connections he's made, and overheard enough quiet conversations, to know that he wants more for every person who looks like us. Every person who has been freed from bondage." She turned to Harrison. "I was angry with him. Now I'm concerned that no one will ever know what he's risking. He doesn't want us to be special. He wants us, Black people with wealth, education, and opportunities, to be common. In the best sense of the word."

Harrison Barton didn't speak. But the expression in his eyes sent a shiver through her body in a room thick with sweat and smoke. "You could never be common, Ruby," he said finally. "You are anything but."

Ruby liked the way he said her name, soft like a caress. "Of course," she said, recovering quickly and unfurling her fingers by her face, as if presenting a magic trick. Then her smile faded.

"They're struggling with the fact that I don't need their permission. Not for what I wear or whom I choose to spend my time with. I'm not like these other girls waiting for a man to ask her parents for *her* hand in marriage." She looked at him pointedly. "Being ahead of the curve doesn't come without its price." Her hand strayed again to her neck. "I had this beautiful ruby necklace," she said. "A gift from my father and mother. My initials were engraved on a tiny charm by the clasp." Ruby replayed the ugly scene of her mother finding it the night of the fundraiser at their home, how Mrs. Tremaine had stood in Ruby's bedroom, choking the necklace in her fist. The thought of someone else wearing her jewel . . .

It had vanished in her mother's hand. In the receiving line later, with teeth clenched, Ruby had endured her mother's words—that she would see it sold. Ruby wondered—if she had begged, reached for her mother's skirts like a child, cried until she'd gasped for air, would she have her necklace now? She doubted it. She had searched the house high and low for it. Her mother was true to her word. And Ruby was inconsolable for days. Her visits with Harrison Barton were among the only bright spots in her week. Olivia's preoccupation with the British bachelor meant Ruby now had plenty of free time. She smiled at Mr. Barton then. "I know how I must sound, but it was mine, and it's worth more to me than a quick buck."

Mr. Barton rubbed his chin. Then he took Ruby's hand in his. His gaze flickered from the cross to her face. "I'm sorry. Any chance you could get it back?"

She shook her head. "I wouldn't know where to start looking for it." The look Mr. Barton gave her eased some of her heartache, and she felt the tension of the memory—her mother's anger, Ruby's own fury and loss—melt away.

She tucked her arm neatly under Harrison's and ushered him away from the bar. She'd shared more than she'd intended. *Dancing, that's what I need right now.* "Let's go," she said, just as a commotion at the entrance caught the room's attention. Heads turned and the chatter died down.

John Davenport had arrived. Beside him were the Greenfield boys. She remembered when the older of the two had tried to court Olivia. The crowd seemed to part around them. Single ladies stepped in and out of John's path to say hello.

The song changed to something slow and dreamy, but Ruby's heart raced. She knew the exact moment John saw them. The muscle in his jaw twitched. Mr. Barton's shoulders stiffened beneath her hands. *Stay calm*, she told herself.

"John, out on a work night?" she teased when he'd reached them. She'd known it was a possibility they'd run into each other. She'd wished for this very thing.

"Hello, Ruby," he said. He dipped his head to her companion.

"Mr. Barton, I'm not sure if you've met John Davenport formally. Our families have known each other since we were children."

"We've met. Miss Tremaine speaks highly of your sister." Mr. Barton's hand hovered in the space between them.

John's hands disappeared into his pockets. He seemed to lean back on his heels. "You two have become very close."

Yes! A rise out of John was exactly what she was hoping for.

Harrison Barton closed his hand over Ruby's. "Good fortune smiled on me the day I ran into Mr. Tremaine at the barber. He offered me an invitation to his party, where I had the opportunity to dance with his lovely daughter."

John's gaze turned to Ruby. "It's not so much luck as it is a privilege." Then he walked away, leaving Ruby's heart racing.

It was working!

Ruby hummed the last tune the band played as she shut the door behind her. Harrison had escorted her home in his carriage. A scandal had anyone seen them, but at this hour, only their set was out and about, and their morals were more relaxed than their parents'.

John had watched them dance a number or two from across the room. Ruby had straightened her back under his stare whenever she inched too close to Harrison. Her companion may be a placeholder, but Ruby quite enjoyed his company. He surprised her with his wit and optimism, had recently come into great wealth but did not show it off like a strutting peacock. He was understated. She especially liked the way she felt around him. Calm. Understood.

Harrison, because how could he continue to be Mr. Barton in her mind after this evening and all he knew?

A light down the hall cast a glow across the walls. Her parents.

Each night she'd spent out since the ball, they'd sat vigil, waiting for the day they assumed would have happened by now. It was getting harder to excuse her failure. Yes, John noticed me, she'd say. No, we haven't made plans. She steeled her spine now and entered her father's study.

She sighed. *Tonight was a good night.*

The light blazed from the fireplace. Her father's study was heavy with mahogany shelves, dotted with books and trinkets. The furniture was large and covered in dark velvet fabric, the thick burgundy Aubusson rug anchored by her father's large desk. Mr. Tremaine sat behind its beveled edge, chair pushed back. He leaned with his forearm propped against his thigh, gently swirling the brown amber liquid in his glass. Ruby realized that they must have been out too. Mrs. Tremaine sat on the couch to his right in a gown with full skirts. Her hair was a pile of curls atop her head. Her father had loosened his cravat and his best dinner jacket hung on the back of his chair.

Their faces greeted Ruby at the door. Her father waved a finger at her. "I heard humming." He turned to her mother and the two seemed to exchange a knowing glance. "Does this call for champagne?"

Ruby halted at the edge of the rug. In her mind, she saw herself, hands pressed against her cheeks, practically glowing with happiness.

"I know you left with Mr. Barton," her mother said. "We've been lax, but surely, he did not put that smile on your face." Her words, though soft, carried her clear disapproval.

"Of course I was with Harrison—Mr. Barton. A lady doesn't abandon her date." Her parents exchanged a wary look. "I'm not some harlot," she huffed. "I have a plan and it is *working*."

Mr. Tremaine regarded her. "Young lady, you will mind your tongue." Ruby suppressed an eye roll. Taking offense at her language in the face of what they were asking her to do hardly seemed just. She felt the same about the reasons they needed her to speed the progression of things with John. It was a challenge, yes, but they could at least give her some credit.

Mrs. Tremaine removed her gloves and Ruby's father sat back in his chair. "What kind of plan?" her mother asked.

Ruby cleared her tightening throat. "Don't worry—"

"Ruby, you do still care for John, don't you?" her father asked.

"Yes!" The force of her answer surprised even her. Ruby took a step back, her eyes focusing on the pattern on the rug. She felt the sudden need to sit down. Just not here, where her parents were sure to continue questioning her. Honestly, she was shocked they even cared to *know* how she felt.

Her mother stood. "You must not lose sight of what's important then, my dear. Never settle."

Ruby, halfway out the door, feeling the weight of their expectation, said, "Don't worry. I know what I'm doing."

CHAPTER 19

Amy-Rose

A man held the door of Binga Bank open for Amy-Rose as she floated into its busy swirl. She felt as if the spirit of her mother cheered her on. She'd taken her time to write out her business ideas on heavy card stock borrowed from Helen. Each letter of her itemized list was penned with care. It was her dreams, her heart, her soul on a sheet of paper that she willingly handed over. "My next deposit is in there too," she added.

"I'll be sure to give this to Mr. Binga," the banker said. "But I'd say you're on the right track." He pushed his glasses higher up on his nose and added Amy-Rose's latest deposit to the ledger on his desk. He continued speaking. She saw his lips moving. *Mr. Binga*, she thought to herself. She couldn't believe her good fortune.

The crisp sound of the receipt he tore from his book jolted her back to her senses.

"Here you are, young lady," he said with a calm smile. "If you don't mind me asking, what are you saving up for?"

"I'll be opening my own shop. To do hair." She'd practiced this statement until the confidence she feigned sounded real. If her dream was going to become a reality, she'd have to treat it like an inevitability.

"Is your husband on board with you spending all that money?"

"I don't have a husband, sir," she replied, keeping her voice as pleasant as before. Her hand remained extended for her receipt, just out of reach. "*I* earned that money."

"I see."

"See what?" she asked, feeling hot under her collar.

"It's unusual for a young woman to go into business alone, with no help or experience."

"I've done my research," she added. "I understand about as much as I can without actually doing it, and I'll have help. Besides, nearly every Black business owner in this city has started where I am now." Amy-Rose wasn't sure why she felt the need to argue. It *was* her money. But she had the desperate sense that if she didn't, something terrible would happen. The change in the banker's demeanor made her stomach clench.

And she'd noticed the way he stiffened when she said Black, as if her lighter complexion negated the part of her identity she'd inherited from her mother. Yes, it allowed her to move more easily in white spaces. That didn't mean it didn't hurt when it was later held against her, when she was made to feel less than. But he was just one person and Binga Bank existed to promote Black entrepreneurship. Amy-Rose sat taller in her seat.

He shuffled through the papers on his desk. None of them appeared to be about her account. But her smile faltered when the banker's brows creased. "And where did you want to open this . . . shop of yours?"

"Mr. Spencer's. It's the barbershop, not too far from here."

He nodded his head slowly. "I know of it." He nodded again. "Best of luck to you," he said.

One step closer. Amy-Rose took the slip and stuck it in the back of the book John had called precious. If her calculations were correct, a few weeks more would do it. She was already so much further along than anyone had expected.

"I don't need luck," she said lightly. Her mother taught her to work hard, that it could get you anywhere. She imagined Clara Shepherd's proud face for the progress made. The heels of Amy-Rose's shoes clacked against the parquet floor as she left the bank. She stopped at the dry-goods store to pick up Jessie's order. Normally, she chatted with other customers and asked the clerk about his family. But today she was distracted by the treatment she had received at the bank. The clerk silently slid packages across the counter, the cost added to the Davenports' tab.

"Thank you," she said, and, leaving, set a brisk pace down the sidewalk. Her shoes began to bite into her ankles as her feet carried her to Mr. Spencer's barbershop.

She paused outside. Her reflection in the glass looked like a businesswoman's. She had debated on her dress and hairstyle all morning. Her thick wavy hair was tucked neatly under a broadbrimmed hat. The A-line cut of the skirt under the simple jacket made her look serious, trustworthy. She hoped her savings and her preparation were enough.

"Clara's Beauty Salon," she whispered. That's what she would call it. All at once it felt so obvious. Amy-Rose stood taller. Forgotten was the encounter at the bank. She could already see her plans taking shape around the façade. She'd tend to the empty planter boxes below the window. A fresh coat of white paint would set it apart from a wall of natural brick on either side. The location saw plenty of foot traffic she hoped would yield regular clients. People seeking her skills.

She pushed inside and found Mr. Spencer with a customer. They were at the grooming station near the back, just before the register. The other stations were covered in white dustcloths. It smelled like wood varnish, cigar smoke, and antiseptic. It was wonderful, and one day soon, would be all hers.

"Well, Clyde, look who's come to visit." Mr. Spencer spoke to the man in the chair, face obscured by a hot towel. "Now, don't you go around looking like you already redecorating," he said, draping a smock over Clyde's shoulders. His words were softened by a grin.

She couldn't help herself. The wood floors were polished to a pale shine, reflecting the light pouring in through the high, arched windows. *Yes, updated wallpaper, new chairs, a lounge up front.* The space would do just fine.

Clyde squinted one eye open as Mr. Spencer removed the towel. "Is that Miss Amy-Rose?"

"Sure is. She's making plans."

"Oh, you *know* I have plans," she said.

Mr. Spencer laughed. His gaze followed hers. "I had a lot of great memories here," he said. His eyes took on a faraway look. The lines etched into his features relaxed and only his salt-and-pepper hair gave any indication to his years. He hummed quietly as he worked on shaving Clyde's patchy beard.

The two men exchanged news of their loved ones and news from around the block, which she knew was old man's gossip. The scene before her was exactly what she wanted: a space to call her own, with customers close enough to be called friends. It would be like when she did Helen's hair: gossip and unsolicited advice shared freely. And a home of some sort, one of her own making.

She bid the gentlemen good evening and began her walk back to Freeport. The sun hung low in the sky and painted everything gold. It also thoroughly baked the road and dried up the last of the rain that had fallen the day before. Heat radiated around Amy-Rose as she tried to ignore the bead of sweat inching down her back. She hefted higher onto her hip the parcels Jessie asked her to pick up, mumbling the grievances she didn't dare tell the cook in person.

She was trying to shift the packages to her other side when she heard a honk behind her. Amy-Rose sidestepped as she turned. A shiny black automobile slowed as it approached. She knew that vehicle. She passed by it most days on her walks to and from the gardens behind the Davenports' kitchen. She glanced at the people around. As they carried on, it became clear. John was slowing down for her.

"Need a ride home?" John asked. The dimple in his cheek made her heart squeeze. Their kiss in the garden replayed in her mind, not for the first time, raising her temperature even higher. But that was nearly a month ago. Just a silly slip, she'd decided. Both of their emotions had run high that night. He held the passenger door open for her now. The interior was all supple leather. She marveled at the craftmanship, the beauty.

"The weather certainly took a turn for the better, but you're miles from home. Why didn't you take a carriage?"

Amy-Rose remembered leaving through the kitchen door with Jessie yelling ingredients at her back. "I thought I'd just pick up a few things. I didn't expect so many orders to be ready. And in such large quantities."

John smiled, and Amy-Rose fell briefly enchanted by the way his lips moved. "Well, I suppose we're lucky I happened to be driving past."

We're lucky.

Amy-Rose thought about those simple words as John pulled back onto the road. His thigh pressed against her knee. His shoulder slightly grazed hers. The breeze itself seemed to be pushing them together. It became easy to imagine this to be her life. Afternoon drives with John after a full day of shopping for their household. No—after they spent their respective days at work. She would not give up her salon so easily.

She sighed and shook the image of the two of them from her mind.

"Did you accomplish everything you set out to do?"

Amy-Rose weighed sharing news of her progress. Regardless of the stolen moment they'd shared, he had shown no more interest in her than before. Nor had she in him. She glanced at his eager look now, his eyes flicking from her to the mostly deserted road before them. The trees on either side of the street seemed to reach toward one another. The dappled light that filtered through the branches created a kaleidoscope of greens and yellows, and the air around them cooled to a more manageable temperature. *He does know I dreamed of opening a salon,* she reasoned.

"I saw a man at Binga's today," she said. "I've been saving up for a storefront—Mr. Spencer's to be exact—for my salon. He's given me a fair deal and I nearly have the deposit." She hesitated, not sure why the next part gave her pause. "Once I do, I'll be leaving Freeport to start on my own."

Several emotions passed over John's face, so quick Amy-Rose couldn't read them. Her palms were slick and her stomach churned. *Why?* She wondered why she was letting his reaction have any effect on her at all. They had lived under the same roof for years. And until recently, she would have said he was nice, polite, but nothing that would warrant the mounting anxiety bubbling in her chest.

John pulled the vehicle to the side. They bounced wildly until it rolled to a stop. He turned to her, increasing the pressure of his leg against hers. "This is fantastic news!" He brought an arm over the back of the seat. It was close enough to feel like an embrace.

She saw his excitement dim. "I'll miss you," he said simply.

His statement, the slightly embarrassed way he looked at her with his heart-melting dimple flashing in and out of sight, made her flustered. She scoffed. "You can hardly expect me to believe that. You will be too busy to notice I'm gone."

John placed a finger under her chin. She felt the chafed, calloused skin against hers and held on to that moment. He looked into her eyes. "I've always had tender feelings toward you," he said.

"No," she replied, in an uncertain tone. Amy-Rose turned to look over the hood of the car, anywhere but his smooth face, the eyes that felt like they were searching her own.

"You don't believe me," he said. "I can see how you think that. But I remember how you always carried spiders outside instead of killing them. When we were younger, you and Olivia made dresses out of a silk sheet set you two found in a linen closet. You got in so much trouble." He leaned back in his seat, eyes narrowed as a heat rose from her neck to her cheekbones. "You are the only person who can convince Helen to do anything. Your freckles and the way you touch the tip of your tongue to your top lip when you're thinking, all of it—"

She immediately stopped and he laughed. *Did she do that so often?*

"So," he continued, "when I say I'm going to miss you being around, I mean it."

Amy-Rose met John's eyes. There was a yearning look there that set her skin ablaze. His full lips were slightly parted, and she remembered the way he smelled, the way they'd kissed.

"I had feelings for you too."

"Had?"

"Yes," she confirmed.

"Amy-Rose, I don't think you understand. My feelings aren't past tense."

He inched forward, waiting for her signal to stop. When she gave none, he closed the space between them. She gasped when his mouth met hers. John's lips were soft against her, gentle. His hands left her skin tingling where they traced her jaw and held the nape of her neck, lighting up the nerves in her spine. A horn frightened them apart. They both looked for another vehicle, hearts racing and breaths coming in ragged bursts. There wasn't one.

"I think that was you," Amy-Rose said, laughing.

John pressed her hand to his chest. His heart beat as madly as hers. "I mean it," he repeated. He released her hand slowly, as if he didn't want to let go, and pulled the automobile back onto the road. She didn't want to let go either. She wanted to enjoy him while she could.

An image of them together, like this, crossed her mind again.

It would not last, she told herself, as hope began to stir.

CHAPTER 20

Olivia

"Miss Olivia, they sent over two." Hetty held a round napkin holder in each hand.

Olivia looked at the silver rings, one with a leaf pattern, the other pearls. In a few days, her parents' friends and the city elite would pack into the ballroom to celebrate the Davenports' twenty-fifth wedding anniversary. The silver celebration. With Olivia's help, Mrs. Davenport would turn the cavernous ballroom into an intimate wonderland. Olivia marveled at all the details her mother juggled, hoping to one day run a household as smoothly.

Ruby leaned over her shoulder. "Neither of these are what you picked."

"I know, and there's no time to place another order." Olivia groaned. "The one on the left." She signaled a footman forward. "When the men arrive to set up the tables, will you instruct them to move the piano to the corner by the windows?" She kneaded the tense muscles in her neck. The party couldn't arrive soon enough.

"You're doing an excellent job," Ruby said, giving her a sympathetic smile. "Your mother wouldn't have given you so much responsibility if she didn't believe you could do it."

Olivia looped her arm through her friend's. She hoped so. She'd been so nervous, she'd hardly eaten all week. "Thank you," she said. She studied Ruby's profile. "How are you doing?"

Ruby shrugged. "My parents have been busy, both working to get as many people invested in my father's candidacy as they can. When I'm not with you or Mr. Barton," she said, tugging Olivia through the ballroom to the foyer where Helen and their mothers waited, "I'm with them. Papa thinks he has a real chance, and people really believe in him." Pride brightened Ruby's features.

"And what do you think?"

"He says the effective force for change in the city are the people themselves."

Olivia pulled free of Ruby's grasp. Mr. Tremaine's words, from the unlikely source of Ruby's lips, rattled deep in Olivia's bones. Of course, he was right. No one would know what the city needs better than those who walked its streets every day. Although she questioned the value of what she brought to the Cause, she knew the men and women who attended the meetings at Samson House to hear news from the South, exchange ideas, and advocate for Chicago were already moving toward more inclusive legislature. "You didn't really answer the question," she said gently.

"I want him to win." Ruby's gaze dropped to the floor. "It's difficult to imagine what you've never seen. A Black mayor."

"Oklahoma elected a Black mayor," said Olivia.

"This isn't Oklahoma," Ruby countered.

"True, but that doesn't mean it can't happen here."

The footman returned. "Miss Olivia, the tables have arrived." He waited for her response. "Miss Olivia?"

"Thank you," she replied, distracted. *This is what I can do.* When the fundraiser at the start of summer arrived, Olivia would have garnered the votes of the wealthy and influential Black and white people her privilege afforded her. The charities her mother championed could be used to her—to Mr. Tremaine's—advantage. The Black progress and community found in the city could only be protected from within.

Olivia joined her mother and sister outside and hugged Ruby before her friend got into the buggy with Mrs. Tremaine. "Thank you," she said.

Ruby's eyebrows pinched together. "I really just watched you work, but you're welcome?"

The buggy was halfway down the drive when Mrs. Davenport asked, "What are your plans for this afternoon, Olivia?"

Helen stared wistfully in the direction of the garage.

"I was hoping Helen would help organize my wardrobe tonight, what with Mr. Lawrence coming to dinner again," Olivia said, trying to catch her sister's eye. Perhaps they could help each other out. Vouch for each other's whereabouts.

"What?" Helen exclaimed. She had straightened quickly and her voice pitched clear across the grounds. She gave their mother an apologetic smile. "I'd rather not, Olivia, dear sister, but thank you for the offer."

Olivia laughed, then hesitated. Washington DeWight's comments rang in her ears. Ever since they'd nearly collided in the hallway outside her father's study a few weeks ago, she had doubled her efforts at the community center, hoping for another chance to hear him or other activists speak. But waiting for that next opportunity was sapping all her energy. And Tommy's patience too, as she often pulled him away from his chores to take her around town. She was glad that her mother was an active member in many charities. At Mrs. Davenport's elbow, Olivia had recently helped organize a book fair, clothing drives, and ladies' luncheons with Black and white women looking to support various initiatives. When scheduling conflicts arose, Olivia had been able to stand in for her mother. Those were the best days.

"I think I'll have a quiet night in after dinner." Olivia followed her mother back inside. They stood underneath a painting of Mr. and Mrs. Davenport embracing and looking at each other instead of at the artist.

"Your father and I appreciate your help and all the work you've done. Mrs. Johnson reports the ladies have nothing but kind words and gratitude." The corners of Mrs. Davenport's almond-shaped eyes crinkled above her smile. Olivia's own felt more like a grimace. It's true, she had been more involved with the charities, but many of her outings had been under the pretense of meeting the other activists. *But they're all working to help the same people,* she told herself, ignoring the tightness in her chest.

"Just don't stretch yourself too thin," said Mrs. Davenport.

"I won't," she promised. She watched her mother head down the hall toward the study. As Olivia approached the bottom landing of the stairs to the kitchen, she heard voices from the other side of the door. She wondered belatedly how many conversations were overheard in this quiet corner, but two words stood out among the rest, and soon Olivia had an ear pressed against the plain pine door: *civil rights.*

"They're gathering at the old Samson House on the South Side again."

"Better you than me, Hetty," Jessie said. "I ain't got time to head down there. Let you young folks feel what it's like to get rounded up and beat on."

"You don't mean that, Jessie," Hetty said.

"I sure do, and I expect you to be as spry as a spring chicken tomorrow. There's still a lot to be done." The door Olivia stood behind suddenly opened. And there was Hetty, carrying a stack of table linens.

"Miss Olivia," Hetty said, "are you okay?"

Was she? Olivia's heart pounded, and just like that afternoon at the community center, she felt a pull toward the South Side. "Do you mean to go to the civil rights meeting tonight?" she asked as the kitchen door swung closed behind Hetty.

Hetty backed away. Olivia held out a hand. "No, don't be afraid. Tonight, when you head downtown, I want to go with you."

"But, miss—" Hetty looked stricken. She glanced behind her as if to the kitchen. "I heard what your father said at that dinner with Mr. Lawrence. He wants your family to stay away from that scene. I don't know—"

"Don't worry. I'll figure something out and meet you in the stables." Olivia suppressed the urge to reach out to Hetty. She didn't know how to describe her need to be there, so she waited, saying nothing more. When the young maid finally nodded, Olivia smiled.

After the main course, Olivia claimed to be suffering a migraine and excused herself. It was such a rare occurrence, her parents barely protested, and her brother and sister wished her well before returning to a conversation about a horse he saw at the track. Mr. Lawrence, ever the gentleman, pulled out her chair and wished her well. She fought her way out of the floor-length silk dress she chose for dinner, the buttons along the back slowing her down. Then waited in her room until she heard them move to the sitting room. Music wafted upstairs.

Leave now, or not all.

She closed her door slowly, careful to muffle every sound. It was easy slipping out the side door, creeping into the garage. Her father had shown each of his children how to saddle, ride, and hitch a horse to one of the simple buggies, for which she was grateful. By the time Hetty arrived, the small open carriage the staff often took into town was ready.

They arrived at Samson House in barely any time at all. Olivia guided the horse to the alley and tied it to a lamppost. Like before, people of all walks of life climbed the steps, crossed the tilted front porch, and entered the nondescript building.

Hetty turned to her. "Miss Olivia, I agreed to come here with you, but if your father ever found out . . ."

"Hetty, I assure you, he would be angry with *me*." But Olivia didn't miss Hetty's look of unease as the two of them entered the house.

The hum from below was louder than she remembered. In her hurry to make it on time and unseen, Olivia had left the house without a hat or gloves. No purse . . . just the simple day dress she wore while making the final preparations for the ball. She had nothing to disguise her or shield her from prying eyes. But there was also nothing about her that marked her as a Davenport. The suffragist Mrs. Woodard had been discreet after Olivia's first night after all.

She melted into the crowd, and though her clothes were of finer quality, she found herself more comfortable than on her first visit, especially with Hetty's familiar face at her side. She felt grounded and eager.

"This way," Hetty said. Olivia obeyed, following her reluctant companion to where a group of women stood. Hetty hugged them. She turned to allow Olivia to join the circle. "This is—"

"My name is Olivia," she said, before Hetty could offer more.

Hetty's eyes widened slightly. Her smile stayed where it was. "Yes, this is Olivia."

"How nice," said the closest woman. A shock of white hair flared from her dark temples and tucked neatly in a bun. "How do you know each other?"

"From work," Hetty said.

Olivia nodded and tried not to fidget under their curious stares. She listened as they made their introductions and spoke their reasons for joining the Cause. When an older woman recounted the abduction and murder of her husband, Olivia wanted to cry, and then became lost in thoughts of *What if?* How many random events had needed to take place for her parents to meet and succeed, for her to be where she stood? She always knew how fortunate she was and enjoyed the work she did, but now more than ever, she wondered what else she had to offer.

"Miss," said Hetty.

Olivia cringed. The small word did not escape the others' notice.

"Do you mind if I meet my cousin over there?" Hetty pointed

to a young man, older than John, a few feet away. "You're welcome to join us."

Olivia shook her head. She needed to find Washington. "Hetty, when we're . . . here," she said quietly, "you can call me Olivia. Actually, I would prefer it." When the dubious frown returned to Hetty's face, Olivia added, "I'll be fine right here."

She watched her companion move toward the young man and hug him, and then she took in the room around her. It was filled to bursting. The attendees glanced around them furtively. The snatches of conversation that floated around warned of increased violence, fear that laws against interracial relationships would spread like the Jim Crow laws.

". . . they're rounding men up at night like cattle . . ."

". . . My sister says she has to walk home to relieve herself. There's no restrooms for the colored girls in the factory . . ."

". . . They've fled north. New York, he said . . . their marriage put a target on their backs. Just the other night, bricks were thrown through all their windows . . ."

There was optimism too. More than one person mentioned Mr. Tremaine and the efforts of former abolitionists working in his favor.

Then she heard a familiar voice. Warm and rich with Southern cadences.

She squeezed between patrons until she saw his face. Washington DeWight wasn't wearing a hat, and the shadow of a beard had begun to show along his jawline. Though he looked tired and a bit rumpled, his eyes shone with an enthusiasm that drew her in. Olivia couldn't deny the magnetic effect he had on the people gathered around him. He was jotting something down in a notebook, stuffed to bursting with brightly colored flyers and cards, some of which dropped like falling leaves to the floor where he stood.

Olivia knew the exact moment he spotted her. His eyes widened.

The gentleman to his left repeated his name. Mr. DeWight thanked him for coming and separated himself from the group.

Olivia couldn't help the smugness creeping into her face. She'd made it. Late, but she was there. Her smile faltered as his grew. *Why does he look like the one who's won?*

"You missed my speech," he said. "Or perhaps you got lost again. The salons are closed at this hour." He pulled a timepiece from his coat pocket and feigned amazement. "I'm surprised to see you," he said, and before she could respond, continued: "Did you have to pay one of your servants to get you here?"

"No." She noticed the crowd around them breaking up into smaller groups. "I snuck out of the house, but I didn't come alone. Unlike you, I can't go and come as I please. I have other commitments, however trite you may find them." She thought about her plan, but doubt crept in. She had lied her way here. She had concealed her last name. And she had placed Hetty in an uncomfortable position. She scanned the room and found her reluctant companion deep in conversation with another young woman. *Does Hetty need compensation?* Olivia wondered if she should have asked Hetty to bring her here in the first place. It wasn't like she didn't know the way here herself.

Mr. DeWight cleared his throat. When he spoke, his voice was gentler. "Well, I'm glad you made it." He rubbed his chin and glanced around the room.

Olivia felt some of her uncertainty fade. "I'd hoped to learn more," she said. "Is it over? No one seems to be leaving."

"It will be like this for a while," he said. "Exchanging ideas and stories." Mr. DeWight led her to a small table of refreshments. He pointed out the prominent leaders in the group. They lived varied lives, served as conductors in the Underground Railroad, fought in the Union Army, and marched on state capitals.

They had all come here because they believed that Chicago was a city full of opportunity and diversity, where the promise of a new start was achievable. They were right. She only had to think of her father and Mr. Tremaine. Now they had to protect it and grow it. Feeling inspired, she realized Chicago was as much a hub of turmoil and change as any place in the country.

"Miss Davenport?" A woman a few years older than her, skin a deep, rich brown, clutched a sleeping infant to her chest. "Oh, it *is* you."

Olivia smiled politely, glancing quickly around to see if anyone had heard her name. "Olivia, please. Have we met before?"

"Not formally," the woman answered. "They told us that your family donated to the children's library, that you delivered some of the books yourself. I just wanted to say, my other little one really enjoys them." She hitched the child higher on her shoulder. "People like you and Mr. Tremaine are truly selfless."

Olivia froze. "Mr. Tremaine?" Her mouth went dry. She searched the faces in the crowd. In all her schemes to escape the house unnoticed, she had forgotten she could be discovered at any one of these political meetings.

"Yes, my husband is working on his campaign until he can find work."

Olivia took in the woman's grateful smile. "Lovely," she managed to say. How could she have been so careless? The small basement seemed to shrink and the voices grew louder. She scanned the faces for Mr. Tremaine, or anyone for that matter, who could report her presence to her parents.

"It's too bad he didn't stay longer. It was nice meeting you," the woman said over her shoulder as she walked away.

Relief flooded Olivia's system. She felt dizzy. Mr. DeWight, as if sensing something off, turned for the exit and asked, "Walk with me?"

She nodded and let him lead her to the door. Outside, the summer air was refreshing after the press of bodies in the basement. It smelled like charcoal smoke. They passed a couple pressed close in an alley. Olivia's ears burned. Washington DeWight was practically a stranger. And no one but Hetty knew she'd even left the house.

"What did you hope to learn tonight, *Olivia*?" he asked.

They'd stopped under a lamppost outside a diner. The soft *clink* of silverware punctuated the chatter wafting through the swinging door.

"I don't know," she admitted. "There is so much I don't know, or understand."

"I find myself learning something new every day." Washington DeWight stuck his hands in his pockets. "You shouldn't be so hard on yourself."

She huffed. "I should leave that to you, *Washington*?" she asked, eyebrows arched.

"That's fair," he said, smiling. "This work is as difficult as it is rewarding."

Olivia watched him look back the way they had come. His gaze seemed to be registering something she couldn't see.

"How did you get involved?" she asked.

"My parents were activists. My father was a lawyer and my mother a teacher. I was always surrounded by fighters, people working toward change for the better."

"So, you always wanted to be a lawyer?"

"No, I wanted to play the saxophone in a jazz band."

Olivia laughed. When he didn't join her, she asked, "Wait, are you serious?"

Mr. DeWight, with a wistful expression, shrugged. "I was very good. Determined. But with parents like mine, school won out."

"I guess living up to expectations is the rule, no matter where you grow up."

"I suppose so. I don't regret it, though. Being part of something bigger than me makes me feel closer to them, to my community and every person I meet." He stood inches away. Olivia stayed still, letting his nearness linger. He was irritating, yes, but interesting. "What would you be, if you could choose?" he asked.

Olivia's eyes snapped up to his. Her heart raced as she tried to come up with an answer. She stuttered, settling on the truth. "I never really thought about it." A sudden coldness hit her. "Um, I never . . ." She trailed off at the realization that no one had ever asked what she wanted for her future. Not even herself. "I— Excuse me," she said.

She brushed past Mr. DeWight. Her feet carried her away from him, from the building full of people so clear in their purpose and passion. She had no idea what she would do with her time if it was not scheduled for her by her mother, society, some days even Ruby. *Have I truly been so thoughtless?*

"Hey," he whispered in her ear. He held her gently at her

elbow and she turned back to face him. "It's okay," he said. His voice was kind. "Good news, there's always time to decide who you want to be."

Olivia blinked back tears. She swallowed the lump in her throat. He still held her elbow, his thumb against the vulnerable flesh at the crook of her arm. She warmed under his touch. It was soothing, which confused her. Days ago, she would have sworn if they ever were to touch, it would be her slapping him for being forward. Now her face burned at the thought of her palm against his bare skin.

He pulled his hand away then and took a small step back. "What do you love to do?" he asked. "Something just for yourself."

She thought back to the moments that she felt happiest and carefree. The wind whipping around her, excitement running through her veins, and no thought but staying seated. "Riding," she said. She thought of the personalities of each of the horses in the stable. And how little time she spent riding since coming out last spring.

"Well, I just met this gentleman who owns a carriage company and seems to have an endless supply of horses on hand. I can make the introductions."

"How kind of you." Olivia laughed. Her breathing eased.

They continued walking. She could see her horse, Chestnut, that had taken her and Hetty here happily accepting apples from two children on the street.

"And does Jacob Lawrence enjoy riding?"

Olivia, rebounding from this last question, glared at him. It was a prying, improper thing to ask. She imagined he didn't heed social niceties unless they suited him. "I don't know," she said.

"I heard things are moving quickly between you two."

"They are."

"Do you love him?"

"Love," she gasped. Her horse waited several feet away. Activists trickled out of the meeting house and parted ways. Hetty slowed her pace when she spotted Mr. DeWight, giving them a wide birth as she climbed into the buggy.

Olivia knew the answer to this. It was the future planned and agreed upon the moment she was introduced into *polite* society, to which Washington DeWight was not a party. No one would ask such an impertinent question. *But we've been honest so far.* "We may not be there yet, but we have a similar background, share the same values. We enjoy the same things."

"What are these *things*? Picnics in the parks and dancing at parties." He crossed his arms over his chest. "They aren't real."

Olivia thought about Mr. Lawrence and their courtship. It *was* real. Their shared experience was real. "You know nothing about our relationship."

For the first time ever, Mr. DeWight seemed at a loss for words. The struggle was clear in the furrow of his brow. "I'm just going to come right out and ask."

"As if that isn't what you've been doing all night?" Olivia laughed in disbelief. It was past time to go home. She should have left when he'd told her she'd missed his speech. She had to get out of here, heaven help her, or she *would* slap him before the night was out. She untethered the reins and coaxed Chestnut forward.

Mr. DeWight placed a hand on the horse's neck. Olivia watched Chestnut nuzzle his shoulder. "Picture your future with him. Are you happy?"

"DeWight!" He glanced to the person calling for him.

He slowly backed up. His eyes stayed on hers, igniting her every nerve. "I can see it. You want passion. Purpose. You won't find that with him." He began walking away, turned, took two backward strides. "What does he really know about you?" he said. He flung out one arm as if to take in the whole South Side, Samson House. "Or you him?"

CHAPTER 21

Helen

The wrench in Helen's left hand shone like sterling, reflecting the light from the bare bulb above. She tried her best not to look at the clock at the end of the workbench. Or think about the hurt look on her sister's face when she hadn't wished to sift through her closet for a husband-snaring ensemble.

She thought of apologizing after dinner. She even went upstairs to see if Olivia wanted dessert. Helen was shocked to see her sister fully dressed and hurrying through the back stairwell to the kitchen used by the staff. Naturally, Helen followed. While her parents and Mr. Lawrence retired to the study, Olivia and Hetty left in a carriage. *What could she be up to?*

Whatever it was, Helen felt a lot less guilty about her own activities. She snuck out to the garage after dinner and began organizing and cleaning the small hand tools left around the automobile John had brought home so many weeks ago now. The mechanics rarely placed things where they belonged, and the task, though tedious, didn't require much thought or effort on her part.

It was soothing. She often wondered if this was how embroidery was supposed to feel.

Her hand was inches away from a set of clamps when the door behind her creaked open. With everyone out or preoccupied, she hadn't thought to lock it. Helen held her breath. Her eyes closed, and she braced herself for the tap of her father's cane and the words that would be her undoing.

"Help me, will you?" John nudged the door open with his foot. He had a tool bag on each shoulder and a stack of files a foot thick in his hands. She dropped the wrench and took the papers. "Put them over there," he said, pointing to the wobbly table they used as a desk.

"What are these?"

"Davenport Carriage's finances over the past decade. I figure the first thing Daddy will say when we try to pitch an automobile line, will be 'How do you plan to pay for it?' I have some reading to catch up on. So do you."

Helen stared at her brother. "Really?" she asked, barely containing her happiness. She threw her arms around him. It was the best news she'd heard in ages. "This is amazing!"

He placed the bags on the workbench. "It will be."

She poked the dimple in his cheek. "Is this why you've been smiling and humming to yourself?"

He laughed and turned away.

"You're blushing! Olivia thinks you fell in love." She'd never seen her brother like this either.

Still smiling, John covered his hands with hers. "Listen, we do this together. I need you to focus. Preferably harder than you do on your etiquette lessons."

"Ugh." Helen frowned and looked in the direction of the

house. Then she whipped around, narrowing her eyes at her brother. "Excuse me, I *do* work hard at them." She sagged. "Sort of? It's the absolute worst. Mrs. Milford watches me like a hawk."

"And yet, you still escaped for an entire afternoon. Did you have Amy-Rose bury the evidence?"

"No." She sighed. "She just helped me get cleaned up. Mostly. Mrs. Milford frowned at me all the rest of the day. We missed a patch behind my ear."

John shook his head, a wistful smile on his face. "Covered from head to toe in mud."

Helen laughed. Then clamped a hand over her mouth. "Stop— you'll get me found out." She sighed and thought back to the way Amy-Rose had looked at her as she climbed the stairs, her shoes squelching with each step. "My, you should have seen the carriage."

In the moment, she had simply been grateful and swallowed every complaint she had about the embroidery she was tasked to complete before the end of the day. But now she thought it strange that only her friend was there when she'd arrived. Mrs. Milford was right where Helen had left her, waiting with her new assignment. Helen recalled her effort to stitch the family name within the embroidery hoop. Her *D* was so large, she had to reset the hoop twice. Now she was stuck with a very lopsided pillowcase.

She looked at her brother and cleared her throat, feigning a dignified expression. "Yes, well, the mud was the least unpleasant part of that day."

"You're lucky it wasn't Mama who found you." John tapped her on her nose. She swatted his hand away, though he was right. "Apply some of that ingenuity to the stuff Mama cares about, and maybe she'll give you a little more leeway—you can use it to go through these with me," he said, fanning the stack of papers before locking them in the file cabinet.

"Yeah, okay," she agreed.

"Good." He gave her the key.

Helen watched her brother unpack the tool bags, the dimple still showing. "John," she said hesitantly. "*Are* you in love?"

He stopped and faced her. She saw a brightness that hadn't been there when he came home from university. Helen wondered what it felt like. She imagined it to be like the relationship her parents shared even though she couldn't imagine wanting to spend so much time with another person. *Is there really that much to talk about?* Still, John looked how she felt when she repaired an engine. "Well?" she prodded.

"I could be," he said shyly.

She looked at her brother, practically bouncing with happiness. *Olivia is right—he is in love.* "Is it Ruby?"

John hesitated. "No, no more questions."

Questions were all she had. Helen took a deep breath, ready to ask them anyway.

"Hello?"

Helen dipped behind the vehicle. The last thing she needed was someone to spot her here and report back to her mother—or her father. She pulled a cap over her head and used John's leg as extra cover. Hopefully, she'd be mistaken for another mechanic.

"Mr. Lawrence," John said. Despite her better judgment, Helen chanced a glance over the car. It was the young British bachelor. He looked out of place in his finely made suit among the discarded oil rags and partially dismantled automobile. His hair was parted to the side and brushed flat. He held his hat in one hand and shook John's with the other.

John turned Mr. Lawrence toward the door and threw a look over his shoulder at Helen that seemed to say *Stay there*. "I lost track of time. I'll meet you at the car." She listened as they left. Every muscle tingled as she eased herself onto her knees. Helen chastised herself for being so careless. She shuddered at the thought of anyone else walking in. Both she and John would have been in enormous trouble. Bitterness at the unfairness of it all threatened to ruin her good mood, but how could she be disappointed? John sought her help and she aimed to be prepared for whatever argument their father might throw at them.

Helen stood. She stretched her arms over her head and immediately saw something that didn't belong.

The hat Mr. Lawrence held moments ago. She stared at it, wondering if she should bring it out to him.

"So it was you hiding?" said a smiling voice.

Helen jumped. Her fingers were inches from the hat. She folded her arms over her chest and gave Jacob Lawrence a wide berth as he reached for it.

"No, I was working." She gestured to the tools and rags across the workbench that hugged the back wall. The new bags of tools brought in by John replaced the clutter she'd removed. When she turned back to Mr. Lawrence, he was looking at her, a bemused expression on his face.

"I like your cap," he said.

Helen yanked it from her head, smiling. "I take it you have plans with my brother," she said.

"We're meeting with some of his friends. The agenda is yet to be revealed," he answered.

She used her fingers to count. "Cards, smoking, boxing."

His eyes widened.

Helen smiled. She liked that she had surprised him. She shrugged. "John's friends aren't very original."

Mr. Lawrence recovered quickly and came around the automobile, leaning his hip against its side. His long legs stretched toward her. "So, this is where you work, when you're not . . . preoccupied."

Helen nodded. "I come down here sometimes. To clear my head, to tinker."

He picked up the wrench she'd had earlier. "Tinker." He shook his head. "I don't know any young ladies who'd willingly touch one of these. In a good way, of course," he added.

Helen's skin prickled. After his help a few days ago, she decided they would be friends. There weren't many people she trusted. It was hard for her to make connections with girls her age. Most wanted to befriend her to get closer to John, and she shared so little in common with them and Olivia. She thought about what Mrs. Milford had said. Though *Jacob Lawrence* wasn't the type of person she'd suggested Helen befriend. *I have to start somewhere,* she thought.

"What do you hope to do with all this tinkering, Miss Davenport?" He examined a screwdriver and watched her off-load the tools from the bags.

"Could you not," she said, straightening. "Helen will do just fine." This was her space, the one where she earned the same treatment as anyone else.

"All right." His voice was softened by his smile. "Only if you call me Jacob."

Helen thought about this for a moment. It was improper, yes, but they were friends, right? Soon to be family. "Jacob, I think about what it would be like to work at the Davenport Carriage Company one day."

There was something in the way Mr. Lawrence looked at her that felt like a gentle nudge to continue. She tried not to think about the way his first name tasted on her tongue. Sweet and unlike anyone else's. "I know John's meant to take over, but I'm sure if I were a boy, there would be a place for me."

"You don't think there's a place for you now?"

Helen threw an oil-stained cloth into a hamper. "If John was in charge, maybe." She sighed. "If I were a boy, I could have done an apprenticeship with a mechanic, undergone formal training, instead of being forced to sneak in late at night when the house is asleep. I would have been carrying the notebooks and manuals instead of my skirts or a parasol." She blushed at her words.

Mr. Lawrence pushed off the automobile. He didn't say anything. Just handed her the screwdriver. His fingers grazed hers. It felt like that first sip of coffee in the morning—smooth, rich, and laced with an energy that shocked her system. Her throat was suddenly dry, the room too hot.

She exhaled. Her reaction confused her. It felt different from her interactions with John's crew. Sure, the twins took her presence in stride, even joked with her. Henry especially shared his knowledge, knowing how desperately she wanted to do an apprenticeship with a mechanic. But an accidental brush of their hands as they passed a tool didn't trigger such a response.

An unexpected friendship. *That's what this is*, she told herself. She returned the screwdriver to the bag, not really seeing, just letting her hands move as she felt Mr. Lawrence's eyes on her. He saw her, she knew deep down, in more ways than most people did.

John appeared at the garage door in a new shirt and his hair slicked back with a fresh coat of pomade. "There you are." His eyes measured the distance between Helen and Mr. Lawrence.

"I forgot my hat," Mr. Lawrence said by way of explanation.

John stared at the gentleman for a beat longer than Helen thought necessary, then asked, "Ready to go?"

Helen, relaxed by the task at hand, faced Jacob Lawrence as he attempted a goodbye. "Don't play poker with Lonnie Lynch," she said. "He cheats."

Jacob laughed. "Good to know. Anything else?"

"Good luck," she said.

Jacob Lawrence bowed like he had that day he'd helped her escape. Helen swore she heard him whisper *Extraordinary* before he left.

CHAPTER 22

Ruby watched the small clock on the mantel. She waited in the foyer, hat and gloves in hand. Harrison Barton was due to arrive at any moment to take her somewhere special, he'd said, piquing her interest. They'd been to all the popular places, where could be left? She sighed now and paced outside her father's study—Mr. Davenport and John were inside. A perfectly timed *chance* encounter between John and Harrison Barton was just the thing her plan needed to get things back on track. The men's voices were muffled. The least they could do was allow her to glean some news worthy to share with Olivia.

She straightened at the sound of movement within, and managed to appear as if she were just walking down the hall when the door swung open.

"Mr. Davenport, good afternoon," she said. Ruby then turned the full wattage of her smile on his son. "John." Both gentlemen greeted her.

John walked to where she stood. She craned her neck to meet

his eyes, which settled on her face. "You look lovely today, Ruby. You always do," he said.

Ruby stood straighter. "It's still nice to hear."

John's mouth twitched. "I haven't seen you at Freeport lately. We've missed you at dinner."

Some of Ruby's confidence deflated at the word *we*.

"Then again, I haven't seen much of Olivia either," he continued. "But I'm glad the two of you are as inseparable as ever."

What is he talking about? Ruby caught her frown and recovered quickly. She and Olivia spent less time together than either of them liked, but she could hardly say as much. Her friend wasn't out with Mr. Lawrence *that* often. *Where does Olivia spend her spare time if not with me?* "We are," she said, "inseparable as ever." Whatever her friend was up to, she wasn't going to expose her.

"I'm sure the volunteering you do together reflects well on your father's campaign."

Ruby smiled. She and her best friend needed to catch up. "It does. And your projects, they are going well? I hope they're not keeping you from more leisure activities."

John returned a grin of his own. "I promise, I will be on time for the next party."

"I should think so," she said. "It's at Freeport!" His laugh was reward enough for the stress eating away at her. His hands were folded behind his back, straining his shirt and waistcoat across his broad chest. The woodsy scent of his cologne nearly distracted her from the events she set in motion. Over his shoulder, her father let in Mr. Barton. They shook hands, and her father introduced him to Mr. Davenport.

"We're headed to the club for lunch to meet some other business partners. I would like to stay here, but we're expected." John followed her gaze. The corners of his mouth tipped down.

"We can schedule something later in the week," she offered, overly bright.

"I'd like that," he said. His eyes tracked Mr. Barton's progress.

Mr. Barton held his hat in his hand. His face lit up when Ruby looked at him. They had been "courting," publicly, and Ruby genuinely enjoyed his company. He shared his past hardships in stride, with an openness that made hers an easier burden to carry. Mr. Barton, she realized, was quickly becoming a close friend. Ruby ignored the nagging worry she may be in over her head. *What if he's expecting more than friendship?* She shook the thought away.

"Good afternoon, Miss Tremaine." He turned to his left. "Davenport."

"Barton," John said coolly.

They stared at each other a beat too long. Ruby's ears prickled. She looped her arm through Mr. Barton's. "Shall we?" She let him lead her past her father and Mr. Davenport.

"Be home for dinner," Mr. Tremaine called.

"Yes, Papa." Ruby waved to the Davenports, noting the sour look on John's face, and her father's.

Mr. Barton turned. "Are you ready?" His grin was infectious.

Outside, Ruby placed a broad-brimmed hat on her head. "Oh, I do love surprises! Can I guess?"

Mr. Barton helped her down the front steps. "You can try."

Her gaze fell to the vehicle parked on the street. It idled loudly. "I get to drive?" She freed her arm and opened the door. The seat vibrated gently as she slid onto the bench. "Will you teach me?"

"Actually, no," he said. "I mean, you can!" He rubbed his chin.

"I can teach you, just . . . not today. The surprise is at a destination only I know." He shuffled from one foot to the other, grinning.

She pouted at him, then slid across the bench seat as he sat down beside her. The way his body grazed hers sent a shiver through her despite the warm afternoon. The Ford model had an open-air top; the breeze skimmed across her cheeks. "So, if the surprise is not driving this magnificent vehicle around the city, and not the destination itself, that means it's a *thing*."

The car pulled away from the curb with a jerk. "Sorry," he said. "I'm still getting used to it."

Ruby clutched her hat to her head. "Harrison, where's your carriage?" It was a luxurious buggy with a ride she'd grown used to.

"At home." The automobile cruised out of the neighborhood. Soon they were a part of downtown traffic. Ruby marveled at this new vantage point. Everything was faster, closer, infused with an urgency she'd never felt before. It was as if the city had doubled in size and population since she was last here and everyone had come to contribute to the music and rhythm of it all. The trollies screeched by and the train above rolled on. She caught snatches of conversation in every direction. The smell of cooked meats from food carts made her mouth water.

"And here we are."

Ruby looked behind him at the jewelry shop. "This is not what I expected," she admitted, ignoring the gnawing in her stomach. Lunch was clearly not on the agenda. A thrill passed through her, though. She missed the luxury of trips like this where she would walk out with a new trinket in a velvet-lined box. Olivia struggled with an unexplained guilt every time she splurged, which made Ruby's attempt to enjoy shopping vicariously through her best friend less than ideal. Mr. Barton had fine taste. His suits were impeccably tailored and made of quality silks and wool. She was curious as to why he'd brought her here.

"C'mon," he said, turning off the engine. He walked around the automobile to open her door. "I'm not a gambling man. I have no wish to return to the hardships of my childhood. That said, through an obscene amount of cigar smoke, I spotted a prize in the pot of a poker game and couldn't pass it up."

Ruby eyed him. *Why is he telling me this?*

"Lonnie Lynch can be a stubborn mule. The buy-in was steep, but worth it."

Ruby returned his smile as she stepped into the shop. The room was dark and heavy under the weight of the wood paneling. The real light came from the glass cases, where precious items glinted under the warm glow of the gas lamps.

A woman stooped over a glass case of assorted jewelry and watched them enter. "Mr. Barton," she said, squinting and straightening a bit. "Perfect timing!" The woman disappeared behind a curtain.

"Do you come here often?" Ruby asked under her breath.

"It was recommended. I was told they appraise and polish precious keepsakes. And I had to be sure my prize was worthy of the wearer." He nodded back to the old woman as she returned.

Ruby's breath caught. On a pillow of black leather sat her necklace. The stone was brighter than she remembered. The chain more delicate and fragile. It was a simple piece of jewelry, but she would have known it anywhere, even if her initials didn't wink at her from the surface of the charm by the clasp. When she spoke, her voice was barely a whisper. "You won?"

"I don't like gambling. But I am quite good at it. Lonnie said he bought it from a friend." He picked at the clasp and slowly lifted the necklace so that the stone gleamed in front of her. Her mother must have given it to the adjuster to sell, then, she thought. And somehow it had found its way back to her. "May I?" he asked.

The shopkeeper placed a mirror before them. Ruby stood silent as he returned her necklace to its rightful home. A chill passed through her, but the stone quickly warmed against the skin below the hollow of her throat. Despite her promise not to ever again cry over a piece of jewelry, she found herself swiping a tear from her cheek. The sight of it had panic bubbling from the depths of her core.

"I can't." Her hand closed around the ruby. She wasn't sure if it was to rip it from her neck or to keep it close.

Mr. Barton placed his hands lightly on her shoulders and turned her again toward the mirror. A flush had spread over both of them. His joy so pure, it hurt her to see it.

His eyes met hers in their reflection. "It's already done." He smiled to the woman behind the case and guided Ruby out. She was floating. Or at least, that's what it felt like. She let him help her back into the automobile as she tested the weight at her neck. The city passed by in a different kind of blur and then disappeared altogether. When her senses fully returned, the car was parked along Lake Shore Drive, where a wide boardwalk separated the road from a short strip of sandy beach.

Have I thanked him yet? she wondered, horrified at her behavior. She opened her mouth.

Mr. Barton blurted, "I'm sorry. I should not have blindsided you like that. You may not have wanted me to intervene and—"

"Thank you," she said. Ruby grasped both his hands, strong and warm in her own.

He relaxed. "It's just, I knew how much you missed it and you didn't seem yourself when you spoke of its absence. Though now you have it back, I'm not sure if you're okay."

Ruby made a choking sound between a cough and laugh. "I promise, I am much better than okay." She squeezed his hands harder, then released them to touch the chain and stone. *Still there.* When she could trust her voice again, she said, "I don't know when I can repay you." *He'd won it in a poker game?*

"I won't hear any talk of repayment. I wanted to do this."

Normally, she would have taken a gift in stride. They were expected, gleefully received and tucked away to flaunt later. This was different. This was personal and intimate. Harrison Barton had restored a part of her. She blinked back tears and nodded as she waited for the tightness in her throat to pass. "I don't think I'll ever take it off again," she said. Her stomach quivered. Harrison Barton was sweet and thoughtful. And she was using him.

She wasn't sure how she could keep this up.

His face broke into a wide grin. He moved closer, his arm stretching behind her. She imagined the pressure of his lips against hers and the air rushed out of her lungs. She faced him, heart racing. Then he pulled away, holding a small wicker basket in his lap. "It's such a nice day. Hungry?"

Ruby shook her mind clear. *"Yes."* She could be friends with Harrison. Friends give each other gifts. They share a picnic. She was famished before. She just needed to eat and her stomach would settle.

The waves of Lake Michigan lapped lazily at the shore. A boy ran along its banks with a toy sailboat, his mother a few feet away. A mix of carriages and automobiles rolled by. They found a quiet spot where wild grasses grew up through the sand and rocks, and shrubs blocked views of the water. There the trees provided a protective canopy, dappling them with light.

Mr. Barton's arm brushed against her shoulder, making her shiver. "Are you all right, Miss Tremaine?"

She wanted him to kiss her even though she knew it would blur the murky line between her feelings for him and her plan. "Yes."

He leaned in, waited. "Even when I do this?" he asked, kissing the skin below her ear.

Ruby's eyes fluttered closed. "Yes." She breathed in the sage that clung to his skin.

"Or this?" A kiss at the edge of her jaw. Then another. Mr. Barton moved toward her mouth at a pace that made her skin sizzle. Heat bloomed at the epicenter of each touch, sending waves of electricity from her jaw to the tips of her toes. They weakened her resolve and fed a need deep within. She wanted more. She had never wanted anyone like this. Ever. It frightened and excited her.

When his lips finally pressed to hers, thoughts of how she would untangle herself from the situation fled. All she could do was savor the taste of him as he kissed her. His tongue slipped past her lips; she gasped and pulled away. Not far, just enough to see his heavy-lidded stare and parted lips. His breaths were ragged. She inhaled his desire and let it meld with hers. And before she could change her mind, she kissed him again. She kissed him until her lips bruised and her heart pounded painfully in her chest.

"Ruby . . ." he said against her lips, her jaw and her neck. She loved the way he said her name. Like a prayer. Then she felt a gentle pressure on her shoulders. Mr. Barton straightened and the world around them snapped back into place. It took Ruby a few minutes to adjust to her surroundings, to hear the sounds of the park over their labored breathing and the pounding in her ears.

Harrison Barton cleared his throat. "I think we should eat."

Ruby laughed. She had forgotten she was hungry.

CHAPTER 23

Olivia

Freeport Manor was a flurry of activity. Olivia completed her last walk through the ballroom while the guests enjoyed dessert. The chandeliers broke the light into a kaleidoscope of colors that danced across the floor's polished surface. The band had been playing quietly throughout the five-course meal. Now they were preparing their larger instruments for music worthy of the celebration. The bar was fully stocked and the lounges and high tops by the patio doors offered refreshments in both drink and air. The silver-and-black decorations continued from the dining room to the patio, creating a seamless transition. Deeming it to be to her mother's exacting standards, she returned inside.

Her mother's encouraging nod made Olivia feel as though she'd passed some test. Mrs. Davenport sat to her father's right, their clasped hands visible above the table. Olivia stole a glance at Mr. Lawrence, who sat opposite her, deep in conversation with Mrs. Johnson. She watched them, the tightness in her chest she felt all day easing. *Everything is falling into place*, she thought.

Clink clink clink.

At the head of the table, Mr. Davenport stood, a champagne flute in hand. "Thank you all for joining us on this special anniversary," he said. His eyes turned to his wife; even from a distance their deep brown seemed to melt with fondness and gratitude. "I am not one for words." He glanced back at his children, his guests. "Let us dance." Laughter filled the dining room. Olivia caught Mr. Lawrence's eye over the rim of her glass. His wink made her forget her exhaustion like a shot of espresso. The guests, following her father's instructions, filed out of the room to enjoy the rest of the night.

Earlier that evening, Olivia had picked at the hem of the chiffon dress she'd laid out on her bed. It was beautiful enough for a bride. The thought had filled her with anticipation and something she couldn't name. It soothed her to know she wasn't the only one in white, per Emmeline Davenport's vision. John and Helen stood out now in the sea of black-tie attire like stars in the night sky. She'd lost Mr. Lawrence in the shuffle.

Nestled in a corner near the ballroom entrance, Ruby waved. "You have outdone yourself," she said. "Twenty-five years of marriage. That's six years *longer* than we've been alive. Can you imagine being with the same person for that long?"

Olivia eyed her friend. It's all they'd thought about for almost two years.

"What?" Ruby asked. "You and Mr. Lawrence have all the old birds in a fit, betting on when the big announcement will come. I say, elope and create a scandal the likes of which they've never seen."

"Elopement is only entertaining in theory." Olivia wondered, not for the first time, what was keeping the British bachelor from making his intentions clearer. He took little interest in the other young women of their set and it was as she told Mr. DeWight: They made an excellent match. Love would come later.

Still, the lawyer's words had rattled her confidence. Since the night of the last meeting, he had slipped into her waking thoughts. He challenged everything she knew. She imagined using all he deemed frivolous and privileged to further the group's reach. He underestimated her. *And Mr. Tremaine's fundraiser in six weeks will be the perfect opportunity to show him what I'm capable of.*

Washington DeWight's lifestyle, so unlike hers, promised a change from her routine that had never occurred to her. Travel. Charity. Purpose.

Above all: Passion.

She had not felt such desire to learn more about anything than she had for civil rights, the elections process, and, yes, *bills*. She'd made more trips to the Chicago Public Library in the past few days than she had in the past year. Questions popped up like dandelions in her mind. If Mrs. Woodard had any say, women would have the vote soon. Best to be informed. She was additionally surprised by Helen's company on these trips. They rode Chestnut together when Tommy or Hetty weren't available, the pair of them forgoing the carriage. They ignored the stares and the honking horns of speeding motorists as they traveled. *How could I have forgotten how much I loved it?* Her sister was content to leave her to her own studies once they got there.

The grin now spreading across Ruby's face snapped Olivia back to the present. "You need to worry about *you*," Olivia scolded her friend. "What's going on with you and Harrison Barton? The two of you have been spending a lot of time together. If the old birds are talking about anyone, it's you."

Ruby's features pinched. "What have you heard?"

Olivia folded her arms. She whispered, "That you may beat me down the aisle, given the way Mr. Barton moons over you. I can't believe you've moved on from John."

"A girl could grow old waiting for your brother to make up his mind."

Olivia reached for her friend's hand. "I don't blame you. He's behaving as if he's got all the time in world. He and Helen are up to something and I fear it's blinded him to everything else." She watched a shadow come over Ruby's face. "Don't give up on him just yet. Unless your feelings for Harrison Barton . . . ?" She let the question trail, but Ruby didn't finish it.

Olivia wanted to admit her disappointment, that they might never be sisters, when she spotted Washington DeWight. His presence filled her with a mixture of exasperation and apprehension. Only the high *ting!* of silverware against glass pulled her gaze away. John in front of the band, dutifully reciting the speech she'd written to introduce their parents. It highlighted their bond and the accomplishments they'd achieved together.

I could do it, she thought. With the right person, Olivia believed she would be able to explore the calling growing louder in her every day. And as her parents embraced to dance for their guests, her attention drifted not to Jacob Lawrence, who gathered a small crowd around him, but to the outspoken lawyer Washington DeWight.

Applause erupted in the grand space, and the party really

began. The band played in earnest. Olivia thought of revealing her doubts. If anyone could keep her secret, it would be Ruby. Her friend was no stranger to sneaking off.

"Ruby, do you see the gentleman making his way over here?"

Ruby followed Olivia's sightline. "Mr. DeWight?"

"You know him?"

"Not well." Ruby shrugged. "He met with my father a few days ago. You should have heard them argue."

"Argue?"

Washington DeWight was almost within earshot.

"Well, maybe not *argue*, but that is how Papa responds to anyone who disagrees with his suggestions. Mr. DeWight had the most pessimistic outlook for the city."

"I have heard his outlook," Olivia confessed. Ruby's eyes grew wide as saucers as she turned to her friend. "He's often at the community center where I volunteer," Olivia said quickly. "We volunteer together," she explained. "We have several acquaintances in common. In fact, one of them is the wife of a man who is working on your father's campaign—"

"Oh yes, *volunteering*," Ruby teased. "I heard you and I volunteer a lot too." She stood taller and nodded to the person approaching their corner. At her friend's tone, Olivia's throat suddenly felt dry.

"Good evening, Miss Tremaine, Miss Davenport." Washington DeWight turned to Olivia and hesitated only the briefest second before asking, "May I have this dance?"

She threw her friend a look she hoped told her to school her features. "You may," she said, accepting his hand. He bowed, allowing her to look at him without the distraction of his high cheekbones. Mr. DeWight had dressed the part. The invitation stated black tie, and although the fit of his tuxedo was a bit off, Washington DeWight was dashing nonetheless.

"Is Miss Tremaine well?"

"She will be," Olivia said. Ruby had found John after all. The pair now moved in a graceful circle not far from where Olivia had left her. "Enjoying the party?"

"It has certainly improved." He held her in a rigid frame, like he had little practice beyond a few lessons, yet his touch was gentle and his smile never wavered. "It's an interesting group of friends and acquaintances your parents have. Black and white union leaders. Teachers, doctors, lawyers, and bankers. It's the kind of social climate we strive for."

Olivia looked around the room and imagined what he saw. The ease with which they laughed, danced, and ate must be frustrating to someone from outside "high society."

"My apologies. It seems I have ruined the celebration," he said.

"No," she replied. "I think you identified what makes it all so special."

"I'm glad to be of service, Miss Davenport," he said wryly. His honey-colored eyed shone under the light of the chandeliers.

"You're not a terrible dance partner either. Not *good*, but . . ."

"Did you expect me to be terrible?" he said, feigning shock. His breath was warm on her neck. "Miss Davenport, do you lie awake at night, thinking about my two left feet?"

"No!" she said. Olivia sniffed. "You're just so serious." She wasn't sure what she expected. She was strongly aware of his hand on the small of her back, the way he guided her with subtle pressure, and the way her temperature rose every time their bodies grazed each other.

"My work is serious. But no person is just their work." He pursed his lips, highlighting the sharp angle of his jaw. Their faces were dangerously close to each other's,

"I've danced with a few lawyers," she said, recovering from his questions. "Few can match your . . . skill."

Washington DeWight glanced around, comically exaggerating his movements, and eliciting a peal of laughter from Olivia loud enough to turn heads. "Where are these fellows? They're out here giving the profession a bad name. Though, I'm sure if they were more skilled, I would not have you in my arms now." He winked and Olivia's heart stuttered.

"I should thank them as well," she whispered, and caught herself wishing they were alone so that she could step deeper into his embrace, let the smell of his aftershave, sharp pine and earthy, envelop her without the distraction of others.

When the song ended, Mrs. Davenport appeared at their elbows without a sound. "Mr. DeWight, lovely to see you again. I do need to steal my daughter. Olivia, walk with me."

Olivia's heart jumped into her throat. She and Washington DeWight *were* standing too close. He congratulated Olivia's mother on her anniversary and withdrew his hand slowly from Olivia's waist, like a caress. She followed her mother as Mrs. Davenport graciously accepted congratulations from Mrs. Johnson, Mrs. Davis, and the family doctor. At the edge of the celebration, Mrs. Davenport asked, "Is there something you want to tell me?"

Olivia's mouth instantly dried. "I'm not sure what you mean." Why hadn't she grabbed a flute of champagne?

Mrs. Davenport leaned close. "I didn't want to distract you from your work, and it wasn't until a few moments ago when I saw you dancing that I became concerned." Olivia followed her mother's gaze, knowing before she found her target whom her mother spied. "If I'm not mistaken, that young man is not the gentleman courting you."

"Mama, we were dancing. This is a party—" Olivia began.

"You stepped out last night. It didn't go unnoticed and—no," she said as Olivia tried to interject, "I don't care to hear about it." Mrs. Davenport's eyes softened. Her hand was warm on Olivia's bare shoulder. "You and Mr. Lawrence," she sighed. "You have a wonderful opportunity at happiness. I don't want to see you throw it away on a whim. So, I will ask once more: Is there something you want to tell me?"

Olivia took a breath. "Jacob Lawrence is a wonderful man. I hope to be as lucky in love as you and Daddy." She kissed her mother's cheek. "Happy anniversary." Her smile felt brittle, but it put her mother at ease, the tension she released sparking a twinge of guilt in Olivia.

"Good," she said, and tucked her arm around her daughter. "Helen is impossible to rein in and your brother can't keep his eyes off the maid." Her mother was so lost in her thoughts, she didn't notice Olivia stiffen at her side. Sure enough, John was tracking Amy-Rose's movements on the fringe of the crowd. "It's a relief to know we don't have to worry about you."

Olivia nodded numbly at her mother's side.

CHAPTER 24

Helen

Helen hated parties. They were even worse when they were hosted by your parents, in your own home. There was nowhere to hide.

The day started early. A long soak in rose-scented water, hours of nearly getting her ears burnt off by the hot comb, and then a corset! It wasn't her fault that the files John brought home were an unorganized nightmare that had kept her up all night, only to have her nodding off while Amy-Rose tried to make her look *presentable*. She much preferred a quick unscented bath and simply styled hair, plaits or twists she could easily tie away from her face.

Once at the party, Helen was beside herself with the customs of being a good hostess. Her hawk-eyed chaperone, Mrs. Milford, appeared at her elbow anytime she saw a means of escape. Like a lion tamer at the zoo corralling her charge. At least at parties held elsewhere, she could sneak away, but as a hostess, she was expected to smile and greet everyone who walked through the door.

Including Jacob Lawrence. She'd be lying if she claimed the

reason she couldn't sleep was completely business related. Sometimes, in the quiet, her thoughts wandered to the British man who'd arrived in Chicago. He was an outsider in all the ways that made her feel less misunderstood, in her world where her last name and relatives seemed to overshadow her wants and desires. Helen liked that he knew she'd rather be in the garage, and the fact that she didn't have to pretend that it wasn't true. She realized he was the only person she cared to see.

And he was attached to her sister.

Even as Olivia graciously danced with other gentlemen, Mr. Lawrence was never far. He watched politely as her sister suffered a dance with Mr. Greenfield and then spoke with a young lawyer Helen didn't recognize, an upstart, if the rumors were to be believed. Olivia danced with the lawyer as well, her expressions dynamic, moving from animated to solemn over the course of the song. They stayed in each other's arms after the band had switched tunes, until her mother interrupted them.

And once again, Jacob Lawrence was at Olivia's side. He played the part of doting suitor perfectly. The whole thing made her sick to her stomach. She knew without a doubt that the awful yet wonderful unnamed feelings she experienced around him were real. The way he watched Olivia, danced with her, was so perfect. How could she compete? Annoyed, Helen angled for an escape. She was content to leave the party, preferably unnoticed. Frustrated, she said to her minder, "I have to powder my nose. May I be excused?"

Helen knew being surrounded by so many cheery people was making her mood worse.

Mrs. Milford frowned. "I trust you can find your way back."

"Of course," Helen said, and suppressed an eye roll. She walked in the direction of the closest powder room. As soon as her chaperone's attention returned to the dancers, Helen raced to the library. The desk was set back, allowing her father, when seated, to gaze down the length of the room. Floor-to-ceiling shelves framed large windows above tufted benches. The two chairs that faced the desk were far less comfortable than the two that faced the fireplace on the opposite wall.

Hoping her tutor didn't know the house, or her, well enough to know where to start looking, she took an atlas off the shelf and sat in a highbacked chair in front of the empty fireplace. She held the book to her chest and closed her eyes, savoring the way the heavy mahogany shelves and books absorbed the brunt of music and laughter. A moment of peace was all she wanted.

A knock at the door jolted her awake. Helen peered around the arm of her chair. Jacob Lawrence entered and closed the door behind him. She'd only just pushed him out of her mind. Now here he stood with his back pressed against the library's door. He studied the shelves, taking in the spines of the leather-bound collections and carefully collected pieces of art that separated them. She ducked as low as she could manage, before cursing under her breath. There was no hiding the bright white gown her mother insisted she wear. Her own reflection had surprised her this afternoon once Amy-Rose had turned her to face her mirror, reviewing the importance of using dinner napkins and the clip to pin up the train.

"This is the perfect hiding space," Jacob Lawrence said, covering the distance between them. He fell heavily into the other chair. *Too close*, she thought. *Yet not close enough. If you had run off to the morning room, you could have shared the divan . . .* Her skin burned like she was caught out in a blistering heat.

He used a hooked finger to undo the silk bow at his throat and popped open the top two buttons of his shirt. "I like a party, don't get me wrong." He gestured to the door. "That is a lot. When I saw you slip out, I knew you must have a secret hiding spot. How long until they find us?"

Helen stared at the base of his neck, at the delicate bone underneath the skin and at the way the knot in his throat bobbed as he spoke. Hardly scandalous, but then why couldn't she look away?

"Helen?" He gently touched her shoulder.

"Uh," she started, pulling his words from the fog in her mind. *Think!* "It depends on who they send to look. John would know where to find me and would lead them in the opposite direction." Her smile dimmed. "Olivia will find me here eventually and bring me back." She stared at the wall, picturing her sister floating across the dance floor and mingling with the guests. "She's at home at these parties. She remembers people's names. She asks about their families, their trips, even their ailing knees. Oh, and she loves dressing up."

Jacob Lawrence angled his head toward her. "Then I guess we're lucky to have found the best spot in the house to wait it out. And I seem to remember a long list of your attributes offered over a pair of cigarettes. Unfortunately, the landlord did have that switch repaired."

His smile sent a delicious wave of gooseflesh across her skin. It also left her confused. Her feelings couldn't be normal. How could he prefer to be here with her instead of with her sister?

"Look, you don't have to entertain the homely sister," she said. "You and Olivia are perfect for each other. She'll be a great wife, like she is at everything else. She's compassionate and beautiful. And—" Helen lost herself in her words. All she could think of were her own flaws. She saw every sharp edge Mama and Mrs. Milford attempted to soften and polish. And how each one would always be jagged next to her sister. There was no point in competing. Not in this. And she wanted her sister to be happy.

Helen's chest hurt with each breath. She stood to create some space and pressed her forehead against the cool wood of the bookcase. Mr. Lawrence rose too, as if to follow, but stayed where he stood.

"Helen." She turned slightly. He took a step forward, hesitated, reached out a hand to her. "May I?"

She nodded, and he stepped closer, brushing a tear from her nose. His fingers turned her face toward his. He looked at her, his eyes boring into hers. "You are beautiful," he said.

He bent his face toward hers. His breath stirred her hair. He smelled of cedar and spiced wine, and faintly of cigarettes. She wondered what it would feel like to kiss him. He was so close. It was as if he was waiting for her to decide.

So, she did.

Helen pressed her lips against his. She had wanted to do this every day since that muddy afternoon. Mr. Lawrence's reaction fueled her desire. He kissed her with the same passion she had desperately tried to hide. When she remembered why her feelings for him needed to remain secret, she faltered. The perfection of their stolen moment began to sour. As if he recalled the reason too, Mr. Lawrence pulled away.

Helen suddenly felt cold and off-balance. Pain replaced longing in his eyes. She felt the change like a blow. She retreated to the chair. And though Mr. Lawrence moved to comfort her, she knew it was the last thing she needed.

"I'm sorry," he whispered to the top of her head. She kept her focus on their feet, watching the way their edges blurred into the floor. "Olivia and I . . ." His voice cracked and Helen felt a fissure open in her heart. "I apologize. That shouldn't have happened," he said.

It was too much. She stood and looked him in the eye. With a voice that was much steadier than her legs, she said, "I have to go."

"Helen, wait," he pleaded.

She opened the door and slipped quickly out, knowing he would not follow.

CHAPTER 25

Amy-Rose

After seeing that the girls were ready to receive their guests, Amy-Rose had removed her severe black dress and white blouse from the hanger behind her door. Harold and Edward, sticklers for protocol, were always nicely starched, but Amy-Rose, Jessie, and the others were not required to wear a uniform. Except on special occasions. Made invisible by her station and attire, Amy-Rose had watched from a distance and tugged at the waist of her dress.

Soon, this will all be behind you, she'd thought.

Olivia looked beautiful in a white chiffon gown, her waist cinched to the size of Mr. Lawrence's hand, which now guided her around the room to everyone's delight. After doing Olivia's hair, Amy-Rose had noticed her old friend had dressed quietly, with as much enthusiasm as Helen, who had disappeared shortly after the gathering moved from the dining room to the ballroom. The night had gone without a hitch; she was happy to see Olivia enjoying herself.

Now Amy-Rose flitted around the room, a nondescript fairy carrying liquid spirits, refilling champagne flutes and carrying away empty dessert trays. The dancers, flushed with drink and merriment, rushed to switch partners as the music changed. Fresh flowers from the gardens decorated the tables, and refreshments flowed freely. Dinner was a success, which was to be expected. It was like watching a painting come to life.

"Amy-Rose!"

"I'm so sorry, Mr. Tremaine," she said, removing the napkin on her shoulder to absorb the champagne soaking into the tablecloth.

"My dear, what *were* you looking at?"

"Olivia?" she said. She hoped her voice carried more confidence than she felt. She was watching the older girl dance, but it was not what captured her attention.

John had walked into her line of sight. Each time she caught a glimpse of him, she remembered the moments they shared, the kisses. They made her pulse quicken. Just the thought of his hand on her bare skin, the way his lips pressed against her own, sent shivers through her. From afar, she admired the fit of his tuxedo. John was by far the most handsome man in the room. His confidence glowed around him as he mingled, charming each guest. As he spun Ruby around the dance floor, she couldn't help imagining herself there.

Snap out of it! Amy-Rose gave Mr. Tremaine an apologetic smile and moved away.

Before she could do something truly stupid, Amy-Rose was pulled aside by an older Black woman dressed in the latest fashion. Diamonds dripped from her ears and flashed at her wrists. Her smile was wide and eyes bright, like she held a secret.

"My name is Mrs. Davis," she said. Her eyes raked over Amy-Rose, setting the young maid into a panic. Three times a widow, Maude Davis had amassed a small fortune that she multiplied with savvy investments along the South Side. *Has she seen me staring at John?* Amy-Rose thought, horrified.

"Can I get you something, ma'am?" she asked.

"The Davenport girls look splendid tonight, even by their standards. Am I correct in assuming you had a lot to do with it?" Mrs. Davis pointed an open hand to Olivia, now dancing with another gentleman.

"Yes, ma'am. My name is Amy-Rose Shepherd." She braced herself. Every maid has heard some horror story of the help being "let go" for getting too close to a man of the house. Mrs. Davenport cared for her, she knew, but loved her children more. A scandal like that would hurt the girls. She tried her best not to fidget.

The older woman nodded. "You're very talented."

Amy-Rose exhaled in a rush. "Thank you." She was aware Mrs. Davenport spoke of her talents to the other ladies, but she never thought they would remember.

"I'll be keeping an eye on you."

As Mrs. Davis walked away, a sudden burst of pride emboldened Amy-Rose. Her encounter with the accomplished businesswoman was proof that her doubts of her capabilities were not too great to overcome. And hers was an opinion that mattered. One that carried weight with the Davenports.

Amy-Rose let herself imagine what it would be like if John Davenport, the ardent bachelor, were to choose her as the girl to call his wife. This was another story among maids. *A fairy tale,* she thought. Still, how could he not see her as more than the help given the quiet, private side of himself he'd shared with her? She was dangerously close to deeper feelings taking root.

And then John smiled at her. The one she thought he saved just for her. Something shifted then. Something deep and vital.

Maybe he wouldn't have to miss her after all.

She picked up a fresh champagne bottle and skirted around the dance floor. The guests, the music, and the warning bells going off in her mind faded into the background. In their brief rendezvous, they did more than embrace. They exchanged sheltered dreams and hidden disappointments, and even the hungry fears they kept at bay with brave smiles and hopeful plans. She arrived at the edge of John's group.

"I'm working on something to present to the board," John said to the small circle around him.

"Champagne!" called one of his friends when she came within earshot.

John laughed. There was that dimple again! "This could be the last bit of fun I have before I return to school, or start full-time at the office," he said.

"So soon?" asked the shorter man to his right. Amy-Rose looked at him. The name Greenfield popped into her head, recalling his face from Olivia's descriptions. "What about our trip this summer?"

John shifted as the group's attention returned to him. "I suppose there's no reason *not* to make plans for the summer. The business is the only thing that could keep me here."

"The only thing?" Half a dozen pairs of eyes whipped back to where she stood. She was cold, though her face burned. She hadn't meant to ask it out loud. Had she misunderstood? No, he'd said he would miss her if she left Freeport Manor. But how could he say that if he might leave too? The plan he made with Helen was bound to succeed. He was sure to stay.

But not for her. And that meant if his plan for the business did fall through, then . . .

Amy-Rose could feel their stares. Their words had dissolved into the music, which now pounded in her ears.

Mr. Greenfield's sharp laugh pierced her ears. "Still breaking hearts, huh, Davenport?"

Amy-Rose cleared her throat. "Forgive me. I spoke out of turn." Her voice was even. She reminded herself that John's plans did not matter. Only hers.

"Don't you know you have to do like the royals and at least take if off the palace grounds?" The laughter erupted anew, the others in the group joining. She glanced at John, a head taller than the rest. His mouth, which explored hers with such tenderness, now split into a grimace.

"That's enough, Greenie," said John. And she knew, whether he truly cared for her or not, he would choose this life. These people. Over her.

Amy-Rose breathed through the painful tightness in her chest as she turned away. She would not wait for him. No daughter of Clara Shepherd would endure ridicule and postpone her own dreams for a man to return. She struggled to keep a graceful pace and slow her breathing. Though there was plenty of champagne left in the bottle, she walked past several guests holding their flutes up for a refill. She kept herself upright long enough to make it to the kitchen.

Had something changed? Had she misread his intentions? No,

he was clear. Mere days ago, John Davenport had said he'd miss her. She did not mistake his feelings for her. She knew in the way he trusted her with his fears, his hopes, that he cared for her. The way he kissed her . . . Amy-Rose barreled into the kitchen. She didn't want to believe he could be so cold. He'd treated her like a—her breath caught in the back of her throat.

The tears she fought to keep at bay finally escaped. Jessie shooed the others out of the kitchen and drew Amy-Rose into a crushing hug. Between sobs, Amy-Rose told Jessie everything from the stolen moments alone with John to the humiliating scene only minutes ago.

Jessie rocked her and rubbed her back until Amy-Rose's breathing evened out and her muscles relaxed. Then she delivered a truth Amy-Rose could no longer ignore.

"He's not gonna marry you, honey. You know this ain't some fairy tale."

CHAPTER 26

Ruby

Ruby searched the crowd for Mr. Barton. She'd taken extra care with her hair, lying to herself that it wasn't to impress him. Neither was the low-cut bodice of the gown she'd picked. It highlighted her figure and allowed an unobstructed view of her necklace that he had returned to her. Naturally, she'd told her parents the truth. Harrison bought it for her to make her happy. If they objected, they couldn't do so publicly without undermining her plan. She very well couldn't sell it again. She wanted him to see her wear it proudly. Her mother eyed it suspiciously. Her father surprised her, complimenting her gruffly before moving on.

When she palmed the stone now, she thought of Harrison's featherlight touch as he placed it around her neck. The way he looked at her made her breath still. The kiss they shared awakened feelings she hadn't expected. It was magical. The world around them had faded away and all she could think about was his lips on hers, hers on his. That kiss was not part of the plan. Neither were these feelings.

Though she was glad to have her ruby back, it served as a reminder that *her goal* was to secure a proposal from the Davenport heir, to make her parents' wish come true. *Your wish too*, she thought. *Once*. Now she wasn't so sure. When she was with Mr. Barton, she didn't want to be anywhere else.

"May I have this dance?" John asked. "I didn't mean to startle you."

Ruby pressed her hand flat against her chest where her heart pounded, though not with the same thrill she usually felt when John singled her out from the crowd. "Of course," she said, offering her hand. Ruby wondered what had brought him to her side. She glanced over her shoulder. Her mother and Mrs. Davenport stood at the bar a few feet away. Between the strokes of their fans, she caught glimpses of their bright eyes and wide grins. She noted the conspiratorial angle of their heads as they exchanged whispers. They were helping. This is what she'd wanted.

Ruby grasped John's hand tighter and followed his lead. His steps lacked the bounce she'd felt in the first dance they'd shared. *What's changed?* She looked around the room. Still no sight of Mr. Barton. She and Olivia had discussed the guest list at length. He had accepted the invitation to the Davenports' anniversary party. *Where is he?* No matter. She needed to focus on John. Ruby had accepted his dance.

He must have felt her studying him, because he schooled his features and said, "I see you've started wearing your necklace again. It suits you." John's dimple appeared as he smiled down at her.

She resisted the urge to reach for it now, focusing on the music of the band and the feel of John's arm around her waist. "I rarely see you out and about," she said. "What's been keeping John Davenport so occupied?"

His face brightened. "I've been working on a project for the company. My father's agreed to hear plans for expanding the business to our own horseless carriage line. It's been challenging, but it's also the closest we've ever come to him even considering it."

"We?"

"Helen and I are working on it together." John grinned, and whatever had clouded his mood cleared. He launched into the finer details of his work. In that moment, she saw a glimpse of the young boy she had known. Tall and gangly, not deterred by the constant company of his sisters and their friends. Even when he grew up and ventured out on his own, he always made time for his family. She practically grew up alongside them. He always made her feel seen. And he was so handsome! She wished his attention now wasn't attached to the pressure she felt from their parents, that they could return to the days when riding across the grounds of Freeport and sneaking treats from the kitchens were all that mattered.

So why didn't she feel happier dancing with him now?

"Ruby?" John looked down at her. They were surrounded by other couples, swaying to the slow strings strummed by the band. "If you're tired, we can sit."

She shook her head. "No, I'm fine," she said. Not too long ago she had savored moments like this. Moments with John. It had been enough to set her heart racing.

But now?

Now she remained lost in her thoughts. Her attention sliding to the entrance. Looking for one face in particular, as John talked about his plans with Helen and the courses he planned to take next term if the proposal they were working on wasn't accepted by their father. Ruby nodded and made sounds to encourage him.

Just when she thought he'd skipped the party altogether, Harrison Barton stepped into the room. The dancers slowed and the music faded away. Everything around Mr. Barton lost focus, bringing him into sharp clarity. Ruby sighed in relief.

The song ended and before she could realize what she was doing, Ruby said, "Excuse me." She dipped out of John's arms before he could reply. She created a path to where she last saw Mr. Barton, around tables of her parents' friends and businessmen she knew only by their pictures in the paper. A hand around her arm stopped her in her tracks.

"You magnificent girl."

Ruby watched her mother flip a curl from her face.

"Your father and I should not have underestimated you," she said. Mrs. Tremaine tapped her nose, like she was harboring a secret. "You and John make such a lovely couple."

"I told you I had a plan," Ruby said. She tried to pull her arm away. She'd lost Harrison in the crowd and didn't want to have this conversation here.

Mrs. Tremaine placed a finger on the stone of the necklace around her neck. "Well, whatever you're doing with Harrison Barton, it's working. John seems absolutely smitten."

Ruby rolled her eyes and finally pried her arm free. "I don't know why you doubted me." She tried to cut around her mother. But Mrs. Tremaine gently took Ruby's elbow. She brushed her daughter's cheek and Ruby softened. This *was* what she wanted.

For the first time in weeks, the strained pinch in her mother's face was gone. Ruby held her mother's hand still pressed against her face. She drank in the change in her mother's features before gently ending the rare show of affection.

"I'm so proud of you," said Mrs. Tremaine.

The words rooted Ruby to the floor. More than Mr. Barton's sudden arrival.

A movement in the corner of her eye made her stomach drop.

"Good evening, Mrs. Tremaine," said Mr. Barton.

"Mr. Barton." Mrs. Tremaine gave Ruby one last glance before stepping out of the alcove.

He stood a foot away, his brow furrowed. He hesitated. "Miss Tremaine, can we talk?"

Ruby managed to nod. She replayed the last few moments of conversation with her mother, her thoughts spinning, trying to gauge how much he had heard. More than enough, she expected.

He let her lead and walked close beside her, the fabric of his new tuxedo grazing her arm. She peeked at his face. He looked calm, but she saw the tightness around his eyes. The music and chatter faded as they entered the cavernous foyer. So late into the night, the guests had gathered in the ballroom or gardens while the household staff moved on to other tasks. They were alone.

Ruby licked her lips. Her mouth felt dry. The words she had rehearsed a dozen times sounded insufficient in her mind. *This has been fun, but things were never going to work between us . . . my hand and heart belong to someone else.* Ugh. She could not say those things to him now. Not after the feelings he'd shared about his family and his life, the secrets she told *him* and not Olivia. Not after their kiss had exposed how desperately she wanted to know she was enough, just as she was. It had awakened a confidence in her that made her feel light, like anything could happen. The happiness she felt when Harrison Barton was near filled her to bursting, and the feel of his hands in hers made her blood sing. The night she returned home with her necklace she was *humming!*

He buried his hands in his pockets and rocked on his heels. He looked no more eager to have this conversation than she was. "What's going on here, Ruby?" He pulled his shoulders in as if preparing for a blow. "What was that in there?" He shook his head. "Please, the truth."

Ruby tasted salt at the back of her throat. She didn't want to answer. She couldn't.

"Maybe I wanted to believe that you were different from the other girls, not trying to get close to me for my money."

Ruby was confused. "I never wanted your money."

Mr. Barton wiped his face with his hands. "Then what did your mother mean? What plan?"

Ruby looked at the pin in his lapel. She hadn't noticed it was a teardrop-shaped stone. A ruby. Her chest tightened and she wished they were anywhere but here. His expression was almost too much to bear. "I—" No, she couldn't tell him the truth. Ruby wasn't fooling herself. She knew once she told him, that would be it. He would want nothing to do with her. Could she lose him now?

Ruby looked into his eyes, eyes that looked at her with such reverence. The truth would change that. Yet, she couldn't bring herself to lie to him. He deserved so much more than she had given him, but most of all he deserved the truth. She licked her lips and swallowed past the dryness in her throat.

"Harrison, when John returned home, he was distracted." No this wasn't John's fault. She started again. "I had hoped to regain John's attention when he returned from school. My normal flirtations weren't working, so I decided to get him to notice me by becoming attached to someone else. To you."

"So you were using me to make him jealous." His eyes searched hers. The longer he stared, the tighter her throat became.

Ruby took his arm. "You must understand—I am my parents' only child and the Davenports are their oldest friends. Our families becoming one is a hope they have had for a long time." Ruby waited while he weighed her words. "I'm sorry," she whispered.

"For what? Stringing me along this whole time?" He paced in front of her. When he turned back, his face was hard as stone. "This was all a lie, then." It wasn't a question.

"At first," she said. "Things are different now."

"How are they different?" He shook his head. "Are you telling me it's over between you and Davenport? You've given him up?"

"I—" She blinked back the tears that blurred his face. She was breathing too fast, and sweat beaded on her temples. Ruby wanted to say yes.

I'm so proud of you. Her mother spoke and Ruby's world had stopped. For a moment, she bathed in the acceptance she'd longed for. She couldn't think of a way to explain it—her parents' expectations, the pressure she felt to please them, how it weighed on her. She couldn't think of a way to explain it without it sounding like a sad excuse, like she didn't know right from wrong. All she could think to say was, "It's complicated."

Ruby forced herself to watch his reaction, the way he bit the inside of his cheek to keep his chin from quivering. "Complicated?"

He cleared his throat. "Uncomplicate it fast. Or I'm gone."

Tears fell from her eyes and she nodded. "I'm sorry." These words, she knew, were true. But when no others came, she felt Harrison Barton pull away.

As if he read her soul, he said, "I am too."

"Sorry," Olivia said, closing the door behind her. "Hostess duties."

Ruby swung her feet off the couch and patted the seat beside her. After the conversation with her mother, and then Mr. Barton, Ruby snagged a bottle of champagne and a pair of flutes. The sitting room between Olivia's and Helen's bedrooms was perfect. Their shared space contained a mix of not only Helen's and Olivia's things, but Ruby's as well. She'd flipped through one of the catalogs while waiting for her friend to arrive, not really registering the images on the pages. It was a familiar place. And Olivia always knew what to do.

Now that Olivia was here, though, Ruby was unsure of where to start. How much to disclose. This wasn't gossip about just any of the young men who wanted to shower her with attention.

Olivia sat beside her on the couch. She kicked her shoes off and tucked her feet underneath her. "I brought dessert." The devil's food cake she placed on the low table laced the air with sugar. In the dim light of the lavender candles, Ruby could see the line forming between her friend's brows. "It's your favorite," she said, holding the plate up to Ruby's face. When Ruby didn't immediately respond, Olivia said, "Oh, Ruby, what's happened? You can tell me."

Ruby leaned against her friend, and decided to go straight to the heart of the thing.

"I think I'm falling for Mr. Barton," she said.

"Well, that's wonderful news," said Olivia. "Why don't you look like it's wonderful news?"

"My parents are completely against it. They have a certain idea of how my life should be, but . . . I don't know what to do." Ruby groaned and slouched against the back of the couch. She felt miserable. And confused.

Olivia was unusually quiet, her eyes distant. Ruby had expected her friend to pepper her with questions. Instead, Olivia stared into the flame of the nearest candle.

"Olivia?"

"Hmm?" Her friend refocused slowly. "I'm sorry, Ruby." She smiled sadly and reached for the bottle on the table. Olivia poured for both of them. The bubbles floated to the top and exploded like tiny fireworks in the glass. "I think the hardest thing we can do is to decide what *we* want, and stride toward it."

Ruby accepted the glass. She was right—Olivia had known what to do. But the pained look on Mr. Barton's face still made it hard to breathe. For now, she wanted to forget. "What did you mean—that you'd heard Mr. DeWight's outlook. Have you heard him speak?"

Her friend gave her a sheepish look. "I stumbled across a meeting," Olivia said. "He was reporting what he witnessed in his travels and garnering support for some demonstrations he's organizing." Ruby listened without interrupting as Olivia spoke. It wasn't anything Ruby had not heard during the countless dinners her father hosted with various political leaders or business associates. She was, however, surprised at the depth of Olivia's involvement and desire to do more. Her friend spoke of women's right to vote. She repeated the things Ruby had heard the outspoken lawyer say, and talked of how he inspired others to act. Olivia may not have wanted to admit it, but she sounded dangerously close to finding herself in the same dilemma as Ruby.

"Be careful. I've heard he never stays in one city long," she said, watching Olivia closely. Her friend wrung the stem of the flute between her hands.

"I know," Olivia said, and sighed. She placed her head on Ruby's shoulder.

"What a pair we make." Ruby held her glass up. "Cheers?" Their glasses clinked together and they settled against the plush back of the couch, listening to the party below.

CHAPTER 27

Olivia

The party was a success. Freeport Manor was alive with music, dancing, and champagne until the small hours of the morning. Olivia crawled into her bed close to dawn with aching feet and burning legs. She was too tired to think about where Mr. Lawrence had disappeared to halfway through the night and why his mood had changed when he'd returned. She fell into a deep sleep only to be awakened too soon.

"Time to rise and shine." Amy-Rose walked into the room. Her footsteps were heavy and magnified the pounding in Olivia's head. The curtains rustled and a bright beam of light cut through the darkness and Olivia's thoughts. She threw an arm over her eyes and groaned.

Amy-Rose tugged at her hand. "It is well after noon and your parents are expecting you for lunch. Mr. Lawrence and your father will be returning from the factory any time now."

"What?" Olivia sat upright. Too quickly, the room began to spin. Too late she remembered sneaking off to the sitting room with Ruby late in the evening—or was it early morning?—where they shared cake and a bottle of champagne, curled up on the couch, only the moon there to overhear their words. Her friend didn't reveal everything that was on her mind. And perhaps Olivia had said too much of what was on hers.

She had found herself in the arms of Mr. DeWight for a second time before the night was through. Ruby's warning, though gentle, rang in her head as loudly as Amy-Rose's entrance. She wondered what Ruby thought of the amount of time she was spending with Mr. DeWight. *Am I in over my head?* Now she reprimanded herself for being so caught up in her own worries that she didn't at least try to find out what ruined her friend's night. And if Mr. Barton had anything to do with it. He came and went too quickly for things to be good between them.

A glance at Amy-Rose revealed her night had likely been no better. Her eyes were puffy and she moved about the room with a brisk gruffness that welcomed no questions.

"Your bath is drawn and your dress is hanging. I can wait or you can ring me when you're ready to be laced up." Amy-Rose kept her eyes averted. There was a time when she and Olivia had shared so many secrets and dreams. They had been close friends who would not have hesitated to comfort each other. Olivia knew she had created this rift between them. She wasn't sure she could mend it.

"Amy-Rose," she said, swinging her feet over the side of the bed. "Are you all right?" She studied her old friend's profile, her straight back, curls tied away in a messy bun at the nape of her neck. Olivia felt strange, almost as if she no longer recognized her.

Amy-Rose smoothed down the front of her apron. Her smile

was brittle and lacked all of her usual cheer. "I'm fine, Miss Olivia. Would you like me to wait for you?"

Olivia stilled. Amy-Rose only addressed her so formally when people outside the household were present. Her mother prided herself on propriety, but otherwise did not hold Amy-Rose to the same standards as the rest of the staff. Their easy friendship felt so far away now that Olivia didn't know if she should pry, if only to determine if there was anything she could do to help. Amy-Rose pulled on her fingers in a way that looked painful. Olivia decided the best thing to do was to let her go. "I can manage," she said, standing and walking to the vanity.

Amy-Rose spread the dress over Olivia's bed. She appeared to be going through the motions. Olivia remembered how they would sit cross-legged at the foot of that same bed and play games, tangling their fingers in a single thread of twine, and making up stories about their futures.

"Do you remember when we spent the night outside, looking for a shooting star," Olivia said. Amy-Rose paused and turned toward the French doors leading onto the small balcony. They had shared a blanket for warmth and fallen asleep propped against each other. "Your mother said if we saw one," Olivia continued, "we could make a wish."

Amy-Rose turned partway, a small smile on her face. "It was so cold. I remember how our teeth chattered." She laughed and tucked her hands into her apron. "John and Helen were jealous they missed it."

Olivia stood up from the vanity. She thought to place her hand on Amy-Rose's shoulder, but changed her mind, curling her arm back. In her rush to grow up, she'd left her friend behind. "You wished we'd always be friends. I did too. I'm sorry I forgot that."

"I remembered for both of us." The tension in Amy-Rose's forehead weakened as did the knot in Olivia's stomach.

"I promise to do better, to be a better friend going forward," said Olivia, returning Amy-Rose's small smile. And though she hesitated before, she didn't now. She grasped Amy-Rose's hand and pulled her into fierce hug.

Lunch was served on the patio outside. It was a mild afternoon for mid-May. A linen tent from the party provided much-needed shade. Jacob Lawrence and Mr. Davenport seemed at ease together, her father's legs stretched out between them. Mr. Lawrence always said all the right things. He made her parents laugh. She believed she could paint an accurate picture of what her life with him would be like: one filled with opportunity and luxury few enjoyed. She would be content. Would he? If she was being truthful, there was a sadness that had crept into his eyes despite his smile and playful banter. Olivia couldn't put her finger on what felt amiss, but something had happened.

Mr. Davenport absentmindedly dug his cane into the ground, disturbing the manicured lawn. Her mother sat opposite her.

"I'd say last night was a success, wouldn't you, Emmie?" Mr. Davenport reached for his wife's hand. Their fingers interlocked and the look they shared made Olivia blush. It was moments like this that made the promise of marriage worth the pressure to make a good match. Her father turned with mischief in his eyes. "When can we expect a proposal?"

Olivia gasped and saw Mr. Lawrence freeze.

"Come now, children, why prolong the inevitable?" he said.

Mr. Lawrence cleared his throat. The wicker chair beneath him creaked with his shifting weight. Olivia stared openly at her parents, her breaths shallow. Surely, they were joking.

Mrs. Davenport squealed and pressed a hand to her cheek. Olivia wasn't sure she'd ever heard her mother make such a sound. "We could have it here, William," she said. "Might I suggest late summer? We can commission an arbor or gazebo for the ceremony. The blazing star and butterfly weed will be in bloom and the reception in the ballroom . . ." Her words were lost to the buzzing in Olivia's ears. *Inevitable*, like she had no choice, no say.

Mr. Davenport straightened in his seat. "We'll have to find you both a suitable place to live. You're welcome to stay here, but a young couple needs privacy."

"And we want grandchildren!" her mother chimed in. Olivia endured her glances with as much grace as she could manage. Her brief conversation with Amy-Rose had left her feeling lighter, but the aftereffects of the champagne, and her conversation with Ruby, lingered. *The hardest thing we can do is to decide what we want,* she'd said.

Olivia's face burned. Mr. Lawrence laughed nervously beside her. She felt as tense as her horse Chestnut before Olivia goaded her over a hedge. She was outdoors, but Olivia felt like walls were pressing in around her. Or maybe it was her skin, stretched too tight. For the first time, she felt the unfairness Helen swore was laced through the expectations of being a young woman. Olivia's jaw clenched beneath her smile and her blood boiled. *How can they discuss my future like this?* Her parents' voices faded to a buzzing in her ears.

As if he sensed her mounting distress, Jacob Lawrence reached for her hand and squeezed it. His gentle pressure kickstarted her breathing. Light-headed from the sudden rush of air, Olivia withdrew her hand and placed it on her cold, damp cheek.

"Olivia dear, you will make a wonderful bride," said Mrs. Davenport, misty-eyed. "Don't you think so, Mr. Lawrence?"

"No one would be able to take their eyes off you." His gaze seemed to skip over her, even as he said the words.

Olivia stood. Her chair tipped back behind her. Mr. Lawrence caught it easily and placed his hand at the small of her back. She realized then what was amiss. When she danced with Jacob Lawrence, when he held her close—it was clear as day. Yes, she could grow to love him, but how long would that take? And what would that love look and feel like? There was no heat drawing her to Mr. Lawrence, no racing heartbeats to signal a deeper attachment. She enjoyed spending time with him. They could live happily together. Without passion. *When did the butterflies stop fluttering?* Olivia couldn't remember. Her feelings for Mr. Lawrence were wrapped up in the happiness of her parents and her desire to please them and live up to the name they shared.

Ruby was right. He was handsome. But Olivia's thoughts returned again to the young lawyer, and the future that awaited her if she continued on the path already set before her.

This is wrong, she thought. *Mr. Lawrence doesn't love me. He doesn't really know me, and we both deserve more.* "Excuse me," she said. Olivia picked up the napkin that had fallen from her lap and dropped it onto her chair. She crossed the patio, torn between entering the house or heading for the stables. Anywhere was better than at that table where her future was being planned without her input. *Helen would have argued back*, she thought. She stopped in a small copse of trees near the stables, ready to turn back, when she heard her name.

Mr. Lawrence approached slowly. He held his hands up near his shoulders like she was a deer that would bolt any second.

"I'm sorry," she said. "That was an ambush. I want you to know that I had no intention of putting you in that situation." Olivia fought to keep her breaths even. "I'm not sure that I'm ready." Behind him, she could see her parents watching them. She turned and began walking along the path between the trees. Mr. Lawrence, hands now in his pockets, fell into an easy stride beside her.

After she got her anger under control, Olivia apologized again. She was mortified.

Mr. Lawrence sighed. "It's all right. I think we both knew there would be some sort of expectation from our courtship." Olivia made a noncommittal sound. He seemed to have relaxed under the canopy of trees. The forlorn look in his features was gone, replaced by mild amusement.

"I'm glad you find this funny, because I don't." His faint smile gave her the courage to ask a bold question. "Do you mind if we let them believe we've arrived at an understanding?"

Olivia watched his pace slow to a halt. His face was now blank, unreadable.

What have I done? she thought.

It was an indecent proposal, not at all what her parents had hoped for. Perhaps not at all what Jacob Lawrence had hoped for. But she needed it—she needed the time it would buy her. Her encounters with Mr. DeWight left her mind muddled. She suspected that Mr. Lawrence was as reluctant as she was. Perhaps she'd misread him? But at least if they were still courting, her mother would not revert to her desperate search to find Olivia a husband. Olivia could take the summer to figure things out.

She turned to Mr. Lawrence again, calm and focused, praying he could not sense the stress at the root of her request. She had expected a proposal, but one that resembled the grand gestures in her novels. Not a thinly veiled nudge from her parents, where her potential fiancé was blindsided. *Where had it all gone wrong?*

Her English bachelor looked now as she felt. Panicked. "There is something I need to tell you, Olivia," he said. "You should know—"

She peered around him. Her parents busied themselves with their lunch, giving them the illusion of privacy.

"Olivia."

Her eyes snapped back to his. He seemed to weigh something then, looking at her.

"Whatever it is," she said at last, "it's okay. At least until the fundraiser? That's six weeks from now."

He regarded her. "I suppose we could," he said hesitantly, "allow them to believe a proposal is forthcoming. That we want to do it on our own terms."

Olivia felt herself relax a fraction. She searched his face, surprised at his gentleness. "Thank you." She glanced behind him again. "We can't tell anyone," she said, meeting his eyes. "Your word, as a gentleman?"

Mr. Lawrence straightened to his full height, his face solemn. "You have my word."

"I'm glad you came with me," Olivia said. After Mr. Lawrence left, she had Tommy take her to Ruby's. Nursing a headache of her own, Ruby first turned down the idea of walking downtown. She was sitting in a lounge chair with a cold compress over her eyes and feet propped up on a settee. Olivia loudly refused to leave until she agreed.

"You hardly gave me a choice," said Ruby. She lightly bumped Olivia with her hip. "But you were right. I do feel better. Was there anywhere in particular you wanted to go, or are we supposed to wander aimlessly down Wabash Avenue?"

"Wander," Olivia replied. Tucked away in her purse was a leather-bound journal for Washington, with his initials embossed on the cover. She hoped he would use it to draft his speeches. They were too important, too moving not to be recorded somewhere special. She'd ordered it after she spotted the tattered one he carried. It was the perfect way to tell him she wanted to be more involved in the Cause, in any way she could. People who looked like her, survived like her father, loved like her mother, they all deserved to build the life they wanted with the same freedoms and protections as any American.

The streets of the South Side were full of people. It was a beautiful day and she hoped if she and Ruby walked along the storefronts near the community center, they might eventually run into him. Sure enough, outside one of the Black-owned bakeries that opened onto the street, she caught sight of him. Or maybe it was the other way around. He stood at the corner, a hand shading his eyes from the sun as he looked in her direction.

"Ruby, do you mind going in and getting us a pair of sweet rolls?"

Her friend rounded on her. "And incur the wrath of Jessie? You know better than to eat pastries outside of your kitchen."

Olivia laughed. "I know, but I have a craving in the worst way. I barely ate anything at lunch." This was true. Olivia found it difficult to take a bite of anything after the enormity of what she'd done—what she'd said to Mr. Lawrence. But the two of them would never truly be happy together. Not while she had feelings for Washington DeWight. As if in agreement, her stomach growled. She handed her friend a coin from her purse. "I'll wait out here." She nearly pushed Ruby inside.

"Your funeral," Ruby called over her shoulder.

Once she was sure she wouldn't be seen, Olivia looked back to find the corner was empty.

Mr. DeWight was already heading in her direction. His steps were sure and measured. As they got closer to each other, he had a hint of a smile that made her stomach flutter. She held her breath until he was close enough to touch. Her hands ached to find his.

"I'm glad I ran into you." She glanced over her shoulder once more before leading him to a nearby tree.

"I didn't think I'd see you so soon," he said, flashing a smile.

"I was hoping to catch you"—Olivia pulled the journal out of her purse—"and give you this."

Washington turned it over in his hands, surprise clear in his face. "Thank you," he said, looking up at her.

Olivia tugged at her gloves, both giddy and nervous. "I want to join—the Cause. I can't stand by and do nothing. Not knowing what I know. And realizing all that I still don't."

Mr. DeWight held her gift over his heart. "Thank you."

She returned his smile, raising her chin high. She was glad to have met him. "What?" she said when she noticed his mouth screw to one side.

"What did it for you?"

Olivia shrugged. There was no chance she was going to tell him that she was growing bored of her routine, that she enjoyed the give and take of what she gleaned among the activists. Definitely not mentioning the stirrings she felt now.

He leaned in. "It was my dancing, wasn't it?" he asked.

Olivia laughed and was rewarded with a look of joy on the young lawyer's face. She smiled long after he continued on his way and Ruby returned with a sweet roll for each of them.

CHAPTER 28

Helen

Mrs. Milford stood at the center of the Davenports' ballroom, hand hovering over the handle of the phonograph. The music sounded tinny in the empty space, nothing like the live bands her parents usually hired for their parties. Without the presence of dozens of people, every step Helen took echoed. And each misstep resulted in her etiquette teacher making her start from the beginning.

Dancing with a partner was ideal. Though it was never her strong suit, a talented gentleman made the endeavor bearable. Alone, Helen stumbled over her own feet. She thought about how gracefully her sister and Ruby moved. She imagined Jacob's arm around her.

And that was where that thought would stay—in her imagination. He and Olivia, it seemed, had an *understanding*. She was not quite sure what that meant except it made her parents immensely happy. And Helen miserable. She flinched.

Helen couldn't think about him without the sting of the library scene replaying in her mind. She'd been so stupid. Behaved so poorly. Throwing herself at him! They were unchaperoned. Olivia had finally found someone after an unsuccessful round the previous year, and here Helen was. Ruining it. Guilt gnawed her insides. The thought of food turned her stomach. She'd skipped breakfast and sat in the garage, unable to focus on the work in front of her.

The record skipped. Distracted by a misery of her own making, she stepped out of her shoe. The pain was hot and sharp. It traveled halfway up her leg before she realized her mistake and fell to the floor. The throbbing in her ankle did nothing to dispel the memory of another time she had stumbled. Jacob Lawrence struggling to contain a laugh, both of them covered in mud. She didn't know then that the stirrings she felt would lead to so much heartache.

"Oh! Miss Helen, stay where you are." Mrs. Milford stopped the music.

"I'm fine," Helen said. Her ankle felt warm under her hand, but the pain receded quickly. She kicked off her other shoe and remained sitting on the floor.

Mrs. Milford walked around her, hands on her hips. "Is this about Mr. Lawrence?"

Helen's head snapped up. Mrs. Milford stared at her. Helen tried to hold the older woman's gaze, but her shoulders deflated. It had been over a week since the stolen kiss in the library and she could think of little else.

Mrs. Milford rolled her eyes. The gesture made her look younger, a less stern version of herself. She sighed and slowly lowered herself to the floor. "I used to have the same look on my face when I met my Robert. I was younger than you. I didn't have any family, living in a tenement with three formerly enslaved in Philadelphia." She smiled and Helen noticed how it softened her features.

"Did you marry him? This was the pastor?"

"I did. We didn't have much, but we were happy." She pulled at the collar at her throat. Exposing the scars at her neck. When she caught Helen looking, she didn't shy away. "They're from a fire. My husband and I moved to Springfield just before the riots. I worked for a white family then, caring for their young daughter." Mrs. Milford stared at a spot on the floor between them. "I could see the flames from miles off. The air was thick with smoke. Hot too. It burned my insides with every breath and stung my eyes." She paused. Her face was as smooth as her voice. But the sadness in her eyes made Helen's throat tight.

She looked at Helen then. "The whole block where we lived was engulfed. Onlookers told me he'd helped a family of three out of the apartment building before running in once more. I don't even remember entering the complex. Or the gentleman who carried me out. All I could think of was my husband and how he was still inside. He didn't come back out."

Helen held her head in her hands, the pain in her ankle forgotten. "Mrs. Milford, I'm sorry." She didn't want to imagine the shock and deep wound of that loss, but she forced herself to sit with it. Her eyes stung. Helen sniffed and said, "And I was so awful when you arrived."

"I didn't tell you this for you to feel sorry. I only want you to know that life is *precious*." Mrs. Milford adjusted her skirts. "Your behavior was surprisingly refreshing. Closest thing to normal since."

Helen swallowed hard and looked around the empty ballroom. She licked her dry lips. "I didn't mean for this to happen," she said. "It doesn't seem real." She watched the dust motes dance in the shaft of light, afraid to look Mrs. Milford in her eyes. "We met at the Tremaines' party . . ." Her voice caught, and she lifted a hand as if to wave away her own words. "It's hardly life or death." This was the last thing Helen wanted—to get emotional about Mr. Lawrence in front of Mrs. Milford, especially knowing now all the woman had been through.

But the older woman offered Helen a handkerchief to wipe her face. "I wouldn't change my life with Robert for the world," she said. "Much of what affects our lives is out of our control. We should always strive to make the choices we can. Life is too short, too full of heartache."

Helen nodded. "But what about Olivia? At first, she seemed thrilled. She and Mr. Lawrence spent nearly every day together. Now—" She caught herself, moments away from divulging to Mrs. Milford her suspicions: Olivia had been sneaking out at night, much like Helen herself had. Only her sister left the *grounds*. Helen cleaned her face and allowed Mrs. Milford to help her to her feet.

"And now," Mrs. Milford prompted, "something has changed?" Her face said she saw more than what she revealed. "Perhaps, your sister has changed?"

Helen thought back to the dinner when Olivia challenged their father. Her sister hadn't pestered her about community work, or complained about attending the charity board meetings with their mother. She had thought it was because Ruby spent so much time with Mr. Barton, and Olivia had nothing else to do. Could it be that Olivia was up to some mischief of her own?

"If you really feel so strongly for the Englishman, then you should tell your sister before they walk too far down the path they're on."

Path *is another word for* aisle. Her tutor raised her brow, as if sensing her conclusion. Helen nodded. Perhaps Mrs. Milford wasn't too bad to have around after all. When the older woman called it a day and gathered her things, Helen escorted her to the front door.

"I see some things are starting to stick," Mrs. Milford teased.

"I guess they are." Helen pulled open the large oak door. The smile on her face slipped when she saw who stood on the other side.

Jacob Lawrence was there, arm raised, hand poised to use the knocker. Helen could not take her eyes off him.

"Good afternoon, Mr. Lawrence," Mrs. Milford said. She edged her way past the two young people. Helen looked at her then, pleading with her eyes for her tutor to stay. Mrs. Milford only shook her head slightly and descended the steps. "Time is scarce," she added.

Helen's heart raced. Her breaths came quick.

She shut the door on him.

She did—she shut the door and leaned against it, putting some distance between them and breathing through the awful tightness in her chest. *I can't do this to my sister.*

She opened the door again.

Jacob Lawrence still stood there, eyebrows raised. Beyond him, Mrs. Milford had paused at the door to the carriage. She gave Helen an incredulous look.

"I came to see Olivia," he said.

"Of course you did," she replied harshly. She immediately

hated herself for it. She'd thrown herself at him during her parents' anniversary party and included him in a betrayal against her sister and slammed the door in his face. If there was anyone who deserved scorn, it was herself.

"Helen, we should talk."

"Fabulous idea." Mrs. Davenport appeared at Helen's side. "Olivia is not home. My, she will be on the board of every social club in Chicago by the end of the year." She adjusted the collar of Helen's shirt. "I think the two of you should spend some time together, get to know each other better. We'll all be family soon." Her smile was brighter than the sun. "Helen, I'm sure you can entertain Mr. Lawrence for a few hours?"

"Mama," Helen started. "I believe you're forgetting that—"

"Whatever it is, I'm sure it can wait." Mrs. Davenport waved to Mrs. Milford. The two women spoke near the carriage while Helen stood on the steps. Her distress multiplied. She mentally urged Mrs. Milford to say she was busy.

Mr. Lawrence worked the muscles in his jaw, like his next words would be painful. "We don't have to, if you don't want to."

Helen sighed and descended the stairs, walking onto the drive. She stopped at an automobile, admiring the detail along the trim. Hearing Mr. Lawrence behind her, she said, "She'll know." She looked over her shoulder at him. "Mama always knows. Where's your carriage?"

"Your brother convinced me to try one of these instead. Not sure how I like it." He opened the door for her. "Where to?" he asked.

Mrs. Milford looked from the automobile to the reluctant pair. "It looks like it'll be a tight fit, but we'll make do," she said, walking over.

The older woman brushed between them and climbed inside, where she arranged herself in the middle of the bench seat.

Helen swallowed around the lump in her throat. "Downtown."

She stood on the front steps of the Field Museum in Jackson Park. Its colonnaded edifice loomed before her. The ride over was torture. Jacob was within her reach, but Helen had never felt so far from another person. She ached with a poison mix of regret and longing. His attempts at small talk made an unwanted interaction even more awkward, especially with her chaperone sitting sentinel between them. Thankfully, once they arrived at the museum Mrs. Milford retreated a discreet distance.

"Shall we go in?" he asked.

"Yes." Helen stepped, then turned. "Actually, not yet. You're right, we should talk." She sat on the stone steps and gazed out to the lakefront. Jacob sat beside her, stretching out one leg and propping an elbow on his bent knee. When she looked back at the entrance, Mrs. Milford was nowhere in sight. She took a deep breath—a mistake, as she filled her lungs with the smell of Mr. Lawrence's cologne or soap. Cedar and spiced wine? She didn't care, it was as unique as him.

"I'm sorry," she said. She forced her eyes up and studied his face. There may never be another chance to look at him so openly. His strong jaw and neatly trimmed mustache. Helen tried her best to push away the memory of how his mouth felt against hers, the way their bodies had fit. Because it could only be just that. A memory. On the car ride over, Helen realized that it was more than her future happiness that hung in the balance. And although

Olivia seemed to have cold feet, this arrangement, this *under-standing*, was something her sister wanted. And it was something Mr. Lawrence had agreed to *after* their own encounter.

His attention moved from Helen's clasped hands to her face. He wore an expression she'd never seen before. It pinned her to the step. "I'm not," he said. "Sorry, that is." They sat close, but not too close. It made her want to shrink the distance between them, regardless of who would see. Her skin tingled as the scene in the library replayed in her mind. She relived every sigh and touch. Before her, his lips parted as his gaze fell to hers. He took deep breaths and she swore she saw her own wants reflected in his eyes.

But what about Olivia?

She watched his fingers intertwine with hers, felt the gentle firmness of his hands. She replayed her sister's behavior in her head. Olivia hadn't looked excited at all about the possibility of marriage now. In fact, she'd looked a lot like Helen did when Mrs. Milford first arrived.

Doubt twitched in Helen's gut. It would be in poor taste for him to swap one sister for another. Bad form for Helen, shameful for Olivia . . . possibly resigning her to spinsterhood.

Unless . . . Olivia walked away from him first. But that would never happen, right?

"If you're not sorry, then . . ." Helen paused. "I—don't understand." She didn't connect how he could be one way with her, but still appear to court Olivia.

"I do wish things were different. And they will be soon. All I can say is, I gave her my word and this pain we're feeling now . . . I believe it will pass."

Helen looked away. She wanted to believe it more than she

could say. She wanted to trust him, that there was some reason he and Olivia welcomed the speculation on their relationship. *Why was this not covered in the etiquette guides?*

"Shall we?" Mr. Lawrence stood and helped Helen to her feet.

"Yes." She slipped her arm through his, afraid to hope, but willing to take a chance.

CHAPTER 29

Amy-Rose

"Did you get any sleep, child?" Jessie lifted a pan from the suds overflowing from the sink. The Davenports' lunch was nearly ready to be served and she was set on putting her kitchen back to rights and prepping for the next meal.

"I got enough," said Amy-Rose. She'd tossed and turned for the better part of an hour. When she couldn't sleep, she'd tried to work on designs for her store. She needed a label to set her apart from the other ladies selling hair-growth formulas and treatments. She'd glanced over partially conceived designs, trying not to dwell on the embarrassing scene at the party that had forced her to hide in the kitchen. She'd stopped when she noticed there were more tears on the pages than ink. She just didn't know where she fit. How could she continue to walk these halls after last night? She'd need to move on from Freeport faster than she'd planned.

Idiot. How could you think there was any version of the future where you belonged on the arm of John Davenport?

Luckily, Jessie had kept her busy for the better part of the day.

Focused on her regular chores and those she offered to complete for Hetty, Amy-Rose could temporarily forget what had happened. The linens were freshly laundered. The silver polished. The wood oiled. Helen had surprised her, sitting still for the first time in ages as she redid her hair. Neither had spoken. The procedure was painless, but free of their usual gossip. Then there was Olivia, who had surprised her with an apology and a promise. Before long, Amy-Rose had moved on to the next item on the list. She'd continued to forget. Before it all came hurtling back like a blow.

"I think that's enough chopping for you." Jessie pulled the knife from Amy-Rose's hands now and moved the diced carrots to a bowl. "Don't want to serve one of your fingertips in tonight's stew."

"Jessie, I'm not sure what came over me."

It was clear the cook knew Amy-Rose didn't mean her knife-handling skills. "Honey, we can't control everything. Sometimes, them feelings take a hold of us and won't let go."

Amy-Rose let her forehead fall to the cool surface of the table. It helped with the aching. Those feelings, despite her best efforts, did grab hold of her. They sank their nails in deep.

"Now, I want you to get out of this house." Jessie began dicing onions. "Don't look at me like that. Just for a couple hours. Walk. Get some air and exercise." Jessie's gaze roamed over Amy-Rose. "Yes, I think that's what you need." She went back to her meal prep as if Amy-Rose had already left.

Slowly, Amy-Rose removed her apron and gathered her things. Jessie was right. There were things in life you couldn't control. Circumstances so big and devastating, they changed your life. Love. A storm. Death. They broke a heart so completely it never fully recovered. They also spurred a determination so sound, it withstood all.

"Fine," Amy-Rose said. "I have to see a man about a shop." Jessie didn't answer as Amy-Rose swung her bag over her shoulder, but the glint in the cook's eye was the only response she needed.

The door at Mr. Spencer's barbershop opened without a sound. Amy-Rose looked up to see the bell above had been removed. An eerie sensation crept up her back as she stepped over the threshold. The large picture windows, which usually flooded the space with light, were dressed in brown paper. The effect created a sickly yellow glow. The station at the end where Mr. Spencer himself cut hair was empty. In fact, all the chairs and sinks were gone. *This will make it easier to redesign*, she thought.

"Mr. Spencer?" she called. Amy-Rose missed the chatter and laughter she always found here. Mr. Spencer's most of all. When no sound came, she turned to leave. The door opened and closed silently behind her. The feeling of dread grew. Her pace quickened as she dodged carriages and automobiles at the intersection on her way to Binga Bank. *He's probably decided to shut down early.*

By the time Amy-Rose pushed her way into the bank, her back was damp with sweat and her breaths puffed out in panicked bursts. Something was wrong. She could feel it. The receptionist, a young Black man in an over-starched suit, took her name even though he'd seen her there many times. He asked her to sit while he checked in the back for the banker handling her account.

Had he looked sad?

She paced the small space in front of his simple wooden desk. Mr. Spencer had said she had more time. He wouldn't leave without telling her. Without saying goodbye. Amy-Rose was well on her way to wearing a trench in the hardwood floor when she heard her name.

"Miss Shepherd?" A different man appeared at the entrance of the hall. "If you'll follow me." He turned as she approached and led her into the first of two offices. She sat in the seat to which he gestured. Through the frosted glass, she could see the bank's other patrons as blurred figures moving in the lobby. Her eyes returned to the banker to find the same regretful look as worn by the secretary. "Miss Shepherd, I understand that you have a savings account with us."

"What's wrong?" Amy-Rose's pulse spiked and sweat broke out at her temples. She had placed all she could spare in her savings account. Nearly everything she had. There would be no way to start over. She stared at the man across the desk, knowing the news he was about to share would be terrible. A chill settled over her.

"It's"—he paused and moved the loose papers on his desk into a neat stack—"that I know you intended to lease a property. Spencer's barbershop, to be precise."

"Not 'intended.' I haven't changed my mind." The cold pooled in her stomach like lead. Her voice shook. "I've nearly saved the amount Mr. Spencer asked for the deposit. Surely you know this. You can check right now."

The banker steepled his fingers. The sigh before his next words sucked all the air out of the room. "We brokered the deal between Mr. Spencer and another patron this morning. I'm afraid the storefront is no longer available."

Amy-Rose held on to the armrests of her chair as the room spun beneath her feet. The man, his desk, even the fern behind him, seemed to blend and wobble to the point of making her ill.

The room was too hot and her heart pounded in sluggish thuds. He apologized for her disappointment and explained her options. She could continue to save and wait for the next opportunity. His words were as muted as her vision. The temperature rose higher.

"I don't understand."

"I'm afraid Mr. Spencer accepted another offer."

"No, I got that part. What I mean is, why? Did they offer him more money? He'd said he cared more about *who* it was leased to, not for how much." Her voice grew more desperate with each breath. The banker watched her, his expression unchanging. She didn't want to hear about alternatives. She needed to know why Mr. Spencer had backed out of their agreement. Then she realized. Snippets of her previous visit rose to the surface of her mind. The prying questions that almost had her second-guessing her capabilities. They saw her as a risky investment. Young. Unmarried. A woman.

"Miss Shepherd, I understand your disappointment. It's just business, nothing personal."

Amy-Rose wished that was all she felt. But it was like a body blow she didn't see coming. "The storefront is leased."

The banker nodded.

"To someone more suitable than me?" Amy-Rose watched the man across the table brace himself. She felt him study her features, which had relaxed in resignation. Even her grip on the arms of the chair loosened enough that her knuckles returned to their natural brown. *Did he expect me to scream and carry on?* His demeanor eroded the rest of her resolve. This was no argument she could win. "Excuse me," she said. "I need air."

Amy-Rose burst out onto the street, where the trolleys squealed on their tracks. The sounds of the city, the strength of the sun as summer approached, snapped her back to the present, to the news that brought her lower than she'd felt in years.

She paid for a buggy to take her back to Freeport Manor. With no property to rent, the splurge was irrelevant. The pressure to be careful with each penny seemed silly. Unnecessary. The ride calmed her and allowed her time to wipe her tears away. *How could this have happened?* Amy-Rose did everything the way she was supposed to. She had laid out her plan. Every extra dollar locked away in a bank vault. And for what?

After the bouncing ride, the solid ground outside Freeport's carriage house felt too firm. Amy-Rose walked to the servants' entrance on numb feet.

"Amy-Rose!" Tommy called from the stables.

Her pace quickened. She felt too raw to talk.

Gravel kicked up to her heels as he came to a stop next to her. "Hey, why didn't you stop?" Tommy stepped ahead of her and his brows knit together. "What's wrong?" he asked.

Amy-Rose inhaled a mixture of horse sweat and the soap he used. The skin around her eyes was tight and puffy. "Mr. Spencer leased the shop." She exhaled heavily, feeling the sting of new tears forming. Tommy's arms held her tight until they'd passed. He waited quietly until she had sniffed away the bitter taste at the back of her throat and began to tell him what happened at the bank. It made it real, recounting the banker and her so-called options, but no less painful. "I was outbid!"

"Hold on. What happened?"

"Mr. Spencer leased the shop to someone else. After the time we spent together. He encouraged me, answered my questions." Amy-Rose shook her head. "How could he lie to me?"

Tommy kicked at the gravel. "You don't know that he did."

Amy-Rose pulled a face. "A purchase like that takes time. I was there not two days ago and he didn't say anything." She gestured to the house, the garage and stables. "And it's not like he doesn't know where I live. He could have broken the news to me himself." Tommy opened his mouth and she felt her temper flare. "Don't tell me it's just business. That's what the man at the bank said. 'Just business, nothing personal.' As if they didn't look at me and decide I wasn't capable." A fresh sob pushed its way past her chest. Tommy stood next to her, a silent salve to the pain and disappointment that escaped through hot tears until she was too exhausted to stand. She leaned against the siding of the house, letting the heat soothe her. "What am going to do now?" she asked, her voice a hoarse whisper.

Tommy shoved his arms into the bib of his overalls. "You can come out west with me. Like I said, there will be loads of opportunities out there. We can start fresh."

California.

It seemed so far away from everything she knew. Sure, once the girls were gone, there would be no real reason for her to stay on. Eventually, she would have to leave the room upstairs.

"Listen, you don't have to decide right now." Tommy smiled. "Just know that it's an option."

Amy-Rose watched him walk back to the stables. He had his head tilted to the sky, whistling to the breeze. He'd made his decision so clear, he seemed to have left all his troubles by the wayside. Opportunities and options. That was what the banker said too. As she pushed her way inside, Amy-Rose wondered what other doors remained to be opened.

CHAPTER 30

"Ruby, dear, if I have to hear you sigh one more time, I will stop this carriage and have you walk home." Mrs. Tremaine stared at her daughter seated opposite her in the open buggy.

"I was not *sighing*," Ruby said. She fought the urge to cross her arms over her chest, choosing instead to readjust her skirt so its leaner silhouette would be free of her mother's fuller one.

"You and Olivia spent the entire lunch nibbling at your sandwiches and gazing into full cups of tea. It was as if Emmeline and I were the only two there." Her mother looked out into the distance.

Ruby wasn't sure when the carriage left Freeport Manor to arrive near Jackson Park. It brought them out of their way to get home. Perhaps her mother wanted to watch passersby. The buggy itself moved at a pace slow enough to lull her to sleep.

"I understand why Olivia was distracted." Her mother's voice dropped several octaves, though they were well out of earshot of anyone. "Emmeline said she and William gave the couple a little nudge." She leaned back in her seat. "She was concerned it may have resulted in a bit of a setback, but I assured her, it will all work out in the end. I bet the ceremony will be grand."

Olivia did look preoccupied, but excited or anxious were not the words Ruby would have chosen to describe her inattention. In fact, Olivia had vented for nearly twenty minutes before she was calm enough to meet their mothers for lunch. Ruby had thought about divulging more of her own troubles with romance, and Olivia had tried to draw it out of her, but there was no good way to explain what she'd done.

Despite all their worries, the teahouse was a treat—a remnant of a time before when it was a nearly daily pastime, if only to stop by and exchange a bit of gossip over a strong cup and a sweet. Ruby especially loved the macaroons. *Did I eat any?* She rubbed her temples. Her head ached. Ruby hated the way she ended things with Harrison. His face, twisted with hurt, haunted her.

"Ruby!"

She flinched at her name.

Mrs. Tremaine leaned forward. "As I said, I understand why *she* was distracted." Her mother's eyebrow slowly crept closer to the fringe of hair that swept over her left eye. Clearly she awaited Ruby's own excuse.

You thought you were so clever, Ruby chided herself. How could she have expected to keep her deepening feelings for Harrison Barton to herself? She should have known better. She did know better.

There was nowhere to go. The reason for this detour was clear. Her mother brought her out here to talk. Ruby shifted in her seat. The day that had passed in a foggy blur now sharpened. A man sat on the bench throwing crumbs to the birds. Two women giggled under a shared parasol. Somewhere, the savory scent of stewed beef thickened the air, and the water lapping the shore reminded her of the tick of the second hand on her father's pocket watch. Her stomach tightened in subtle warning before she spoke. "Harrison Barton, the young man I've befriended—" she started. *Of course she remembers!* "He suspects something is amiss between us. I don't think we'll be spending as much time together."

"And is that something you want—to spend more time with him?"

Ruby's answer: absolutely. Time spent with Mr. Barton felt like another life, one where the pressure of the everyday lifted for a time. She could relax, feel free. Her skin warmed at the thought of him at the jewelry shop, with her on the beach, the two of them dancing.

"But I think it's wise to continue the courtship until my situation with John is settled, see this to the end," Ruby said cautiously.

"My dear, there is only one way this will end." When she didn't respond, her mother continued. "You know, your father wasn't my first love." Ruby gasped and her mother cocked another eyebrow. She watched her mother's face soften around a sad smile. "There was a young man who thought the world of me. And I of him. We made plans." Mrs. Tremaine picked at the leather piping along her seat. It was as if she wandered into a memory.

Ruby wondered what her mother was like when she was Ruby's age. They rarely spoke like this anymore. She waited, afraid to ask questions. A part of her mother must still love this other man. Why else would she bring him up? Was her father the safer choice? They both turned to watch a couple walk past. Their arms linked through each other's, creating a unit, moving as one. *Like you and Papa*, Ruby thought. They never tired of each other's company and decided everything together. *Isn't that the goal?*

"We were young," her mother said. "And when you're that age, you don't realize there are many types of love. I chose your father and have never regretted it." Mrs. Tremaine signaled the driver to move on. "Enslavement is rooted in our history, Ruby. I wanted something we could build, as far away from that past as we could get without forgetting it."

"What happened to the young man?" Ruby asked.

"He married someone else. Had another family."

The response was so matter-of-fact, it knocked Ruby back. She tried to imagine Harrison marrying someone else, giving another woman his last name and fathering her children. It put a sour taste in her mouth. She wasn't sure if she wanted to live in a reality where she thought of him as in the past. Ruby wondered what about her father had swayed her mother from this other man. She bit the inside of her cheek, debating whether knowing was better than wondering. Her curiosity won out.

"Why Papa?" she asked.

Mrs. Tremaine never took her eyes off the street passing by. "He was the better choice."

The buggy jerked away from the curb, rattling Ruby's jumbled thoughts. Harrison Barton surprised her. She liked the version of herself she was when with him. She breathed easier around him. Their outings were the highlights of her week, and now the days stretched out before her. The thought of spending every dinner, function, *day* without him felt like too much to handle. How could she have been so stupid? And so cruel? He deserved the truth, yes, but the whole truth: That despite the reason she pursued him, her feelings for him were real—and she was a fool for not realizing it sooner.

She looked at her mother. *The better choice.* Deep in her bones. Ruby knew the better choice for her was Harrison Barton.

Her nails bit into her palm as she replayed the confrontation in her mind. *I will make this right*, she thought. *I must.*

CHAPTER 31

Olivia

"Are you going to save these?" Olivia pointed at the lunch tray of untouched sandwiches.

Her father frowned. "You don't mean to take these with you?"

"The schoolhouse roof is being repaired by volunteers, and some women are gathering to discuss the vote. I thought it would be nice to add these to the others Jessie prepared and bring them over." She didn't wait for a yes. Olivia began wrapping the sandwiches in cheesecloth. She avoided eye contact with her mother, keeping her hands busy and concentrating on staying relaxed.

Mr. Davenport leaned back in his chair, watching his elder daughter. There was a small smile on his face that made the lines there deepen. He stood and embraced Olivia. "You've been spending a lot of time on the South Side. I'm sure they appreciate the help."

Olivia's hand knocked over a teacup. She quickly righted it while her father laughed. Her own smile was stiff. Helen had nearly caught her twice coming back home, and Jessie was beginning to wonder why she couldn't keep the pantry stocked. The community center was as close to a perfect excuse as she could muster. Plus, it served as a meeting place where volunteers for the Tremaine campaign and activists overlapped and worked together. Her presence there as her mother's proxy or as a close friend of the Tremaine family was not unusual. *Hiding in plain sight.*

"Will Mr. Lawrence be meeting you there?" Mrs. Davenport asked.

Olivia paused. She looked at her mother then. Mrs. Davenport's eyes were shrewd; she knew something was amiss. Olivia hated deceiving her parents. She'd convinced herself she wasn't quite lying. What she, Mr. DeWight, and the others were doing was in the service of their people, if not exactly charity. But each time she stepped out of the house, her stomach tied up in knots.

All the knots loosened, though, each time she saw Washington DeWight, whether onstage or in the street, encouraging the activists to keep hope alive in their struggle for equality.

"Mr. Lawrence will not be there today."

"Olivia, I don't like the idea of you traveling by yourself."

"I won't be alone," Olivia said. "Tommy will drive me. There will be a host of other people where I'm going, and Tommy will wait for me outside until I'm ready to leave. I'll be late for dinner, though. I may stay to serve in the soup kitchen. They've been so short-staffed these past few weeks."

"Maybe I should go with you," Mrs. Davenport said.

"No!" Olivia smiled brightly. "I appreciate the offer, but I think we'll manage. It is only a possibility I may need to stay." She tucked the last sandwich away, picked up her skirts, hoisted the basket, and walked away before they could hold her any longer.

She had nearly made it to the stable when Helen stepped into her path. "Where are you going, Livy?"

Olivia started. "The community center," she replied. Tommy was waiting for her out front and she didn't want to keep Mr. DeWight wondering where she was.

Helen's eyes narrowed. "You spend a lot of time there. Are you trying to atone for some scandalous transgression?" Olivia froze. "Ha! You should see your face," said Helen, laughing.

"I'm glad you're amused, Helen." Olivia shouldered past, heart racing. She spent the carriage ride with the echo of her sister's laugh ringing in her ears and thoughts of the various narrow escapes she'd made over the past few weeks. Until now, she'd been able to avoid suspicion, but she could tell time was running out. Her parents made the expectation of Mr. Lawrence's official, and preferably public, proposal very clear. Mrs. Davenport was set on a ceremony in autumn now, to give them more time. To everyone on the outside, the pieces were finally falling into place.

Olivia worried about more practical things. Like where they would live. Was she meant to move to England? Mr. Lawrence's family was in Europe, where he was set to inherit a business of his own. And what would he think of her involvement with the protestors and activists? She would be of no use to the people in Chicago when she was married and out of the country.

The carriage came to an abrupt halt in front of the community center.

"I'll be here, in this spot, in two hours," Tommy said.

"Two hours? That isn't enough time."

"It is if all you're doing is bringing food to day laborers."

Olivia bit the inside of her cheek. He was right. "I'll need you to stall. Please? I need more time."

"Miss, I do not think this is a good idea, and I reckon we'll both be in a sorry mess if you get caught. I admire what you're doing. It's why I agree to help, but you're tempting fate."

Olivia knew word would get back to her parents eventually, but she wasn't doing anything wrong. And what was the worst that could happen? They continue to hide the ugliest of the truth and shelter her? It was far too late for that. "I'll try to make it back in time."

Tommy nodded and drove away. Olivia walked into the community center. The energy inside was magnetic. She was a regular now, and recognized many of the faces around her. It filled her up to have a purpose outside of her household, and one that mattered, a place where she'd become more than her last name. In the small classroom used for adult education, she found Washington DeWight hunched over a table with two gentlemen reading a paper. She enjoyed watching him work from a distance and the effect he had on people. He'd removed his jacket, and his shirtsleeves were pushed up above his elbows. The man to his right tracked his fingers along the page, mouth moving with each word. Mr. DeWight stood quietly, patiently, as the man read.

"Olivia, we weren't expecting you today," said Mrs. Woodard.

Olivia handed her the basket. "I brought sandwiches. Clarence said they spent three days in a jail without bread or water last time."

Mrs. Woodard placed a hand on her arm, "They'll appreciate this. The papers that came reported more lynching over the weekend. We're to march. We'll need full bellies, especially if trouble starts. The sign you made is against the wall."

Olivia's eyes settled on the single-ply wood board she'd painted last week.

EQUAL OPPORTUNITY IS HUMAN DIGNITY

The words came to her with a rush of emotion. Her hand, made steady by hours of needlepoint, created a banner she hoped was worthy of the unified message.

Mr. DeWight picked up her sign by the wooden post added later and handed it to her. "Ready?"

She nodded, not trusting her voice.

He rubbed her shoulder. With his free hand, he grabbed his own banner off the table. "Let's go."

Hand in hand they emerged from the community center to a crowd that had doubled in size since Olivia had arrived. The street was full of people who fought what was expected of them, damn the consequences. Now she was one of them. Olivia wondered if this was what her sister felt. *She's never given up*, she thought. Helen's time spent in the garage was the poorest-kept secret of Freeport Manor. Yet knowing the disappointment and eventual heartbreak her disobedience would bring, Helen still fought to do what she loved. Olivia smiled at her sister's courage—at how much fulfillment could be found in doing what you were passionate about.

Mr. DeWight squeezed her hand and together they walked to the front of the crowd. People quieted as they passed. The hush around her heightened the nervous excitement now rushing through her limbs. Olivia no longer felt tired or clumsy from lack of sleep. No, it was the opposite—a spark of wild energy that threatened to burst through her skin.

"Brothers and sisters," Mr. DeWight called to the people gathered. Olivia let the confidence and conviction of his voice lift her up. "Remember, this is a peaceful demonstration. We're here in solidarity with our brothers and sisters in the South. The burden and horrors of Jim Crow are not theirs alone. There will be no violence. Our voices"—he held up his sign, I AM A MAN—"are the only sword and shield we need." The hand that still held Olivia's shot up to the sky. Together, their raised hands stood as the joint signal to begin. The crowd held up their signs and posters, banners and flags, and moved forward, parting as they passed Olivia and Washington DeWight as if the pair were a stone in a river. She watched men and women of all shades and ages move as one. Without waiting for him, she grasped her post with both hands and held her own sign high. He joined her, matching her pace.

At the edge of the group, people handed out copies of a blue pamphlet to anyone who would take it. The same blue pamphlet she received the afternoon she first stepped into Samson House. Its reception was as varied as the people of the city. She noted each tiny burst of pride when a passerby stopped to ask questions. Another person threw it on the ground. Still another reached out to gather more. Mr. DeWight's mission at work.

Mrs. Woodard sidled up next to Olivia. The older woman's dove-gray suit had a white rose in the lapel. Its perfume mingled with the smell of horses and exhaust. "I thought there would be more ladies here." Mrs. Woodard sighed.

Olivia glanced at the crowd. "Fewer than we expected, to be sure, but enough." Hetty was up ahead with her cousin and some of the working girls.

"A good group of them from the garment factories were warned they'd be forfeiting their jobs if they came here today. Even if they were not scheduled to work." Mrs. Woodard tutted. "More like sweatshops, if you ask me." She shook her head and lifted her sign higher. Her voice joined the others, chanting, "Equality is dignity."

Olivia's heart raced, her throat hoarse from the power of her own voice. Her eyes couldn't take in her surroundings fast enough. Though she recognized the route they marched, everything appeared brighter, larger in the river of people that buoyed her body, her mind, her soul. They stopped along the way to speak to passersby. It was as if the meeting from the basement had spilled out into the streets, only exponentially larger. In the light of day, everyone seemed sharper, bolder, and so did she. The nervousness she felt leaving the house had evaporated—no—transformed into something else.

You are exactly *where you are meant to be.*

"Not bad for your first time, eh?" Mr. DeWight gave her a lazy smile.

She couldn't contain the wide grin on her face, even if she wanted to. "This is amazing," she said as the nearly completed façade of city hall and Cook County Circuit Court came into view, casting its shadow over the activists. Her muscles burned from holding her sign, but the solidarity of the people around her bolstered her confidence. Laughter, despite the seriousness of what they were gathered to share, swirled around her. North La-Salle Street thrummed beneath her feet. Automobiles, carriages, and the vibrations from within the twelve-story building going up behind her. The crowd parted for the construction crews. It was here Olivia noticed a shift. The street was crowded. Some people had stopped to stare, jeer. A brick came tumbling through their column of marchers. It skittered about their feet, but the crowd regrouped and continued moving forward.

Olivia only had to look at the people beside her for strength. They ignored the looks from shopkeepers, some of them heckling the marchers, their shouts indecipherable in all the noise. Some of the demonstrators walked in circles. Their signs bobbed up and down to songs Olivia didn't know. High above them, a boy about three years of age, sat on the shoulders of his father. He held on to his father's chin and smiled down at her.

"What was your first rally like?" she asked Mr. DeWight.

"Much like this," he said. "Smaller group, though. We stood outside a county jail until the sun went down." He smiled. "I was so scared. I was fourteen then, and some of the older guys told me stories about being locked up." He dipped his chin. "There are worse things in life than to be imprisoned for standing up for ourselves and others."

Olivia nodded. Her eyes scanned the street.

"Chicago is a new place for most of us," he said, "still untouched by what I've seen. Part of the reason we're here, in daylight, under a short time frame, is to avoid some of the dangers of rallies." He placed a hand on her back. She allowed him to tuck her against his side, his lips a breath's distance away, when a scream ripped the air.

As one, the crowd turned. Bodies pressed into Olivia. Her sign fell from her hand. Mr. DeWight pushed through. He gently removed people from his path as he made his way to the epicenter of the commotion. Olivia followed.

"Stay off our streets." A man in a dark suit spit at the feet of one of the protesters. He replaced his hat on a shock of white-blond hair and looked up. Olivia ducked behind Washington's shoulder. She didn't know his name, but she recognized his face. Chicago was as small as it was large, and she didn't want to risk him seeing her. When she looked up, the young boy stood in front her. *Don't look at me like that*, she thought.

The boy's eyes widened into two brown saucers as his father scooped him up with one arm and ran. Everything after that happened in a blur. A whistle pierced the air and the shoulders that brushed hers moments ago slammed into her with a force that knocked her down. The palms of her hands burned as they skid over the sidewalk. A knee struck her head. When a hand closed around her upper arm she swung blindly.

"Ow!" Mr. DeWight rubbed his jaw, but held on. Around her was turmoil. The police had arrived. They blocked both ends of the sidewalk, pushing the activists against the building behind them. Olivia searched for the father and child, hoping they'd made it out safely.

"Are you hurt?" Washington quickly scanned her face.

"No," she breathed. Luckily, her hat had absorbed most of the blow to the top of her head, but her palms stung and her wrists throbbed from the impact. The others had warned her. The last thing she wanted to do was complain. Olivia blinked back surprised tears and swiftly returned his determined smile. Around them, the activists linked their arms. Their signs were a discarded heap on the ground. And their songs began anew. She watched Mr. DeWight, uneasy, hesitate to join them. But she was here for a purpose. She twined her fingers with his. "Don't you want to rejoin?"

"Run!" shouted Mr. DeWight. He released her hand and guided her behind him.

High against the setting sun, a baton came down on a man in the line. With his hands linked in peaceful defiance, he could do nothing to protect himself from the blow. Olivia flinched in horror as he fell to the ground. The crowd tried to leave then. But it was too late. They had waited too long and now were penned in.

Her toes pinched when Mr. DeWight stepped back. "Sorry," he said over his shoulder. He had pulled her behind him, effectively blocking her vision. The chants had turned into shouts and screams. The press of bodies made panic rise in her throat. She felt him flinch.

"What's going on?" she asked. Her hands were sweating and stinging. Her breath came fast. She could feel the pounding of her heart over the cries from every direction. "Washington?"

He turned and said, "We need to get out of here." His eyes darted up and down the street. *How can he be so calm?* "There's George," he said, nodding to a man behind them. Olivia recognized him among the regulars at Samson House. He was the tall gentleman who stood at the top of the stairs at the first meeting she attended.

"This way," said George. He picked up a sign and led Olivia and Mr. DeWight through the crowd. "Washington, when I charge, you and your lady better run." Before either of them could stop him, he charged the nearest officer, creating an opening. Olivia and Mr. DeWight surged through, along with a few demonstrators with shots and cries chasing them.

Olivia ran. She ran with Washington DeWight pulling her arm with an urgency she knew would leave bruises in the morning.

Darkness descended around them with a quickness that chilled her bones. The sun was set now. The air was considerably cooler than before. As shouts bled into the night, Mr. DeWight again grabbed her stinging hand and led her away. Over the uneven ground, she followed him. Their harried breathing became the loudest sound in the night. His warm, rough hand kept her focused on their escape. Still, her thoughts returned to the boy and his father. Did he see the violence? Were they able to flee?

He led her farther. They were blocks away from the community center now. He insisted on taking a winding route back. Every sound was amplified by her fear. Fresh sweat stung her palms. Her feet burned. And with every minute that passed, she wondered what excuse she or Tommy could give for her returning in this state.

Mr. DeWight stopped. Held her back. There was a sound of hooves striking the pavement. The mounted officer turned, his light shining across the street. "In here," Mr. DeWight said. Olivia followed him into the adjacent alley. She stared at his shoulders, hunched as he took them from shadow to shadow, stopping in an alcove no wider than the servants' passage at Freeport Manor. There they waited, a few blocks from where her carriage should be. She didn't protest his arms around her.

"You're hurt. Why didn't you say anything?" he said, turning her hands palms up with a featherlight touch. They were red and puffy. Olivia took in the state of them and knew she'd have a hard time explaining it the next morning. Perhaps she could steal away to the stables and claim to have been thrown from a horse. She chewed her lip, her mind racing when he removed the handkerchief from his jacket and wrapped it around her hand. He covered the deeper gash and where her skin was most tender. Then he pulled her closer, clearing her mind of worry for just a moment. Her muscles relaxed. She looked up to catch him staring at her.

"You have been fully initiated," he said. "Every man and woman out there today has a scar and a story to tell."

Olivia thought of her parents. The scars her father kept hidden, even from his children. Her injury was less than minor. She knew in a few days it would heal and fade. She hoped that the impact she and others made would last longer than that.

He smoothed her hair away from her face. Olivia breathed. The electric current spreading through her grew. She didn't know if what they did today reached many people, how many hearts or heads they turned. But she knew, this is where she wanted to be. On the side working for a better Chicago. Next to a man who valued her spirit more than her last name. Olivia stared at Mr. DeWight, bare of his usual fire and drive and charm, and saw tenderness in his eyes.

It was his turn to gasp, because Olivia kissed him, pulling him by his lapels down to her lips. He stiffened briefly. Then his arm tightened around her. She felt herself drawn to his body, his to hers, eliminating all space. Despite her boldness, Olivia was aware of her inexperience. She let him lead, matching his pressure until a sigh parted her lips. She felt his muscles tense at the sound. His tongue slipped over hers, exploring her as she savored the taste of him. They should keep moving, she knew, but the way he leaned into her displaced all reason. She nipped his lip, so soft against hers, and coaxed a moan from him that made her warm all over. Her pulse roared in her head.

She wanted to be even closer to him. He was handsome, yes, strong, not just in looks, but in his conviction. And Olivia felt, more than ever, firm in her own.

"Thank you," Olivia said outside the carriage house.

"I'm just glad we found you." Hetty smacked Tommy on his arm. "Aren't we?" she asked, squinting at him. The pair had been searching for her when she hadn't arrived back at the center on time.

"Of course," he said. He looked over Olivia's shoulder at Freeport Manor. When his eyes met hers, they seemed to tell her *Stop tempting fate.* "Are you sure you don't need help?"

Olivia held up her injured hands and said, "Thank you, but no." Grateful for their help, she stole back to the house. She removed her shoes and tiptoed through the kitchen and up to the bathroom she shared with Helen. The events of the day felt surreal, but the people who stopped to hear their calls for support made it all worth it. She washed her hands in the basin and counted herself lucky. Then her thoughts wandered to the kiss between her and Washington DeWight. Water dripped from her hands onto her bare feet, jolting her back to the present. She saw movement down the hall.

"Olivia Elise," Helen said, shaking her head. "I am sorely disappointed." Olivia could hear rather than see the smile on her sister's face. Helen stood in the doorway, the arms of the dark blue coveralls she wore knotted around her waist and a plait peeking out from the silk scarf tied around her head.

"Shh. Someone might hear you," Olivia whispered.

"Relax, Mama and Daddy went out for dinner." Helen walked farther into the room. She took Olivia's wrist, turning it to expose the gash. "There's rubbing alcohol and some bandages under the sink.

Olivia watched her dig inside a cabinet and pull out a small box. She let her younger sister clean her wounds, sucking in a breath when the sting of the alcohol met her skin. "Where did you learn to do this?"

"The mechanics. Car parts can be sharp," said Helen, wrapping a fresh strip of linen around Olivia's hand. "Do I want to know how this happened?"

Olivia met her sister's critical look. "I fell." Not, technically, a lie.

Helen's mouth opened. Olivia watched as a strange emotion changed her sister's features. "Were you with Mr. Lawrence?" Helen asked.

The question caught her off guard. "I—" Olivia said. She and Mr. Lawrence agreed to let her parents believe things were progressing quickly. Neither one of them had thought of the long-term consequences. Sticking close to the truth now seemed the safest choice. "No, I wasn't," she said. Helen's shoulders relaxed. Olivia felt a twinge of guilt. Her sneaking around, if discovered, could not only disrupt her own ability to come and go, but her sister's too.

"Are the rumors true, then? About the engagement?"

Helen's interest confused her. Her sister had never shown any interest in Olivia's relationships. Then again, Olivia had never been this close to settling down before. *Could she be worried that I'll leave her?* She hugged Helen then. "Not officially. I promise, if I'm going anywhere, you'll hear it from me first." Olivia tightened her arms around Helen until at last she felt her sister soften, and return her hug.

CHAPTER 32

Amy-Rose

Amy-Rose paced outside the stables, ignoring the dust clinging to her boots and the hem of her skirt. She replayed her conversation with Tommy a thousand times. Each time, she arrived at no good reason to stay.

Binga Bank was reluctant to support her bid to open a salon, but without a space to call her own, the dream of opening a shop seemed more out of reach than ever. Tommy was convinced that the growing need for businesses of all types out west was too good an opportunity to pass up. And it wasn't like she had clients beyond the Davenports to entice her to stay. She would be starting from the ground up. Why not start somewhere new?

With a shake of her skirts, she entered the stable. It was a mixture of light and shadow. The sounds of many breaths and shuffling created a soothing lull that helped ease her nerves. Dried hay rustled underfoot and she placed her palm on a rough wooden beam for support. The smell of horse, hay, and sweat tickled her nose. "Tommy?"

Tommy stepped out of a stall. His shirtsleeves were pushed up and his skin glistened with a thin sheen of sweat. He smiled broadly when he saw her. His reaction and the way it made her feel reminded Amy-Rose of why she was here. She needed a friend.

"Amy-Rose, grab a brush," he said.

She glanced at the table and took a brush. He led a mare out of a stall and spoke quietly to her. "Amy-Rose here is an expert in all things fashionable. She'll get you up to snuff quick."

"Tommy, I'm used to the two-legged variety of girls in need of hair care." The mare looked her way with large, watery eyes, tail whipping the air.

"I'm sure Bess won't mind. Plus, she is an excellent listener." He patted the horse's neck and gestured to Amy-Rose to follow his lead, with broad strokes. She turned the brush over in her hand. Bess's ears twitched. Her feet shuffled closer to Amy-Rose as if directing her to where she needed the most attention. Soon, the quiet of the barn had worked the magic Tommy always boasted it did. The rhythmic motion of each stroke was like a deep calming breath. The heat of the horse enveloped her, relaxing the tightly coiled muscles of her neck. Even the smell of manure and hay acted on her senses in a way that made it easier to quiet the doubt and disappointment she felt.

Amy-Rose weighed her options. Without the distraction of the house and its occupants, Jessie's loud but well-meaning interjections, and the memories of her mother tugging at her heart, she'd made her decision. She cleared her throat. "I thought about your offer."

Tommy stepped closer, slowly, as if a sudden move might startle her.

Amy-Rose tucked her hands behind her back. "I'd like to go to California. With you."

"Truly?" he asked, his disbelief clear.

"Yes."

Tommy whooped, throwing his hat into the air.

Amy-Rose laughed to cover her relief. Then genuinely laughed when he raced to her and lifted her off her feet. He spun her around. She stretched her arms wide and enjoyed the feeling of weightlessness that filled her.

"I'm so glad," he said, setting her down again.

Amy-Rose tried to hold on to his words as he spoke about the opportunities out west. There were beaches and sunsets, new homes and work. It was a place they could start fresh. She latched on to his ideas like a lifesaver. His optimism bubbled over and fed the relief rising in her. *This is the right decision.* She knew that she was destined to open a salon of her own, run a business dedicated to Black beauty in a way that brought her joy and used her skills. She wanted that for herself.

"Will you be ready? The train leaves tomorrow night."

His question hung in the air, simple, yet heavy. It would be short notice. And Mrs. Davenport would be sad to see her go so suddenly, but Tommy was right: They needed a fresh start.

"Yes, but I should go pack."

Tommy walked her to the servants' entrance of the manor. He talked the whole way, most of it lost to the wind.

Once inside, Amy-Rose hurried up to her third-floor room, cataloguing everything in her path like it was the last time she'd see it. Perhaps it was. Before long, the dresser drawers hung empty, their contents draped across the narrow bed. Simple sensible dresses mixed with the higher quality cast-offs of the Davenport girls. Rough-spun cotton and silk. Only so many could fit in her mother's suitcase. She wished for the full-length mirrors the girls had in their rooms. She did her best with the small round one on her nightstand.

In the end, she decided on the nicer dresses. She was going to be a hairdresser and salon owner. It was time she dressed like the successful businesswoman she wanted to become. They would be the only piece of this life she would take with her, aside from the memories.

Amy-Rose carefully wrapped her mother's belongings in old newspaper and sat on the suitcase to latch it closed. The bed creaked under her weight. She let her head fall into her hands. She knew she couldn't stay at Freeport forever, but a small part of her still felt like leaving with Tommy was wrong. That it was running away.

There was a knock on her door.

"Jessie, I don't want any more scones," she said, rubbing her temples.

"That's good," John said from the doorway. "I don't have any."

"What are you doing here?" Amy-Rose's voice sounded small and hoarse, even to her own ears.

"Can we talk?" He stood in the doorway, waiting. He was out of breath. The top button of his shirt was undone and his hair, normally slicked back into place, was starting to stick out at the temples.

"This is my room." She looked around the space, imagining what it must look like. The odd mix of old and new garments, an overstuffed suitcase and her mother's letters. She wanted him out. Needed him out.

John's face fell. "I'm sorry." He drew back, and she took an unthinking step forward. She could tell it gave him pause. From the hallway, he said, "What I did at the party was unacceptable. I never should have treated you—or let others—treat you that way. My mother and I had just had a row about how I spend my time. She accused me of being distracted and I guess—"

"That doesn't make what you did okay."

"I know. Can I come in?"

She sighed and sat down on the bed, clearing the doorway. She pulled her mother's letters, bound by a white ribbon, close for comfort.

He stepped deeper into the room, hunching under the angled ceiling. She watched his eyes scan the room: the suitcase, emptied closet, the small bundle cradled in her arms. "You're going somewhere."

Amy-Rose placed the letters on the bed, stood, and picked up the dresses she planned to leave behind. "Yes, I'm leaving for California." She faced him and fought the urge to smooth down the front of her dress.

John passed his hands over his face. "California?"

Her eyes flitted to his. This was happening all out of order. She was supposed to tell Mr. and Mrs. Davenport first. They didn't need her. They kept her on out of generosity and fondness for her mother. Surely they wouldn't have objected to her moving on, when they'd done the same to start their own lives here. Amy-Rose plucked at a loose thread in a dress she held and tried to quell the emotions tumbling through her. She hadn't exactly come up with a plan to tell the girls. Or John. A part of her thought she wouldn't have to.

"Amy-Rose?"

She pulled Tommy's reason from a thousand things she could say. "I need a fresh start, and California seems a place as good as any to do it."

"You can't throw everything away to move halfway across the country."

"You can't throw away what you don't have," she shouted, shocking even herself. She took a breath and her vision blurred. She had gone a whole two days without crying over Mr. Spencer's barbershop. She had packed away those painful, awful feelings into something smaller and more manageable. "The salon space was leased to another." She watched his eyes shutter closed and felt her heart break, not only for the store, but also for what had been growing between them. *He understands the depth of this blow,* she thought. He looked at her now, silent. And if there seemed to be some other, puzzling emotion alight in his eyes, she couldn't afford to wonder about it. "I don't have a reason to stay," she said. "It's time to move on, start fresh, in a new town where I won't be known as *the maid*." Tommy's own reason for leaving had never been so clear.

John took a breath. "What if—what if that space wasn't your only option?"

"I'd say you're grasping at straws. I've combed downtown looking for a new spot I can afford. It doesn't exist."

His eyes sparkled—that puzzling look returned to his face. "But it does." John's face split into a boyish grin. He pulled a bundle of papers from inside his jacket.

Amy-Rose took them. "What is this?" Her breath hitched. The papers rustled loudly as she unfolded them, her eyes still on John.

"Read it."

She did. She tried. Tears quickly obscured the text after she saw the deed to a salon, and her name on the first page. "I don't understand."

"Greenie works at Binga's," John said. The nickname made Amy-Rose's stomach turn. She recognized it as the name of John's friend who'd played a hand in her public misstep. John continued, "He's sorry too. He mentioned you had your heart set on Mr. Spencer's old space and that the barber had leased his store to someone else." His voice softened. "I know how much you wanted it."

"You knew . . . ?" She trailed off. Read the deed again.

"Don't go. You're not *the maid* and . . . just stay."

Amy-Rose couldn't believe her ears. "Why?" she asked.

"Because I can't handle you not being here," he said, his eyes pained, his steady gaze holding her own.

He began to pace her room, which was so small, he appeared to be turning in a tight circle, neck bent. She considered his face, and moved toward him until she was close enough to touch him. He stood very still, except for the rapid rise and fall of his chest, his breaths just as shallow as hers. She placed a hand on his chest. Beneath her palm, his heart raced.

It would not undo her embarrassment at the party. But he'd done this for her. Her dream. And because he knew what that store meant to her. Amy-Rose shook her head in disbelief. "Where did you find—where did you get this?" She couldn't believe her eyes. The property was much larger than Mr. Spencer's place. And bought, not leased. *It must cost a fortune.* She brought a shaking hand to her forehead. Her breaths were shallow and uneven.

"This is too much." Amy-Rose folded the papers up and held them out to John. He gently pushed her hand back. She shook her head. "I can't accept it."

John's dimple appeared. "You can, Amy-Rose. All it needs is your signature."

Amy-Rose blinked her vision clear and reread the documents. Her dream was in her hand. And John had given it to her. A giggle escaped her lips. She could hardly keep up with the surge and swirl of emotions. She was overwhelmed. Overjoyed. In John's eyes, she saw her reason to stay. Amy-Rose kissed him, and let all the heartache melt away.

CHAPTER 33

Helen

The crisp white napkins formed a bridge over the saucer and plate, framed by meticulously polished silverware. The mahogany table beneath the embroidered tablecloth was set for six guests and five courses. Helen had polished the silverware herself. Arranged the flower centerpiece and planned the menu.

I did this.

Helen stared at the hours of hard work she'd put into meeting Mrs. Milford's exact standards. She'd prepared tonight's evening down to the minutest detail.

Penance, she thought, for lusting after her sister's suitor.

But really this table, this night, was for her parents. And it was far from the last hoop she would need to jump through to earn back their confidence. They worried about her the way they used to worry about Olivia, as if being unmarried, despite doing something she loved, was the worst of all possible futures for her.

Helen only hoped she could convince them just enough to allow her to return to afternoons free of her etiquette lessons.

She'd grown tired of adjusting the progress the other mechanics made on the automobile at odds hours of the day and night. It frustrated her that she wasn't allowed to work where she pleased, doing something that actually interested her. The surface of the sideboard rattled under her fist.

"Has the table offended you?"

Helen jumped.

Jacob Lawrence stood in the doorway. He was beautiful. So beautiful it made her breath catch. They drank each other in under the dim lighting. She didn't understand why he had this effect on her. She steadied her thoughts. "Offend me? No. The idea that this is how I'm expected to spend my time offends me."

Mr. Lawrence reviewed her work. He removed his hands from his pockets and crossed his arms. Helen tried not to notice the way the fabric of his jacket rippled with the motion, and the way his mouth puckered in thought. Each breath she took to steady herself filled her head with the scent of his aftershave, which left her feeling lighter than the sips of sherry she sometimes snuck at dinner.

"I don't know," he said. "I quite like it."

"I don't intend to make it a habit," she said.

"Maybe just a backup plan?" he offered. She scowled at him, and he smiled. "Only teasing." He placed a hand on her elbow and they walked out of the room, a few feet away from the dining room entrance. He shielded her from her family as the group made their way from the sitting room to the table. Mrs. Davenport's exclamations of surprise only served to annoy Helen more. *How could this be more important than learning the family business?*

"It wasn't at all amusing," Helen said to him. She rolled her shoulders. Her elbow escaped his touch and left her chilled. "Where are we going? We should head back in."

"Helen, wait." Mr. Lawrence looked at her with one of his rare expressions of doubt. "I'm not sure how much longer I can pretend that there isn't something happening between us." He brushed down the neatly trimmed hairs of his mustache.

Helen found herself thinking about his lips. She quickly shook her head. "Jacob, you said yourself, you gave Olivia your word. And she is my sister."

"And not the woman I want to be with," he countered. "I want to be with you."

Helen's ears rang with his confession. Her mouth dried, all her words lost in the whirl of her feelings, too great and awful for her to contain. She licked her lips before answering, her voice barely above a whisper. "I have feelings for you too." She watched as his face brightened; the sheer joy of it broke her heart. "But even though we aren't as close anymore, I won't do this to Olivia." She watched silently as her words sank in. The pain was worse than what she felt moments ago. At least she could spare her sister feeling this too. Olivia would have the chance to live out her life the way she'd dreamed, with a devoted husband at her side. If that's what her sister wanted. Helen couldn't tell anymore. One moment Olivia was skulking around at night, keeping mysterious company, the next she was promising Helen she'd be the first to know when her engagement to Mr. Lawrence was official.

Helen forced herself to ignore his whispered protests. There was nothing either one of them could do. Well, there was some-thing Mr. Lawrence could do—he could break his attachment to her sister. Perhaps call it a mutual uncoupling to minimize the damage Helen feared they could not avoid. Of course, she wanted happiness for Mr. Lawrence too. Olivia could make him happy.

She lifted her hand, her fingers not quite touching his arm. "I won't destroy her chance at happiness. Please, if you care about me, do this. Remember Olivia. Forget about me," she said, her voice steady.

"I could never."

His words felt like a challenge, the first Helen had no desire to meet head-on.

Helen eased the door to the library open to find a single lamp on. John sat in the corner. The book in his hand hung from his fingertips as he stared into the empty fireplace.

"I didn't think anyone was in here," she said.

The book fell to the floor with a thud. John straightened. "I wasn't ready to go to bed."

As Helen drew near, she noticed her brother looked unusually tired. He was almost as quiet at dinner as she and Mr. Lawrence were. Luckily, their mother carried the conversation well enough for them all.

"No plans to head to the garage?"

Helen shook her head. The late nights were starting to catch up with her. "I'd rather stay here. I love this room. This is where I come to hide during social functions," she said. She ran her hand along the shelves, taking in the mix of leather-bound books and small crafts her father picked up from street vendors. His favorite was the little wooden horse whittled by a freed enslaved person he had known, whose eyes were clouded by cataracts, but whose fingers were agile enough to produce a mini masterpiece. Helen plucked the piece up and sat in the chair opposite her brother. "People don't think to look for me here."

"Oh, on the contrary," he said with a wry smile. "It's not as big a secret as you think. Sometimes your presence is so unpleasant, we leave you to your books." He grinned when she delivered a half-hearted kick. "I needed somewhere to think."

Helen leaned forward on her elbow, chin on her fist. "Want to tell me what's on your mind? Like how a certain conversation with Daddy went?" She welcomed any distraction from the raging thoughts in her head and she desperately needed to know what progress was made.

John adjusted himself in the chair. He opened his mouth, then closed it.

She didn't dare hope. "John? Did you and Daddy talk about the automobile manufacturing?"

His face fell. The silence stretched so long between them, Helen didn't think he would answer. When he finally spoke, his voice was hoarse and defeated. "The lunch with the board members went well . . ."

"But?"

"But he's still not convinced."

"Ugh!" She wasn't surprised. She had hoped against her better judgment.

John tugged on her ear. "Don't worry. We'll keep trying." Though he still looked sad.

"I know." Helen slumped back, then sat up. "Wait, what *else* were you thinking about?"

Her brother sighed. "Amy-Rose was going to move to California."

"What?" This was news to Helen. Amy-Rose had been a part of Helen's life for longer than she could remember.

John nodded. "She wants to open a business, a salon, and she believes that getting far from here would be her best shot."

"That doesn't sound like her." Helen replayed her last interactions with Amy-Rose in her head. *Has she been unhappy and I've been too self-absorbed to notice?* As if he read the question on her face, John spoke.

"I think I'm falling for her, Helen. And I almost lost her." Her brother sighed and Helen thought she had never heard such a lonely sound. "At the party, I shunned her in front of my friends . . . Even if she felt then a fraction of what I felt when she told me she was moving—"

"John! How could you?"

"I know." He wiped his face with his hands.

"It'll take a lot for her to get over a slight like that. She must have felt awful . . ." Helen knew it. The other girls her age— The nausea and dizziness that came with the humiliation they waged. She'd decided long ago to stop trying to fit in.

"It was a betrayal. I know that," he said, "but I think we're on our way past it."

She narrowed her eyes at her brother. "She's forgiven you? How did you manage that? And don't say your *charming* personality. I don't think you have one."

He flashed her an exaggerated smile, which made her roll her eyes. His expression sobered and he said, "I don't think I'm forgiven yet. She plans to open her own salon here in the city. I'll have time to make it up to her and convince Daddy to hand over more business responsibilities to me. I'm not sure how Mama and Daddy will take our relationship, but the fact that Amy-Rose is staying gives me a chance."

Helen's gaze traveled to the dormant firebox. "Mama and Daddy you can work with. If they accept her, everyone else will fall in line. Life is too short and the choice too important." She thought of what Mrs. Milford had told her—how you should hold on to your happiness, however long you have it. *Even if it's a few short hours in a museum where no one knows who you are.*

"Thanks, Helen," he whispered. Minutes passed. The clock on the mantel was the only sound in the room. "Do you plan to tell me what's on your mind? I shared, so can you."

Helen covered her face with her hands. Her encounter with Jacob Lawrence had left her feeling too raw. The last thing she wanted was to relive it. Her nerves were on edge from dinner and her stomach bubbled with hunger as she thought about all the carefully planned courses she'd ordered and barely tasted. John didn't give up. He asked questions, the next more ridiculous than the last. "Have you decided to join a traveling troupe as a tight-rope walker?" He nudged her with his foot and she slouched in her chair like a rag doll.

"Ugh, I'll tell you, but you can't interrupt me or say anything until I say so." Helen narrowed her eyes at her brother. He sat straighter in his chair and nodded. His serious expression made her more nervous. *This is John.* Helen knew she could tell her brother anything. So, she did. Every detail and confused feeling, as she stared into the fire.

"Now I feel awful, and I know it's my fault," she said when she came to the end of her story, because what it felt like was the end of things with Jacob Lawrence.

John had done as promised. He'd listened without stepping in or asking questions. When Helen was finished, she felt more exhausted than ever. She remained composed. The threat of tears, though, was not far away. "Okay, you can speak now." She braced herself for a scolding that would support the guilt and unhappiness she felt.

It didn't come. Instead, her brother asked, "Do you believe what he said? That he might love you?"

Helen didn't doubt it for a moment. "Yes."

"Then he and Livy shouldn't get married. It'd be a sham, a loveless future for them both. And then what? We all live miserably ever after? You'll end up avoiding each other to escape heartache and you'll lose love *and* your sister. You will tell her, right?" John got up and squeezed himself into the seat beside her. His words needled her. He was right. She hated when he was right, especially now that he was smothering her.

Her hip began to ache under his weight. He sat and waited for her answer as if he wasn't planning to move until he got it.

"I will," she said, flustered.

John kissed the top of her head, rubbed her shoulders, and left Helen staring into the cold firebox, more confused than ever.

CHAPTER 34

The air smelled like fresh cut grass. It soothed Ruby's frayed nerves as she scanned her surroundings. She held her parasol higher against the midday sun and stood near the copse of trees by the lake, where she and Harrison Barton shared a kiss that nearly did her in. Her pulse quickened at the memory. With Olivia's help, he had received her note in time to meet her here. She hoped the spot would remind him of how happy they'd both been that afternoon.

As far as her parents knew, she and Mr. Barton would continue their courtship until John was secured. What her parents didn't know was that there would be no her and John.

A bead of sweat ran down Ruby's back. A sudden breeze brought much needed relief and the woodsy scent of Mr. Barton's cologne. She turned, and the sight of him made her ache. The dappled light through the leaves sent sunlight dancing across his face.

"Miss Tremaine," he said politely.

Ruby swallowed and straightened her spine. *If he didn't want to see you, he would not have come*, she told herself. "Thank you for meeting me." She didn't know where to start. Her mouth was so dry. This may be her one chance to convince Harrison Barton that her feelings were true. When she saw his eyes dart to the copse of trees, and the spark of recognition, she knew she'd made the right choice. He needed to hear it all as much as she needed to say it.

"Why are we here, Ruby?" he asked, his voice strained.

"I want to apologize. For everything."

He shook his head. "You already did. This"—he gestured toward the trees—"wasn't necessary." He took a step back.

"I haven't stopped thinking about you, Harrison," she blurted.

He paused and relief flooded every inch of her. Her fingertips tingled. Ruby licked her lips. She met his hazel eyes with determination, and all the feelings she couldn't put into words.

"I trusted you."

"I know," she said. "I can't change why I did what I did, but I will never regret meeting you and . . . knowing you. You are one of the best people I have ever met." Ruby cleared her throat. She stood firm as he studied her face. Finally, she asked the question she feared most: "Will you give me another chance?"

He closed his eyes as hers filled with tears. "Yes."

Ruby's knees gave way and she sat hard in the grass. He settled next to her, drawing her to him. She rested her head on his chest, hearing his heartbeat. Her fear of rejection had occupied a space so great that the next breath shuddered. They held on to each other. Mr. Barton rubbed small circles in the middle of her back. Ruby wasn't sure how long they stayed like this. Long enough for her neck to ache and her feet to fall asleep in her heeled boots. Gently, he created space between them. Ruby brushed away the salt and moisture from her cheeks.

He held out his handkerchief to her. "And what about your parents?"

"They'll come around. They just want me to be happy," she said quickly, not ready for anything to puncture this bliss. *I'll tell Mother the full truth today*, she thought. *No John. Only Harrison. There's plenty of time.*

He hesitated a fraction, then stood, pulling her to her feet. He searched her eyes. And then he kissed her, cool and gentle, and then firmer, deeper. The tension that had gripped Ruby released, pushing her on to her toes and closing the gap between them. His arms went around her. She tasted the salt of her tears and the sweetness that was Harrison Barton and the hope she dared to hold on to.

Ruby held fast to the post in the dressing room, trying not to exhale as the attendant laced up the corset. She needed every breath if she was going to survive a dress fitting with her mother. What had suddenly loosened her mother's grasp on the family purse strings was a mystery. It left Ruby uneasy. But finding the answer was low on her current list of priorities. Ruby was hours into her second chance with Mr. Barton and didn't plan on building this one on a lie too. *At least not for long.*

From the other side of the curtain, Mrs. Tremaine talked, presumably to Mrs. Davenport but mostly to herself, about Ruby's father and the upcoming campaign event to be hosted by the

Davenports themselves. They'd invited the Chicago elite as well as prominent Black politicians from Springfield to New York. Some of her words were lost in the thick fabric that divided the anteroom from the smaller dressing area where the dressmaker now pulled a rather heavy silk over Ruby's head.

They were at Madame Chérie's, next door to the milliner's shop. No one knew the dressmaker's real name, but she was the best on this side of Lake Michigan. She had an eye for pattern and color like no other. And after she was turned out of every factory job she'd tried for, she, like many recently enslaved, began working out of a small apartment, financed by odd jobs until the work could support her. Now ladies all over Illinois, northern Indiana, and southern Wisconsin sought the deft fingers of the Black dressmaker. She worked her magic over Ruby now, gathering the fabric, draping and pinning it in place. Satisfied that everything was where it should be, she threw back the curtain to reveal Mrs. Tremaine on a settee between Olivia and Mrs. Davenport.

Mrs. Tremaine gasped. She pressed a hand to each of her cheeks.

Ruby's shoulders relaxed. She'd tried on half a dozen dresses. Her feet ached from standing in one spot for hours and her stomach roared with hunger. Perhaps a custom-made original would please her mother.

"Now, this is just the general shape I was thinking of," Madame Chérie said, readjusting the fabric pinned at Ruby's shoulder. "What do you think?"

"She is a vision," Mrs. Tremaine said. She stood and leaned in close, intending only Ruby to hear. "John won't be able to take his eyes off you."

Ruby ignored this, focusing instead on the memory of Mr. Barton's arms around her, the feel of his hands on her back. The promise of being able to do this openly was worth an uncomfortable conversation with her mother. *Maybe I should tell Papa first?*

Ruby glanced at Olivia. Her best friend stared at her wide-eyed, as if she knew exactly where Ruby's thoughts had wandered.

Ruby had always wanted a big family. She'd spent much of her childhood surrounded by the Davenport siblings, but had always returned home to her parents in their large home and quiet corridors. Marrying John would have more than doubled her family *and* kept all the people she loved close. Ruby had dreaded confessing to Olivia that she no longer had feelings for John, and that they could never be sisters. The two friends had shared a carriage from the park to the shop and Olivia agreed—Ruby's parents should be told as soon as possible. "They'll be thrilled to see you so happy," she'd said. "Just as I am. And you and I—we will always be family."

We will always be family. Those were Olivia's words.

The only thing holding Ruby back was the guilt of disappointing her parents. She took deep, calming breaths. She was another step closer to the life she wanted.

Olivia stood now and came to her side. "You look beautiful, Ruby." She rubbed the silk between her fingers, a genuine smile on her lips, a speaking look in her eyes.

Ruby slitted her gaze at Olivia. Her skin prickled with a panicked sweat. There were too many people in this room. She couldn't tell her mother here. Or maybe she should. Certainly her mother wouldn't start a scene in Madame's shop. Oh, she really did want to get this over with.

"There's something missing," Mrs. Tremaine said. Her mother's head was tilted to the side, eyes narrowed and lips pursed.

"Oh, I don't know," Mrs. Davenport said. "I agree with Olivia. Once it's finished, it'll be beautiful."

The attendant gave a sigh. Madame Chérie hid her annoyance better. They'd been here all afternoon. Each dress had some minor fault—it was the wrong color or the cut was off.

"Mother, no one will be paying any attention to me," she said. "This is a fundraiser. People will be there to hear what Papa has to say, his plans. Not to see what I'm wearing."

Mrs. Tremaine hmphed. "There will be reporters from *The Defender* and the *Tribune*. Who may want a photo of the candidate and his family and any news we may have to share." She gave Ruby a meaningful look. "We must look as successful and capable as we are."

Ruby picked up her skirts and stepped off the dais. "I'm going to see if the red dress we saw on the way in is my size."

"I hope not the one with the empire waist," her mother said. "Those are better suited for girls with narrower hips." Ruby's grip on the dress's skirt tightened. Mrs. Tremaine followed her, just as Ruby knew she would. She signaled for Olivia to stay behind. At the front of the shop, away from the others, Ruby steeled herself to tell her mother the full truth.

"Mother, I want to talk about John." Her mother seemed to perk up at the sound of his name. *Steady.* "John and I have known each other for so long. We went on a few outings before he left for school—"

"Yes, dear, I know." Mrs. Tremaine sniffed at the red dress. "I must say, he's been hot and cold, but grew much more attentive after Barton's interest."

"Actually, this is about him too." This is it. Ruby took a breath. "Harrison Barton and I have grown close. It wasn't part of my plan, I know—"

"Ruby, you are a very pretty and charming young lady." Her mother tugged at the bodice of the dress. "You'll just have to let Mr. Barton down gently. I'm sure he'll find a girl to settle down with. Girls like you deserve the best. Your father and I won't have it any other way." Ruby's feelings for Harrison Barton sat on her tongue, which had turned to dry rope in her mouth. Her parents *wouldn't have it*?

Panic rose in her chest. Surely they knew how much happier she had been with Mr. Barton. Olivia had called it obvious in the way they looked at each other. Ruby stared at her mother in shock. What would become of her if she refused to marry John? Her stomach clenched. It seemed clear by this excursion they no longer needed the influx of capital from the Davenports' business to fund the campaign. But the Davenport name had wider recognition than the Barton one. The crest was emblazoned on luxury carriages across the city and country. The Davenports moved in and out of many different social circles and wielded more influence bought by the company's success. The women at her parents' party so many weeks ago were right. Her father *would* need the white vote to win.

Mrs. Tremaine pouted at the red dress on the mannequin. "Try it on. I'm curious."

Ruby watched her mother walk away and numbly reached for the dress, shame settling beneath the stone hanging around her neck. She touched it then, and remembered how lost she had felt without it. Maybe her instincts had been right. This place—it wasn't the right time.

Later, I'll tell Mother and Papa together. Tonight.

Ruby threw the red dress over her arm and made her way back to the dressing room.

CHAPTER 35

Olivia

Thirty minutes after retiring to her room, Olivia picked up her shoes and tiptoed down the servants' stairs. The house creaked restlessly as she made her way through the house. She had claimed a headache again before dinner and silently paced around her room, listening to the clock ticking above the mantel of her fireplace until it was time. She'd reread the letter Hetty delivered to her that morning from Washington DeWight. She'd pressed it to her chest and tried to quell the lightning crackling over her nerves. It smelled of his cologne and tobacco and fresh ink. She imagined him writing it in a crowded corner of the café.

After that, it was easy to pretend to be ill. All she could think of was how she was going to get away.

As she gathered her belongings to leave the sitting room that joined her room with Helen's, her sister walked in. Olivia took in Helen's grease-smudged face and sighed. "If Daddy finds you, Mrs. Milford will be the least of your problems."

"You're one to talk," Helen teased, pulling the bandanna from around her head. "Why are you always heading into town with the staff and returning with no packages?" Olivia crossed her arms over her chest. "Fine, don't tell me. I just need you to keep this"— Helen gestured to her clothes—"to yourself. Just until after John meets with Daddy again to talk about our plans to manufacture horseless carriages of our own."

The desire to obey their family and to be part of something bigger than themselves was the unlikely foundation of this truce between sisters.

Olivia's thoughts turned to the women who had shared their lives with her. They recounted the harsh working conditions of the sweatshops and the paltry pay they received. Others shared news from the Southern states. They arrived on trains by the dozens each day, traumatized, hungry, and looking to start fresh.

She couldn't help thinking of how her father must have looked decades ago still healing from the wounds on his back and the horrors of the plantation. He had a skill, a keen eye, a desire to work. A determination to not only survive, but to thrive. Not until she saw the faces of the migrants, witnessed their fear and confusion for herself, did she realize the sheer amount of hardship he had had to overcome once he'd made it here. Her heart ached for a young William Davenport.

She wished she could express all of this to Helen. Keeping her work secret weighed on her, but it was safest this way. She reminded herself that she wouldn't have to hide it forever. And neither should Helen.

"Fine," Olivia said now, mirroring Helen's earlier tone. "I won't tell anyone you're working on John's automobile. For now. But the two of you better come up with a better way. I can help. If you'll let me."

Helen threw her arms around Olivia's neck. "Thanks, Livy." She held her sister tight.

"You smell," Olivia said. Helen held her tighter and laughed.

The warmth of that hug still clung to Olivia as she stepped off the streetcar at the busy intersection to meet Washington DeWight.

She spotted him immediately. His face was turned up toward the setting sun, his hat hanging precariously on his head. The restaurant behind him was a flurry of activity. Tables spilled out onto the sidewalk, filled with diners. The smell was intoxicating. Her stomach reminded her of the skipped meal that made this rendezvous possible. She removed her hand from her angry abdomen as she approached, and tapped his shoulder.

"You made it." His face broke out in a grin. The sight of it made her heart flutter in her chest.

"I did," she said, smiling.

He offered his hand. "Hungry?"

"Starved." His fingers closed around hers and the electricity that had thrummed in her all day arced.

He led her down a winding path between the outdoor tables and into the hole-in-the-wall restaurant, where every square inch seemed to be occupied. Behind the counter, she saw the cook waving a spatula like a conductor before an orchestra. The sound of a dozen voices pressed in on either side of them. The dining room was alive. It lacked all the decorum and pageantry she was used to. People sat with elbows on the table, grabbed from one another's plates, and spoke too loud so as to be heard over each other. It was intimate in its chaos. And she loved it.

"Is something wrong, Washington?" she asked when he stopped abruptly. All the seats around them were filled and there was no space at the counter. He still held her hand. His felt like a torch in hers, radiating heat that traveled up her arm.

Mr. DeWight lowered his voice to match hers. "They lost each other in 1906, during the riots in Atlanta." She followed his gaze to a couple in the corner. Their heads tilted close to each other. The look they exchanged made her blush for witnessing it. "A chance meeting at the Loop near Wabash brought them back together. You missed the ceremony, simple vows, but now's the time to celebrate." Olivia saw her favorite side of Washington DeWight: hopeful.

"A happy ending," she said. "My father is still searching for his brother. It's hard to believe that he's still out there after so much time." She thought of the letters and the meetings, dead-end leads and all the disappointments. "They were lucky enough not to be separated as children. It wasn't until they escaped the plantation that they lost each other. He has people following rumors of my uncle's last known location, men who fit his description. We pray for his return. With each year, though, it seems less likely."

Mr. DeWight drew circles in her palm with his thumb. "They are proof that it can happen. Have faith." His gaze lingered on the couple a moment longer, then he tugged her hand for them to move on. Olivia took one last look, hoping he was right.

They wound around the boisterous kitchen, down a thin hall, and finally up a narrow set of steps. A warm breeze cleared the savory and sweet aroma that had filled her head. Olivia stared in wonder once they made it to the roof. All of Chicago was laid out before them. The sun, setting in the distance, painted everything in warm, broad strokes. A small round table, set for two. A cluster of candles served as a centerpiece. Music traveled on the breeze and a sun-bleached couch created a cozy nook in the corner.

"It's beautiful," she said.

He came up beside her and placed a hand on her back. Instinctively, she fell into step with the music. He trapped one of her hands between his chest and his free hand. Olivia pressed her cheek to his. "Someone's been practicing," she said.

"Turns out I just needed the right partner." His voice sent shivers down her body. Olivia was acutely aware of the weight of his hand, the gentle pressure a little lower than decent. The heady scent of him muddled her thoughts.

The rooftop door swung open then and two servers came into view carrying steaming dishes. "Ya'll better be careful of that door. It only opens one way," said the taller of the two. He was a lanky man with a long, lazy stride. He murmured instructions to the other man. The taller dipped his head as he passed Olivia, still tucked close to Mr. DeWight. He kicked a small wooden wedge on the floor under the frame of the door so that the same sliver of space she noticed on the way up separated the two of them from the rest of the world.

Olivia and Mr. DeWight walked to the edge of the rooftop and watched the last of the sun's light disappear between the buildings. The setting sun seemed to melt like an amber flame behind the city. "It truly is beautiful," she said. She looked at him. "I don't think I slept a wink the night before or after the rally." Her voice became firm. "It felt right being there, like I was exactly where I was meant to be, even though I had no idea what I was doing. It wasn't until we had to run for our lives that this thing that's been slowly dawning on me made sense. It was love. For this city. For—" She cleared her throat. "For the me I am when—I'm with you."

Twilight had fallen around them, but Washington DeWight's eyes sparkled in the candlelight. "Love for just the city and yourself, huh?" His lip twitched.

Olivia laughed. "I mean, there is this relentless lawyer I'm starting to grow fond of."

"I see," he said. He swept her up close and held her there, searching her face. She freed her hand and gently ran her fingers across his brows, his high rounded cheekbones. She gasped when he laughed to reveal bright, white teeth. The knot in his throat bobbed as her touch dipped and they both shivered. She wanted to hook her fingers into his collar and pull his lips to hers, but he released her. Her stomach protested her hunger loud enough for both of them to hear.

"Let's eat before it gets cold," he said, a laugh in his voice.

They sat at the table and tucked into the thick soup and hard-dough bread. Washington recounted stories of his activist up-bringing. Raised by a teacher and a lawyer, he was forever full of questions and a yearning for answers. After, they danced and lay on the couch, where he pointed out the stars, explaining how to find your way by the constellations. She felt warm and safe tucked beside him. He'd removed his jacket and placed it over them to keep their body heat close. Olivia was sure that she produced enough to chase the chill out of a banquet hall. Mr. DeWight's legs tangled with hers and she cuddled in tight.

"Will you be at the suffrage meeting next week?" she asked. Olivia struggled to keep her mind from wandering as Washington traced lazy circles on her arms, leaving gooseflesh in his wake.

He stilled. Olivia felt cold the first time all day.

"We'll be heading to Philadelphia in a few days, then on to the Capitol."

Olivia pushed up onto her elbows. "What? When were you planning to tell me?"

"Tonight." His disarming smile made an appearance. "You can always come with us."

Olivia's next words evaporated. *Go with him?* No, not with him. Them. "You're *all* moving on?" *What about Chicago?*

"We'll come back," he said.

Her stomach felt like a lead weight. She'd never been outside the city. Never been out from under the sharp eye of her mother or her friends. Oh, but the energy that fueled her when she helped organize such trips for others and the thought of marching in the nation's capital! It filled her with a longing she couldn't voice. And to do with Washington DeWight at her side.

She could do it.

I can find a way. She could room with another female activist.

Mr. DeWight's smug grin grew. He'd read her as easily as she had the primer set out by her first tutors.

"I'll have to think about it," she said with as much insouciance as she could muster. "And you really should have told me sooner."

"I should have, yes. I was worried you'd say no."

"I still haven't said yes." But warmth spread through her then. Her mind raced with all the tasks that would need completing. Plans whirled in her mind. Olivia settled her head back on his chest and imagined how she'd manage lodging, among other things.

"Olivia," he said into her hair.

"Hmm."

"Look at me."

She tilted her face up, the to-do list in her mind multiplying.

"Try not to overthink it," he said. And then he kissed her.

Olivia arrived back at Freeport Manor without incident atop a borrowed horse. She could still feel Mr. DeWight's arms around her as she sat, sidesaddle across his lap. She held her breath until her bedroom door closed shut, listening to the house.

"Where have you been?"

Olivia nearly screamed into the night. Or was it morning now? She whipped around to see Helen. Sitting at her vanity.

"What are you doing here?" Olivia whispered. Helen's constant attention was setting her on edge, but better her sister than either of their parents. Her eyes burned and her hip and neck ached from the awkward way she'd fallen asleep against Mr. DeWight. *It was worth it*, she thought, remembering the way his body felt against hers. She touched her lips, swollen and tender. She didn't know two people could kiss for so long and never get tired of it. After they discovered the wedge had dislodged, they had no choice but to return to the couch and wait for rescue by the morning shift. Olivia blushed at how they'd passed the time before falling asleep in each other's arms.

Helen narrowed her eyes. "I got up for a glass of milk and saw your empty bed *after* you claimed to be ill. Are you avoiding my question?"

"No!" Olivia whispered back. She grabbed Helen's hand and

dragged her sister to their shared sitting room. Helen wrenched her arm away and sat on the chair with a huff. Her book was open and candles were lit. She must have been waiting for Olivia to return. Helen had that stubborn set to her jaw that warned she would not leave until Olivia indulged her. "I went to the South Side. To see someone." Olivia watched Helen frown. "Why were you in my room?"

"I'll tell you when you tell me who you met. And don't say Ruby. She was here looking for you too."

Drat! There would be no easy way out of this conversation. Olivia sighed and sat down. She started from the beginning: the first meeting she stumbled into, the community's efforts to march, mobilize, and educate. She talked about Washington DeWight, the passionate lawyer who challenged her and expected more from her than what she'd been taught. Olivia felt her pulse quicken when she glossed over the details of their most recent night together. Helen's eyebrows still nearly arced to her hairline.

"I never would have guessed you were a secret rabble-rouser romantic." Helen giggled.

"We're activists, Helen."

Her sister grew serious. Her gaze was steady as she lifted her chin. "I didn't think you had it in you."

Olivia glanced at the closed door behind her. She hadn't even begun to iron out the details of her departure yet. The last thing she needed was to be found out before she'd even had the chance to decide she was truly going.

"Do you love him?" Helen asked.

The question made Olivia pause. She enjoyed being around Mr. DeWight. She wanted desperately to travel with his group to the capital to protest, to march, anything except talk about needlepoint or parties. So much of her future was predetermined, she had never allowed herself to think about the many ways it could be different. Before now, before him, there was no sense in wondering what could be.

Does he feel the same way? He certainly took every opportunity to challenge her, pushed her to evaluate her privilege, see her responsibilities. But he also appreciated the strength and determination she valued in herself. And he most definitely kissed her as though he did.

"You do love him!" Helen grasped her wrist with both hands. "You should see your face right now." Her sister grew wistful. "You look just like Mama thinking about Daddy when he's away. Mopey and happy at the same time." Helen's expression became serious. "Olivia—what are you going to do?"

"I don't know," Olivia said. A sudden wave of nausea hit her. "Everyone expects me to marry Jacob Lawrence. Or someone just like him."

Helen turned Olivia toward her, their legs crossed and knees touching like they used to when they were younger, only she remembered there being a lot more room on the couch. "I'll take care of it," Helen said. She squeezed her sister's hands. "You've always done the right thing. If you have to commit to marriage before the end of summer, you deserve to see what's out there in the meantime. And have a little fun too."

Olivia gasped. "Helen!" Again, her eyes darted to the door.

Helen shrugged. "Think of it as my way of saying sorry for leaving you to weather the brunt of the matchmaking pressure."

"You're here now, and it's hardly your fault."

"Ugh, just let me do this," said Helen, smacking Olivia's arm with a pillow.

"You don't have to make up for it. I've enjoyed it." Then Olivia thought of all the chores and outings she was saddled with when Helen failed to show. "Mostly," she added.

More than anything, Olivia had just missed her sister. It was only a matter of time before she did marry and had to leave this house and her sister behind. Her future was as uncertain as Helen's. There was no telling when or where the Davenports' youngest would find love and where it would take her. *How many moments like this do we have left?* She pulled Helen into a fierce hug.

Helen tolerated it for a while and then pulled back, averting her eyes. "I think I've fallen for someone too."

Olivia hid her shock, and smiled instead. The day she had warned Helen about, the day Helen had so dreaded, had finally come and caught Olivia off guard. She pushed aside her surprise for a moment to gloat. But her outspoken, rebellious sister suddenly seemed shy. Olivia really looked at Helen and the *I told you so* died on her lips. "Oh no, Helen, does he not feel the same way?"

"I think he does. Only, he's attached to someone else. Or maybe he's not anymore?"

"Well, who is it? Maybe it's not as serious as you might think."

Helen looked up, eyes bright with unshed tears.

Olivia squeezed Helen's fingers and pressed their foreheads together. "Oh, Helen! You can tell me. Who is it?"

Helen took a shuddering breath. "It's Jacob Lawrence."

Olivia's hand slackened around Helen's. She sat back hard against the couch. She had so many questions without any ability to voice them.

Helen eyed her warily. "We met at the Tremaines' party . . . because I missed that lunch."

"You always miss lunch," she said; she couldn't help it.

"Hey! If I'm remembering clearly, so did you," Helen said. They both glanced at the door. Then Helen continued. "He gave me a cigarette. I gave him a light and we talked about faulty electrical wiring and . . ." Helen trailed off. "He admires that I follow my interests. We make each other laugh." Helen exhaled loudly. "I've never felt this way before, Livy. And he—I know he feels the same." Olivia listened in stunned silence as her sister caught her up on the brief but intimate encounters shared with the man her parents had chosen for *her*. Helen was hiccupping by the time she finished. She covered her face in her hands. "Are you mad at me?"

Mr. Lawrence's distant behavior began to fall into place. It was never anything Olivia had done. It wasn't who she was—it was who she wasn't. As good a match as she and the British bachelor made in theory, the spark Olivia had hoped for was not there. A weight felt lifted from her shoulders. She cupped Helen's tear-streaked face and lifted it so their eyes met. "Helen, I could never be mad at you." She wrapped her younger sister in her arms again and held on to her tight, the pressure in her own chest dissolving as Helen relaxed against her. "At least, not for long. Anyway, Mr. Lawrence and I are not attached."

Helen leaned back. "You're not?"

"I panicked after Mama and Daddy made it sound like our marriage was a done deal. We decided to let them think that a proposal was imminent. I needed more time, and he was nothing but a gentleman. I swear, if I'd known how you felt, I would have never asked him to do that. Why didn't he say anything to me?

He must have felt so caught in between." Olivia frowned, then laughed. "I can't believe you're in love."

"Neither can I." Helen looked dazed.

Olivia brushed her sister's cheek. "Tell him I want you to be happy. Both of you." She watched her sister's face brighten, and she savored their weightlessness.

CHAPTER 36

Helen

There was no time to think about the scandal of her actions. Helen knew where Jacob Lawrence was staying from their conversations, from back when she thought she had no chance.

She dressed quickly that morning in a simple white blouse under a dark blue jacket and skirt. She removed the pins Olivia had placed in her hair and secured it as neatly as she could.

Long after her sister had gone to bed, Helen had lain awake, thinking.

He'd seen her in a pair of John's old coveralls and hadn't batted an eye!

Now it was the bright light of morning and Mrs. Milford's day off, and Helen used a distraction set by Olivia, plus the fact that her parents rarely checked for her, to walk right through Freeport's main gate and take the closest streetcar into downtown. Everything about the city seemed shiny and new to her. Summer was quickly approaching. The couple beside her unfolded a map of the city, the man flipping through a small guidebook printed in another language. Along State Street, the number of horseless carriages had doubled. Many were Ford's sturdy Model T, but she saw a few from the smaller Ohio companies like Studebaker and Patterson. All the more reason to push John and their father to modernize.

By the time the streetcar arrived at her stop, Helen had calmed her nerves. She was sure of Mr. Lawrence's feelings for her.

Helen stood at a stone-faced building at the end of the business district. *This is it*, she thought, bounding up the few stairs. The lobby of the hotel was sparse. Tall plants at the door were the only pops of color in the poorly lit space, weighed down by deep, dark wood furnishings. She approached the desk. This was not at all what she'd pictured, but then Helen remembered the quip Mr. Lawrence had made about the faulty lighting in his room.

At the desk, the squat man with deep frown lines read the newspaper. She waited to be acknowledged. Coughed into her hand. Finally, she said, "Excuse me, I'd like to speak to the guest in room 309."

The receptionist peered over the top of the page. "Sister?"

"No," Helen said, blushing, all her feelings for Mr. Lawrence plain on her face.

The attendant refused to let her up. It was improper for a lady to go up to man's room who wasn't family or accompanied by a chaperone.

"But it's important," she pleaded.

"I'm sure it is."

"Well, couldn't you at least let him know I'm here?"

"If it's so *important*, doesn't he know already?" He returned to his paper, humming a tune she couldn't place. Helen resigned herself to pacing the lobby. She wrung her fingers.

"You'll have to look out for the postman," said the attendant, taking pity on her, and, giving clear instructions to delay the mail carrier should he arrive, went upstairs himself to announce her. Minutes later Jacob Lawrence came down the stairs, ahead of the attendant. He was fully dressed, but his hair was mussed, missing the pomade that kept his tight waves flat and neat.

The man resumed his seat behind the desk, pretending to read his paper as he watched them almost embrace. "Let's go outside." Mr. Lawrence opened the door for her and they began walking with no particular destination in mind.

"To what do I owe such an unexpected surprise?"

"I wanted to see you." She did. It was a different feeling entirely to stare at him without stealing glances from beneath her lashes or when she thought no one else was watching her. Oh! To look at him freely, knowing that the only person who could truly be hurt by her feelings for Jacob Lawrence was already in love with someone else. Helen was simply here to tell him how she felt. They walked, hands just grazing, to the community garden around the corner. The canopy of trees transported Helen to a page in a storybook. In the privacy of all that lush greenery, she took Mr. Lawrence's hands in hers.

Now that she stood before him, Helen found her tongue tangled with all the words she wanted to say. It didn't help that he had taken a step closer—close enough that she could smell the faint scent of his soap. She was mesmerized by the sensation of his skin on hers, and it was just his hands!

"Helen." He lowered his voice. "I wish I had met you first. I can't deny what I feel, but I know that you—and Olivia—"

"I love you," Helen blurted out. Her pounding heart rammed

against her chest with a force she feared would break her ribs. She had prepared a speech. She had a plan and it wasn't confessing in three words, but she couldn't contain herself. Olivia had given her blessing, after all. She felt giddy and light as she waited for his response.

Mr. Lawrence's grip on her hands loosened, and the pained sadness she knew she had caused creeped into his eyes. "And I love you, Helen." The words had scarcely left his lips before she kissed him. She inhaled deeply as he returned her pressure after a moment of surprise. She dropped his hands to grab fistfuls of his lapels, angling herself to his height. His arms encircled her and pressed her against the hard planes of his chest. Helen's feet swept off the ground and she surprised them both with a "Whoop!" smiling against his mouth.

"Helen, we can't. You said—Olivia—"

"Is in love with someone else," Helen finished for him. "She told me everything. She gave me a letter relieving you of the promise." She closed the space between them again and placed one hand over his heart, which beat just as quickly as hers. With the other, she held the letter up to him. The emotions playing over his face were worth getting up early and racing across town for. Helen gasped as he pulled her onto her toes and kissed her. They laughed and kissed again.

"We'll have to keep this to ourselves until Olivia and I find a way to break it to our parents," she said.

Jacob Lawrence dropped his arms, but not the boyish grin on his face. "I will wait."

CHAPTER 37

The drawing room shared by the Davenport girls had been transformed into Olivia's party-planning headquarters. Swatches of tablecloths, various place setting examples, and food samples from various restaurants occupied every available surface. Ruby watched her friend make notes in a book between bouts of pulling at her hair, which was braided into two plaits, one on either side of her head.

"I still think you should have Jessie make the desserts," Ruby said, gracelessly spitting a lemon tart into a napkin. "We want people to vote for Papa, not accuse him of food poisoning."

Olivia laughed. "No to the lemon tarts," she said, dragging a pencil across the page. "Anything else I should know?"

Ruby knew her friend meant her opinion of turning the Davenports' annual masquerade ball into a campaign fundraiser. The fact was, the tart wasn't so bad. It was just that nothing could overcome the sour taste in Ruby's mouth. The mess she'd created spoiled everything, including her excitement for this party.

"Harrison thinks my parents know about us," she said, closing her eyes, trying to think of what she would say when she saw him.

He also believed that they made no objections. That Ruby's single-minded pursuit of John Davenport at her parents' urging was over, and that she and Harrison Barton were free to move on with their lives. They had spent as much time together as they could manage. And all the while, she'd sidestepped conversations about her parents.

"And why would he think that? Have you told them the full truth yet?" Olivia's stare felt like needles against Ruby's skin. It was awful. "Oh, Ruby, you didn't." The disappointment in Olivia's voice was even worse. "You have to tell them the truth! What if Harrison Barton runs into your father at one of the gentlemen's clubs? How you've managed to avoid such a disaster—"

"I know!" Ruby said. She fanned herself in front of the window. The air was still and muggy, which only served to sour her mood further. "It's just—I hate to disappointment them. I don't know when I went from 'doing no wrong' to everything being a disaster. And it feels like this campaign has taken so much of their attention—it's so important, Olivia, I just can't compete."

Olivia stood and walked across the room, tugging Ruby back to the couch. "I understand feeling afraid of losing your parents' esteem. It can lead to rash, foolish decisions. Trust me," she said, smiling. "But in this situation, deception will lead to more pain than the truth will. For all of you."

Ruby slouched against the pillows and covered her face. Olivia was right.

"Ruby! Tell them."

"All right!" she said.

Olivia picked up her novel from the table. "You should leave now if you want a ride into town with Hetty."

Ruby stood up from the couch and gathered her things. She stopped at the door, turning to her friend. When Olivia looked up, she said, "Thank you."

Except, instead of confronting her parents, Ruby accepted an invitation to the museum.

I'm late.

She raced up the stairs to the museum's grand doors. Harrison Barton was already waiting for her inside. She slowed her pace so she could watch him unnoticed. He was dressed in a new suit, immaculately tailored to hug every inch of him. He swung a bouquet of deep red roses while he paced, appearing about as nervous as she felt.

He whipped around at the sound of her footsteps, which echoed loudly in the cavernous room. Ruby's breaths came in little puffs that doubled in rate when he looked at her. He smelled of fresh aftershave and sage, and his shoes were shined to a polished gleam. She decided to focus on calming herself, each breath slow and deliberate.

"Good afternoon, Miss Tremaine," he said formally, handing her the flowers.

She noted his tone, the way he tugged at the sleeves of his jacket and shifted his weight from one foot to the other.

"Thank you, good sir. They're exquisite." She glanced at the painting behind them, two lovers embracing beside a river. "This painting—" she began.

"Ruby." He said her name with such tenderness, her own voice quieted.

He stilled, inhaled, then closed the space between them. "I want you to know, Ruby, I never stopped thinking about you either. You surprise me, every day, with your wit, your laughter. I admire your passion and your strength, especially in the quiet moments when we've shared thoughts revealed to no one else. And I admire your bravery in choosing what you want." He cleared his throat. "I love you, Ruby."

Harrison Barton knelt before her, a velvet box held aloft. Any words Ruby might have had fled. Her skin tingled all over. Her hands felt numb. It took all her strength to hold on to the bouquet. Beyond the box, he looked at her as if she were the sun. Her heart felt enormous, making it hard to breathe.

"Miss Tremaine," he said, "will you make me the happiest, luckiest man in the world?" He opened the box to reveal a large ruby, haloed by bright sparkling diamonds, and set on a fine gold band. "Ruby, will you marry me?"

"Yes!" The word burst from her lips. There was no need to think it over.

Mr. Barton leaped up and caught her around the waist. A sense of weightlessness overtook her that had nothing to do with the way he held her aloft and spun her about the room. Their laughter rang out.

This is true joy.

It was a feeling Ruby wanted to hold on to for as long as possible.

CHAPTER 38

Amy-Rose

The trees in the small orchard were starting to bloom. Amy-Rose always loved this time of year. Freeport Manor and the sprawling grounds that separated it from Chicago's white elite felt like a slice of paradise, a quiet haven from the rest of the city, even if the balance between work and her own time was not always clear. It was hard to think of what she would have been doing if John Davenport, who walked beside her now, had not asked her to stay by delivering her dream on a silver platter.

Tommy had left several days ago with much pomp and circumstance. His going-away party lasted well into the evening and Jessie had packed enough baked goods to hold him through the week-long journey. "You know there's food in California?" he choked out as the family cook pressed him into her bosom like he was still a child.

Amy-Rose's own goodbye was bittersweet. Long after the others had gone to bed, she and Tommy had stayed up telling stories of their childhood, *Remember when* as essential as *Once upon a time.* She accompanied him and his father, Harold, to the train station the next day, and she held her objections when he pressed the business card of his contact out west into her hand. Later, she and Harold rode back to Freeport in silence. She pretended not to notice the tears in Harold's eyes as they neared the stables, knowing Tommy would not be there to receive the tired horses or help her down from the carriage.

"I'm glad you're here," John said now. He held her hand as they ambled through the trees, far from the house, where they could talk unseen. His thumb drew circles in the palm of her hand. Hers looked small and pale against the deep richness of his. Their interlocked fingers created a fine tapestry, she thought.

It felt strange but right, knowing Tommy had moved on. "Leaving was part of Tommy's plan," she said. "It doesn't have to be part of mine."

John exhaled. The tension in his posture relaxed. Had the prospect of her moving caused this? Amy-Rose chewed her bottom lip, not sure how she felt about having such a powerful effect on another person.

"I admire your determination," John said. He looked at her and slowed their pace. "I have no doubt it will succeed."

"Much like you," she said.

"I do have all these ideas. And we have to act soon. Automobiles are the future. We can open another factory so we don't impact operations for the carriages."

"Helen told me. She's thrilled. I think it's wonderful."

John's smile was grim. "I want to take Davenport Carriages into the future. Update our whole business model." He'd released her hand to pace. His steps were quick, and he kneaded the muscles in the back of his neck. The tension of her possible departure replaced by another.

She grabbed him by his arms and turned him to face her. He stilled under her touch. "What's stopping you?" she asked. It was the same question Tommy had asked her when she broke the news that she would not be joining him. She couldn't quite answer him, but she suspected it was the same thing preventing John from taking his own leap.

He inhaled a deep breath before he answered. "Nothing," he said. "I'm ready."

Amy-Rose grinned. "I'm happy for you."

John pressed a gentle kiss to the back of one of her hands. He held it under his chin as he spoke. "My father is set in his ways. He waves my words away as if I'm still in secondary school playing pretend in one of his showrooms. It's like no matter what I do, that's the only way he'll see me. But the proposal Helen and I are working on is sound. It will work . . . I just have to convince my father . . . That is the real challenge."

Amy-Rose understood. His fears were her own. What did a maid know about opening a salon, making and selling hair serums, balancing books and paying wages? She'd been laughed out of more rooms than she cared to admit. Still, she knocked on that next door, and that next door. She would until she had the keys to her own. She too was ready. Nothing would stop her.

This was why she'd stayed. Despite their uneven footing, John understood her like no one else could. He was the other side to her coin—no, a mirror. Someone who would understand her drive, forgive her long hours, and know from the beginning that her dreams, her voice, were non-negotiable. *And more.* She hoped, against the lead sitting in her stomach, that she could trust him with her whole heart and he would protect it.

"My father—"

"Your father was once standing where you are right now. The crossroads of fear and hope. He didn't know anything about running a business when he came to this city. But he learned. He'll see the value of your plan."

A hesitant smile tugged at John's face. He stared at her. In his deep brown eyes, she saw his desire to believe her.

"Helen will certainly be excited when you succeed," Amy-Rose continued. "Will she have a greater role in this plan of yours?"

John rubbed the back of his neck. "That might be a harder sell than the automobile." A crease appeared between his brows. He had gone still. "I wouldn't have gotten everything prepared without her help. She's deserves a chance just as much as I do."

Amy-Rose squeezed his hands in hers. "Maybe . . . instead of continuing to try to change him, you should consider going out on your own. You and Helen. The two of you can create your own legacy."

He studied her face for a beat. "No, we can do this." John pressed her knuckles to his lips. It was a chaste gesture that sent a jolt through her. He inhaled deeply. "Together."

CHAPTER 39

Olivia

Olivia's secret collection of political pamphlets and newspapers littered her bed. Helen's feet dangled off the end as she read them, asking Olivia "did you know" about whatever piece surprised her next.

"How did you get all these?" her sister asked.

Olivia tried to arrange the newspapers back into some semblance of order. "Hetty usually brings them to me when she's done." She pushed Helen's hip to get the paper underneath her. "Remember to return that book to her when you're finished."

"Of course," Helen said, rolling onto her stomach and disrupting the tea tray between them on the duvet. Olivia moved it to the vanity before it spilled. "What about the rest?" She looked at Olivia, her chin propped on a fist. Helen had grown, filled out. No longer hidden in their brother's cast-off coveralls, her cleavage pushed against her bodice, accentuating a tapered waist that flared to rebellious hips. Their father's proud nose suited her. Her skin was a deep rich brown. And her laugh was contagious, better suited to pull Jacob Lawrence out of his shell. They were a well-matched pair.

Helen mouthed the words as she read, hitting Olivia with a sudden wave of nostalgia. She'd missed this, time with her sister. She envied the time Helen and John spent in the garage, tinkering and talking. The thought caused a pang in chest. So much wasted time. Now Olivia and Helen had quite a few secrets between them. *And I'm leaving*, she thought with a heavy sigh. Helen in love. She shook her head in disbelief.

Helen widened her eyes and gave Olivia a questioning look.

"Right, I get most of them from Washington or other activists." Olivia scanned the mess.

"I can't wait until we can vote." Helen moved the piece on the suffragettes to the side. Her hand lingered over the photo of women marching, signs held high. Helen looked up and seemed to study Olivia's face. "I can't believe this is what you've been up to instead shopping or volunteering."

"Oh, I'm still shopping," Olivia laughed. "Just not always for myself. Some of the clothing drives needed help, clothes for interviews, children. Good, sturdy shoes are popular. The larders at the soup kitchens empty a few days after the Sunday services. And it's all still volunteering. Technically." There was always more to do. An exhausting circle that brought about as much joy as frustration.

"Hey." Helen pulled her close and nestled her head in the space above her shoulder. "Don't look like that. I'm sure they appreciate it."

"I know. I just wish things moved faster. I'm impatient for change . . . in the good sense. Most of all, I wish there was more I could do."

"You'll think of something."

"I suppose," she said, not entirely sure it was true. Staring up at the canopy, Olivia tried to imagine what it would be like to walk arm in arm with the women in the photograph or to speak out at town hall meetings as Jim Crow legislation was discussed. She knew money helped. But she also knew, no matter how many checks signed *Davenport* she turned over, there would always be a barrier between her and most people she'd meet. After the rally had ended in violence, the work of Mr. DeWight and his group had come to rely on newspapers and magazines.

"Olivia, what are we going to tell Mama and Daddy? About you and Jacob?"

Olivia flopped back down on the bed. "You mean, *you* and Jacob?"

Helen poked her side. "Now is not the time to develop a sense of humor."

Olivia drew the pillow over her head. Her sister crawled closer when she rolled away, her finger a persistent pressure in her arm. She didn't know if she was going to laugh or growl.

Helen uncovered her face. "Livy."

Olivia sighed. "We should tell Mama and Daddy the truth."

"But after you leave, right? You are obviously in love with Mr. DeWight *and* this whole other life the two of you share. How are you not plotting your grand escape?"

Olivia sat up too quickly, leaving her simultaneously dizzy and clear-headed. Helen was right. She was in love, the type of love she dreamed about. Washington DeWight's face eased into her mind. His easy smile that highlighted his strong jaw, and cheekbones any girl would covet. There was his kindness, his passion, even the ways he provoked her. Thinking of him rose her temperature. How could she hesitate? She looked at her sister grinning at her. "You're right," she conceded, tossing the pillow at Helen. "I don't think they'll let me out of their sight once they find out about you and Mr. Lawrence. The scandal. Then I'd be just as trapped as you are. Daddy wants us staying clear of protests, anything that may cause us physical danger." Olivia paused. "If they found out about Washington . . ."

"You know . . ." Helen rolled her eyes. "Mrs. Milford may be able to help us. She saw this coming way before either of us did."

Helen gave Olivia a subtle nod, her signal that their parents were too deep into a conversation with the pastor and his wife to notice her slip away from the church. Thanks to her sister—and, Olivia suspected, her tutor—a note had made its way from Olivia to Mr. DeWight yesterday to meet her after the service.

While her family exchanged pleasantries and news with the congregation, she walked the few blocks to the apartment building where Mr. DeWight rented a room. It was a simple brick building, lacking a doorman or any of the amenities she was accustomed to. It served a purpose, he said, when they walked past it a few weeks ago. She stared at the listing next to the door and was lucky that someone exited so she could slip past the tall wrought-iron gate. Olivia climbed up the three flights of stairs, cursing under her breath at the way her church shoes pinched her toes.

The door to his apartment was at the top of the third landing. Olivia stared at the large 3A mounted at eye level. She paused with her fist inches from its surface. What she was doing had consequences. Not just for her, but Helen, her family's reputation. It was one thing to daydream about running away with a handsome young gentleman lawyer and an entirely different thing to enter his apartments. *It will be much worse once you board that train*, she scolded herself. Her mind was made up.

Her rap on the door went unanswered. Olivia stepped back to check the number on the door. This was the correct address. "Washington," she called. Still no answer. Dread began to pool in her stomach. Olivia glanced over her shoulder, and with a shaking hand, turned the knob. The door gave easily, though it screamed the whole way open.

It was one room. A narrow bed was pushed up against the longest wall. A chair and desk nestled opposite it, and immediately to her right was a small kitchenette, barely enough to prepare the essentials. He said he lived simply, but this was beyond what she expected. She stood in the room, smaller than her sitting room, and grasped for what to do next. She couldn't look for him. There was nowhere *to* look.

Her palms prickled. She removed her gloves before her damp hands could soak into the silk. Panic began to set in. Washington DeWight lived here. It smelled like him. Olivia threw open the wardrobe. Empty. The cabinets in the kitchenette empty. Had he left without her? Spots began to crowd her vision. Olivia tried to slow her breathing, but her nose stung with the threat of tears. *Did I miss my chance?*

Her next breath caught in her throat, she coughed, and the breath after was filled with a whiff of pine so strong, it made her look up.

"Olivia, are you okay?" Mr. DeWight stood in the doorway.

She stared at him. "I thought you'd left without me."

"I would never leave without saying goodbye," he said, crossing the room to her.

"Then where are all your things?"

"Reverend Andrews offered me the room in his attic until I leave for Philadelphia. The previous occupant moved out. I'm just returning the key," he said, placing it next to the stove.

Relief hit her as swiftly and forcefully as the panic. He pulled her close. His arms wrapped around her and every muscle in Olivia melted into him. She felt his smile on her forehead when he kissed it, his skin fresh and smooth from a shave. "Does this mean you've decided?"

Olivia focused on a knot in the wood floor, with the full knowledge of her inadequacy from her place of privilege. "That night I came to see you at Samson House I missed your speech, but I did listen." Olivia shook her head. "I listened to people speak of their greatest tragedies without an ounce of surprise or anguish. It was spoken as a matter of fact."

She looked up into his honey-colored eyes and said, "Yes, I want to go with you."

Mr. DeWight lifted a hand to stroke the sensitive hollow of her neck where her pulse jumped in response. He took both her hands, and she inhaled. Coffee, pine, and the warmth of his skin. She was drunk on the smell of him, stronger than any champagne cocktail.

"It's a difficult life," he said. "The risk of injury or imprisonment— or worse—is always present. The accommodations are unpredictable. And there's a lot of heartache mixed in with the wins. That rally . . . it was nothing compared to what I've seen. I want you to be sure."

His words, though true, had the opposite of the intended effect on Olivia. She didn't crave danger, but the thought of doing nothing . . .

"I'm sure."

He hesitated a moment before kissing her. The kiss started slow, but Olivia was greedy. She pushed onto her toes and arched her back until they fit together like two pieces of a puzzle. She sighed and his tongue slipped into her mouth, skimming the tender underside of her lip. The kiss deepened and she pulled him even closer. The taste of him made her head spin. Olivia broke away, stepping back and gasping for air. Her skin felt tight and clammy.

"Maybe we should slow down," he rasped.

Olivia placed her hand on his chest. "Like your heart." His raced beneath her palm as if challenging hers to keep pace. He watched her with half-closed eyes while she took in the liquified depths of them, the shape of his lips, and the high cheekbones that framed every smile. He was beautiful. She ached to have his lips on hers again. He shuddered as she kissed along his jaw. Her hands pushed his jacket off his shoulders. It fell to the floor with a soft thud. When their lips met again, Olivia's body hummed with anticipation. She didn't want to slow down. And even if she did, she wasn't sure if she could.

CHAPTER 40

Helen

Helen watched florists and contractors walk in and out of the house from the railing of Freeport's wide veranda. Bouquets of orchids and lilies would adorn the corners of the grand ballroom, redecorated in gold and black for the masquerade ball. Trying to guess which guests hid behind each elaborate disguise would dull the sting of having to attend. And, because no one would recognize her, Helen could slip away early and easily.

This was also the first big social event since she and Jacob Lawrence had revealed their true feelings to each other. Sure, they still had to keep their intentions secret, but at least she didn't have to dodge him to avoid heartache.

"Young lady, what are you doing here?" Mrs. Davenport asked. "You should be getting dressed." She crossed her arms and gave Helen a speaking look. The band had arrived. A string quartet from the Negro Orchestra. Their instruments preceded them in shiny black cases. They greeted her and Mrs. Davenport with deep bows. Their arrival meant that last-minute touches were underway, though they still had plenty of time. Her mother directed them to the ballroom, where Amy-Rose showed them the waiting room reserved for the entertainment. When Mrs. Davenport returned her gaze to Helen, she regarded her daughter with some suspicion.

"Mama, we have at least four hours before the first set of guests arrive. Jessie's already kicked me out of the kitchen."

"Why don't you see what your sister is up to?" Mrs. Davenport asked.

Helen pushed off the railing. "That is a splendid idea." She smiled at her mother and followed the band inside.

Helen knew exactly what Olivia was doing, closed up in her room, trying to decide what, if anything, in her closet was suitable for a trip to Philadelphia. They had pooled their allowances for her to use for lodging and essentials. Neither knew what Olivia was walking into, only that Washington DeWight would be at her side. So, the younger Miss Davenport took the most roundabout way to her sister's rooms as she could think of.

Though she dared not enter the kitchen, she listened to the clang of pots as the air filled with the scent of a savory broth and Jessie's roasted chicken. Helen's stomach protested and she made a slight detour for a sweet roll before she continued her tour of the first floor. Below the grandfather clock in the foyer, a linen-draped table was organized with face masks of varying shapes and sizes. Some were jeweled or covered in a thick crust of glitter—they promised to be a sparkly mess. Others resembled animals with horns and whiskers.

In the ballroom, the silver and frosted chandeliers and table pieces were replaced with brass and iron fixtures that gave the space an Old World feel softened by the flowers she'd seen carried in. All the doors leading to the courtyard were open. Dinner would be served outside. The weather was calm and comfortable—perfect for the Davenports' nearly two hundred guests to enjoy. A light breeze picked up, blending the fragrant bouquet of the lilies with the scent of fresh cut grass and woodsmoke from the outdoor fireplace.

"Helen!" Mrs. Davenport's voice from across the way jolted Helen and startled several staff brought on for the evening. "Please, get dressed."

She suppressed a groan. "Yes, Mama." Helen took one last look at the setup around her. *Perhaps next year, Jacob will be here as my guest.*

She was torn between descending upon Olivia and hiding somewhere her mother wouldn't find her. The garage was out of the question—though she had placed all the parts back in the Model T, she had not had a chance to start it.

She chose her sister.

Helen had spent the morning watching Olivia direct the staff as efficiently as their mother. She was ready to lead her own household, and she was a marvel to watch. In her room, however, Olivia was a different story.

"What happened in here?" Helen asked as she stepped into the chaos that had become her sister's bedroom. Olivia had turned her entire wardrobe inside out. Garments lay strewn about every surface. Helen sifted through the piles and found a fold of bright fabric still wrapped in tissue. It was pretty. "Can I have this?" Helen asked. The silk spilled onto the bed like liquid sunshine.

Olivia looked her way. "Of course." She walked over to Helen and took the material from her. A quick shake later, it fell like a cape about Helen's shoulders, the silk settling over her skin like a warm whisper. She felt glamorous and grown up until she spotted Olivia's frown.

"Spit those out, Helen. That's a disgusting habit." The pearls fell from Helen's mouth. She caught them before they could touch the bodice of her dress. "Here," Olivia said, handing her a handkerchief.

"Will you relax," Helen said, watching her sister tug on the matching strand around her neck. She caught Olivia's arm. "We've gone over this countless times. Mama and Daddy will understand. You're going to be with the man you love." She stood up and wrapped her arms around her sister. "And to save both our reputations, Jacob can't trade you in for a newer model, not immediately at least."

"Helen! I knew you were cheeky, but when did you become so wise." Olivia sniffed.

"Mrs. Milford is an excellent teacher," she said.

They had been doing this a lot the past few days. Helen couldn't remember a time in recent memory where they embraced so frequently. Her heart felt heavy. She feared this would be the last hug they'd share for a while and she wanted to enjoy every moment of it.

Olivia gently pulled away, keeping her arms on Helen's shoulders. Helen felt her sister's eyes roam over her face.

"My goodness, you're acting like we'll never see each other again," Helen said, as if the same sentiment hadn't just crossed her mind. Olivia's eyes were already red, the skin around them shiny and puffy. "If you start crying, I'll have to join you, so stop."

"All right," Olivia said. "I'll stop, if you promise not to start. Are you sure you don't want me to at least tell Mama and Daddy that Mr. Lawrence and I aren't together anymore?"

"And have them lock you in this room until they find out why you've changed your mind?"

"I hardly think they'd do that."

Helen raised an eyebrow. "You honestly want to find out?" Olivia pinched her bottom lip between her teeth. "*I* will tell them. When the time is right," said Helen.

Olivia pressed her cool hands to her cheeks. After a few deep breaths, she returned to the task at hand. Helen watched her sister pull out a small suitcase from under the bed. The clasp of the luggage popped open and Olivia turned to the clothing draped over the furniture.

"I love you," Helen whispered as she hugged her sister from behind. "Now, get to packing."

Helen left Olivia in her room, singing loudly and off-key. Her lack of any skill hid the shakiness of her voice.

Helen again considered a stop-off in the garage, but her conversation with her father about how she spent her free time was still a sore subject. Today, she'd stay away. She walked past the morning room when strange movement outside on the patio caught her eye. Helen entered the hall and walked quickly to the nearest exit. She rattled the French doors open.

Jacob Lawrence stood there, squinting into the bright sun, pebbles clinking in his hand. He threw one. It bounced off the windowpane with a clear, high *ping*.

"What are you doing?" she said, staring up at the window above.

Mr. Lawrence started. He rubbed the back of his neck and tossed the remaining stones into a bush. "I was trying to get your attention."

"By throwing rocks at the linen closet window?"

He chuckled. His sheepish grin made him seem not so adult as she thought when he'd first arrived. He'd grown more relaxed in the weeks he'd spent in Chicago. Helen wondered what other sides of him might be revealed in the coming months, years even.

"Is she really leaving?" Mr. Lawrence looked through the doors Helen had left open.

"Yes," she said, a bittersweet feeling tingeing her words. She closed the doors and led them out of sight. She couldn't believe they had a chance. Helen always thought love was for other girls. Her passion for the family business, no matter how many obstacles stood in her way, was the only thing she had going for her. It was the only thing she wanted. Now, with Mr. Lawrence by her side, she would have someone to share it with.

She reached up onto her toes and found air where she expected his mouth to be. Helen opened her eyes to a pained look on his face. "What's wrong?" she asked. Her insides felt cold. As soon as the question left her lips she wished them back. She wanted to stay in this blissful bubble of possibility.

"I have to tell you something."

Helen laughed nervously. "Don't tell me there's *another* fiancée I have to help escape town."

Mr. Lawrence didn't seem to hear her. His gaze was fixed on the spot in between them. She could feel it widening the longer he stared.

She touched him then, taking his face in her hands and forcing him to look at her.

"I love you, Helen," he said.

"I already know that." Her words sounded harsher than she'd intended over the alarm bells ringing in her ears. Whatever he was working up to saying, she didn't want to hear it.

"I have a confession to make." His body tensed. "I lied to you, your family. I'm broke. The Lawrence shipping tycoon is my great-uncle. My father abandoned the family business when he was my age and was cut out of my grandfather's estate." He sighed. "I'm what they call the poor relations. I was—" He stopped. All his swagger and bravado had disappeared.

"Looking to marry a girl with means?"

"No, I intended to buy myself back in. With help or employment. Meeting your father at the newsstand was merely a coincidence. Fate."

Helen let go of his face. A chill had spread from her core, leaving her fingertips stinging with pins and needles.

"I do love you. All my feelings—they're true. But I don't have much to offer you now. Will you have me anyway?"

He reached for her, but Helen felt numb. Her nose stung with the threat of tears and her vision became watery. He waited for her to say something. For the first time in her life, Helen Marie Davenport was at a loss for words. No textbook or etiquette manual prepared her for his revelation. She remembered the hours they'd spent talking, sharing parts of themselves they rarely shared. Did he not trust her? Why would he have not told her this sooner? Would he still have married Olivia if she hadn't fallen for the lawyer?

He did touch her then and her reaction was reflexive. She stepped beyond his reach. Helen found her voice, stronger than she would have imagined.

"I don't know. You're telling me you've lied. To everyone. You're telling me you used my sister, my parents." She wrapped her arms around herself as if she could keep her pieces from falling apart. "I care about *you*, Jacob, not what you can offer me. I *fell* for you. Now I don't know. What am I supposed to do with this?" A sob disguised as a hiccup escaped her chest, which heaved uncontrollably. "I want you to go."

"Helen, please—"

"Please, just go," she said, relieved she alone knew what he had done. She hated the way her voice sounded now. Small and fragile. Not at all like herself. Why had he not trusted her with the truth? Mr. Lawrence held her gaze, pain written over his features.

He composed himself, and with a nod, turned away.

Helen, too hurt to wipe her tears, watched him go.

CHAPTER 41

Ruby

"My, they certainly have outdone themselves." Mr. Barton's eyes traveled across the ballroom, where every inch was meticulously decorated. Ruby watched him soak in the room. His tuxedo fit him well, the white waistcoat and bow tie contrasted beautifully with his skin and the bright black and gold of his mask. Ruby placed her arm on his and stared at the spot where he had tried to place a ring on her finger. It was a beautiful piece modeled after her namesake pendant that couldn't make it past the last knuckle. It was now in the care of the same jeweler who had polished her ruby, getting sized.

She was overjoyed. And not having the ring on her finger bought Ruby some time, though precious little of it, to come clean to her parents about Harrison. Did they not think their friendship with the Davenports strong enough to secure their support? Two hundred guests had arrived in disguise to the Davenport family home to support her father's campaign!

Ruby kept her eyes peeled for her parents, who chose to arrive with another couple. She prayed she would be able to intercept them before dread caused her to sweat through her crimson bodice. Surely they'd understand love is preferable to whatever her relationship to John was now. She wanted to believe that they wanted more for her than just the Davenports' last name.

"Would you like to dance?"

Ruby smiled. A dance couldn't hurt. She let Mr. Barton lead her into the center of the floor. His palm settled low on her back and they began to move. He really was a fabulous dancer. It was one of the reasons she first enjoyed his company. The music enveloped them. The couples around them turned in blurs of colors, of silk or satin, spinning wheels.

"Do you remember the first time we danced?" she asked.

His lips twitched and he leaned in. "To be honest, I think I fell for you right then." He gently turned her underneath his arm. When he pulled her close, it was to press her back to his chest. The heat of him devoured her doubts. "I knew," he whispered against the sensitive part of her neck, "that I would never find anyone else like you." He spun her away and when they met again, Ruby placed her head on his shoulder. She imagined a lifetime of dances like this. Maybe they could spend the whole evening here, hidden in the crowd.

They spent two more dances doing just that, and then Mr. Barton wanted to get a drink. Ruby walked beside him, her focus darting in every direction. Her breath stuck in her chest. All she could see were bursts of color between tuxedo black, faces shielded by masks. She held tight to his arm, searching for her parents. A breath escaped her lips when she saw the refreshments table blessedly free.

"Are you all right?" he asked. He pressed a hand to her damp forehead. "We'll take our drinks outside. Some fresh air might do you some good."

Her agreement was on the tip of her tongue when a sharp pain erupted at her elbow. Her mother had appeared like the specter she feared and pulled Ruby to a secluded alcove, Mr. Barton in tow. Ruby tried to untangle herself from her mother, but it was too late. She stood her ground between them now, hoping that whatever came, he would still be holding her hand afterward.

"Mrs. Tremaine, lovely to see you," he said. His voice was warm, if a bit uncertain. Though her mother smiled, there was nothing friendly about it. The three removed their masks and Ruby saw that her mother's errant eyebrow had shot up to her hairline.

"What is this nonsense about you being engaged? Mrs. Davis is walking around telling everyone who will listen that you and Mr. Barton are engaged."

Harrison turned to Ruby. "We are."

Mrs. Tremaine narrowed her eyes at her daughter.

Ruby's heart pounded in her chest. "Harrison and I are in love."

"Love?" Mrs. Tremaine said. "Ruby, we've discussed love and marriage, and you are marrying John Davenport."

"I don't understand," said Mr. Barton. "Ruby, you did tell them how we felt about each other before I proposed."

Mrs. Tremaine inhaled sharply. "My word, you aim to disappoint us at every turn. You will fix this mess," her mother said. Ruby and Mr. Barton watched her replace her mask and glide back into the crowd.

Slowly, Ruby turned to face Harrison.

"You said they approved, that you, in no uncertain terms, were done with Davenport."

"Harrison, I'm sorry. I was planning—I tried once—"

"Once?" He pulled his hand from hers. It felt like he'd ripped her arm out with it.

"I did, really. Everything has been so stressful with the campaign. They were always so busy, worried. I didn't want to add to it."

"Too busy and worried for you to tell them . . ." He worked his jaw before he spoke. "Are you sure it's not because you're still in love with John Davenport?"

Ruby recoiled as if struck. "How could you think that? Of course I'm not."

"I never know where I stand with you, Ruby. I think I do, but then—" He threw his hands up. "Why can't you just be honest with me? This scheming—" He turned to the dance floor, his back rigid, his face cold. "I don't think you know what you want."

"I do."

"Do you? From where I stand, the only thing you want or care about is their approval. On their terms. There isn't room for anyone else. Your bravado, all your talk about how you don't care about anyone's opinion—it's a lie." His voice dropped so only she could hear how it shook. "And now it's one only you believe. You're a coward, Ruby Tremaine." He stepped back, his jaw as rigid as his spine.

She felt hot tears on her face. "Harrison, wait." Her fingertips grazed his sleeve. The music drowned out her call. Her vision blurred. And just like that, he was gone.

CHAPTER 42

Amy-Rose

Amy-Rose placed her bowl into the sink with the dishes Hetty put to soak. *Where has that girl gone?* "Jessie, do you know where Hetty went?" Her stomach was full and her body ached. Days of preparation went into making sure everything for this fundraiser would be perfect. It was the social event of the summer and critical to Mr. Tremaine's campaign. Amy-Rose kept herself busy all evening behind the scenes. She didn't want to risk another spectacle. Oh, it was agony staying sequestered in the kitchen. She longed to see the finery, how the women's hair was done up. The masks. It was better than flipping through a catalog.

"That girl run off as soon as the dessert was served." Jessie shook her head. "I know that face." She gave Amy-Rose a telling look. "I'm sure you can behave yourself long enough to take a peek."

"A tiny one wouldn't hurt." She shrugged out of her apron and smoothed her hair down. The steam from all the cooking had her curls more unruly than usual. She opened the kitchen door to the sound of hundreds of voices mingling with the brassy notes of the band. It drew her closer, beckoning with the promise of Black excellence and opulence.

She was not disappointed. The scene was out of a painting. The sparkling beauty of it elicited a sigh. Hair was elaborately coiffed, complete with precious stones or fresh flowers. The pictures in the Sunday papers wouldn't do any of them justice. She was proud of her work on the Davenport sisters. They shined like twin suns. Helen looked beautiful in a pale green sheath that slid off her shoulders, gathered around her bust, and cinched her waist, before falling like a column to her feet. It was a more modern style than what Olivia wore. The older Davenport girl wore a high-collared gown in ivory. The crystal beading around her throat and fluttering sleeves made her look angelic. Their hair she styled simply. A low chignon for Helen and a high French twist for Olivia. They appeared to be too deep in conversation to notice the way they commanded the attention of their guests.

Amy-Rose caught a glimpse of Mrs. Davis and made her way to where the older woman stood. "Good evening, Mrs. Davis."

"Miss Shepherd," she said. The older woman lowered her crystal-covered mask. "I was sorry to hear about Mr. Spencer's barbershop."

Amy-Rose remembered the pain of that news. Her dream was not unfolding as she planned, but it was still on track. "It was a terrible disappointment, yes, but I've found another location that will serve just fine." Her chest puffed up with pride. She scanned the crowd for John's broad shoulders and dimpled smile, the gaggle of girls who usually followed in his wake.

Surprisingly, he was not near the dance floor or the refreshments. His parents were missing too.

"Why, that is fantastic news!" Mrs. Davis said. "I can't say I'm not a little disappointed myself."

Amy-Rose brought her attention back to the widow.

Mrs. Davis laughed. "My dear, I'm a wealthy woman with no children and an eye for business. I thought to lure you into a joint venture with a trip to New York. Now that I think about it, it does make me sound like quite the villain."

New York? Amy-Rose pivoted to the thrice-widowed woman beside her.

Mrs. Davis laughed again. "I am truly happy your fortune has turned for the better. Do keep me informed of your progress, yes?"

"Yes," she whispered.

"Good." Mrs. Davis replaced her mask and disappeared onto the dance floor.

When Amy-Rose had her fill of the pageantry, she wandered outside to the bench at the edge of the garden. It was where John had first revealed his feelings for her. Their first kiss. She hadn't felt so close to another person since her mother passed away. She had felt hope here, and thought tonight this spot might renew her resolve. She imagined coming here to steal romantic moments with John in the future, to revisit the memories this place held. With her eyes closed, she could almost hear him.

"I tried to do things your way."

No, that is him. She opened her eyes and peered into the darkness beyond the brightly lit courtyard. From behind the hedges, John and Mr. Davenport came into view. Mr. Davenport leaned heavily on his cane while his son walked circles around him. John's agitation unsettled Amy-Rose. His cool and aloof demeanor had peeled away. The pair stopped at the edge of the courtyard, their backs facing Amy-Rose. She thought of announcing herself, coming out from behind the trees so that she couldn't be accused of eavesdropping. Hetty was the one for gossip. But something in the way John's shoulders crept up to his ears gave her pause.

"Ruby and I have known each other since we were children. It's not like that between us," John said, in a tone that suggested it was not the first time he'd said that. Amy-Rose felt a flutter in her chest. "She doesn't love me. She has feelings for Barton."

"Your mother and Mrs. Tremaine were quite sure that it was a passing infatuation." He patted John's face and smiled.

John stopped moving at the touch, as if the feel of his father's hand stilled the churning inside that wound him up. Amy-Rose couldn't see his face from where she stood, but his shoulders sagged, his head bowed.

"What did you say?" Mr. Davenport asked.

Amy-Rose slipped out of the protection of the trees and walked along the hedges. She kept her footfalls slow, careful with each step, and using the shadows to conceal her.

"I don't love Ruby." John's words were clear. He straightened and looked his father in the eye. "My choice is Amy-Rose. I know she is not who you and Mother had in mind for me, but I don't care. Ruby and I will not make each other happy."

"And you think this girl will make you happy?" Mr. Davenport shook his head. "Do you think the wives of your friends will welcome her? Wish to socialize and dine with a woman who used to serve them? What about your children? She is the daughter of a *slave owner*. One look at her will have people wondering. It is hard enough to get that table in the back of the restaurant or the end of the counter in public spaces, without reducing the spaces among our own. Some may accept her, prefer her, but many more will fawn over her while they accuse her of putting on airs. It will only bring you both heartache and resentment."

John shook his head. "I choose Amy-Rose. Damned what other people think."

"And what about your mother and myself. Are we to be damned?"

Amy-Rose still couldn't see John's face, but he stiffened at his father's question. Her stomach lurched as he remained silent. She felt sick in the back of her throat. As much as she didn't want to admit it, Mr. Davenport was right. Things would never be easy for them. He was always kind to her. Now she wondered if she was a walking reminder of the life he ran from. *I live in his home.* Her knees buckled as she lowered herself to the damp ground. She knew she should leave, but she found herself unable to stand.

"People like the man that got her mother in trouble, they take what they want." Mr. Davenport's voice shook. "She is a nice girl. No one would say otherwise. If you want to marry the daughter of a slave owner, your mother and I will not stand in your way." He placed both of his hands over the top of his cane. He straightened to his full height. From where Amy-Rose stood, he appeared to tremble with anger. "We will also not pave the way for you. You will have to support yourself, and her, on your own. Without any help from us."

John flinched as if he had been slapped.

"Are you sure you want to give up everything," Mr. Davenport asked, eyes sweeping the manor house and grounds, "for a girl?"

Amy-Rose held her breath, waiting for John's reply, for him to say she was his choice once more. Sweat began to bead above her lip. She squinted. *Maybe if I could get closer?* She forced herself to continue on wobbly knees to the edge of the darkness that concealed her. Amy-Rose looked at the ground, avoiding the dry leaves and twigs. When she looked up, Mr. Davenport was making his way back to the house. "John," he called, "I thought you were serious about school. The business. I still have the final say."

John remained where he was. He'd said nothing. The realization stopped her. Mr. Davenport dangled the one thing his son wanted more than anything. *Even more than me?* Amy-Rose's feet refused to go any closer. Breathing was suddenly difficult. She no longer cared if she was discovered. Her eyes stung with fresh rejection and heartbreak. Mr. Davenport had offered John the perfect alternative. If he wanted to start out on his own, enter the automobile business from the ground up, create a new future with her . . . that was it.

But his silence was her answer. John Davenport was not ready. He may never be.

Before she knew it, she was stalking across the garden to where he stood.

"I'm never going to be enough, am I?" she asked to his back.

John started. He glanced over his shoulder like he was checking for an audience. "Amy-Rose, I—"

"Didn't know I was here?"

"You heard?" He rubbed the back of his neck.

She felt a fire rise within her as hot as her tears. "He was right. A future with me would be difficult. But my whole life has been difficult. You think I don't know what people call me? What they called my mother for sleeping with a white man and having his child?"

She didn't wait for him to answer. She couldn't. Though Mr. Davenport treated her kindly and hadn't meant for her to hear, his words cut just as deep as John's reaction. It was another reminder that people like her never knew where they stood. The uncertainty that accompanied her into unfamiliar places still plagued her, even though she'd mastered her mother's ability to act like she belonged everywhere.

Deep down, Amy-Rose feared there was nowhere she belonged.

She looked at John, furious that he had shaken her resolve to leave with a promise and a gift. How could she have let herself fall for him so thoroughly? Her anger turned cold and bitter as the hurt she felt turned inward. *You let him*, she told herself. She had thought there was a chance. That as long as she had John on her side, they'd weather any obstacle thrown at them.

"Every time I leave through those gates," she said, pointing to the entrance of the estate and struggling to keep her voice steady, "I brace myself for the stares, the comments, the slights. Most of the time, it's not needed, but I've learned the hard way that it's better to armor my skin than to be caught off guard. I am Black and white, and sometimes, in *some spaces*, neither. But I thought, here, with you, I could remove that armor. I wouldn't feel the need to scrub the freckles off my face, make myself small, or apologize for what I look like or the work I do here. Apologize for who my father was. I could just be me."

Amy-Rose steadied herself. "You didn't stand up for me; worse, you didn't stand up for yourself." She was already backing away, out of his reach, with his friends calling his name in the distance. John looked torn.

No, he isn't ready.

"I feel sorry for you." She heaved a breath between words. "You can keep your building and turn it into a store, salon, or a showroom for your automobiles. I don't want it," she said, and left before he could see her fall apart.

CHAPTER 43

Olivia

Olivia circled the ottoman and sat on the suitcase. Narrowing down the "essentials" to a single unit of luggage had proven difficult—*she was leaving home*—so difficult, in fact, that against her better judgment, she had pulled on the slippery ivory gown and made an appearance at the ball. Her presence would have been missed, she told herself.

She had briefly seen Helen, puffy-eyed but stoic. Something had happened, but Helen had refused to discuss it. Her sister's hands had shaken while she flatly refused Olivia's offer to stay. In fact, she nearly chased her out of the ballroom.

"What's going on?"

Mrs. Davenport stepped into Olivia's room, her mask dangling in her hand at her side. Its intricate gold pattern matched the crown woven through her hair, standing bold against the deep burgundy of her gown. She looked like a queen. A tired monarch. Her gaze flitted around the room and settled on the suitcase under her daughter. She walked farther into the room.

Though Olivia had replaced the items she pulled out when packing, she could hardly hide the bulky luggage case. As her mother made her way to the vanity, Olivia took one long breath after another. Her body hummed with anxiety, twisting her stomach in knots. She had hoped to be gone, but maybe this was better. Helen wouldn't be left to pick up the pieces while dealing with whatever else she now had going on.

"This is a train ticket to Philadelphia. Olivia, explain, please?"

"I've decided to travel south with some of the activists I've met." She watched shock change to determination on her mother's regal countenance. "I know this isn't what you and Daddy wanted for me, but this is the life I choose."

"You mean, the young man you choose." Her mother sighed and placed the ticket back on the vanity. "I was young once too." Her mother gave her a sad smile.

"I won't deny that along the way, I fell in love." Olivia walked up to her mother. "With Washington DeWight, and the work he does. Mama, our family philanthropy only goes so far."

"It's dangerous, Olivia."

"I know."

"No, you *think* you do. You may think the worst that could happen is a beating, jail." Mrs. Davenport shook her head. "You were too young to remember the bricks wrapped in threats when the carriage business began to leave others in the dust. After the riots in Springfield, Black-owned business here were attacked. We didn't redo the showroom for the aesthetic. Someone threw a flaming liquor bottle through one of the windows." Mrs. Davenport sighed. "Perhaps I should have heeded Mrs. Tremaine and not have sheltered you children so much."

Olivia's heart raced. She watched the pain of the memories flit across her mother's face. She felt cold, despite the balmy night air wafting in through the window. The commotion from downstairs faded into the background.

"Before John was born, your father and I tried to do what you and Mr. DeWight are doing. We marched." She grabbed her daughter's hand. "But there are other ways to affect change without risking your life. And with better results."

"Why haven't you told me this before? You and Daddy keep so much hidden." Olivia tried to shake away the bubbling anger. "Instead you had us tutored here. In town, we practically flaunt our wealth in circles where we are sometimes the only people of color, where our best is better than everyone around, and some still look down their noses at us. Then we cross over to the South Side. Where we are as likely to be praised as cursed. A basket of pastries or a check in hand when all our people want is a chance."

Mrs. Davenport sighed. "By helping one, you can help many." She tucked a stray curl behind Olivia's ear. "I'm sorry. Our only intention was to protect you and your brother and sister from the worst of it. However we could. Do you really know what you're signing up for?"

Doubt found a crack in Olivia's resolve, widening the crack, and making it harder for her to focus. Her mother still held her hand, the pressure warm and reassuring. The same hands that soothed her when she was sick, wiped her tears. That tucked her hair away moments ago.

She glanced down. Her bag was packed.

"I want you to think carefully about this decision," said Emmeline Davenport.

"I have. All I ever do is think. This is the time to act. Maybe Mr. Tremaine will win his election and can make a difference that way, but it's not a guarantee."

"Give it until the end of the summer."

"Mama, I don't need to wait until the end of the summer."

Mrs. Davenport's eyes glittered and her mask wrinkled in her hands. "And what if it doesn't work out with this man? You would come home from"—she waved her mask at the door—"wherever, with your reputation ruined and unable to find a suitable husband. Mr. Lawrence is downstairs. He is a fine man and will make a wonderful husband."

Olivia's face heated. "Husband? Mama, I know this isn't what you wanted—"

"It's not!"

"But it is what *I* want. I know what I'm doing."

"I hope you do." Mrs. Davenport pressed her lips to her daughter's forehead. "Your father and I may not be unable to undo the damage when you return."

"Who's to say there will be any damage to undo?"

"It's a wonderful thing to hope," Mrs. Davenport said, before her voice turned to pleading. "At least, wait until morning. If you still want to go, your father and I will arrange for someone to go with you."

Olivia chewed her lip. It was a similar plan she had considered, though she'd rather find someone among the group of lawyers and activists. She suspected her parents would try to delay her as well. *Wouldn't it be better to leave with the group tonight?* She looked at the mess around her. "Okay," she said. "I'll wait."

Mrs. Davenport sighed. "Good. I'll see you downstairs."

"Yes, Mama." Olivia watched her leave and then gazed around the room, cataloging the possessions she would leave behind. Her heart ached as she picked up each of the framed photos from their spots on the mantel.

"Drat!" The small clock next to the picture of her father told her she was late. There was no time to change. Olivia grabbed her long traveling coat and threw it over her shoulders. She listened at the door for footsteps. When she heard none, she picked up the suitcase and stole silently out of the house.

Olivia arrived at the train station with moments to spare. She bade her borrowed driver and carriage goodbye as he made his way back to Freeport Manor to await his employer—one of her parents' party guests—and she sprinted up the stairs. She paused once inside, craning her neck to examine the eighty-five-foot arch above the Van Buren Street entrance. The cavernous expanse of the concourse made her feel small. The people rushing about made her feel invisible. *I could easily disappear, become a new version of me right here.*

Already the weight of society's expectations of her began to lessen. She marveled at the group of day laborers carrying large canvas bags, their toolbelts clanging at their hips. Businessmen read their papers on benches and ladies swung shopping bags after naughty children. Olivia felt like she was walking through a snow globe before inversion. Her heels clacked against the polished marble and through plastered columns until she emerged at the La Salle Station platform and the crowd. She looked for Washington DeWight's familiar face.

The air vibrated with the intensity of the train idling at the edge of the platform. It was alive, as much as she was. Her palms were slick with sweat. She readjusted her grip on her bag, wishing she had allowed the porter to take it when she'd arrived, but it was too close to her departure time. She looked around, panic creeping in.

At last she spotted Washington DeWight standing on the step into the train, arm outstretched as he held fast to the rail. The flutter in her stomach only heightened the mix of emotions she was feeling. She'd never been to Philadelphia or Washington, DC. Never been out of the county without her family. Now she was traveling halfway across the country.

"Miss Davenport?" A young man approached, pressing a bloodied handkerchief to his brow. "Are you Miss Davenport?"

"Yes," she said uncertainly. His face was familiar. Olivia had met so many people over the past few weeks, she couldn't place him. Then there was something in the way his mouth moved. *Hetty.* The man before Olivia was her cousin. "Are you okay?"

He blinked with one eye, as the other had swollen shut. "Looks worse than it is. I'm here for Hetty. She needs your help."

"Is she hurt?" Olivia looked around. "Where is she?"

"In jail, miss. I paid her bail, but they won't release her to me."

"All aboard!" the conductor yelled from two cars away.

"They don't believe in the relation?"

He refolded the handkerchief and placed it back on his face. "They took my money, *then* told me they would release her to immediate kin only. On account of her age." His expression told just how he felt about their excuse.

The longer Olivia stood on the platform, the harder it was to convince herself to keep moving forward. When she looked back, Washington DeWight had finally found her in the crowd. His face lit up. His arm raised, waving her forward. Excitement and relief was plain on his face.

Olivia felt caught in a storm. His words came back to her. He traveled from city to city, rallying the masses before leaving them informed with the tools to carry on. The rest of the work, the kind that sparks lasting, meaningful change, is carried out by the community.

The ones who stay.

She watched disappointment change his features.

The smile went first, taking with it the sharp angles of his cheekbones. He pulled back his wave and his dark brows knit together. She was too far to see the crease that formed between them when he was deep in concentration. She used her imagination. With one final nod, he ducked into the car.

She said, "Goodbye," tasting the tears that burned tracks down her cheeks.

The ball was at its peak when Olivia and Hetty returned. Thankfully, Hetty's only injuries were from the struggle of the arrest. Jessie and Ethel hugged them both. Neither commented on the suitcase Olivia carried. Or how she knew that Hetty was in need.

"Thank you, Olivia," Hetty said. "Will Harold take you back to the train station?"

Olivia smiled, though it felt hollow. "I think it's too late."

Hetty opened her mouth, then closed it. She pressed her hand to Olivia's face. "Thank you," she whispered. They embraced.

Long after Hetty disappeared inside, arm in arm with the other women, Olivia decided to return to the party. Guests milled about the porch and drive. The smoke from their cigarettes clawed at her raw throat. She'd made the right decision, she was sure of it. She was just so very tired. Her suitcase and coat fell to the floor in a discarded heap. With the help of the foyer mirror and a napkin, Olivia removed the smudged mascara under her eyes. Then she swiped a fresh champagne flute from a passing tray and rejoined the ladies on the divans.

"Another successful event, Mama," she said, posture perfect and shoulders back.

Mrs. Davenport drew her daughter close. "Yes, you should be proud."

CHAPTER 44

Helen

Helen endured the embrace of Josiah Andrews, hoping Olivia had taken her leave and was on her way to Philadelphia. She only had to occupy their parents until it was too late for them to do anything to stop her. *What we do for our sisters.* From over the shoulder of the younger Mr. Andrews, Helen watched Jacob Lawrence. He stood at the fringe of a group of gentlemen. Every time she let herself look in his direction, his eyes found hers. They seemed to be trying to tell her something. All she felt was hot and angry. What she wouldn't give to be in the garage right now.

"Green is a very lovely color on you," Mr. Andrews said.

"How very kind of you to say," she replied through clenched teeth as she lifted his hand higher on her back. He'd been dropping it closer to her bottom since the song began.

He turned red and stepped on her foot. "Sorry," he grumbled.

When the music finally stopped, she twisted from his grasp. "Pleasure dancing with you," she said, leaving him in the middle of the dance floor. She'd had enough.

"Miss Davenport?" Jacob called to her. Helen increased her speed but she was no match for his longer stride. "Please, Helen," he said. "I'm sorry, for all of it."

"You lied to me and to my parents. To Olivia, then *for* her. I just don't know what to think anymore."

"I have plans. I just need time. Please," he said again.

The pain in his voice made Helen feel hollow and exhausted. She'd never wanted to disappear as much as she did now. But Olivia needed her to make sure their parents stayed in the ballroom, enjoyed the party, and didn't notice her leave. She swallowed her tears. "I'd like you to leave," she said. And remembering all the instructions Mrs. Milford had taught her, she said it with a smile. "Thank you for coming." She averted her eyes so she would not see his face. Eventually, he retreated from her vision and faded into the crowd.

Time to go to the library. Helen skidded to a halt. Her father stood between her and freedom.

"Helen, looking to escape already?"

Her eyes darted beyond his shoulder. "Of course not, Daddy," she said, grasping for words. "I was wondering if you'd like to dance."

His surprised smile sent a twinge of guilt through her. Helen had not remembered when her father last looked so moved and lost for words.

Mr. Davenport held his hand out to his daughter and led her back into the fray. In his arms she felt like a little girl again. She felt his eyes on her, gleaming. He was steady on his feet, despite his limp. "Do you remember when you were small enough to stand on my toes?"

"I can hop on, if you'd like," she teased.

He laughed. Helen couldn't help joining him. The knot in her stomach loosened enough to make room for happiness among the guilt. Is this what she missed, locked in her room or the library or the garage? Father-daughter dances? Is this why his patience with her was so thin? Why every idea she had was so easily swept aside?

"What's the matter, sweet?" he asked. He tilted her head to catch her eyes. She looked at her father, the newer wrinkles lining his brows and the proud nose they shared.

"Nothing," she said. "This is nice."

"We should do it more often."

The song ended and Helen escorted him to where he'd propped his cane.

"When you see your sister, send her my way. I'd like to dance with all my girls tonight." He kissed her gently on her cheek. When he stood back, Helen's mouth was still parted with Olivia's alibi out of reach. "Helen," he said sternly.

"Yes, Daddy," she said quickly. She looked at the entrance to the hall.

"What's going on?"

"Nothing! I think Livy went to bed—she wasn't feeling well." Helen slipped her hands behind her back so he couldn't see her pick at her nails.

"She's been quite unwell lately. Perhaps I should check on her."

"No!" she said. Helen stepped into his path. *At least you're closer to the door.* "I can check on her and report back to you." She fumbled for what to say next. She usually wasn't this clumsy in talking her way out a mess. Her etiquette lessons had jumbled her mind! She was sure, in this moment, they had honed all the wrong skills. Mrs. Milford would be proud, but now she was on her way to disappointing her sister. Olivia would be devastated.

"Olivia is there," he said. The statement was as much a surprise to her as it was to her father's delight. Along the far wall where her mother and other matrons relaxed on couches, her sister floated like a vision in white.

"I'll go tell her you're looking for her." Helen didn't wait for her father to answer. She weaved through the crowd and dodged Greenfield, keen as he was to ask her to do a picnic or something equally dull.

"Livy."

Her sister turned at the sound of her name. "Helen, you and Daddy made quite the pair." Though her tone was bright, Helen heard the shakiness in her voice. Mrs. Davenport eyed her daughters from her perch on the couch.

"I thought you were ill," Helen said.

"I feel much better now. I just needed to rest for a while." Olivia smiled tightly at Helen. Something was wrong, so very wrong.

"Fantastic. May I speak to you?" She said, threading her arm through her sister's and dragging her in her wake.

In the privacy of the library, she demanded an answer. "What are you doing here?"

"I don't know," Olivia said. "I was standing on the platform when Hetty's cousin found me. He told me she'd been arrested—"

"Hetty was arrested?"

"I went to the station to get her. She's with Jessie and Ethel now."

"You went like that?" she asked, looking at her sister's gown.

Olivia's laugh was hollow. "You should have seen the officer's face." Her chin quivered and she sank into the nearest chair and placed her face in her hands.

Helen sighed. "What are you going to do, Livy?"

She shrugged. Helen had never seen her sister so unsure of herself.

"Mama caught me before I left. She told me how she and Daddy tried living the life of activists and how little impact it made. Did you know they did that?" When Helen shook her head, Olivia said, "I barely made it to the station on time and all I could think about was that they tried." Quieter, she added, "And then I realized there is so much left to be done, including seeing this campaign through, how can I think of leaving now?" She stopped short. "I saw him looking for me, and when he found me, I couldn't move. That's when Hetty's cousin came up to me." Olivia cleared her throat. "I'm going to keep working here. Just because he moved on doesn't mean I have to." Olivia hugged herself. "What happened with Mr. Lawrence?"

The sound of his name felt like the reopening of a wound barely on the mend. Tears began to fall.

"Helen." Olivia rushed to her side and smoothed her hair away from her face, making her feel young and small again. Helen fell onto her shoulder, and told Olivia all of it. By the time she was done, Helen's face felt tight and puffy. She should have just gone to the garage, stayed there. But as her sister rocked her and whispered soothing words she was too upset to understand, Helen knew that this moment was priceless.

CHAPTER 45

Amy-Rose

The first tears began to fall as Amy-Rose passed through the kitchen's swinging door. One look at her face, and Jessie set the rolling pin to the side. Amy-Rose rounded the table and embraced the cook. Jessie wordlessly held her while she sobbed. "I'm just a maid," Amy-Rose said into Jessie's shoulder. "I'll always be a maid."

Jessie took Amy-Rose's face in her hands and took a step back. The small gesture silenced Amy-Rose, who couldn't believe she had any more tears to shed.

"Ain't nobody *just* anything. Especially you. And you don't need any man to make your dream come true. I expect that's what this is about."

Amy-Rose took a deep breath, though it hurt. She remembered her mother and how she found a way. So would she. The weight of the notebook in her apron grounded her. Jessie was right; she could do it. But she couldn't do it here at Freeport Manor . . .

Good thing her bag was still out. This time, she would go east.

CHAPTER 46

Ruby

The tearoom was blissfully empty except for a few older women, Ruby, and her mother. The walls were painted in a robin's-egg blue and framed by large bay windows that stretched from floor to ceiling. The crisp white linens were too bright. The fundraiser had knocked everyone out, yet Mrs. Tremaine insisted they still attend Sunday brunch today.

After Mr. Barton had left the ball, all Ruby had wanted was to return home and sulk. The events for the campaign were bearable, sometimes fun. Now she only saw what this last commitment had cost her: Harrison Barton, a shot at love, her freedom. Months ago, Ruby would have been gloating to have secured the first proposal of the season. Instead, she felt a hopeless sort of sorrow.

The idea of Harrison Barton doting on another girl was so much worse. And yet, it was a pain she knew she deserved. She had hurt him. She had thrown away their chance at happiness together and possibly her chance at real love. A marriage to John would be one of convenience and their parents' nostalgia and her father's need for validation. Already she and her family were ben-efiting from the Davenports' realm of power and influence after her parents made it clear that the union of the two families was still in the cards.

"Drink your tea, dear. We don't want to appear like we don't enjoy the refreshments here. They are strong supporters of your father," Mrs. Tremaine said through her teeth.

Ruby obeyed and played with the pendant hanging from her neck.

"Next we'll go to the milliner. I think we need new hats. Oh, and what do think about Marshall Field's?" When the two of them were alone, Mrs. Tremaine whispered, "Your plan has worked in more ways than one. In addition to your necklace, Mr. Barton made a sizeable donation to your father's campaign."

"He did?" Ruby said. Her breath hitched at the mention of his name. "When?"

"Several weeks ago. Mr. Barton didn't want you to know, and of course, you were confused enough already . . ."

Given his upbringing, Mr. Barton's interest in her father's campaign made sense, but she had not expected him to help her family. He believed her father could make a difference. To be the first Black mayor meant something.

For once, she had no interest in fashion or shopping, but her mother was true to her word. She ordered each of them a new hat, then they made their way to the large department store. Mrs. Tremaine stopped to talk to every shopkeeper, newsstand owner, and acquaintance on the way. It was like she was practicing for her victory tour. The journey was peppered with Ruby-focused encouragement. Ruby needed to smile more, Ruby needed to be more engaging in conversation.

Her chest felt tight at Marshall Field's. And it wasn't just because the bodice of the dress her mother suggested she try on was pulled taut over her chest. Her temper flared at the callous way her mother was spending money, like the last couple of months of penny-pinching didn't happen. Or couldn't happen again.

The shop attendant spread the skirt around and adjusted the frills around her shoulder. Ruby marveled at the fine fabric draped on her skin. The severe plunging neckline was made modest by the lace running from one shoulder to the other, its scalloped edges just grazing her collarbone.

"Miss Tremaine, would you like flowers along the waist?" the seamstress asked, holding a silk arrangement about the size of her palm at the gown's empire waist.

I don't care, Ruby thought, wondering how many dress fittings were in her future. She said yes, if only to buy her some time to compose herself. A heat had risen beneath her skin and her heartbeat spiked with each passing moment.

She glanced once more at her reflection, took a deep breath, and hid her true feelings behind her best smile. The sample dress was too wide and far too long. Clips and pins, cinched far too tight, gathered excess fabric at her shoulders and waist, revealing her curves. Ruby fought the urge to turn her nose up at the design. It was outdated and made her look short. The material was nice, though. With a nod, the salesgirl opened the curtain.

"Oh, Ruby," her mother said. "The lace is exquisite."

The seamstress draped a measure tape across her shoulders, her flaxen curls looping around it. Her face was bright and rosy. She looked from Ruby to her mother expectantly.

Mrs. Tremaine adjusted the flowers at Ruby's waist. Ruby

squeezed her eyes shut and resisted the urge to claw her way out of the dress. But when she opened her eyes, she noticed the softened look on her mother's face.

"My beautiful girl," Mrs. Tremaine said, patting her cheek.

Ruby grasped her hand. It occurred to her fully then, the true weight of it, that she'd have to break her mother's heart if she herself wanted to be happy.

"May I have a glass of sparkling water?" she asked.

"Right away, miss." The shopgirl dipped out of the room.

"Mother, could you pick out a broach for comparison? I think it would be better suited for this dress."

"I know just the one!"

"Actually, I changed my mind." There were enough pins sticking her through the dress.

Mrs. Tremaine pressed her hands to the pearls around her neck. "All right, but I must say, I do not care for that tone. I doubt John will welcome such behavior, and children need a good example."

"I do not care about your plans, Mother," Ruby said evenly. "I will not be marrying John. I love Harrison Barton and I do not care if that throws a wrench in your plans. I want to be happy. It's my life *and* my decision. I will not let you and Papa bully me anymore."

By the time Ruby finished speaking, her pulse was the only sound she could hear. She stuffed her feet back into her shoes. Air. She needed fresh air. Ruby walked in the opposite direction of the broaches, ignoring the stares of shoppers and attendants.

Aren't there any windows?

"Is that Ruby Tremaine? I do say it is."

Ruby cringed.

Agatha Leary stood a few feet away, arms crossed, as she sized Ruby up. "That's an interesting frock," she said.

"Agatha, lovely to see you, though I do think you could have used a few more hours of sleep."

Agatha laughed. It was a tinny sound and framed by a glare. "I was hoping you could clear something up for me. I heard you and Mr. Barton ended things. Does that mean he's back on the market?"

For a moment Ruby saw red as deep as the stone dangling from her neck. She had a mind to throttle Agatha Leary right there in front the makeup counter. If it weren't for the glorious blast of cool air from the entrance, she might have.

"Actually, I heard he's taken." Ruby straightened and followed the breeze to the exit. She let her feet carry her to where her heart led. She ignored the strange looks she received. The clips and pins holding the dress in place had begun to fail. Ruby didn't care. A short streetcar ride later, she climbed the stairs of the brownstone nestled behind a large flowering tree. She knocked on the door, pounding her fist until a stooped woman opened it. Beyond her, on the staircase to the second floor, Harrison Barton gaped.

Ruby hesitated. "Excuse me," she breathed, smiling. She squeezed herself between his housekeeper and the door. Her strides matched Mr. Barton's until they met at the bottom of the stairs. "I know what I want. I want a life with you. I do not want to keep going back and forth. I have told my mother. You can take a page out in the paper for all I care! I love you, dammit!"

He was so still, Ruby was afraid she'd frightened him beyond any repair of their relationship. Then he scooped a hand at the nape of her neck and brought her lips to his. Ruby's toes curled in her boots. She parted her lips as their kiss deepened. This was her only choice.

A clatter broke them apart. The older woman had slammed the door. Ruby and Harrison Barton stared at each other, eyes bright and grinning from ear to ear.

"Anything else you'd like to tell me?" he asked.

Ruby looked down at her chest. "I think I stole this dress."

CHAPTER 47

Olivia

The early morning sun painted the horizon in blue and gold, chasing away the stars in their purple blanket of sky. What Olivia told her sister last night was true: Everything would look different in the morning. From her window overlooking the courtyard, she noticed the flagstones had been cleared of the party debris. The tables where dinner was served had since been carried away, along with the linens, the centerpieces, and other trappings of the meal. The glasses and discarded bottles of champagne that cluttered the corners of the lounge furniture tossed. The results of her hard work swept clean.

Olivia exhaled deeply and watched her breath fog the glass of the now-shut window. When she closed her eyes, she was transported to the train platform. Hidden in the press of the crowd, she watched Washington DeWight search for her. Her heart ached as her feet remained where they were. The disappointment in his face left her queasy. It was the hardest thing she'd ever done. Returning home to see the party still swinging like she hadn't even left had only made it worse.

Mama and Helen know, she thought to herself.

Helen had seemed stricken, while her mother was both relieved and triumphant. Olivia felt drained.

She was surprised to hear the knock at her door long after she had crawled beneath her duvet and settled in to stare at the canopy above her. Sleep had also eluded Helen, who, still wrapped in a blanket of her own, burrowed beside her. They had stayed up late into the night, talking about everything and nothing—all the things they should have been sharing the past few years.

They had talked until their voices were hoarse and the candles burned out. Helen wanted to make plans. A plan to get Olivia back to Mr. DeWight and another to break the news of Mr. Lawrence's betrayal to their parents. Olivia wanted her sister to wait. If they ruined Mr. Lawrence's good standing in their parents' eyes, there would be no way for him to earn their trust again, if ever Helen should want him to. Plus, propriety also had to be considered since he was so recently attached to Olivia. Helen claimed not to care. Olivia knew that was the pain speaking.

"You're awake." Helen's head appeared in a gap between the mix of their bedding.

"Well, someone snored uncontrollably all night."

"I don't snore," Helen said.

"And she also hogged all the covers."

"I wouldn't have to if you slept with your windows closed like a normal person." Helen threw the blankets to the floor and stretched like a cat. "Have you decided what you want to do?"

Olivia wanted to get back to work. Find Hetty and regroup. She wanted to make plans of her own. Her feelings for Washington DeWight helped her to see that. "We can plot on full stomachs," she said, pulling her sister to her feet.

"Good. I think I smell eggs."

When they entered the breakfast room, John was already there. His plate was laden with food, smeared like he was onto his second round. Steam from the fresh pot of coffee he poured in front of him made his expression difficult to read. He was dressed like he was going out.

"Where's Mama and Daddy?" Helen asked, sliding into a seat next to John.

He shrugged. His eyes looked red, like he was up all night. The tightness around the corners of his mouth let Olivia know his night had been just as unpleasant as theirs. He handed them each a plate as Olivia sat down. The spread in front of them made Olivia's mouth water. Eggs, bacon, and copious amounts of buttered toast, the Davenport siblings ate in silence.

"What is it, Helen?" John said, annoyed. She had been kicking the leg of the table for the past few minutes.

"Don't snap at her like that," Olivia said.

"I wasn't snapping," His face softened and he apologized, cutting Olivia a look to remind her he was the oldest. She rolled her eyes.

Helen took a slice of toast off his plate. Before he could say anything, she asked, "How'd it go with Amy-Rose?"

Olivia's head perked up.

John flinched. "Daddy didn't take it well. She overheard and now . . ." His voice trailed off. He shook his head. His eyes seemed unfocused as he gazed at the plate in front of him.

"Uh, what am I missing?" Olivia asked. "What did Daddy not take well and what does it have to do with Amy-Rose?"

"John is in love with her," Helen provided.

Olivia really had been missing out. She felt an odd lurch as it dawned on her that her relationship with Helen wasn't the only one she had neglected.

"I let her down. Again." He scrubbed a day's worth of beard growing in. "I don't think I can make it right."

Helen grasped his forearm. "What did you do now?"

"I didn't step in soon enough when Greenie embarrassed her, and then again when Daddy leveraged my inheritance against a relationship between us." Both Helen and Olivia gasped. "I thought buying her a salon would make her stay . . . and then she heard last night . . ."

Helen now kicked his shin. "You bought her a *salon*? Oh, John. Did you think you could just bat your eyelashes and Amy-Rose would forget everything she's been working for? That she'd let someone else control what she has every right to earn? Would you expect that of me?" She shook her head. "Men."

"She was so disappointed about losing Mr. Spencer's barber-shop."

"So you thought buying her one would solve everything," said Helen.

Olivia was still confused. "So, you're in love with Amy-Rose, and you're in love with Mr. Lawrence—"

"You told her?" John's eyes snapped to Helen's.

"You knew?" Olivia's mind was reeling. There was so much she didn't see. Her gaze fell to the stack of letters she'd brought to the table from the basket in the foyer. "This is addressed to Amy-

Rose. It's from Georgia. Maybe you should bring it to her. Apologize. Again."

John grabbed the letter. "I recognize this seal. It was broken on all the envelopes she had from the letters her father sent to her mother. I think it's his family's crest. They didn't know it then, but they stopped coming when he died." His whole body bounced with his knee, all the tension of a coiled spring.

"It's unopened." Olivia tried to take the letter back, but he pulled it closer, as if holding it would make Amy-Rose appear. "And that looks like a woman's handwriting."

He stood and left the room. They listened to his frantic footsteps echoing through the house. Then quiet.

The coffee was strong and bitter; Helen drank it without hesitation. Olivia poured sugar and cream until the liquid in her cup was as pale as unvarnished oak. She was about to reach for the bacon on John's plate when her sister tapped her arm and pointed over her shoulder.

John re-entered the room. His hands shook. A torn sheet of paper in his hand trembled like a leaf in the wind. Olivia and Helen exchanged glances as he crushed the page in his fist and threw it on the table. Olivia watched helplessly as he collapsed into the chair. His eyes filled with tears. Helen smoothed out the paper, her own eyes filling as she read.

"She's gone?" Olivia breathed.

John nodded. He still held the letter addressed to Amy-Rose. "I'll have to find a way to get this to her."

"Where did she say she was going?"

"She didn't."

"John—"

He waved away their words. "I'll get this to her," he repeated, holding the letter from Georgia, determination now etched in his face. "What's the next problem to solve?"

Helen wiped her eyes and spoke around a mouth full of food. "We need a plan to get Olivia to Philadelphia."

"Helen, I'm not going. It's too late now and it's not where I should be. There's plenty of work to do here. I told you there's no need for a ruse, or some elaborate plan. I choose to stay. You can't get rid of me that easily." Olivia knew she'd said the wrong thing as soon as the words passed her lips. "Can't" sounded like a dare. And there was nothing her siblings loved more than a challenge.

Helen smirked despite her watery eyes, and John asked, "What's in Philadelphia?"

Before Olivia could answer, Helen jumped in, eyes bright and a little breathless as she relayed what she'd been up to the past couple of months. Her sister painted her as an awe-inspiring activist, ready to take on any challenge. It reminded her of Washington DeWight and the way other people, herself included, spoke of him. Fresh tears stung her eyes and Helen's voice trailed off. "Can't you see she loves him, John? We have to help her."

His brows furrowed. "What about you and Mr. Lawrence?"

Olivia's eyes darted to Helen, whose face blanked at the mention of the British bachelor.

Helen placed her head on the table. John looked at Olivia with a question in his eyes.

"It's a bit more complicated," said Olivia. "Mama and Daddy think he's about to propose to me." She turned to her sister. "He was only trying to help, buying me time. Now we're afraid they'll see him as opportunistic."

"He lied," Helen said.

"I did too." Olivia squeezed her arm, hoping it offered some comfort.

John leaned back in his chair with his fingers laced behind his shaking head. "Well, aren't we three peas in a pod?"

They were quite unlucky in love, Olivia thought. And for some odd reason, she started laughing. The sound began deep in her belly and rose until her shoulders shook.

"I think she's lost it," John said, his deeper laugh joining hers.

Soon, Helen lifted her head. Though there was a watery glint to her eyes, she smiled. Then giggled. Then cackled.

Olivia wiped under her eyes. Her feelings for Washington DeWight hadn't changed, but the sudden surge of mirth chased away some of the sorrow. "What do we do now?" she asked.

John shrugged. "Let's go for a ride. There's a newly repaired Ford in the garage, thanks to someone I know."

Helen brightened. "Can I drive?"

The Davenports is inspired by a forgotten history—by the instances of Black success across Midwestern U.S. cities like Chicago during the early 1900s, places then as full of progress and possibility for Black people as they were inequity and segregation. It's inspired by the story of the C.R. Patterson & Sons carriage company, founded by a proud patriarch who escaped enslavement to become a wealthy and respected entrepreneur.

Charles Richard Patterson was born into slavery in Virginia in 1833. It's unclear how or when he was able to relocate to Greenfield, Ohio, but we know he found early success as a blacksmith in a carriage company. In 1873, he partnered with J. P. Loew to open a carriage manufacturing business, building and selling no fewer than twenty-eight types of horse-drawn carriages and buggies, some of them as luxurious as those depicted in *The Davenports*.

Twenty years later, he was wealthy enough to buy out his partner and rename the company C. R. Patterson & Sons. When his son Frederick Patterson took over, cars were newly on the rise, and the business was converted to an automobile manufacturer. Unfortunately, after three generations of wealth and success, C. R. Patterson & Sons closed under the pressures of industrialization.

I wondered about C. R. Patterson's family—about his daughters especially. Few articles made mention of his them, and fewer still shared their names: Dorothea (Dollie), Mary, and Kate. I wondered, what was life like for women in their position? I wanted

The Davenports to hold up examples of representation I wish I'd had as a teen, to focus on young Black women discovering the courage to pursue their dreams—and loves—at a time when Jim Crow, fear, and distrust threatened both.

The four young women in *The Davenports* are a work of fiction. But their dreams, fears, and ambitions are real. They are determined and passionate as they try to balance the expectations of their circumstances with love and happiness found in surprising, and not always approved of, places. (And really, who doesn't adore a grand estate, a glamorous ball, and a juicy romance or four?)

In my research for this novel, I found the Patterson family's success to be one of many. Following the Reconstruction in the South, Black Americans, both free-born and formerly enslaved, carved their own paths into a society once barred to them. They became lawyers, doctors, and elected officials. Some, like Madam C. J. Walker, built empires large enough to become household names in their time. Her tenacity and resourcefulness provided the foundation for the character of Amy-Rose and her entrepreneurial aspirations.

After the Civil War, Chicago, in particular, became a hub of African American culture and business, which is why I selected it for the setting of this story. At the turn of the twentieth century, Chicago was growing, and its demographics were changing. In 1910, several Chicago newspapers claimed the corner of State and Madison Streets, known as the "Great Central Market," to be the busiest corner in the world. The city became a popular tourist destination, as Americans and Europeans alike flocked there for its lively night life, beaches, and beautiful lake.

What would later be called The Great Migration—the influx of newly freed people to cities like Chicago, New York, Boston, Los Angles, Detroit, and Philadelphia—resulted in predominately African American neighborhoods where Black-owned businesses and art could flourish. For the purposes of this story, the effects of this mass exodus were moved up a decade to aid Olivia's realization of her own privilege and foreshadow the oppression that would spark the Civil Rights Movement.

As inspiring as it was to read about the contributions of Black people throughout history and at this moment in particular, I was saddened that so little made it to the pages of my own schoolbooks. Instead, I had been guided through the same handful of biographies and a few highlights each year: *Brown v. Board of Education*, the speeches of Dr. Martin Luther King Jr., and Rosa Parks's famous bus ride. Today, there are textbooks that have rebranded slaves as "workers" who "immigrated" to fill agricultural jobs. The true horrors of slavery and the early push toward equity is a footnote in American history, and stories of Black success, like the Pattersons', are all but erased. I believe this erasure is why people of color and their allies still march.

And though it would be easy to become disheartened by the violence enacted against Black people in this country throughout history, I was reminded in my research of Black resilience too. For every Tulsa Race Massacre or the razing of Seneca Village, there is a Harlem Renaissance. The Springfield Race Riot in 1908 led to the establishment of the National Association for the Advancement of Colored People (NAACP). Barriers to education resulted in the creation of Historical Black Colleges and Universities (HBCUs). In the wake of modern technology, Black Americans and other minorities are documenting their truth, sharing their art, and amplifying their voices. There is a push to be seen and rediscover parts of America's history that have been largely overlooked. Books like Isabel Wilkerson's *The Warmth of Other Suns: The Epic Story of America's Great Migration* and *Unspeakable* by Carole Boston Weatherford highlight the triumph and tragedy Black Americans experienced during a critical time in history, full of hope, sacrifice, and loss. Juneteenth, celebrated in ways as varied as the people who honored their traditions, is now a national holiday. And Americans of all races gather in city streets, calling for change and equality.

Dr. LaGarrett King of the University of Missouri-Columbia said, "In many ways we wouldn't have a Black Lives Matter movement if Black lives mattered in the classroom." We can speculate how different our nation would be if curriculums better illuminated the highs and lows of our past as well as the diversity our of society. But I believe, dear reader, that like me, you are optimistic that the spotlight on BIPOC representation and books like this are just the beginning.

I hope you had as much fun reading the stories of these young, determined women—Olivia, Helen, Amy-Rose, and Ruby—as I did writing them.

Thank you for reading. See you next time at Freeport.

Krystal Marquis

ACKNOWLEDGEMENTS

Thank you, reader, for staying with me this far. This book is my wildest dream come true and I am so happy to share it with you. I am incredibly grateful for the love and support of everyone who has made *The Davenports* possible.

To my parents: I love you. Thank you for believing in me and providing a safe space to believe in myself. Daddy, thank you for letting me hover over your shoulder every time you worked on a car and for your quiet pride, which helped push me forward. Mom, thank you for reading to me until I could read on my own. Then reading every version of this novel until it was ready to share with the world. You are my ideal beta reader and your perceptiveness is invaluable. My love of stories, I learned from you.

To the best siblings I could ask for: thank you, Anthony and Hillary (and Miles) for your joy and confidence. Cake will always be appreciated. Kimberly, thank (and sorry) for your patience as I spoke *at* you about all the things running through my mind, keeping me humble, and for the beautiful author photo. Brandon, thank you for daring me to try, challenging me and bringing me along on your NaNoWrimo journey. This has truly been the greatest adventure yet. Love you, gremlins.

Tamar Rydzinski, thank you for taking a chance on me. Your wisdom and guidance found *The Davenports* the perfect home. Thank you for being the champion of my work. You were my dream agent.

To my editor, Jessica Dandino Garrison: Thank you for your brilliant insight. And for taking in stride, the drastic changes to the last third of this novel between drafts. Your care and passion for these four young women and Chicago helped bring this story to life. I can't wait to geek out on history and romance IRL. You are amazing!

Many thanks to the stellar publishing team at Dial Books. Regina Castillo, aka "Mistress of Logic and Continuity," your attention to detail allowed this novel to really shine. Thank you, Deanna Halsall for the striking cover, Theresa Evangelista for the beautiful cover design, and Jenny Kelly for the interior—your designs went above and beyond my imagination. To Lauri Hornik and Jen Klonsky and everyone else at Dial and Penguin Random House, I appreciate the time and passion invested in me and this novel.

Viana Siniscalchi, your enthusiasm was everything! Thank you for always being available to talk through any block. You organized my thoughts and I am so grateful. To Sara Shandler, you were a voice of reason that kept me grounded. The rest of team at Alloy Entertainment: Les Morgenstein, Joelle Hobeika, Romy Golan, Josh Bank, Matthew Bloomgarden, Laura Barbiea, and anyone else working behind the scenes, thank you.

The amazing people behind NaNoWrimo and Pitch Wars: You opened a door to a world that welcomed me and introduced me to some of the most wonderfully supportive people I've ever met.

To Paulicia Jean Baptiste, my St. Lucian family and anyone who sent well wishes and shared this book, who told me to keep going and cheered me on: Thank you! Ale Barzola, Kendriana Gonzalez, Fiza Awan, Candice Dodd, Jessica Santiago, and Nkechi Wamou. Thank you for your words of encouragement, the memes, and working around my schedule. You are my diamonds.

Thank you to BDL-who? The BDL2 community for your support (#safetyfirst), especially Meghan Flynn, who never let a met deadline pass without an airhorn celebration, and Chris Eaton for the midnight-thirty pep talks and junk food care packages. I appreciate you.

Thank you to the many teachers who fostered my love of reading, particularly Mrs. DiMassa, Mrs. Gallagher, and Mrs. Gibson at Lauralton Hall. Mrs. Gibson, you read an essay about a confirmation dress (and later a cheerleading ribbon) and told me I had true talent. (I still have that blue binder.) To teachers, librarians, book bloggers, and booksellers: thank you. I hope you know how special you are.

Reader, if you're still here, don't give up. Keep dreaming.

Krystal Marquis happily spends most of her time in libraries and used bookstores. She studied biology at Boston College and University of Connecticut and now works as an environmental, health, and safety manager for the world's biggest bookseller. A lifelong reader, Krystal began researching and writing on a dare to complete the NaNoWriMo Challenge, resulting in the first partial draft of *The Davenports*. When not writing or planning trips to the Book Barn to discover her next favorite romance, Krystal enjoys hiking, expanding her shoe collection, and plotting ways to create her own Jurassic Park.

Connect with Krystal on Twitter @KrystalMarquis
and Instagram @krystabelle_reads.